ONE DARK, TWO LIGHT

RUTH
MANCINI

HEAD
of ZEUS

First published in the UK in 2020 by Head of Zeus Ltd
This paperback edition first published in 2021 by Head of Zeus Ltd

9 7 5 3 1 2 4 6 8

A catalogue record for this book is available from
the British Library.

ISBN (PB): 9781788543361
ISBN (E): 9781788543330

Typeset by Silicon Chips

Printed and bound in Great Britain by
CPI Group (UK) Ltd, Croydon CRO 4YY

Head of Zeus Ltd
5–8 Hardwick Street
London ECIR 4RG

WWW.HEADOFZEUS.COM

For Dad

PROLOGUE

The voices are all around, taunting him, almost.

'Ten, nine, eight...'

His fist clasps the handle and pulls open the door.

'Seven, six, five...' they chime in drunken unison as he steps out into the cold night air. 'Four, three, two, one...'

The door swings shut. The street is empty, but the sky above him is alive – glowing, iridescent orange on black, the sound of fireworks like gunshots piercing the air. There is a disorderly roar from the small building behind him, followed by the muffled beat of music. Another simultaneous clatter of gunshots breaks out above him followed by an eruption of colour: pink, purple, yellow, green.

He pulls up his collar against the cold and pushes his hands into his jacket pockets. He turns the corner into Packington Street. He'll cut through the Pear Tree Estate; it's always quickest – fifteen minutes and he'll be home. First, get home, then he'll call, tell her he loves her – and that she should give that boy a big hug from him. This can't go on. He only ever wanted to be with them. He'll tell her everything – it's time she knew the truth.

The estate is huge, sprawling and incongruous. On the one side, there's the prosperity of Packington Street, with its huge brass door-knockers, its white pillars and arches, its BMWs and its Porsches. On the other side, beyond the small park, there's the council flats, with their frontage of pale blue metal panels, their PVC... and their trash. His eye moves to a row of garages, where an old Rover and two white Transit vans are parked. A broken armchair lies on its back next to an overflowing green metal skip, a swivel desk chair and several broken planks of wood thrown carelessly on top.

He walks up the street a little, quickening his pace. There's no traffic, so he steps out to cross the road – and then he feels it. His neck cricks under the weight. He's dazed, disarmed. Slowly, he turns to face his attacker. Their eyes meet, momentarily, but before the horror can register fully, his legs buckle underneath him. The back of his head hits the pavement. There's a split second of immense, crucifying pain – and then he's gone.

When he comes to, he remembers but he can't move. He's on his side, his arm bent at an awkward angle beneath him, his cheek pressed hard against the cold paving slab. There's a hand on his upper thigh. It's patting him down, lifting his wallet and his phone. He tries to speak but no words will come. He feels a hand on his wrist and his watch is unclasped. Footsteps, running and fading into the distance. More gunshots overhead.

His eyelids flicker open, his head is blurred and spinning. He slides one leg back and rolls onto his stomach, freeing his trapped arm and pushing himself onto his knees. With his good arm, he pushes hard and staggers to his feet. He glances round. There's no one; they've gone.

He rubs his cheek, feels the sticky wetness there and realises that he's bleeding. He'll be OK. He needs to get home, that's all. He steps off the kerb and spots a glint of metal against the blackened tarmac. It's his door keys; they've dropped his door keys. Thank Christ. He bends down to pick them up, but the effort is too much and he stumbles and falls, his head smacking the ground for a second time.

For a few moments he drifts in and out of consciousness, while the sky continues to crackle and light up above him. Somewhere, somewhere outside of him, there's a growling sound. In his dream-like state he at first thinks it's a lion but then... of course not – it's a car. He forces himself to swim up out of the murky waters of unconsciousness and listens hard. From the direction of the pub, the vehicle is cruising slowly along the road. Soon, the headlamps are on him, blazing brighter and brighter until he is blinded by their yellow glare. But his head is so heavy. He's going to sleep again... he can feel himself slipping away.

With a sudden roar, the engine accelerates. The car is almost upon him. It's going too fast – it's not going to stop. For a fleeting, surreal moment he feels the metal of the bumper as it smacks, scrapes and rolls him sideways, followed by the incredible, crushing weight of a tyre against his back. Then, nothing. Just blackness – and the distant scream of an engine, as the car speeds away.

1

I'm in court when my phone rings. It's a Tuesday, just after three. We're all sitting in silence – the court clerk, the prosecutor, myself and the usher – while District Judge Long peruses the papers for the next case. The judge is a tall, thin-framed man in his sixties with wavy grey hair, kind, intelligent eyes and a soft-featured face. We call him Lock-'em-up Long because, in spite of his gentle appearance, he's known for being tough. You could say he takes no prisoners but, actually, he does – a lot. I sometimes wonder what he's like at home, what happens when he falls out with his wife. He must feel annoyed that he can't lock her up. Maybe they don't argue; I wouldn't. No, that's not true – I probably would.

The judge finishes reading and looks up as Cathy from the Youth Offending Team walks in. He asks her if my client, Jerome, is complying with his Youth Rehabilitation Order. Cathy shakes her head. 'No, sir, unfortunately not. He's not been engaging well, I'm afraid—'

She pauses and glances in my direction. We can all hear it: there's a deep buzzing noise from beside my feet and a familiar tune now starts to play. My heart sinks. I reach down, grab the handle of my bag and leap to my feet.

'Turn it off, Ms Kellerman.' Judge Long looks hard at me from the bench.

'Yes, sir. I just have to find it, sir.'

I'm rummaging as quickly as I can. My bag doesn't seem to have anything in it apart from an inordinate quantity of half-used tissues and a tangled-up mobile phone charger lead. 'I'm so sorry, sir. Can I just…?' I nod plaintively in the direction of the courtroom door.

'Turn it off, Ms Kellerman,' the judge repeats, his voice booming across the room.

'Yes, sir. Of course.'

The phone's in the side pocket. Just as I find it, it stops. I lift it up a little and try to sneak a peek at the screen – I can't help myself. But it's a withheld number; goddammit. Out of the corner of my eye I can see Malcolm, the usher, shaking his head.

'Ms Kellerman,' says the judge, enunciating my name as if it contains two separate sentences.

'Sir,' I mutter. 'I'm so sorry, sir.' I turn the phone off and sit back down.

'Stand up,' the judge orders.

I stand up again.

'Ms Kellerman, I have the power, do I not, to deal with you immediately under section 12, subsection 2 of the Contempt of Court Act 1981 and Criminal Procedure Rule 48.5. I can imprison for one month anyone who wilfully interrupts the proceedings of the court.'

I take a deep breath. 'It wasn't wilful, sir. I thought I'd turned it off. It has to be wilful. Section 12, subsection 1.'

The judge leans forward. 'It was wilful when you looked at it just now. It had already stopped ringing.'

I nod. 'Sir, that might be true. But if it was, it was a split second of wilfulness, as set against a strong background of compliance with the protocol of the court.'

'Is it a man?'

The court clerk covers her mouth and coughs. Cathy bites her lip and looks pointedly down at her papers.

I give him a long, hard stare. 'Sir. The number was withheld.'

'Very well.' The judge's face relaxes suddenly and his mouth curves into a smile. I'd forgotten that, whilst tough on crime, Judge Long has a wry sense of humour. 'I was young once,' he tells me. 'Sit down.' He turns to the usher. 'Call on the next case.'

The usher disappears and a moment later my client, Jerome, enters the courtroom, with Georgina, his mum. Georgina looks fed up, and not without reason. She's a good person and a loving mum; I know that about her. But she's up against it. This is the third time already this year that Jerome has been before the Youth Court. Stealing cars, or vehicle interference (when he doesn't manage to steal them, that is) – it's the same thing every time. The kid's been obsessed with cars since I've known him. He can't stay away from them. I keep telling him he needs to get himself some junior apprentice job in a garage – and then in just over a year's time he could get his driving licence and get paid to fiddle with them, all legit. Georgina tells him to listen to me, and he almost does, but we both fear that he's heading down a different route.

The court clerk lifts up her head. 'Take your hands out of your pockets, please.'

Jerome does as he's told. He takes a seat at the bench in

front of me and Georgina sits down beside him. Jerome is fifteen. He's British Jamaican. On the surface he's unemotional, but deep down he's angry. He's angry because none of the white people in this courtroom (myself included) knows what it's like to be a black kid growing up on Finsbury's Pear Tree Estate. He's angry because he's a teenager, and because his dad left when he was small. Georgina has three other children besides Jerome, all under the age of ten. She's lost control. The only men in Jerome's life with any authority over him are the drug dealers on the estate.

I'm not going to tell the judge any of this. He already knows it – but what can he do? The law is the law. You break it, you're punished, you get so many chances and then: 'Take him down.' Judge Long's favourite phrase.

'Stand up.'

Jerome shuffles to his feet. Now that his hands are no longer in his pockets, his trousers are falling down. From my seat behind him, I can see the band of his red underpants along with an expanse of unblemished skin. There's something about it – that youthful skin, that curve at the small of his back, the bright red underpants – that makes my heart melt. He's so young. He's just a kid. He's my Ben, but bigger. And black. And – of course – brighter. Much brighter, I concede. For a start, Ben's not yet ready for underpants. And at five years old, he still can't talk. Although, right now, Jerome's vocabulary range appears to be almost as limited as Ben's.

'So, why shouldn't I send you to youth detention?' the judge asks Jerome, directly.

'Dunno.' Jerome shrugs his shoulders. Georgina, next to him, hangs her head and sighs.

'Well, you haven't cooperated with the Youth Offending Team, have you?' the judge asks him.

Jerome shakes his head.

'Why not?'

'Dunno,' says Jerome, again.

'All right. Sit down. Ms Kellerman?' The judge turns to me.

I have just one shot at this, I know; the judge has limited patience. If I launch into a lengthy mitigation he'll cut me off sharp. I need to make my best point – and quickly. Sum it up in just a few sentences. Economy of words is everything here.

'Sir, it's the groupwork,' I tell him. 'Jerome lacks confidence. When he's in a group with others he feels inadequate. He can't speak – it mortifies him. He dreads these sessions because they always leave him feeling so low. He constantly compares himself to others and, in these groups, he comes out second-rate, every time.'

Jerome's head dips. He hasn't told me any of this, not in so many words – he wouldn't have thought to, nor would he have known how to articulate it, but I know Jerome, and I know it to be true. I also know that this is what counts in the eyes of the judge. This is the only thing that will persuade him not to revoke the Youth Rehabilitation Order and send Jerome 'downstairs'.

I study the judge's face; there's a flicker of interest. 'By contrast,' I continue, 'when he's behind the wheel of a car he feels *really good* about himself. In control. It's not an excuse, but it's a reason – that's why he keeps slipping back. He needs a way to feel good about himself; a way that's legal, of course. Youth detention won't do that. It will only reinforce his negative self-image. When he comes out the problem will still be there – but multiplied by ten.'

The judge says nothing for a moment. He picks up a pen and writes something down. He then looks up and gives Jerome a thoughtful stare before turning to Cathy. 'Is this group issue something that can be worked on?'

Cathy nods. 'We can offer one-to-one sessions initially. Resources are limited but we may be able to get him onto a mentoring programme. I'll need to do a further assessment, but, yes. There are definitely options we can look at.'

'Very well.' The judge turns to Jerome. 'Stand up.'

Jerome grabs hold of his waistband and wriggles to his feet.

'On this occasion,' says the judge, 'I will allow the order to continue. Jerome Thomas, for the offence of aggravated vehicle taking, I'm sentencing you to a two-year Youth Rehabilitation Order. This is your last chance. Do you understand? You will be sixteen in a few weeks' time and then things will be different. If I see you before the court again, I will send you to youth detention, make no mistake about that.'

I finish tapping into my iPad and look up. Jerome's head is bobbing up and down as the judge speaks. He won't admit to it, but he's overwhelmed with relief. Thankfully, he hasn't yet reached that stage – the stage that some of them do – where he *wants* to go inside for a bit, to big himself up in the eyes of the older kids on the estate.

The judge sits back in his chair. 'Go with your mum and make sure you see someone from the Youth Offending Team before you leave.'

I pick up my bag and my iPad and we all follow Cathy out of the door. As soon as we're out on the concourse and Jerome and Georgina have gone into a room with Cathy, I pull my phone out of my bag and turn it back on. I quickly check to see if there have been any more calls.

There's nothing, no alert from my voicemail service either. I tap the screen and dial the number for my voicemail anyway, but the caller hasn't left a message. I still have just the one saved message; the one I've already listened to a dozen times. I exhale deeply and curse my optimism. Why would he withhold his number, anyway? It doesn't make any sense. It can't have been him – and if it was the school, calling about Ben, their number would show, it always does. Besides, they'd have left a message, without a doubt.

I sink into a seat to wait for Jerome. Beyond the staircase that leads down to the foyer, I can see that, outside, it's raining steadily, the glass doors to the entrance obscured by beads of water which are streaking downwards to form runny, broken lines. I lift my phone up again and scroll back through my messages to check the date of my last text to him. And then I dial voicemail again.

'Hi, Sarah.' Will's lovely, smoky barrister's voice. 'I'm really sorry, I can't make it tonight. Something's come up. There's somewhere I have to be. I'll... I'll call you tomorrow, OK?'

Only he didn't. He hasn't. Not a call, not a text. Nothing. Not for over a week.

I end the call and push my phone into my bag, my heart sinking a notch deeper, the way that it has done with each passing day. He's lost interest; it's obvious. Oh well, there you go. It's not as if things had really got off the ground between us, anyway. It's only been a few weeks; we've seen each other a few times – that's all.

But on the other hand, I thought we had something. And it's not as though we've only just met. An involuntary bubble of excitement rises inside me as I cast my mind back, as I try to pinpoint the precise moment when I realised that we were going to transition from work colleagues into something more. But there wasn't a single moment. It was a slow, gradual realisation – for me at least. A joke, a smile, a lingering look. The deep concern that Will showed for me – the passion with which he defended me – when I ran into all that trouble on the Ellis Stephens case. The daily texts and the long, late-night phone calls. Dinner at mine. A second dinner. And a first kiss that told me that I'd been far more to him than just his instructing solicitor for a long time now.

It'll be Ben, of course. I lean back in my seat and fold my arms, fixing my eyes on the empty stairwell ahead of me. He can't deal with Ben. That'll be it. He liked me well enough when it was just me and him at court each day. He liked me when I was 'fun Sarah'. He even liked me when I was 'Sarah-in-distress'. But, now that he's been to my flat a few times, met Ben, seen what the real deal is… he can't get far enough away. He just doesn't know how to tell me. After all, what could anyone say that didn't make them look like a complete dick?

The door to the Youth Offending Team office opens and Jerome and Georgina come out. I pick up my bag and stand to greet them. Georgina gives me a friendly wave and Jerome's mouth curves into something approaching a smile.

'So, all good?' I ask.

'Yes. I think so.' Georgina gently shoulder-barges Jerome. She's a large woman, with a big bosom and a wide waist, and the motion knocks him off balance slightly. Her dark eyes flash as she glares at him, but I can see the love that's there. 'If this one can keep himself out of trouble from now on, we will be just fine. Won't we?'

Jerome pouts. 'I told you, Mum, it weren't my idea, anyway. I was just getting a lift, then my mate, he gets out and he asked me if I could just drive to—'

'And like Sarah told you, that's the same thing. You knew that car didn't belong to them. You don't never learn, Jerome. You just got to walk next time. Use your head. Use your bicycle. And stay away from that lot. Don't you think I got enough to be worrying about?' Her voice rises a little higher with each sentence as she continues to reprimand him. Eventually she stops, looks at me and shakes her head. 'Thank you, Sarah. I hope we don't see you again. You know I mean that well.'

'I know, Georgina. I know you do.' I momentarily place my hand on her shoulder and then hold it out to Jerome. He offers me his fist, so we exchange fist bumps instead. He then walks off down the stairs.

Georgina pauses at the top of the stairwell for a moment then looks back at me. 'He acts so tough, but inside he's still just a kid, you know?'

I nod. 'I know he is.'

'He wouldn't cope inside that place.' Her eyes glaze with a mild swell of tears and I take a step towards her. I put out a hand and stroke her fleshy arm. 'What you said,' she continues, 'about the other kids at those meetings, about him thinking he's being judged all the time. It's right. That's the way he is. No matter how much you tell him you love him, he just don't believe it. He won't ever believe anything good about himself.'

'I know.' I give her arm a squeeze. 'But hang on in there. And don't blame yourself. You've done the best you can; I know that.' I nod towards the Youth Offending Team office. 'And they know that too.'

She gives me a half smile. 'Sometimes that's just not enough though, is it? Some kids, they're just born needing so much more.'

I think about this for a moment. I think about Ben. I nod my agreement as she heads off down the stairs.

The rain has eased off, thankfully. I open the gate to my front yard and manoeuvre the buggy through before unstrapping Ben and standing him upright on the narrow path. I hold him steady with one hand while I try to unclip the folding mechanism of the buggy with the other, simultaneously trying not to collide with the handles of several bicycles which are protruding over the wall from the neighbour's front yard. Ben wriggles impatiently and I give up and slide the buggy off the path with one foot. It rolls across the tiny patch of grass and into the spindly branches of my overgrown rosebush. I'm too tired to fight with it this evening. I'll come back for it later, once I've settled Ben.

Inside, I slip a *Teletubbies* DVD into the Panasonic and sit Ben on the floor with his sippy cup. I tip some crisps onto a plate and place them on the rug beside him. Ben's fist darts out onto the plate and immediately upends it, the crisps flying out and landing in a heap on the rug. I instinctively leap down onto my hands and knees and, with both hands and in one swift movement, scoop the crisps up off the rug and back onto the plate again. Five second rule, I tell myself. If I threw away every item of food that Ben dropped on the floor we'd run out pretty quickly. I'd be visiting food banks. I'd probably go bankrupt within a year.

But there are limits. An uncomfortable image comes into my mind: me and Will in a restaurant (the one and only meal we've ever had in a restaurant together, while Anna babysat); me knocking a basket of bread to the floor as I brushed past the table on my way back from the loo. Me dropping to the ground and cheerfully declaring, 'Five second rule!' whilst scooping the bread up and back into the basket again. Will's face as he said, 'I think perhaps we'll just order some more.' I can feel the heat creeping its way across my forehead as I think about it now. I wouldn't have eaten that bread! Of course I wouldn't – I acted on instinct, that's all. But lord knows what he thought of me. No wonder he hasn't called. He's probably found himself someone with a little more class.

Seeing me still sitting back on my heels beside him, Ben picks up and passes me his sippy cup, even though it's still full. Ben likes to find me things to do. I hand it straight back to him. 'You've got juice,' I tell him. He takes a sip and then drops the cup on the floor. Some juice spills out of the spout onto the rug. As I push myself to my feet to get a cloth, there's a knock at the door and it nearly makes me jump out of my skin. Logic tells me it's not going to be Will; why would he turn up without calling first? Although, maybe he's lost his phone, I wonder suddenly. Maybe that was him who tried calling earlier, from his chambers, perhaps? But more likely it's just a neighbour with a parcel that's been delivered to the wrong house.

I grab my bag and blot the puddle of juice with one of the half-used tissues before jumping up and heading out into the hallway. I pull the catch on the door and it swings open. I feel my knees go weak as I step back in surprise.

'Andy?'

For a moment I'm speechless. I haven't heard from Andy for… ages. I thought he was in Australia. How can he suddenly be here, on my doorstep?

'Hey, Sarah.' Andy – my ex – smiles a straight-mouthed, hesitant smile which lets me know that he's nervous.

I shake my head. 'What are you doing here?'

As I wait for him to reply I take in his appearance. He looks really well. He's lean and tanned. He's wearing a navy-blue polo top and light brown jeans. He's shorter than I remember – but not too short – and stocky, still, like a rugby player. He's had his hair cut, his lovely, long, wavy, fair hair, but it suits him and the overall impression is now much more 'established man' than 'surfer dude'.

He shifts from one foot to the other as his big blue eyes seek out mine. As I meet his gaze, my heart leaps: I can see Ben's face staring right back at me. It's unmistakable; he's the image of Ben – or Ben of him.

He shrugs. 'I'm back.' He smiles a little and his left cheek twitches slightly – a very mild nervous tic he has, which I'd always loved and had forgotten about. It transports me back in time, as does his accent. 'I mean… I'm back in the UK,' he qualifies his statement and laughs, nervously.

He waits for me to speak. I hold onto the door catch and continue to stare at him in stunned silence. Andy presses his lips together and then pops them open again, and grins – another mannerism I'd forgotten about and yet one which now feels so familiar to me again.

'You've let your hair grow.' He nods, still smiling. 'I like it long. And I like the colour.'

I push my hair back from my shoulders awkwardly. He can tell that it's dyed. Dark blonde, the packet said. Has he also guessed that I'm trying to cover up the grey that's started to sneak its way through at the roots? My hand moves self-consciously from my hair to my mouth. I've noticed a few lines around it recently. Do I look *very* much older than I did when he left?

Christ! What am I thinking? Why should I care? This is the man who walked out on me – on me and *Ben* – the man who left me to deal alone with the daily slog, the sleepless nights, the sickness and the worry. He has no idea how hard the last two years have been. If I look older than my thirty-five years, then it's his bloody fault.

'You're looking good, Sarah,' he says. 'Really good.'

I shift, uncomfortably, in the doorway. His voice. That Australian lilt when he says the word 'looking' – when he pronounces my name. I cast my mind back. When did I last speak to him? We've WhatsApped and emailed a number of times over the past year or so, but I can't remember when we last spoke on the phone.

'Why didn't you let me know you were coming?' I ask him. 'Wait – was that you who called earlier?'

'What? When? No.' He shakes his head. 'I'm sorry. I…' He takes a long breath and his chest heaves. He looks up and fixes his blue eyes on mine. 'Look, the truth is I didn't know how you'd react. I thought you might say that I shouldn't come. But I wanted to see you and Ben. I wanted to—'

'Surprise me?' I finish for him, frowning.

'Yeah, kind of.'

'Well it worked,' I tell him. 'You really did surprise me.'

Andy cocks his head to one side. 'Were you expecting someone else?'

I nod, slowly. 'Ah. So that's it. You wanted to find out for yourself if I was living with someone?'

He purses his lips – the exact same way that Ben does. 'And are you?'

'Am I what?'

'Living with someone?'

I shake my head. I think about Will. Let's face it: if Ben's own father couldn't stick around, why would anyone else?

He tries to mask it but, just for a second, the relief is clear on his face. 'Can I come in, then?' he asks.

'Sure.' I step back into the hallway and open the door a little wider.

He points to a white Laguna that's parked just up the street. 'Is my car all right there?'

I follow his gaze. 'Have you been sitting in the car, waiting? Were you here when I got home?'

Andy smiles. 'Well, yeah,' he admits. 'I figured you'd be home around this time.'

I nod at the car. 'It's fine.'

Andy steps into the hallway. The sound of the *Teletubbies* emanates from the front room. He stops in his tracks and grins. 'He still listens to that?'

'Oh, yes. We're into the sixth year of the Tubbies, now.' I search his face for the old, haunted, disappointed look that always accompanied any evidence of Ben's limitations, but he simply smiles. He stops in the doorway for a moment and points out into the garden. 'You want me to get the buggy?'

'Sure.' I feel a pang of something I can't quite place. Was I expecting Andy to fight his way in? Was I hoping he'd push past me into the front room before gathering Ben up in his arms, sobbing and lamenting the day he ever left? But then I realise how nervous he must be, and what it must have taken for him to come here like this, unannounced, after everything he's done. Or not done, more to the point. He's trying to be helpful. He's trying to make up for not being around. I almost want to laugh.

But he's acting so differently. So normally. He's a far cry from the hollow-cheeked, broken man that I said goodbye to almost two years ago. He seems... mended, somehow. And more grown up. But why is he here? And what does he want?

Andy steps back outside into the front garden. I go back into the living room to check on Ben. He's standing up now, his hands and nose pressed up against the TV screen. His glasses are on the floor.

'No, Ben, too close,' I tell him, bending down to pick up his specs before leading him away. I sit him down on a chair at the computer and flick the monitor on.

The front door slams and Andy appears in the living room.

'Hey, Ben,' he says gently, brightly. There's genuine emotion in his voice and his face has softened. Ben glances at him, fleetingly, then turns back to the computer, opens up a browser window and double clicks on the YouTube icon. He starts up a video: 'Five Little Monkeys Jumping on the

Bed'. 'Jeez.' Andy moves forward and crouches down beside him. 'Look at that! When did he learn to use a computer?'

'A few months ago.'

I feel a trickle of pleasure as I wipe Ben's specs on the edge of my blouse and place them back on his nose. Keep going, Ben, I urge him, silently. Find another video. Show him what you can do.

Ben moves the cursor and scrolls up and down the options in the sidebar. He selects another video, then another. Andy watches for a moment, then looks up at him, admiringly. 'Well, how about that?'

'More to him than meets the eye.' I smile.

'You can say that again!'

'He can walk now, too.'

'Really?' Andy looks genuinely delighted.

'Well, not brilliantly,' I correct myself. 'He's a bit unsteady and you have to hold his hand outdoors. But he's getting steadier and stronger every day.'

Andy nods slowly. 'That's amazing. Well done, buddy!' He puts an arm round Ben and gives him a squeeze. Ben wriggles free of his grasp, but Andy just laughs, leans forwards, plants a kiss on his cheek and says, 'I missed you, little fella.' He turns to me and grins. 'He looks like me, huh?'

'Yes.' I nod. 'He really does. He makes the same expressions that you do. It's uncanny.'

Andy grins. 'His hair is... wild!'

'I know,' I agree. 'It needs a cut, but...'

'I like it. He looks like a... like a mad professor.' He chuckles and strokes Ben's thick blond hair back from his forehead so that it's standing up even more.

A strange knot has formed in the pit of my stomach. In

spite of everything, I can't help feeling happy that Andy is so impressed with Ben. I realise that, the minute I'd seen him on the doorstep, I'd been gearing myself up for disappointment, that I'd been holding the door shut to protect Ben, to stop Andy from noticing his lack of development, from commenting on all the things he still can't do.

'He's autistic,' I tell him. 'I mean, obviously, his learning disability is still there. But we've had the autism diagnosis now. So, that's why he's ignoring you. He probably doesn't remember you too well, either. But he *can* get attached to people. He can show love. He will—' I break off. I have to stop mitigating. What am I doing? Am I trying to persuade Andy to love his own child?

'That's OK.' Andy smiles and ruffles Ben's head a little before standing back up. 'We've got plenty of time.'

My heart leaps. Plenty of time? What does he mean?

He turns to me and sees the look on my face. 'Things have changed, Sarah. I wasn't in a good place, back then. I...'

'What do you mean?' I ask. 'What do you mean, we have plenty of time?'

Andy moves over to the sofa and sits down. 'Like I said, I'm back. I have a job back here in London. I start next week.'

I sink down into the chair next to him. 'What? For how long? Is it contract work?'

'No. It's permanent.' His eyes meet mine and flicker back and forth a little, trying to gauge my reaction. 'Well, we'll have to see how it goes, obviously, but... things weren't really working out for me in Perth. I needed a change and I... Look, Sarah, I know this is a bit sudden and everything, and I'm not expecting to walk back through the door just like that.' He lifts one hand and clicks his fingers. 'But I missed you guys. I think I made a big mistake, leaving—'

'No!' I cry out in alarm. 'No. You can't do this! You can't just waltz back in like this and—'

Andy lifts up both hands in a gesture of surrender. 'It's OK. Stop. I don't mean anything by that. I don't expect anything from you. I'm just telling you how I feel, that's all. When I saw you walking down the road with Ben earlier, I just knew... I just knew that I'd never stopped loving the both of you. I thought to myself, "That's my family, that is."'

I'm stunned into silence for a second time. My head is spinning. I just can't think of anything to say.

Then the phone rings. It's on the coffee table. Andy passes it to me.

It's a withheld number again. I push the slider with my thumb before putting the phone to my ear.

'Is that Sarah Kellerman?' A woman's voice, which I don't recognise. My heart stops in my chest. An inexplicable instinct tells me that this is not going to be good news.

'Yes.' My voice croaks as I speak. I clear my throat. 'Yes, this is Sarah.'

'Sarah, my name is Joanne Gooding. I'm a charge nurse on the Critical Care Unit at St James's Hospital. I'm afraid I have some bad news for you. We have William Gaskin here.'

2

Dusk has set by the time I exit the Tube station at Westminster and cross the road towards the bridge. In front of me, the Houses of Parliament are lit up brightly, their ornate walls and turrets encased in an orange glow. In contrast, just one wing of the building on the southwest side is in darkness, casting a black shadow across the silvery blue waters of the Thames. I pause on the bridge for a moment as my phone retrieves its GPS signal. Up above me, Big Ben's luminous clockface tells me that it's a quarter past eight. Visiting hours run until ten; I still have plenty of time. But if only I'd known, I berate myself. If only I'd gone to Will's flat or called his chambers... or rung around the hospitals. If I'd done that, I could have come sooner. How could I have not known? How could I have just carried on with my life and not even sensed that something was seriously wrong?

I tap the hospital address into Google Maps and then follow the directions up the street and into Parliament Square. As I pass the entrance to the Commons, I wonder, yet again, what kind of a state I'm going to find him in. All they've told me is that he's been in an accident and that he's in a 'serious but stable condition' – but what does that mean, exactly? What kind of an accident was it? A road traffic accident? Or something else? Will he live? And even if he does, might he have… I think about the police reports I've read so many times: 'The injuries are life-changing.' Might Will have life-changing injuries? Selfishly, and feeling ashamed as I think it, I can't help but wonder… what is this going to mean for me? For us? For me and him?

As I cross the road opposite the abbey, my phone bleeps, then rings. It's Andy. I pull it out of my pocket and answer the call, simultaneously sidestepping a black cab, whose driver seems intent on mowing down anyone in his path now that the traffic lights have turned to green.

'Andy?' My voice is tight and breathless. 'Is everything OK?'

'Yeah, it's fine. But he's, erm… he's done a… there's a bit of a mess. It's all over his trousers. And his T-shirt. Are there any more wipes anywhere?'

'Yes, in the hall cupboard. And there's a bucket under the sink. Just give his clothes a rinse through and leave them to soak.'

'They're in the garden. I put them out the back door. Sorry. The smell.'

I sigh. 'OK. Is he in his PJs now? Did you give him his meds? Like I told you?'

'No, I'm going to do that now.'

I think about the time. Ben should have had his meds. He should be in bed, asleep by now. He's going to be really tired tomorrow. 'Make sure you do,' I say. 'Please don't forget. It's five mils. You just use the syringe, like I showed you.'

'I remember, don't worry. He'll be right. It's not that long since I last gave it to him.'

'It's nearly two years, Andy.'

'Really? Is it? It doesn't feel that long.'

I think: not for you, maybe. 'And then he needs to go to bed,' I tell him. 'This is very late for him.'

'OK.'

'And just while I remember… don't leave anything lying around, like money.'

'Money?'

'Coins. I mean coins. Or peanuts.'

'Huh? Peanuts? I don't have any peanuts.'

'All right… jewellery, then.'

'*Jewellery?* Since when have I worn jewellery?'

'I don't know, do I?' I let out a wail of exasperation. 'What do I know about you these days, Andy? I'm just talking about anything small that he could put in his mouth, and then choke on. That's what I mean!'

'Oh, right. Got it. Yeah, don't worry. I'll take good care of him. We'll be fine.'

'OK. Sorry. I'm just… worried.'

'Well, don't worry about us,' he reassures me. 'And your… your fella. I'm sure he'll be OK.'

'Thanks. I'm nearly there now. I'd better go.'

As I end the call and turn off Millbank towards St John's Gardens, I spot the red brick of the hospital and the entrance up ahead where the ambulances are parked. The back of one of the ambulances is open and a small group of paramedics are standing nearby, their green uniforms and hi-vis jackets causing the hairs on the back of my neck to rise. Danger. That's what those uniforms, those ambulances say. In my mind's eye, I immediately see images of Will on a stretcher, Will in the back of that ambulance, Will bleeding heavily, struggling to breathe or writhing in pain.

The Critical Care Unit is on the third floor. I run up the staircase rather than waiting for the lift. I announce myself through an intercom and, a moment later, I'm buzzed in. I give Will's name at the nurses' station and am shown to a sink where I'm asked to put on a plastic apron and wash my hands.

'Sarah, is it?' A nurse appears behind me as I'm drying my hands with a paper towel. 'I'm Becky. I'm looking after Will.'

I drop the paper towel into the bin and turn to greet her. 'How is he?' I ask her, anxiously. 'Is he going to be OK?'

'We're doing all we can,' she replies. 'Right now, he's comfortable. But he's been in theatre. He had surgery this morning, so he's going to be very—'

'Surgery?' I repeat, my mind racing. 'Surgery… for what?'

The nurse looks at me with a slight awkwardness. She's wondering exactly who I am to Will; she's thinking about what to say. She's young, slim and pretty, I notice, with even features and soft clear ebony skin. She has a small piercing in the side of her nose and tousled platinum pink hair, which is tied back in a ponytail.

'So, what happened to him?' I prompt her. 'Please. I need to know.'

Becky hesitates. 'I can only tell you what's happened since he's been in hospital,' she says. 'I'm afraid he's in a critical condition. That's all I can say.'

'Is he awake? Can he talk?'

I look at her expectantly. I wonder, does Will even know that this is his nurse?

'Yes,' she says, and I breathe a sigh of relief. 'But he's going to be very tired.' She looks at me kindly. 'And he's been quite confused. Don't expect too much from him.'

I think for a moment. 'How did you know to call me?'

'He asked for you.' She smiles.

'So, he'll know who I am, then?'

'Yes. I think so.' She says this confidently, and smiles again, but it's a tight-lipped smile. 'So,' she asks. 'Are you ready?'

I follow her through the main ward into a bay to the left. The air is heavy with the smell of sickness, mingled with ethyl alcohol gel. The bay has six beds, four of which are occupied. Will is in the far corner, near the window. I catch my breath as I take in his appearance. He doesn't look like Will at all. He looks pale and thin. And frail. And unshaven, I notice. His lovely dark hair looks lank and dishevelled. He's wearing a hospital gown and his left leg is propped up on a pillow, wrapped in a crepe bandage. There's a machine at his feet which is inflating and deflating in a steady rhythm. There are countless tubes coming in or out of his neck, his nose and his arms into machines beside the bed.

'What are all the tubes?' I whisper to the nurse, my voice breaking a little as I try hard not to cry.

'Fluids. Antibiotics. Noradrenaline. The pump on his feet is to keep the blood circulating and to prevent clots.'

I bite my lip, afraid to ask any more.

She moves ahead of me towards the bed and I blink back my tears before following her. 'Will?' she calls. 'Look who's here to see you.'

As his head turns towards us and he opens his eyes, I can see that Will's eyelids are swollen. His face appears clammy. He gives me a look which tells me that he's pleased to see

27

me, but that he's embarrassed, all the same, to be found here looking like this.

'Hi, you,' I say, softly.

'Hi, yourself,' he replies. His voice sounds gravelly.

'Shall we just make you a little more comfortable?' Becky adjusts Will's tubes a little then reaches for his right elbow, lifts his hand and places it on top of the bedclothes. She then smiles at us both and leaves.

I tentatively reach out and touch Will's hand, then stroke back the hair that's sticking to his clammy forehead while he fixes his dark, swollen eyes on mine. I pull a chair up closer to his bed and slip my hand into his, careful to avoid knocking his cannula.

Will curls his fingers around mine. 'This wasn't how I imagined it.'

'Imagined what?'

He smiles, weakly. 'Waking up in bed with no clothes on and finding you next to me.'

'Me neither.' I let out a quiet giggle, my chest heaving as the tension inside me lifts a little. Whatever's happened, he hasn't lost his sense of humour. Does that mean he's going to be OK? 'So, how are you feeling?' I ask.

'Not too bad. Although, I've felt better, that's for sure.' He swallows heavily. I watch his Adam's apple as it moves up and down in his throat, beneath his unshaven chin. So many times I've watched it as it moves; when he's sitting across a table from me, talking authoritatively about our trial strategy, or standing up in court, cleverly cross-examining a witness. I think of him in his wig and gown, looking handsome and strong as he strides across the courtroom. Now, the lump at his throat appears fragile, his neck pale and slender as if it could break.

'Christ, Will, what on earth happened?' I ask.

He heaves a sigh. His eyes flicker towards the cabinet beside his bed. 'Could you…' He releases his fingers from my hand and eyepoints towards the jug of water.

'Of course.' I stand up. 'Shall I sit you up a little?'

'Yes please.'

I pour a glass of water and then use the remote to raise his head just a bit. I help him take a few sips through a straw that's on top of the cabinet, wrapped in plastic.

The effort of sitting up and drinking is clearly exhausting for him. When he's finished, I sit back down and wait until he's ready.

'I don't remember,' he says finally.

'What… nothing? Nothing at all?' I gasp. 'You don't know how you got here?'

Will moves his head slightly and closes his eyes. I wait until he opens them again. 'I collapsed in the street. Or so I'm told.' He speaks slowly. 'I remember feeling really unwell. I thought I had the flu. I went home, to sleep; I don't know how long. I remember getting up, going out. Milk. I wanted to buy milk. I was very thirsty. Then… then waking up here.'

'Oh my God, Will. Why didn't you call me? Or… or someone?' I correct myself, not wanting to sound as though I'm berating him for keeping me in the dark.

Will looks at me in silence for a moment. 'I don't know,' he confesses, eventually.

'How long have you been here?' I ask.

'Since Friday, they said – although it's all a bit of a blur. They say I was delirious. Up until yesterday, I thought I was on a film set. I remember congratulating one of the nurses on her acting.'

I laugh and Will smiles too. He looks up and fixes his dark, puffy eyes on mine. 'I'm sorry,' he says.

I lean forward and take his hand again. 'Don't be silly. Why are you sorry?'

'I didn't call.'

'Well… you weren't well,' I say.

'No.' Will looks relieved. He closes his eyes again.

'So, what is it?' I persist. 'What's wrong? What was the operation for? They told me you'd been in an accident.'

A shadow crosses Will's face and he frowns. 'Who told you that?'

'The charge nurse – when she phoned.'

'No.' Will shakes his head and closes his eyes again.

'Then…'

'I have an infection,' Will says, with his eyes closed.

'What kind of infection?'

'In my leg.'

'What happened to your leg?' I ask him, nodding at the bandaged leg which is on top of a pillow, protruding from his bedclothes.

Will opens his eyes and glances down at it. He looks puzzled, as if seeing the bandages for the first time. 'They had to operate,' he says. 'I had a… a scratch on my leg. It got infected.'

'A scratch?' I ask, incredulous.

But Will has closed his eyes again. He releases his grip on my fingers.

I sit still for a few moments. Eventually, realising Will's asleep, I take the bed remote and lower him back down. I lean over to kiss his forehead, then get up to see if I can find his nurse. Becky. That was her name. I need to find Becky. I need to find out what's wrong with Will. She might not be able to tell me what brought him to hospital, but she can tell me about his treatment, surely? I need to know how serious this is. What kind of infection would need an operation – and for him to be kept in intensive care?

She's in a bay at the end of the ward. As I pass each bay, I peer in until I see her platinum pink hair moving around next to a bed in the corner near the window. I pause in the doorway and wait for her to finish what she's doing. As I do so, the man in the bed nearest to me starts coughing loudly. I notice that he has a tracheostomy tube in his neck, which is attached to a ventilator at the side of the bed. The ventilator is noisy – it's bleeping and whirring. It has a large screen which looks like an old-fashioned computer game. The man lifts his hand and tries to tug at the tube in his neck.

'No,' I say, quickly, flustered. 'Nurse! Becky. He's trying to take his tube out.'

Becky appears beside me. She reaches over and gently unpeels the man's fingers from the tube. She places both his hands on the bedclothes. 'No,' she says, gently but firmly. 'We need to leave that there.'

The man stops coughing and looks at her. I can't help being drawn to his face. Despite his pallor, he is very attractive – and young, too. Well, not *young* exactly – but not old. Definitely not old. I'd put him in his mid-to-late forties, no more. Will's age, in fact. Although in contrast to Will's olive skin and dark looks, this man has startling blue eyes – and a scar underneath his right eye which, now I come to think of it, looks familiar. I step forward and study his face more carefully. And then I realise – I know him. I know him well.

'Oh my God. It's… it's… I know him!' I step right up to his bedside. 'Mark?' I ask him. 'Are you OK?'

The man turns his head to look at me but doesn't respond.

'Mark?' I repeat. 'It's me, Sarah. Sarah Kellerman.'

The man continues to look at me in silence. At first, I wonder if I've got it wrong, but… no. My heart skips a beat. It's him. It's definitely him.

I turn to Becky, who's standing behind me. 'Can't he talk?' I ask her. My mouth feels dry with shock. 'Is it the trache… the breathing tube in his throat?'

Becky stares back at me for a moment, her eyes flickering from Mark to me and back again. 'You know him?' she asks me, her brow creasing.

I nod. 'Yes. His name's Mark Felding, right? He's a police sergeant. Or was.' I turn to Mark for backup, but he's looking at… I'm not sure what he's looking at, actually. I realise with alarm that he's not really looking at anything, that his eyes are just moving aimlessly around in his head. I watch in horror for a moment as it dawns on me: he's not fully conscious. He's awake, but he's not able to communicate. He doesn't know who I am.

I turn back to Becky for reassurance, but she appears to be as stunned as I am. 'Are you sure?' she asks eventually.

Now, I'm really confused. I turn to look at the man again. It's true that I haven't seen him for quite a while and he looks a little different. For a start, his head is shaved, which it isn't normally, and he's not acknowledging me in any way. But I know him! I definitely recognise him. I know his face; I know it well.

'Yes,' I insist. 'Definitely. His name's Mark Felding. He used to be a custody sergeant at Farringdon police station.'

In fact, he was one of the best custody sergeants I've ever dealt with, and certainly the nicest. He was kind, and approachable – and fair. I used to enjoy having a bit of a chat and a laugh with him when custody was quiet, and I found that I missed him when he suddenly wasn't there any more. 'I used to see him every day, almost, at the police station. I'm a solicitor,' I explain. 'In fact,' I recall, 'he once saved me from a violent client... a man being detained by the police, who I was there to represent. I was in a holding room with him. One minute everything was fine and then, suddenly, he switched – and he went for me. Before I even knew what had happened, Mark was there in the room, pinning him to the ground. I've never seen anyone move so fast.'

'So, when did you last see him?' Becky asks me.

I cast my mind back. 'I can't remember exactly. A year... eighteen months ago... maybe more. I just noticed, one day, that he wasn't there any more. I asked around at Farringdon but no one seemed to know where he'd gone.' I pause and look at Becky's face. 'Why? What is it?'

Becky hesitates. 'Look, I'm not his nurse,' she says. 'But... can you wait, while I go and get her?'

'Sure.' I nod, puzzled by her reaction.

Becky leaves the ward. I sit down on a chair next to the bed. Mark turns his head to look at me and I smile, but he looks blankly back at me. Even though he's not behaving like himself, or acknowledging me in any way, I know it's him. It's definitely him. I remember those eyes, that scar under his eye... I remember watching his face many a time and wondering how he'd got it, as he tilted his computer monitor to show me a custody record or passed my client a bail sheet to sign.

Then he lifts one hand and I see that he's going for his breathing tube again. I lean forward and gently take both of his hands in mine. I'm a little worried that he might fight me, that I won't be able to restrain him, but he just wriggles a little, before relaxing. He seems to like me holding his hands. They're big and warm, his palms soft, his fingers a little calloused. It feels good to hold them, although strange, at the same time. A mixture of emotions is rising up inside me, churning me up. First Will, and now... this: Mark Felding, of all people. He was always so... solid. Authoritative. Reliable. And astute. Able to make sensible decisions quickly, to restrain violent prisoners or to protect the self-harmers. He was good at his job, at looking after those in his care. And now, here he is, in his hospital gown, needing restraining himself, like a child. I fight back tears for the second time. I move his hands firmly downwards and sit them on top of the bedclothes. Mark responds by squeezing my right hand. I look up quickly, in mild anticipation: has he realised who I am? But his face is impassive still and his eyes are again moving back and forth without any apparent focus.

A moment later, Becky is back with two more nurses. One of them has what looks like a pair of boxing gloves in her hands. She immediately moves over to the bed and I let go of Mark's hands. I watch for a moment as she takes them in her own and pushes them into the boxing gloves, before fastening them. Mark tries to resist at first and Becky steps forward to help. 'They're to stop him from pulling out his tubes,' Mark's nurse explains. 'We need to do this. Just until he settles. If he removes the tube, it could be life threatening.'

I nod. 'Sure. Of course.' I notice that she's talking to me as if I'm a relative, someone whose opinion counts.

'Sarah?' says the third nurse from behind me. I turn to face her. She's wearing a navy-blue tunic with red piping. She's around my age – late thirties, I'd say. 'I'm Jo Gooding, the ward sister,' she says.

I nod. 'We spoke on the phone, I think.'

'Yes. That's right. I wonder if we could have a quiet word?'

'Yes, of course.' I glance at Mark, who appears to have accepted the boxing mitts and is now looking up at the ceiling. My eyes automatically track his, as they do with Ben's, to see what he's looking at, what he wants or what it is that's bothering him. But there's nothing there.

I stand up and follow the ward sister out of the bay and along the corridor into a small room behind the nurses' station. The room is empty except for a small table, two armchairs and a plant. It has white flowers which remind me of lilies. Something tells me that this is the room where people go when there's bad news to be delivered by the nursing staff. I'm not completely sure if I'm here because of Will or Mark, and my stomach is in knots. The ward sister waves me into one of the armchairs and sits down opposite me, with a pad and pen. She takes a pair of glasses out of her top pocket and puts them on.

'So,' she says. 'You know the man in the bed as Mark...?'

'Felding.'

'Mark Felding,' she repeats. 'F-e-l-l-d-i-n-g?'

'One "l", I think. But, yes,' I agree, confused. 'Don't you?'

She doesn't answer my question. 'So, how do you know him?' she asks me, instead.

'Like I said, through work.'

'Do you know his family?' she asks.

I stare at her for a moment in bewilderment. 'You didn't know who he was, did you?'

She shakes her head. 'No.' She looks up at me. 'It's really very fortunate, you being here and recognising him. We're very grateful. Hopefully we can now take steps to contact his next of kin.'

I look at her in horror and confusion. 'How long has he been here?'

'Since New Year's Day,' she tells me. 'The early hours.'

'All that time?' I gasp. 'He's been here... what, nearly three months, without anyone knowing who he was?'

'He was in an accident. A road traffic accident. He's suffered a severe brain trauma,' she explains. 'He hasn't been able to tell us... And he had nothing with him – no personal effects, nothing with which we could identify him. There was nothing we could do. We were hoping that you might be able to tell us about his next of kin.'

I think about this for a moment. 'He has a wife and... two children, I think. I couldn't tell you their ages, but his daughter's named Sophie... or Sophia. Yes, Sophia. He used to talk about her. I remember once he was thinking about getting her a rabbit for her birthday and he asked my opinion.'

'OK. And do you know where they live?'

I shake my head. 'No, but... but the police do. Surely they were called to the scene of the accident? Surely they're involved?'

She nods. 'Yes, of course they were. They *are* involved. But they haven't been able to identify him, unfortunately.'

'But he's a police officer!' I protest. 'Or at least he *was* a police officer. Didn't the other nurse... Becky... didn't she tell you?' I peer at her, trying to read her expression. It feels as though she's not quite sure that I've got any of this right. I think about this for a moment, questioning myself. 'I suppose if he's left the police,' I continue. 'I suppose... but they would know him, still. Or someone would. This doesn't make any sense.'

Her face is impassive. 'I'm sure there's an explanation. And they'll be called, don't worry. Which police station was he based at?'

'Farringdon.'

'OK. We'll speak to them and see if we can get some further information. And they may want to speak to you, too.'

I nod. 'OK.'

She takes her glasses off, stands up and smiles. I reach down to pick up my bag and stand up too and we move towards the door.

'Will he recover?' I ask her.

She looks at me sympathetically. 'We really don't know at this stage.'

I nod, knowing that this is all she is going to tell me. 'And Will,' I say. 'Will Gaskin. What about him? Will he be OK?'

She says, 'Again. It's hard to predict at this stage. He has a serious infection. He's on a full course of antibiotics and we are hopeful that surgery has got ahead of the infection at the moment. He's in the best place for treatment. We'll continue to monitor him.'

'He said it started in his leg,' I blurt out. 'From a scratch. How can that have happened?'

For a moment, she doesn't say anything, but then she says, 'The infection is called necrotising fasciitis. It's relatively rare, but several things can cause it. We've operated to remove the infected tissue in his leg and we've made him comfortable. We will do everything we can to prevent it spreading.'

'It could spread?' I say, in alarm.

'As I said, he's on a full course of antibiotics. He'll stay in the ICU for as long as is needed. There may well be more procedures, going forward. But we're doing everything we can.'

I nod and heave a sigh. 'Thank you.' I open the door. As I turn to leave, I reach into the side pocket of my bag and hand her a business card. 'For the police,' I say.

When I turn my key in the lock, I can smell food. Andy's cooked dinner, by the looks of things. He's in the front room, watching some quiz show on the telly. It feels strange but somewhat comforting, I realise, to walk into my own front room and find the lights on and him sitting there, intermittent bursts of laughter coming from the TV. He has a bottle of beer in one hand and a foot up on the coffee table. He's removed his shoes, and I feel a strange surge of emotion at the sight of his socks, his toes wiggling inside them, the way they always did when he was happy and relaxed. When he sees me in the doorway, he immediately picks up the remote and flicks off the TV.

'Sarah. You're back. How'd it go?'

I take a deep breath in and out. 'He's not too good. I mean, he's awake and he's talking. But he's seriously unwell.'

'What's happened to him?'

'He has an infection. It's called necrotising fasciitis. It causes tissue damage.'

'How did he get it?'

'I'm not completely sure.'

Andy frowns. 'They didn't tell you? Or they don't know?'

I hesitate. 'The infection's in his leg. He said it was from a scratch.'

'A *scratch*?'

'That's what he said.'

'Oh. OK.' Andy smooths back his hair, then stands up. 'I made you dinner. You must be hungry. Want to sit down and I'll get it? I bet you could do with a glass of wine.'

I nod and shrug off my coat. 'Thanks. Is Ben OK?'

'He's good,' Andy reassures me. 'He had his meds. Five mils. Like you said,' he jumps in quickly, before I can ask. 'And then we put on his music. That nursery rhyme one, he still likes that, huh? "Little Mousie Brown". He hasn't got tired of that yet!' He smiles, and I can see that he's feeling nostalgic, not critical of Ben. Instead of being upset that Ben's still listening to the same old music he was listening to as a baby, he's glad. Although he's pleased that Ben has learned new things, he's also glad about the things that haven't changed too much while he's been away. This wasn't what I was expecting at all.

Suddenly, everything feels too much. All the emotion that's been building up inside me for the last few hours finally spills out.

'Hey. Come here.' Andy moves over to the doorway where I'm standing and puts his arms round me. I remember, now, that he was always really good when I cried. Some men find it awkward and want you to stop. *My bloody father.* But not Andy. He always knew how to make me feel better when I was upset. I could always be myself with him.

He rubs my back and hugs me tight. Against all my better judgement and reasoning, I find myself sinking into his arms, my face pressing against his neck. He feels solid, comforting and familiar.

'Come on,' he says. 'I know it must be really hard. But you have to believe that everything's gonna be right.'

'But what if it's not?' I sob. 'What if he dies?'

Even whilst I'm saying this I feel torn up inside. Suddenly, it feels wrong to be in Andy's arms while I'm talking about Will, especially while I'm talking about Will not making it. And especially knowing that I can't trust that *anything* that's here today will still be here tomorrow. That's what it boils down to, isn't it?

I pull myself away.

'You OK?' he asks me, peering into my eyes, his forehead etched with concern.

I nod.

'He's in the best place,' Andy says. 'Really. He is.'

I wipe my eyes with the back of my hand.

'You're tired,' Andy tells me. 'You need to sit down, have some food.'

'OK. In a minute. I just want to check on Ben.'

I kick off my shoes and tiptoe down the hallway and into Ben's room. He's fast asleep, wearing his stripy blue and white PJs, snuffling softly, one arm flung out above his head.

I lean forward and kiss him, gently. His cheek is soft, and real, and warm. The old hurt seeps back into my lungs as I watch him sleeping, as I recall the first days and weeks after Andy left, how I stumbled through them like an automaton. Poor Ben. Did he notice, I wonder? Did he miss those strong male arms as much as I did? Or was he still too busy trying to make sense of the world around him to notice that his father had gone?

I whisper goodnight, then go into my bedroom and slip out of my work clothes and into a T-shirt and tracksuit bottoms. I can hear Andy moving around in the kitchen. When he sees me come in, he opens the oven and pulls out a hot plate of pasta with some kind of sauce. On the table is a bowl of salad and a glass of white wine. The table is set for one.

'You've done well,' I comment, trying not to mind that there are several dirty pans on the stove and yet more crockery piled up in the sink. 'Did Ben eat all of his?'

'Yep. He loved my pasta. I gave it to him with some cheese.'

'That's good.' I sit down at the table and pick up my fork.

Andy pulls out a chair and sits down opposite me. 'So, have you googled it?' he asks. 'This infection?'

I nod, through a mouthful of pasta. I get up and pull my iPad out of my bag, open the browser and push the iPad across the table towards him. I take a large gulp of wine and continue to eat in silence as Andy reads. He taps the page a few times and scrolls up and down.

'So, you see, it can be caused by a scratch,' I say, finally.

Andy looks up. 'Amongst other things.'

I take another sip of wine. 'Well, yeah. There are lots of things. Insect bites.'

'In March?' Andy raises his eyebrows.

I shrug. 'The point is, necrotising fasciitis is rare, but scarily easy to get if you have the bacteria living in your skin already. All it takes is a scratch.'

'But he didn't tell you how he got that scratch?'

'No.'

Andy nods, silently. He scrolls back and forth a few times more, hits a few more links.

'What?' I ask him.

'Well, it's just that...'

'What?' I insist. 'Tell me.'

Andy puts the iPad down on the table. He sits back in his seat and folds his arms. 'Well, it says that one of the most common ways you can get it is from puncture wounds.'

I put down my fork. 'Puncture wounds?'

'Yes.' Andy's eyes meet mine. 'You know. From injecting drugs.'

I shake my head in disbelief. 'Drugs? You think Will takes drugs?'

Andy shrugs. 'I don't know. I don't know the guy, do I? But it's an explanation, isn't it? A reason why he's not telling you how he got this "scratch".'

I look at him in horror. 'Andy, what are you talking about?' I cry out, scornfully. 'He's a lawyer. A professional!'

'That doesn't mean anything,' Andy says, dismissively. 'Take ice, for instance,' he continues. 'It's a really big problem amongst professionals in Australia right now. It's the new heroin.'

'Ice? You mean crystal meth?' I ask, alarmed.

'Although, I'm not sure about here,' Andy says.

'It's not,' I say. 'I deal with Class A drugs cases all the time. It's mainly heroin or cocaine here.'

'So, heroin. Or cocaine.'

'You don't inject cocaine.'

'You can inject anything,' says Andy. 'If you want the bigger high, that's what you do.'

I shake my head. 'Why are you saying all this? Why would you automatically assume that it's drugs?'

Andy shrugs. 'Is he diabetic?'

I shake my head. 'No.'

'Is he an alcoholic?'

'*No.*'

'Then it's the most likely explanation.' He slides the iPad back across the table towards me. 'See for yourself.'

I grab it from him and switch it off. 'It can't be that. I've worked with him. He's brilliant at his job. If he was doing something like that, I'd know.'

'Are you sure about that?' Andy looks me in the eye. 'Ice is highly addictive, but many people back home seem to be able to function and hold down a job.'

I glare at him. He's starting to annoy me now.

'OK. Forget it,' he says. 'It was just a thought.' He pushes his chair back and gets up. 'I'd better get going.'

'Yeah. You better had.' I make no move to get up.

Andy walks over to the door, then appears to have second thoughts. He comes back over and stoops down in front of me. 'Sorry. I didn't mean to upset you. Just ignore me. I don't even know him, do I?'

I look back at him. His eyes are level with mine. 'No, you don't,' I agree.

I watch as Andy springs up, satisfied that all is well between us. I follow him out to the hallway as he locates his car keys, finds his jacket and slips on his shoes. No, you don't, I think to myself as he opens the front door and waves goodbye. You don't know Will at all. The question is, do I?

3

When I arrive at the office on Friday morning, there's a message for me.

'It's Jerome Thomas's mum, Georgina.' Lucy, our receptionist, hands me a yellow telephone attendance note. 'Oh, and your friend called again.'

I look up. 'What friend?'

'The woman who called yesterday.'

'What woman?'

Lucy looks up at me. 'Didn't I tell you?'

'No. I don't think so.'

'Oh. Maybe I haven't seen you since then.'

'Did she leave her name, or a number?'

'Uh-uh.' Lucy shakes her head and starts typing.

'You didn't think to ask?' I press her, knowing at the same time that this will rile her. I'm normally exceptionally forgiving of Lucy's uncooperative attitude towards me. I've never completely understood what I've done to upset her. She's nothing but sweetness and light when it comes to my boss, Gareth, or to my colleague, Matt – or any of the other members of the team, come to that.

Lucy stops typing. Her fingers remain poised over the keyboard as she shoots an intransigent look at me, her green eyes flashing and her cheeks flushing. 'No. I didn't. I'm too busy to be taking personal calls.'

I remain standing in front of her as she starts typing again, her fingernails clickety-clicking against the keyboard. If it's a personal call, I've no idea who it could be. Why would any of my friends call me at the office? Was it a nurse? I wonder. About Will? But I spoke to the ICU night shift this morning – and Will had had a good night. And why would they call me at the office? They'd call me on my mobile, wouldn't they?

'So… what did she want?' I persist.

Lucy sighs and drops her hands into her lap. 'I don't know. She just wanted to know where you were. I told her you were at court and that you should be back at the office by lunchtime.'

'OK. Thank you. That's helpful,' I say, pointedly. 'I'd better go and see what Georgina wants.'

'Jerome's been arrested again,' she says. 'Last night.'

'Last night? Why didn't he ask for us?'

'He did. Matt was on call. He went out for him. He says he couldn't get hold of you.'

'Oh. I see.'

I head up the stairs to my room and dial Georgina's number. She picks up on the first ring. 'Sarah?'

'Hi, Georgina. What's happened?'

'You're not going to believe this!' Her voice is loud, her pitch raised. 'Jerome's only gone and got himself into trouble again!' I can hear a child crying in the background. Georgina sounds at her wits' end. 'Well, when I say *again*, it's not something new. They said it happened a few months ago. But this is really stressing me out, you know? Kaleisha, you put that down, now!' Her voice becomes muffled as she reprimands the child in the background. The child's crying intensifies for a moment or two, then stops. 'Sorry about that, Sarah. I'm starting to lose my patience here!'

'So, what is it?' I ask her. 'Another car theft?'

'Yes. Same old, same old. Only, this time, Jerome says it wasn't him. I just don't know what to think, to be honest. You know Jerome. If he's done it he puts his hands up, always. But he swears blind, this time, he was not in that car.'

'OK. So...'

'Your colleague, Matthew,' she continues, her voice irate, 'he said, just say nothing. No comment. So that's what Jerome did. Jerome said that he had nothing to do with it. He wanted to explain himself. But Matthew said no, that he should just keep his powder dry. I don't know if that was the right thing to do. We wanted you, but Matthew said you don't come out in the evenings, that it's always him.'

'Right.' I scratch my head. 'Well, I do often have trouble in the evenings...'

'I know. It's OK. You got your boy. I understand, Lord help me, I do. I had to get my sister to come over last night and she weren't none too happy about that.'

'Oh dear. So, what happened?'

'Well, they gave him bail. But I don't know whether he did the right thing. It makes it look like he's guilty, doesn't it? And he says he's not. Not this time.'

'Not being funny, Georgina, but if it was a few months ago, how can he be sure he wasn't involved?'

'Because of the car. It was a four-by-four, they said, with blacked out windows. Jerome said that's the sort of car that the drug dealers drive. He wouldn't be stupid enough to steal one of them, he said. It would be more than his life was worth.'

'Where was it stolen from?'

'They wouldn't say. They just said they found a fingerprint that may or may not be Jerome's.'

'Where did they find it?'

'They weren't prepared to say.'

'Hmm. That's odd.'

'Is it?'

'Well… yeah.' I think about this for a moment. 'If it was a few months ago they'd have got the forensics back by now. If it was his fingerprint, they'd know. And if that was the reason for arrest, they'd say.'

'Well, they didn't. All they said was that he matched the description of one of the persons seen running away from the scene: a black kid.'

'So, what was the description?'

'It was a kid. And he was black.'

I sigh. 'Really? That's it?'

'Pretty much. Oh, and of course, it happened on the estate where we live.'

'Hmm. That doesn't sound like sufficient grounds for arrest,' I murmur. 'And the fingerprint is interesting. If they had a match, they'd have enough evidence to charge him. And yet, they haven't. So maybe they were bluffing. Maybe Jerome is telling the truth.'

'That's what I said! But your colleague Matthew, he said—'

'I'll speak to Matt,' I tell her. 'I'm sure he had his reasons. I'll make sure I'm there on the bail date. In the meantime, leave it with me.'

I end the call, switch on my computer and sit down. I log onto our case management system and search for Jerome's police station file. There's nothing there. Matt hasn't uploaded it yet. I open my bag and take out my iPad to start uploading my own cases from this morning. As I do so, the office phone rings, a single ring. It's Lucy. I pick up.

'She's here,' she says. 'Your friend. She's in reception.'

'Oh. OK. I'll be right there.'

I switch off my monitor, grab my iPad and head down the stairs. When I reach reception, a woman stands up. Lucy stops typing and watches us both. The woman is tall and slim and has striking features: straight, light auburn hair, cut into a neat, shoulder-length bob, a long roman nose and lips painted deep red set against pale porcelain skin. She's wearing a belted, brown wool coat and high-heeled black boots. I've never seen her before in my life.

'Hello,' I say. 'I'm Sarah Kellerman. Can I help you?'

The woman takes a step towards me and scans me with her eyes. She takes both my hands in hers and squeezes them tight. Her hands are cold but her smile is warm and friendly. 'Sarah. It's so good to meet you. My name's Karen. Karen Felding.' For a moment it doesn't register with me. 'Mark's wife,' she explains.

'Oh. Oh, gosh. I see.' I turn to Lucy. 'Is the conference room free?'

'Yes,' Lucy agrees, but gives me a disapproving look. She knows this isn't to do with work.

I usher Karen into the conference room and wave her into a seat. 'I'd offer you a drink,' I say, 'but...'

'Oh, no, that's OK,' she smiles. She takes her handbag from her shoulder and places it on her lap. Her voice is soft as she says, 'I'm interrupting your working day. I don't want to keep you. I just wanted to thank you, for finding Mark.'

I shrug. 'It was a coincidence. Really. I was visiting someone else and I walked past his room. I'm so sorry. It must have been a terrible shock for you.'

She nods. I can see the pain in her eyes, in her expression. But no tears. She's putting on a brave face.

'When did you find out?' I ask her.

'The police contacted me yesterday morning.'

I look at her in silence for a moment. 'I don't get it, though. He'd been missing for nearly three months,' I say. 'How did you not...?'

'We're separated,' she explains. 'We've been separated for over a year.'

'Oh. I see.'

She lifts her hand and takes hold of a pendant that's hanging on a chain round her neck. She rolls it back and forth between her thumb and forefinger. 'How well do you know him?' she asks me.

'Not well,' I admit. 'Just from the police station when he was a custody sergeant at Farringdon. I'd see him almost every day, sometimes, but you know how it is when you work with people. You don't always know that much about them.'

She lets go of the chain. 'Yes, well, it can be like that when you live with someone, too. He was a workaholic. He was always at work – or out drinking with his police buddies, or whatever he was doing. But the police came first, at the end of the day.'

She sighs heavily and falls silent.

'He often talked about his children,' I say, to comfort her. 'He seemed very proud of them.'

'I'm sure he was,' she agrees. 'But that doesn't mean he was a father to them. We never saw him. Especially after he moved out.' She grips her handbag with both hands. 'The last time I heard from him was just before Christmas,' she continues. 'He told the children he'd spend Christmas Day with them, but he never showed. When I finally got hold of him, he was full of apologies, said he'd be over on New Year's Eve, that he would bring the children their presents, make it up to them. When he didn't come, when we didn't hear from him, I just assumed he was being his usual unreliable self.'

I nod, although this image of her husband is so at odds with the solid, caring, seemingly reliable Mark Felding I'd thought I'd known that I'm struggling to make sense of it. For a moment, I even wonder if we're talking about the same person.

'So… what happened to him?' I ask her. 'What did the police say?'

'He was run over. It was a hit-and-run. The car had gone right over him.' Her voice wavers and she hesitates for a moment, before taking a deep inward breath. 'He had two separate head injuries, a fractured pelvis, two collapsed lungs, multiple broken ribs and a fractured shoulder blade. It's a miracle that he survived.'

'Jeez. I'm so sorry,' I say.

Karen places her elbows on the table and puts her head in her hands, her hair falling forwards. For a moment she doesn't speak. 'Me too,' she says, finally, lifting her head.

Her eyes are red-rimmed and her face is pale. 'Poor Mark. Whatever our differences, he didn't deserve that. And he's the children's father at the end of the day. They're going to be devastated.'

'They still don't know?'

She shakes her head. 'Sophia was away on a geography field trip. She got back last night. She was so happy, full of stories about her week away. I couldn't bring myself to tell her. And Jack had a chemistry assessment at school today.' She lets out another sigh. 'He's got his GCSEs in two months' time. Lord only knows how this is going to affect him. Anyway, I wanted to wait until the weekend. I'll tell them both tonight.'

'Of course. So, who found him?' I venture, after a moment.

'A member of the public, apparently. Someone who lives in the street. He looked out of his window and saw Mark lying in the road, then called the police.'

'Did he see what happened?'

'No. But they think he was already unconscious when the car hit him. They think he was mugged.'

'Mugged… and then run over?' I ask, incredulous.

She nods, slowly. 'Because of the nature of the head injuries. And because he had no ID – no watch, no wallet, nothing.'

I sit back in my chair and fold my arms, while I take this in. 'So where did he go?' I ask her. 'After he left custody?'

'Back to CID,' she replies. 'That's the way it goes. They all do their stint in custody, and then it's on to bigger and better things.'

'So… how could the police have not known who he was?'

'The response team was from the Met. Mark worked at Farringdon, which is...'

'City of London Police,' I finish for her.

'Right. They didn't know him, he wasn't on their beat. Their own CID got onto it apparently and it was a crime scene at the time. They did house-to-house enquiries, put boards up... but no one came forward.'

'What about CCTV? There must have been CCTV.'

She shakes her head. 'No. There was no CCTV. There isn't always.'

'Really? Nothing at all? Where did it happen?'

'Finsbury. Packington Street.'

I look up sharply.

'It's near the Pear Tree Estate.'

I nod. 'I know where it is.'

She heaves a sigh. 'Rough area, right?'

I think about this for a moment. 'Do they know what he was doing there?'

She shakes her head. 'They didn't say. But his flat's near King's Cross, around a fifteen-minute walk away. He may have been out for the evening; on his way home from somewhere, I suppose.'

'I still don't understand it,' I tell her. 'I don't understand how no one missed him – for three months!'

Karen lowers her head. 'I feel bad. I guess I should have realised—'

'I don't mean you,' I say, quickly. I think about Will, and how I'd immediately assumed that he'd lost interest in me, was maybe seeing someone else. It had never occurred to me that something had happened to him. 'But what about his colleagues, his bosses? When he didn't turn up for work...

surely someone would have noticed? He's a cop, for Christ's sake!'

Karen looks up and nods, slowly. 'I asked that too.' She hesitates. 'It seems he was facing disciplinary proceedings at work. He'd been suspended. Just before Christmas. Pending a full investigation.'

I frown. 'Into what?'

Her face flushes. 'They found drugs in his locker. They think he was supplying.' She shrugs. 'Who knows? Maybe using too.'

I shake my head, incredulous. 'Drugs? Mark? You're kidding me?'

She sighs. 'I wish.'

There's a bleeping noise and a lively jingle emanates from inside her handbag. 'I'm sorry,' she says. 'Can you excuse me, please. It's probably one of the children.'

'Of course, take it,' I insist. 'Do you want me to step outside?'

She shakes her head and pulls her phone out of her bag and glances at the screen. 'It's my son, Jack.' She answers the call. 'Jack? Everything all right?' She pauses. 'Yes, all right, but I'm with someone at the moment. Can't you just stay with her a bit longer?' She pauses again, then sighs. 'All right, all right. Calm down. I'm on my way.' She ends the call and snaps her phone case shut, then stands up. 'I should go. They're both home. I need to talk to them.'

'Of course,' I agree, and stand up too. 'I hope it goes… well, I'll be thinking of you,' I say, knowing that I will.

'Thank you.' She slips her handbag over her shoulder, before tightening the belt on her coat.

'I may see you at the hospital,' I suggest.

'Oh, gosh. Of course. You have... someone there?'

'My boyfriend,' I say. 'He's in intensive care. It's a combined ward, so he's just a few bays down from the HDU.'

'I'm sorry.' She reaches out and touches my hand.

'He has an infection. I don't know much more than that right now.'

She nods and sighs. 'Well, I'm planning on taking the children up tomorrow morning,' she tells me. 'If they want to go, that is. I think it's the right thing to do.' She doesn't say, 'In case Mark doesn't make it,' but I know that's what she means.

'I think so too,' I agree.

When I get back to my desk I immediately do a Google search for 'Hit and run Pear Tree Estate New Year's Eve'. When nothing comes up, I search again for 'Injured man St James's Hospital London' and 'Accident Packington Street New Year'. There are no results – not a single one.

The door opens and Matt walks in.

'Hi, Matt,' I say. 'I hear you represented Jerome last night?'

'Yeah.' Matt shrugs off his coat and sits down. He pulls his laptop out of his bag and sets it on his desk.

'Georgina rang,' I say. 'Jerome's mum. She seemed a bit upset.'

Matt swings round to face me. 'Why? What's she got to be upset about?'

'She's just wondering if Jerome should have answered questions. I said I'd speak to you.'

Matt frowns. 'She's an interfering old cow.'

I shake my head. 'No, she's not. She's a concerned mum of a fifteen-year-old boy. She's at her wits' end. We just need to reassure her, that's all.'

'Well, I reassured her last night.' Matt turns back to his desk and switches on his laptop. 'So, if you want to have a go, then be my guest. But my advice was spot on. They had nothing, disclosed nothing. No case to answer.'

'I thought that's what you'd say.'

Matt looks up. 'What, so you think he should have talked?'

'No.' I shake my head. 'Not necessarily. I just wanted to know your reasons.'

'Well, I'll tell you my reasons.' Matt leans down, opens his bag and takes out a battered counsel's notepad. 'One, the kid was *not* going to be a good advocate in his own defence. Yeah, he was sure he didn't nick that car. But he couldn't tell me anything else, couldn't remember where he was.'

I shrug. It was a few months ago. Why would he?

'And, two,' Matt continues. 'The cops.' He slaps the notebook down on top of an already burgeoning pile of paperwork on his desk.

'What about them?'

'They were having a laugh.'

I glance across at the notes in his hand. 'Who was the OIC?'

'So, here's the fun part,' says Matt. 'This wasn't traffic. It wasn't even CID. It was the MCU.'

I look up at him. Matt looks back at me, triumphantly.

'Major Crime?' I ask him. 'For a car theft?'

'Exactly,' says Matt. 'And yet... zip. Zero disclosure.

No VRN, no loser statement, no evidence the vehicle was reported missing – or where from. Where was it found? Nothing. Any damage to the steering lock? Not prepared to disclose. Those cars ain't cheap, anyway. Sixty-five K up, new. Even if it's older it's gonna have an immobiliser. Thief would need the keys. How did he get the keys? Oh. Guess what?' Matt looks up and rolls his eyes. 'Not prepared to disclose.'

'So what grounds did they give to arrest him?'

'Description.'

'Oh yeah,' I recall. 'That.'

'So, now you know why I told him to keep his mouth shut.' Matt connects a mouse to his laptop and clicks open a web page. 'No case to answer. And, yes, I challenged the grounds for arrest.'

'What did they say?'

'The usual. Early stages of an investigation, intel they're… wait for it… not prepared to disclose.'

'A fingerprint,' I comment. 'Georgina said they had a lift.'

Matt nods. 'So they said. But then they just glossed over it. Nothing was put to him in interview.'

'OK.' I lean back in my seat. 'You all right with me taking over?'

Matt frowns. 'What, you don't agree with my advice?'

'No, no. It was bang on. Obviously,' I say. 'It's just that I know Jerome, I've dealt with him a few times, and I promised Georgina…'

'Fine.' Matt shrugs. 'Whatever.'

'So, can I have your police station notes, then?'

'I have to upload them first.'

'It's OK, I'll do it for you,' I offer.

Matt looks up. He hates admin. 'OK,' he agrees.

He pulls the notebook off the pile on his desk, opens it and flicks through the pages, selecting and tearing out a handful before passing them to me.

I flick through the disclosure notice and notes of interview. Matt's handwriting is legible, just. Matt's right, though, that there's nothing here to indicate that this is anything more than a bog-standard TWOC – a 'taking without consent'.

'Can I ask you a question?' I say.

'What question?'

'What do you think would happen if a man was found lying in the road, with multiple life-threatening injuries, having been mugged and left for dead, then run over. A hit-and-run. He's got no ID. So, they can't identify him. House-to-house reveals nothing. No CCTV, no witnesses come forward.'

Matt looks at me as if I'm stupid. 'Well, they'd release photos to the press.'

I nod. 'Right. And what if – at around the same time – a copper goes missing.'

Matt pulls a face. 'What do you mean, goes missing?'

'Disappears,' I say.

'Well… a balloon would go up. There would be national press coverage. They'd give it all they'd got.'

'What if he was already suspended from work? Being investigated by Professional Standards.'

'Well, they'd still notice he was missing, wouldn't they? How can you investigate someone if they've disappeared?'

'Right.' I nod.

'Why? Who are we talking about?'

'Mark Felding. Used to be a custody sergeant at Farringdon. Do you remember him?'

'Oh yeah. Him. Arrogant twat,' says Matt.

'No, he wasn't!' I protest. 'He was really nice.'

'There's no such thing as a nice cop.' Matt turns back to his laptop and starts typing. 'He probably deserved it. Probably someone who he gave a good kicking in the cells one day.'

I can't imagine Mark Felding giving anyone a good kicking, but this isn't the first time Matt and I have had completely different experiences of the same person, or opposing views as regards to their character, or what they 'deserve'.

I turn back to the police station notes in my hand.

'Oh. Here.' Matt passes me the custody front sheet.

I take it from him and glance down at the page. I scan down past the arrest, arrival and detention times to the circumstances of arrest. I read: 'Received credible information that DP is main suspect in a TWOC involved in a collision in early hours of 1 Jan.'

'First of Jan?' I say, stunned. 'This happened on the first of January?'

Matt looks up. 'Yeah. That's right. New Year's Day. Why?'

I think about this for a moment, my mind racing. 'Nothing. No reason,' I say.

4

The air in the ICU is thick and warm. I shrug off my coat as I'm buzzed into the entrance near the nurses' station. As I head over to the sink to wash my hands, I can hear my name being called. I turn to see Karen Felding's head looking up at me from a glass-walled waiting area that's set back from the ward. The door is already ajar, so I wander over and poke my head inside. Sitting next to Karen is a young girl of ten or eleven, who looks up as I appear in the doorway. She's wearing a glittery pink T-shirt and light grey leggings and is kicking one fawn Ugg-booted heel repeatedly against the chair leg. As she does so, her coat slips off from the seat next to her and onto the floor. Karen leans down to pick it up. She looks tired, I notice, and fraught.

The little girl continues to watch as I enter the room, her forehead furrowed. Her eyes meet mine briefly and then she drops her head, her golden, waist-length hair falling over her shoulders.

'I'm not going,' I hear her mutter, softly.

'Sophia,' her mum protests. 'Are you *really* sure about this?'

'*Yes.*'

Karen folds her daughter's coat up in her lap and places

it back onto the chair next to her. She looks up at me and gives me a half-smile.

'She doesn't want to go in,' she sighs.

'Well...' I glance out through the glass window at the nurses' station, at the nurses sitting there. I remember how it felt to walk in here for the first time a few days ago, to see Will for the very first time, hooked up to all the tubes and machines. And then Mark, his eyes staring, but not seeing. The shock of it. And Sophia is just a child, after all. 'It's a hard thing to do. Maybe when she's ready...'

Karen nods. 'Yes. I'm not going to push her.'

'No,' I agree, glancing at Sophia. She's staring at the ground still, but she lifts one hand and pushes her hair back. I can see that her mouth is set in a straight line, one stray tooth creeping over her lip as she tries not to cry. She has freckles on her nose, I notice. A small section of her hair has a lilac-coloured braid threaded through. I ask, 'And Jack?'

'He's there now, with Mark. He was keen to see him.'

'How's he taken it?'

'He's devastated,' Karen says. 'As you'd expect. But he couldn't wait to get up here today to see him. I guess, in some small way – no matter how bad it is – knowing where he is, being able to be with him, is better than the not knowing. For him, anyway.' She glances at Sophia. 'At least he knows now that his father had a very good reason for not being in touch.'

'Of course.' I hesitate, recalling Mark's wandering, vacant eyes. 'Is he on his own in there?'

'There's someone with him,' she says.

I nod. 'Well, I'd better...' I shrug my head towards the door.

'How's your boyfriend doing?' Karen asks.

'No change, as far as I'm aware,' I tell her. 'They said on the phone that he's recovered well from his surgery. I guess I'll find out for myself in a minute.'

Sophia turns her head in my direction, her blue eyes now expressing mild interest as she realises that I'm not just another interfering adult, that I've got problems of my own.

'I hope he's OK.' Karen smiles.

'Me too,' I tell her. 'And... well. Likewise. I'll see you. Bye, Sophia.'

'Bye,' Sophia mutters back.

The air on the ward feels stifling now. My lungs are heavy with it. When I reach Will's bay, I stop in the doorway to shove my coat between my knees so that I can remove my scarf and jumper.

'Ah. He has visitors already, I'm afraid,' says Becky, looking up from beside the bed nearest the door. The occupant is asleep and doesn't stir at the sound of her voice.

I pause in the doorway, my stomach sinking in disappointment as I survey the small crowd around Will's bed. On the opposite side near the window, facing me, is a tall, well-dressed man in his late sixties or early seventies. He's sporting a smart, navy-blue blazer with gold buttons and a hankie in the upper pocket. Will's father, I'm guessing. On the other side of the bed with her back to me and blocking my view of Will is – I assume – his mother. A younger woman is seated alongside the older woman, her back to me also. I can see her arm stretched out across the bed. She's touching Will – holding his hand. His sister, maybe? No. I cast my mind back to our evening out in the restaurant, when I'd asked Will about his family. No brothers or sisters, that's what he'd said. He's an only child. 'They fuss over me a little,' he'd added, with a self-conscious grin.

Becky's eyes track mine for a second and then she turns and takes a clear plastic feed bag from a drawer and attaches it to a tube which she then hangs onto a frame by the side of the bed. Her pink hair is plaited tightly on each side of her head and I can see her light brown roots sneaking through. 'Sorry, but it's three to a bed, maximum. That's the rules,' she tells me. 'They've not been here long.'

I feel a moment of irrational irritation. Of course Will has near ones, dear ones. And of course they're going to be here, fussing over him, now of all times. What did I expect? I've only just begun my relationship with him; I'm way down on the list of people who are entitled to care about him. But bang goes any chance of me talking to him in private, of quizzing him about the 'scratch' on his leg, of asking him to tell me, truthfully, what's happened.

I consider my options.

'You could go and get a coffee… come back in half an hour, maybe?' Becky suggests.

Yes, I could do that. If I lived in the normal world, like normal people, that's what I could do, what I *would* do, of course. But Ben's at home with Anna and, when I called and asked her to babysit, I promised her I wouldn't be long. Anna's a good friend, but looking after Ben is far from easy. Her day is on hold, waiting for me to get back.

'I don't think I can. I have a child waiting…' I point towards the exit, but I'm not quite sure where I'm pointing. It's hard to explain why I can't just sit around drinking

coffee when someone else is looking after Ben. 'Could I...
could I just go and say hello to him?' I venture. 'Just let him
know that I came? I've brought him some chocolates.'

Becky pulls off her rubber gloves and drops them into an
industrial-looking bin with a clatter, before reaching out for
the dispenser on the wall and squirting alcohol gel onto her
hands. She wriggles her nose a little while she considers my
request. Her piercing has been removed, I notice. There's
just an empty hole there now.

'Well...'

'Please? I won't stay long.'

'Go on then,' she agrees. 'Just this once.'

As I approach the bed, Will's father spots me first. He
says something I can't hear to his wife, who in turn swings
round to face me. Will looks up at me at the same time and
his face widens in surprise, then – almost imperceptibly –
falls. He quickly corrects himself and forces a smile, but
his expression is unmistakable: he's wishing I hadn't come.
He quickly – under the pretence of a short coughing fit –
extracts his hand from the young woman's grasp, but this
then causes the woman to lift her head in my direction. Her
eyes glare at me in undisguised hostility as she sees that
I'm female, and that I'm on my own. Her small chin tilts
upwards and her thin mouth sets in a hard line.

Will's mother cocks her head to one side, anxiously, as
if she's unsure if I've come to the right bed, but radiating
the impression that she rather fears I have. It's more than
obvious that I'm interrupting something, that my presence
is unwelcome. But what do I do? I'm here, now. I can't just
say, 'Sorry,' and leave again.

Will has recovered from his coughing fit. His dark,

swollen eyes move back and forth from the young woman at his bedside to me, as I stand there self-consciously clutching the small bundle of clothing – my coat, scarf and jumper – that's scrunched up in my arms. I want to put them down, but there isn't anywhere. The young woman is sitting on the one and only chair. She looks me up and down and I do the same to her. She's really pretty; thin boned, I notice, with tiny wrists and a slender neck. She has delicate even features: big brown eyes and neatly plucked eyebrows, olive skin and honey-coloured hair that hangs in tiny ringlets over her brow and down her back.

Will's father speaks first. 'Hello. Who's this, then?' He's peering at me with interest over gold-rimmed half-eye reading glasses. He lifts a hand and strokes his bearded chin.

Will's mother forces a quick smile, and gives me a searching look. The young woman turns to Will. 'Well?' she presses him.

Will's voice is gravelly and tired, still. 'Mum. Dad. This is my friend Sarah. Sarah, these are my parents. And Veronica.'

'Pleased to meet you, Sarah. I'm Nick.' Will's father steps forward. He's now the only one smiling. He circuits the bed and offers me his hand. I take it and allow him to pump it up and down. He stoops to retrieve my scarf, which has fallen from my arm, and hands it back to me with another sombre, half-smile.

Will's mother stiffens and her neck flushes. 'This is not really—' she begins.

'So, how do you two know each other?' Veronica interjects.

Will looks up at me, beseechingly.

'Just from work,' I say, my eyes meeting his. 'I'm just a colleague.'

I can see the relief wash over Will's face.

'Same set?' asks Nick.

'Sorry?' I shake my head.

'Five Temple Square?' Nick persists.

Veronica's big brown eyes dart from me to Nick and back again.

'Oh. No.' I shake my head again. 'I'm a solicitor.'

Nick's smile fades a little. Veronica looks pleased.

'Sarah instructed me on my last big case,' Will says, his voice still gravelly and hoarse. *Not, Sarah and I worked together on our last big case. Sarah and I were a brilliant team. We were so great together, in fact, that we started dating. And now, here she is: my girlfriend.*

I stand there awkwardly for a moment. 'Oh. I brought you these.' I rummage around under the bundle of clothing in my arms and locate my handbag. I pull out the chocolates and step forward to place them on Will's bedside table, but his mother blocks my way.

'How *very thoughtful*,' she announces, with far more emphasis than the box of Maltesers warrants. 'But it's a little too soon for sweets. Why don't you take them home for now?'

She suggests this gently, her face softening, as if she's trying hard not to hurt my feelings. I happen to know that Will adores Maltesers, and that you only have to suck them until they melt on your tongue and disappear into thin air. You don't need teeth. You barely even need to be able to swallow. You definitely don't need maternal intervention. But I don't say any of this.

'How are you?' I ask Will, instead.

'He's doing well,' says his mother. 'But he's still very weak.'

'Yes,' I agree. 'Well, I only wanted to…'

Nick beams at me. 'It's good of you to come.'

'Oh, I was just passing,' I say, brightly. 'But I can't stop. I need to get back to my son.'

'Of course.' Will's mother smiles, fully, for the first time. 'Children come first.'

'Right then,' I say.

I look over at Will. He fixes his swollen eyes on mine. *I'm sorry*, he's saying.

'I'm glad you're doing well,' I tell him.

He nods and says hoarsely, 'Thanks for stopping by.'

Back in the waiting area, Sophia is sitting alone. She has a pair of white headphones in her ears and is watching a video on her phone, which is framed horizontally between her thumbs and middle fingers.

I deposit my bundle of clothing onto a chair just inside the doorway and pull out my jumper. 'Are you OK?' I ask her.

Sophia doesn't appear to have heard me and her eyes remain glued to her screen, so I put on my jumper and wind my scarf back round my neck, then pick up my coat.

Sophia looks up and pulls out an earbud. 'Where's my mum?' she asks.

'I haven't seen her, I'm afraid.'

'She went in to see my dad.'

'But you didn't want to go?'

She shakes her head, tight-lipped, and turns her head away from me.

I hesitate. 'Do you want me to go and get her?'

Sophia looks back at me and nods. Her eyes are glistening. She turns her head away again, looking up at the TV in the opposite corner of the room, which isn't on.

'OK. Sure.' I put my coat back on the chair and unwind my scarf. 'Can I leave these here with you?'

Sophia turns and nods again.

I pick up my handbag and put it over my shoulder, then pause as I remember the Maltesers. I glance at Sophia out of the corner of my eye and can see that she's now watching me with interest, her lips parted slightly and her gappy front teeth resting on her bottom lip. I open up my bag and pull out the box of Maltesers, then slide them onto the chair, underneath my coat.

'And please look after those, too.' I glance up at her and press my lips together to stifle a smile.

Her mouth twists up as she tries not to smile, herself. She blinks her tears away.

'Whatever happens,' I tell her, as I head out of the door, 'do *not* let anything happen to that box of Maltesers. Or the cellophane around them.' I wag a finger at her. 'That mustn't come off, whatever happens. I'm counting on you to make sure that no one – I repeat *no one* – comes along and...' I pause and scratch my head. 'Oh, I don't know. Accidentally takes them out from underneath my coat and... accidentally pulls on that bit of cellophane and opens the box and...' I look down my nose at her sternly.

'Eats one!' she finishes for me, with a smile.

'Yes. Exactly,' I nod. 'That must *not* happen.'

I turn on my heel and march out of the room, making a big pretence of not noticing her through the glass window as she reaches over and slides one hand underneath my coat. She looks up at me and pulls a funny 'you can't stop me' face. I shake my head and pull a fake angry one back at her.

I follow the corridor down to the HDU at the end, and peer into Mark Felding's bay. His bed is empty, the sheets neatly tucked and folded, the heavy machinery and breathing equipment gone. I step back with a start. Have I got the wrong bay? But, no. It was definitely the last one along. I step back out into the corridor.

'Are you looking for someone?' asks a nurse, who's walking towards me.

'Mark Felding,' I say. 'He was on this bay the last time I came.'

'Two doors down, on the right,' she tells me. 'He's got his own room now.'

I walk down the corridor a little and tap on a semi-open door, then peer inside. A large man in a beige suit jacket and jeans steps forwards as I enter and blocks my path.

'Can I help you?'

I can feel myself getting annoyed with all the hostility towards me. I sidestep around him and catch Karen's eye. She's seated in a chair on the opposite side of the bed. 'Sophia wants you,' I tell her, before turning on my heel and heading back towards the door.

My words come out a little more curtly than I'd meant them to and Karen jumps up. 'Sarah. Wait! Come back.' She makes her way round the bed towards me. As I turn, my eyes meet those of the man in the suit jacket and I can see his face harden, but after glancing over at Karen, he takes a step back.

I can now see Mark. He's lying down, asleep it seems, although his head is moving restlessly from side to side and his eyes aren't completely shut, the whites of his eyeballs still visible as they move around. I feel a surge of renewed shock and grief as it hits me once again what this man has suffered, what he has lost; and what the tall, slim boy sitting on the edge of his bed – who must be his son – is seeing, for the very first time.

'Jack, this is Sarah,' Karen says to him. 'This is the lady who found your dad and told the police where he was.'

Jack glances over his shoulder at me with red-rimmed eyes. 'Hi,' he mumbles. 'Thank you.'

'You've nothing to thank me for,' I tell him. 'It was pure coincidence. I just walked in and there he was. But I'm so pleased that I did, that you're with him now.'

'And so are *we*,' says Karen, insistently. She nods her head towards the bed and beckons to me. 'Come. Say hello.'

I move nearer. The man in the suit jacket steps out of my way, but Jack remains sitting sideways on the bed with his back to us, just the nape of his young neck and one blotchy red cheek visible above the collar of his smart denim shirt as he defiantly hunches over his father.

Karen puts a gentle hand on his shoulder. 'Jack. Go and sit with Sophia for a bit, will you?'

Jack shrugs his mother's hand from his shoulder and remains where he is. He continues to watch his father intently as he thrashes around on the bed.

'Jack,' his mother persists.

'I want to stay with Dad.'

Mark continues to move his head from side to side for a moment, then his eyes open fully and he looks directly at his son.

'Hey, Dad,' Jack says, his voice rising hopefully, as if he's said the magic word that's brought his father back to him. He tentatively reaches out and takes Mark's hand. I watch as Mark clutches it and squeezes it tight. He stares back at his son for a moment, his expression sombre. He then turns his head, training his eyes on a fan-shaped ceiling vent near the window.

Karen tries again. 'Jack, I need to talk to DCI Hollis—'

'He knows me,' Jack cuts in, breathlessly. 'He knows it's me.'

Karen sighs and says gently, 'Maybe. But don't get your hopes up too much, love. The doctors said—'

'He squeezed my hand,' Jack protests.

'That's just a reflex. It happens when...' She stops mid-sentence, then draws both hands up to her mouth and sighs.

Jack continues to hold his father's hand in silence. His mother glances up despairingly at the man in the suit jacket. DCI Hollis. I should have guessed he was a copper. He has that hard-nosed, self-important look about him that many of them seem to adopt, the more senior they get. His eyes soften a little as he looks back at Karen, but his jaw is set tight behind his moustache and goatee beard, and his back is straight, his posture unyielding.

'Jack. Your mother and I need to talk.' DCI Hollis speaks firmly, loudly, with a thick London accent.

Jack swings his head round and glares at him, angrily. 'So, talk! I'm not stopping you,' he retorts, his teenage voice breaking slightly as it rises.

'But someone needs to sit with Sophia,' Karen pleads with him. 'She's on her own out there. This is hard for her too.'

She waits a moment then turns to me and rolls her eyes, as if I know what this is like, although I don't, obviously. I doubt Ben would take much notice if his father keeled over right beside him and never got up again.

Karen lets out a weary sigh and reaches for her handbag, which is on the trolley at the end of Mark's bed. I feel a tight stab of pity; the poor woman must be going through hell. Mark's still her husband, after all. Seeing him like this, so fragile and vulnerable, must be stirring up all kinds of emotions within her. But she has to stay strong for her children; that must be incredibly hard.

'I can sit with Sophia for a bit, if you like?' I suggest.

Karen says, 'Oh, I don't know. She's a bit...'

'It's OK,' I insist. 'I think we're friends. I've ingratiated myself with the help of a box of Maltesers. I hope you don't mind?'

'Of course not,' she smiles. 'And that would be a real help, if you're sure?' She lowers her voice. 'I don't really know what I'm doing here, if I'm honest,' she confides, before shooting a quick glance in Jack's direction.

'You're doing just fine,' I reassure her. 'And it's no problem at all.' I think of Anna and hope that's true, that she and Ben are OK. But now that my visit to Will has been cut short, I have a few minutes to spare; she won't be expecting me just yet.

'How's your boyfriend? You didn't stay long?' Karen reads my mind, as I turn to leave. She looks at me expectantly and I notice DCI Hollis casting his eyes over me, too.

'He seems OK,' I tell her. 'It's early days, I guess. But he's got his parents with him, so I've left them to it.'

'Made you feel in the way, did they?' She gives me a sympathetic frown.

'A bit.' I smile, glad for that nugget of recognition. I don't know for sure why Will's parents – well, his mother – were so unfriendly towards me, but it's not that hard to guess. Veronica. The woman Will's mother either wants for Will – or worse, he's already in a relationship with, and his mother wants to keep it that way. I'm hardly the stereotype of the attractive divorcee, I know; I'm not nearly glamorous enough for that role. But I was clearly unwelcome, and it feels strangely comforting to imagine that I have an ally here at the hospital, in Karen.

She follows me out of the room and DCI Hollis joins her in the corridor. I leave them to talk and head back towards the waiting room.

When Karen appears through the glass window fifteen minutes later, Jack is behind her. He casts his red-rimmed eyes in the direction of me and Sophia and then carries on walking towards the exit.

'Jack!' Karen calls after him.

'What?' he snaps back at her. 'I'll be outside!'

'Alcohol gel,' she reminds him, nodding to the dispenser on the wall.

Jack heaves a sigh then turns and steps over to the dispenser. A moment later, the doors click and slam, and then he's gone.

Sophia stands up and pulls her coat on and I do the same.

'So?' asks Karen, wearily. 'Everything OK?'

'Everything's fine,' I say. 'Sophia and I have been

comparing rabbit stories. We both got a rabbit for our ninth birthday. How about that?'

'Hers is called "Tallulah Louisiana",' Sophia snorts derisively, but she's smiling.

'I don't have her any more,' I clarify.

'I'll never get rid of mine,' says Sophia, decisively. 'She's family. And my guinea pig. And my tortoise. And my hamster – and the cat.'

'And now she wants a horse to add to the menagerie.' Karen turns to me, a hint of a smile playing on her lips, although her eyes are glassy and tired.

'So, are you getting one?' I tease, gently.

Karen leans over and tugs at Sophia's coat, which is hanging loosely around her upper arms, and pulls it over her shoulders. 'We live in a three-bed terraced townhouse in Clerkenwell,' she says. 'So, in a word – no.'

'Mum!' Sophia protests. 'I've already told you. You can hire stable space.'

'You can hire a lot of things,' her mum smiles back at her, 'like maths tutors.'

Sophia glares at her in disgust and heads for the door in the direction her brother has just gone, stopping, pointedly, to squirt alcohol gel onto her hands.

Her mother turns to me. 'Thanks for keeping her occupied. You've obviously taken her mind off things for a while. It was just what she needed. She's still young enough to... distract a little. Whereas with Jack... well, everything's all-consuming at that age, isn't it?' She lets out a puff of air, which blows her fringe upwards. 'The moody silences have been pretty deafening of late,' she adds with a wry smile. 'Along with the intermittent bursts of rudeness.'

I give her a sympathetic smile back as I wonder fleetingly what's in store for me once Ben's teenage hormones kick in. 'It must have been so hard for him,' I say, in Jack's defence. 'Not knowing where his dad was all this time, then finding him like this.'

Karen sighs and lowers her eyes. 'It's hard to know what Jack's thinking at the best of times. He just won't open up to me.' She smiles, wistfully. 'It's funny; he was my boy until he hit thirteen, and then suddenly, overnight, he shrugged me away. Wouldn't hug me, didn't want to get close to me. I was suddenly the embarrassing one, and he and his dad were now the best of friends.' She looks up. 'I've read all the parenting books and it's normal, apparently, with boys. It's all part of him embracing his male side and rejecting his feminine side, his vulnerability. But it's hard not being able to comfort him.'

'I'm not sure the police presence helps much,' I say, speculatively.

'No.' Karen ties the belt of her coat and gives both ends a sharp tug. 'But he's going to have to get used to that.'

I look up at her, questioningly.

'Well... you know,' she says. 'Mark's been seriously injured. They need to keep an eye on him.'

'Do they?'

Karen looks at me awkwardly.

I shrug. 'I just mean that... well, you told me that they think it was a hit-and-run. A random mugging, then a hit-and-run.'

'Yes. That's right,' she agrees.

'So why would he need a police presence at the hospital?'

'Well... because they're investigating him, I suppose.'

Karen's cheeks flush slightly. 'Because of the drugs they found in his locker.'

'Are you serious?' I shake my head. 'Why would that matter now? Shouldn't they be focusing their efforts on the crime against *him*? What leads have they got? Have they said?'

'No.' Karen shakes her head. 'I don't know.'

'I mean… they must be able to access his phone records, surely?' I persist. 'Find out where he'd been that night, who he was with; the last person to have seen him? There must be *some* CCTV from *somewhere*? If not from the street, then from the last place he was seen?'

Karen looks flustered. 'I… I don't…' she mumbles, but leaves the sentence hanging.

I've overstepped the mark, I realise. I reach out and touch her elbow. 'I'm so sorry. It's none of my business. I hope you're OK?'

'It's fine.' She takes another long, deep breath, her chest rising. 'It's hard, isn't it? All of this?'

'Yeah,' I agree, firmly. 'It is.'

She nods at the door. 'So, are you going to go back in and see him?'

'Mark?' I frown.

'Your boyfriend.'

'Oh. No.' I shake my head, feeling stupid. 'His parents are still in there. And I need to get home now anyway.'

'Well, don't let them boss you around,' she smiles. 'He's going to want to see you, isn't he? Spend some time with you alone?'

'Actually, I don't know,' I admit. 'There was someone else there; a woman. A younger, much prettier one than me.'

'Sheesh. Sorry.' Karen winces sympathetically. She looks at me thoughtfully for a moment. 'People can behave strangely when something life-shattering happens,' she comments. 'But sometimes it's just because of the shock.'

I nod. 'Yeah. We'll see.'

I follow her out of the waiting area. As we take turns to gel our hands, DCI Hollis appears behind us and says, 'Karen. A word, please, before you go.'

Karen's face hardens and there's a slight edge to her voice as she tells him, 'I need to go. The kids are waiting.'

The officer watches her silently for a moment, then nods solemnly and walks back down the corridor to the HDU.

'Coming?' she asks me.

'Sure.' I slide my bag up over my shoulder. 'Don't you want to know what he wants?'

Karen looks straight ahead of her as she presses the door release button. 'It'll keep.'

I follow her out of the door and down the staircase to where the children are.

5

I'm back in Judge Long's courtroom a few days later when I notice a man sitting there. A cop, by the looks of things. Slicked back dark hair, smart black suit and tie, solemn expression, and a mildly humbled demeanour as he squeezes his bulky frame onto a bench in the public gallery where everyone else has to sit. There's no special seating area for the police in a courtroom. *You're on my turf, now*, I always think to myself, when I see a detective sitting there. *You can't play your mind games here.* They don't all play mind games, of course, but some of them do. Summoning us to the police station for interview (at their convenience, not ours), then leaving us sitting at the front desk for an hour, to put us on the back foot. Telling the suspect that it could be a long wait for a solicitor in the hope that he'll say he doesn't want one, that he'll go into interview by himself.

Judge Long finishes reading the papers in my case, then looks up. 'Ms Kellerman, this man has an appalling record. He's committed this offence whilst on bail to the Crown Court and he's interfered with a witness. You're not seriously going to ask me to release him on bail?'

I glance round at my client, who's in the dock behind me. He raises his eyebrows at me hopefully and I give him a grim smile back.

I say, 'I'm instructed to do so, sir.'

'Very well,' says the judge. 'What have you got?'

'A condition of residence, sir, at an address outside London, with an electronic curfew and a reporting condition. He's learned his lesson. He's already getting help with his alcohol problem. He won't try and talk to the witness again.'

The judge nods. 'Thank you, Ms Kellerman. Bail is refused. Take him down.'

There's the usual rattle of handcuffs from behind me and I turn back to face my client, who gives me a benign shrug of resignation as he allows the cells staff to lead him away. I turn to leave, to follow my client out through the door that leads down to the cells.

'Ms Kellerman,' calls a voice. 'Just a moment.'

It's the man from the public gallery, who's now standing behind me.

'Can I have a word, please?' he asks.

I think back to the facts of the case I've just dealt with. It was a domestic. A straightforward 'he says, she says'. No reason that I can think of for an investigating officer to come to court.

'You'll have to wait,' I say. 'I need to see my client.'

The officer nods. 'I'll be outside on the concourse.'

'OK,' I agree. 'But I don't know how long I'll be.'

I wait at the door to the cells before being buzzed through and heading down the steps. The metal gate is unlocked and I'm shown into a room. My client's handcuffs are released and he's shown in to join me. I find out which prison he's going to, talk to him about his right to a second bail application and then take his final instructions for his forthcoming trial. When I'm finished, the cells staff let me out of the back gates and I have to go back in through security and up the stairs. The officer is waiting for me in a seat outside the courtroom. He looks up as I make my way along the concourse towards him. When he sees me, he immediately stands up and waves me into a nearby conference room, which he's already secured, by the looks of things; the door's wedged open with a pocket notebook, which he now bends down and retrieves, before following me inside.

He holds out his hand. 'I'm John.'

I take it. 'John who?'

He gives me a single, firm handshake before sitting down at the table opposite me. 'Sinclair,' he clarifies. 'Detective Chief Superintendent John Sinclair.'

'From… where?'

'Please. Take a seat,' he says, but not without warmth.

I pull out the plastic chair in front of me and sit down. Sinclair responds by linking his fingers together loosely on the table in front of him and fixing his dark eyes on mine. His face is deeply lined and weather-worn, I notice, with a single pockmark on one cheek.

'Sarah,' he says. 'Can I call you Sarah?'

I nod. 'Yes.'

'OK, Sarah.' He smiles, genially. 'I'm the chief commanding officer at SO21, the Home Counties Regional Organised Crime Unit, which is headed up by my senior investigating officer, DCI Steven Hollis, who you met at the hospital. You won't have heard of us,' he pre-empts my question. 'It's a small, specialist unit, a joint initiative between the capital's territorial forces and a number of regional squads. The unit's been formed specifically to combat organised crime in the south of England at the most senior level. We're dealing specifically with a multimillion drugs op running between the City and a number of coastal locations.'

'County Lines,' I suggest.

Sinclair nods. 'Yes, but on a massive scale. We've been tracking the activities of a highly organised syndicate which is effectively sub-contracting out to a number of smaller crime groups. Our focus is trans-regional, the top end of the supply chain. We're not interested in the runners, or even the generals. We're after the commanders-in-chief at the top end of the hierarchy.'

I shake my head. 'Why are you telling me this?'

He looks at me sombrely for a moment, then says, 'Because you appear to have taken an interest in Mark Felding's well-being. Because Mark Felding's life is in danger. And because we'd therefore like your…' He pauses and his eyes seek out mine. 'Your cooperation.'

He flashes me a tight, tolerant smile.

'Carry on,' I say.

Sinclair's eyes bore into mine. 'I hope it goes without saying that the information I'm about to give you must be treated in the strictest of confidence.' He watches my expression. 'I think you'll agree that you already have a conflict of interest in acting in defence of any perpetrators of violence towards DS Felding.'

I think about this for a minute. I'll be the judge of that; it's none of his business. If he wants my cooperation, then talking to me is a risk he'll have to take. But if I want to know what he's about to tell me – which I do – then I'm going to need to play ball. So…

'Fine,' I agree.

Sinclair inhales deeply. He lifts his hand and scratches behind one ear, then leans his large frame back in his seat and folds his arms. 'Mark Felding was…' His face is expressionless as he pauses, then corrects himself. 'Mark Felding is central to the investigation. He's been working with us at SO21, as an undercover operative.'

'Mark's a UCO?'

Sinclair nods.

I consider this for a moment. That's why no-one at Farringdon knew where Mark had gone. And that's why there was nothing about the hit-and-run in the press. So much that's happened now makes sense.

Sinclair continues, 'He'd been working on this op for nearly two years. He'd successfully infiltrated one of the drug-dealing networks and obtained intelligence about the syndicate which has in turn enabled us to secure valuable evidence against them. We were on the verge of bringing the organisers to justice, with DS Felding as our chief prosecution witness.'

My eyes level with his. 'And they got to him. Is that what you're saying?'

Sinclair surveys me in silence for a moment. 'We don't know for sure. But what we do know is that DS Felding had begun to engage in risk-taking behaviour. He'd stepped away from his brief and become… cocky. Arrogant,' he finishes, then adds, 'I'm sorry, there's no better way of putting that.'

'You think he blew his own cover?'

His mouth tightens. 'All the evidence is pointing that way. He was meeting the informant regularly in unknown locations, without authorisation. His handler was struggling to keep tabs on him, to rein him back in. At the beginning of December, he was removed from the op and from the unit. He was presenting as too much of a risk to continue, both to himself and to the op itself. We'd already begun to put together our file for the CPS. We considered that we had enough evidence to bring charges. Mark was reassigned to a desk-based role at the territorial force he'd come from. But he didn't adjust well to his repositioning. He found it difficult to slip back into normal duties. So, we had to remove him again.'

I nod, slowly. 'Karen – his wife – told me he was based at Farringdon CID. That he'd been suspended on a drugs allegation.'

'He'd been suspended from duties,' Sinclair agrees. He clasps his hands together. 'The details are by the by.'

I look up at him. 'Did Karen know? That he was undercover?'

Sinclair looks back at me in silence.

'I need to know what I can and can't say to her,' I remind him.

Sinclair hesitates for a moment, then says, 'His wife knew at the time that he'd been asked to work undercover. She had no idea about the nature or extent of the op.'

I sigh. 'So, are you going to tell me that you knew all along who it was lying in that hospital bed?'

Sinclair nods. 'At a senior level, yes, of course we did. But the circumstances of the attack against him meant that we were able to conceal it at a lower level. Our strategy was to continue to "hide" him in hospital, to keep his identity hidden from everyone outside our unit that came into contact with him, including the hospital staff. It was the only way to ensure his complete safety while we secured the operation and preserved the evidence, put right whatever damage he'd done.'

'And then I came along.'

'Precisely.'

His face is expressionless as he says this, but I can imagine his reaction when the charge nurse called him, told him I'd identified the anonymous hit-and-run victim and – as far as SO21 was concerned – blown his cover for a second time.

'What about Karen?' I ask him. 'Did *she* know?'

'No.' He shakes his head firmly. 'As I said, that information was tightly controlled. No one knew outside of the unit. But once you'd made the nursing staff aware of his identity, it then became impossible not to inform his wife.'

Sinclair's tone is neutral, not critical, and he has the good grace to remain silent for a moment while everything he's told me sinks in.

'So, what *really* happened?' I ask him. 'On New Year's Eve?'

Sinclair looks down at his hands and examines his fingernails. 'As I said, we still don't know for certain. But we do know that DS Felding had failed to stand down. We know that he was still in contact with the Dex network and was associating with the—'

'The Dex network?' I interrupt him. 'What's that?'

His eyes meet mine. 'Dex is the name of the drugs line.'

I nod. 'Oh. Yeah. OK. Go on.'

He looks down at his fingernails again. 'At around eleven p.m. on the thirty-first of December, he'd gone to meet the informant at a venue—' He breaks off, then corrects himself. 'At a location where he could be compromised. It was too close to his own neighbourhood.'

'What was the location?'

Sinclair's eyes flicker up to meet mine. He hesitates for a second, then ignores my question. 'We have reason to believe that he may have been recognised at that location by a person, or persons known to him,' he continues, 'and that this may then have led to the subsequent threat against his life.'

'So what leads do you have?' I ask him. 'What about CCTV?'

'There's no CCTV in Packington Street. The response team that dealt with him initially and their own investigation department did door-to-door enquiries with a view to obtaining householder footage, but unfortunately these enquiries were negative.'

'But you know where he'd been, right? You said the location was compromised. What was it? A pub? A club?'

He doesn't answer.

I watch his face carefully. 'There'd be CCTV,' I insist. 'From inside.'

Still no reply.

'So, what did it show?'

Sinclair hesitates before saying, resignedly, 'The footage for the time and date in question had been overridden.' My eyes meet his. He gives me a look which says, 'Don't make me explain this to you.' I continue to look him in the eye. He surveys me wearily for a moment, then continues, 'The venue in question is effectively run by members of the criminal fraternity. It's no more than we'd expect. You can't rely on ordinary lines of investigation in situations like this.'

'OK,' I agree. 'So what *are* you doing then?'

'We've brought in a highly experienced surveillance team from another force. We've extended the operation. We're "on it", as they say. So, there's no need for you to get any more involved than you have done already. We appreciate your concerns, Sarah, but, with all due respect, this is our investigation and we know what we're doing. Now that you're a little better informed, perhaps you can get on and do *your* job.' He nods out through the door of the conference room towards the general direction of the courtrooms. 'And leave us to get on with ours. Does that sound fair enough?'

I survey him in silence for a moment. Sinclair pushes his chair back; it screeches along the floor. He tilts his chin forward and his gaze intensifies. 'I'm sure you appreciate that we need to restrict the number of visitors to DS Felding's bedside. Goes without saying. And his wife, Karen.' He pauses momentarily. 'She's been told that what happened to her husband was an accident. She has no idea that there's any threat to her or her family. I'd like it to stay that way. I need to ask that you avoid contact with her. We don't want to alarm her unnecessarily at such a difficult time; it could put the investigation in jeopardy. I hope you understand.'

'What about his kids?'

Sinclair looks genuinely confused by my question. 'Yes. Them too,' he agrees.

I shake my head. 'No. I don't mean that. I mean that Mark Felding's their father. You've known for three months where he was, that he had life-threatening injuries, but you kept it from them,' I say, accusingly. 'He could have died at any time.'

Sinclair's eyes flash, and his mouth gapes momentarily,

but he quickly composes himself. He rises slightly as he drags his chair back towards the table and places himself in front of me again. 'I thought I'd made myself clear. DS Felding's identity had to be concealed for his own safety. Protecting him had to be our priority. There was an immediate risk to his life.'

'His life?' I argue. 'What if he doesn't have one for much longer? He needed to be with his family. And they needed to be with him.'

'Sarah...' Sinclair lowers his head for a moment, then looks up at me and smiles. 'Sarah. You're not stupid.'

'No,' I agree. 'I'm not.'

'Then you'll understand the position we were in.'

'They had a right to know.' I shake my head, angrily. '*All* of them. She's still his wife. And they're his kids.'

He hesitates. 'They're kids who go to school with other kids,' he says. 'And they live less than a mile away from the Pear Tree Estate. We have intelligence to suggest that the Dex network was using children from the estate as drug mules. It was essential that word didn't get out as to Mark's whereabouts.'

He looks at me in silence for a moment and I feel a small stab of shame; has word now got out – because of me? But on the other hand, how would Karen and the children have felt if Mark had died before they'd had a chance to say goodbye?

Sinclair locks eyes with me. 'I am one hundred per cent confident,' he continues, firmly but kindly, 'that we made the right decision. That in keeping his identity hidden we were acting in the best interests of his family; and, in fact, Mark was very specific in his instructions—'

'What instructions?'

'—when he first agreed to the assignment. His instructions were that his family were to be protected at all costs. That they had to be kept as far away as possible from him if anything went wrong.'

I think about this for a moment. I have no way of knowing if what he's telling me is the truth, but I do know that the Mark *I* knew cared deeply about his children, and would not have wanted them in harm's way.

'OK,' I concede. 'So, is that it?'

Sinclair scratches his cheek, pausing with one arm folded across his chest and one thumb under his chin. 'So long as we understand each other. Do we?'

I nod. He starts to get up. 'Just one more thing,' I say.

He hesitates, then sits down again.

'These children. These drug mules. Do you know who they are?'

'Yes.'

'You have names?'

He hesitates again. 'What is this?'

I think carefully for a moment about what I'm about to say. Jerome steals cars; he's not a drug runner, surely? But if he is…

'They've arrested my client,' I tell him. 'His name's Jerome Thomas. He's a fifteen-year-old kid who lives on the Pear Tree Estate. They said it was a TWOC. A four-by-four with blacked out windows.' I look at him pointedly. 'There was a collision. It happened in Packington Street in the early hours of New Year's Day.'

Sinclair's face is impassive. 'Which team is dealing?'

'Finsbury. Major Crime.'

He looks thoughtful for a moment.

'So... what's that all about?' I ask.

Sinclair leans his elbows on the table and presses the tips of his fingers together. 'We've had some help with our enquiries from some of the local investigation teams. I think some wires may have been crossed.'

'They said they had a lift. A fingerprint, which may or may not be Jerome's,' I counter.

Sinclair stands up again. 'Like I said, I think some wires may have been crossed. Someone's got ahead of themselves. Put two and two together. I'll look into it. I'm sure we can sort it out.'

'But you've got the vehicle,' I persist. 'You've got forensics. You'd know if it had been in an accident. You'll have examined it for crash damage. And... and well... blood. Fibres from Mark's clothing. DNA.'

Sinclair's forehead creases and he shakes his head. 'No,' he says, finally. 'There's no vehicle. We had a *sighting* of a vehicle, but that's all.'

I frown back at him.

Sinclair straightens up. 'Like I said, someone's got their wires crossed. It'll be an NFA on that. No further action.' He raises his eyebrows. 'All right? So, leave it with me. I'll see to it personally that your Mr Thomas is released from bail in the next couple of days.'

I open my mouth to object, but I think of Georgina and Jerome and I close it again.

'Do we understand each other?' he asks me.

I nod.

'Are we sure?' He smiles.

I nod again. That's all he's getting from me.

6

Andy's waiting outside again when I get home. I can see his Laguna sitting just across the road as I push Ben's buggy up the street and open the gate. He looks up and smiles when he sees us, then removes his reading glasses and opens the car door.

'G'day, buddy.' He smiles at Ben as he strides across the road towards us.

' 'Ello, Dad,' I ventriloquise back, in a gruff, fake-Ben voice.

'Ah-ha,' Andy laughs and points at me. 'You nearly got me there. How are you?' He leans across the buggy and plants a kiss on my cheek. 'Here. Hop the little fella out. I'll get the buggy.'

'Sure.' I lean down to unstrap Ben, and lift him out and onto the pavement. Ben takes a hesitant step, then two, then wobbles ahead of us through the gate and down the path towards the front door. I run after him and try to take his arm in case he falls and hurts himself on the concrete, but he pushes me away.

'Get off me, Mum, I can do it by myself,' Andy says from behind me in a silly, squeaky voice.

'That's so not his voice,' I protest. 'He does *not* talk like that!'

'Well he don't talk like this either,' says Andy, mimicking my own gruff, fake-Ben voice and exaggerating my London accent.

'If you think he's got an Australian accent,' I shoot back at him as I stride up the path after Ben, 'you can forget it.'

'Why?' Andy snaps the buggy shut and follows me. 'He's half Aussie, isn't he? In fact, maybe that's it; he just doesn't understand the lingo you're teaching him. I reckon he's thinking to himself right now, "I hope someone slips me into me trackie-dacks, gets me a nice bit of tucker, sticks the *Teletubbies* on – and I'll be stoked."'

I laugh as I catch Ben lightly under one arm and help him up onto the doorstep, then lean over him to push the key into the lock.

Andy crouches down beside Ben and holds him steady. His face softens as he asks me, 'You think he remembers? That I'm his dad?'

'Well, he knows no one else is,' I say. 'If that helps.'

Andy nods and gives me a grateful smile. 'Yeah. It does.'

I take Ben's shoes and coat off, then follow him into the living room. I switch on the computer monitor for him, before sitting him down in his chair.

'So, what's up?' I ask Andy as he first hovers in the living room doorway and then follows me down the hallway to the kitchen.

He pulls out a chair and sits down at the table. 'What do you mean?'

'Why are you here? Don't you ever phone?'

He grins. 'Yeah, sorry about that. I was nearby and I just thought I'd see if I could catch you. I have something for Ben.'

'Oh yeah? What's that?'

Andy leans down and pulls a box out of the rucksack at his feet. He hands it to me. 'It's an iPad.' He grins at me. 'It's all set up and ready to go. You just need to stick in your Wi-Fi code and—'

'Wow.' I take the box from him. 'That's... well, that's fantastic. I was actually thinking about getting him one, but money's been a bit tight.'

'Well, now you don't have to.' Andy smiles and jumps up. 'Want me to do it?' he offers.

'Sure. Code's on the back of the router – in the front room near the computer.' I hand it back to him and fetch the chopping board from the sink. I open the microwave and take out the fruit bowl.

Andy stops in the doorway and laughs. 'You keep your fruit in the microwave?'

I select a banana and an apple for Ben and then put the fruit bowl back into the microwave again. 'I have to hide it from Ben, otherwise he'll eat it. All of it. Banana and orange skins. The lot. So that,' I nod towards the microwave, 'is where the fruit bowl lives. Unless you're microwaving anything, of course, in which case it lives in the oven.'

'Gotcha.' Andy nods, then heads down the hallway into the living room. I can hear him talking to Ben. 'Raided the fruit bowl, did you, you little monkey?'

I follow Andy into the living room with the plate of fruit. 'Watch where you're treading!' I call out to him as I spot that Ben's not wearing his glasses. 'He's thrown his specs off. I can't afford to lose another pair.'

Andy backs down onto the sofa and puts his socked feet up onto the coffee table. He puts on his glasses and taps the

Wi-Fi code into the iPad while I drop down onto my hands and knees on the floor.

'So, how's your bloke?' he asks, as I peer underneath the computer table. 'Is he doing any better?'

I think about this for a moment, feeling something akin to shame that I don't quite know the answer. I want to know what happened to Will every bit as much as Andy does – and I want to know who Veronica is and what she means to him, too. But I don't want Andy to know that there's a problem between us. I can just see how he'll read it: 'Sarah's boyfriend is a womanising junkie; she can't half pick 'em.' I'm not in the mood for a conversation about my love-life that ends in an 'I told you so.'

'He's OK,' I say. 'Seems to be recovering from his surgery.'

'So, did you ask him? About the scratch on his leg?'

I push myself back up to standing. 'No. It wasn't the right time. He's still very unwell.' I add, for good measure, 'He could barely speak when I saw him.' Which is not exactly untrue.

'Poor guy.' Andy frowns.

I put my hands on my hips and heave a loud sigh as I scan the room, hoping he'll get the hint and change the subject.

'You don't have a spare pair?' Andy asks, mercifully, as his eyes track mine.

'I have three spare pairs,' I tell him. 'But they're all broken. I haven't had a chance to get to the opticians.'

'Oh. Where is it? Can I help you out there?'

'Angel,' I tell him. 'And yes, maybe you can. It can be quite tricky doing stuff like that with Ben. Ah.' I spot Ben's specs in the corner of the room behind the doorstop. As I bend down to pick them up, Ben slips out of his seat and heads over to the sofa towards his dad.

'Hey, buddy,' Andy says, happily, as Ben wriggles behind the coffee table and reaches one hand out towards him. I turn to watch with surprise and interest; this is unprecedented. Ben never initiates this kind of exchange – at least not with anyone but me and his teachers, people he's known and trusted consistently over a long period of time. But then, 'Hey,' Andy exclaims, as Ben swipes his glasses off. Both Andy and I watch in bemusement as Ben turns them the right way up, wrestles with the arms for a moment then straightens them out and hooks them over his ears.

I clap my hands. 'Clever boy, Ben!'

'Why's he clever?' Andy objects, in mock indignation. 'They're not his, they're mine.'

'I mean, he's never put them on all by himself before. His. Anyone's!' I laugh, and as Andy and I both start to giggle at the comedy spectacle of Ben – who's standing in front of us wearing a pair of glasses that are two sizes too big for him – Ben can't resist the merriment, and joins in. I glance from Ben to Andy and it flashes through my mind how happy he looks, how different to the way he looked when he walked out of the door two years ago. Is this really enough for him? I wonder. A happy moment with his family? Does he truly understand that his son is never going to be able to play a proper game of footie or cricket with him? That he might never call him 'Dad'?

Ben soon realises that he can't see any better with this pair of glasses than he could before, and grasps then flings them from his nose. Andy lurches out like a wicket keeper and catches them before they hit the ground.

'At least he noticed me, huh?' Andy asks hopefully.

I feel an unexpected tug at my heartstrings. I hesitate, then ask, 'Do you want to stay for dinner?'

Andy looks pleased. 'You don't have plans?'

I give him a wry smile. 'Strangely enough, I don't get to make "plans" all that often. I really only have one person I can call on to look after Ben. My friend Anna,' I clarify, as Andy looks up at me, regretfully. 'She's very sweet. But I don't like to ask too often.'

'What about your dad?'

I snort. 'You've got to be joking. I wouldn't ask *him*.'

'Why not?'

'You know why not.' I follow Ben over to the computer and give him his glasses. I watch, pleased, as he turns them around in his hands and, a little clumsily, puts them on. 'Anyway, he wouldn't have a clue how to look after him.' I shrug. 'He didn't have any time for his *own* children. Why would he be interested in Ben?'

Andy hesitates, then says, 'Well, things need to change, then, don't they?'

I spin round to face him.

'With me, I mean.'

I raise my eyebrows.

He leans forward, looking up at me, earnestly. 'I told you, Sarah. I want to be a proper dad to Ben. I want to help you. To make things up to you.'

'OK.' I nod.

He smiles at me for a moment, then slaps his hands against his knees and stands up. 'So what're we having? Pizza? Curry? Or how about good old English fish and chips?'

*

While Andy's out, I get out of my work clothes and into my 'trackie-dacks'. I'm surprised to see that I'm smiling as I catch sight of myself in the mirrored wardrobe doors. As I fetch Ben from the living room and lay him down to change him, I recall how things were between me and Andy in the good old days, how at ease in each other's company we always were; how much fun we had. It was only when Ben's disability crashed into our lives that our relationship hit the rocks. It's early days, and I still can't trust completely that Andy has come to terms with Ben's limitations, that his wish to get to know his son is unconditional, that he's not going to decide that it's still all too much for him, turn around and bolt out of our lives again. But I can't help but feel relief in the knowledge that I'm now not the only one looking out for Ben. Andy owes me. He owes me big time, in fact. I don't have to feel grateful for his help the same way I do with Anna, or the after-school club staff. This is Andy's son. He's the only person in the world that I don't have to say 'thank you' to for looking after him.

He's the only person in the world who could ever love Ben as much as I do. The thought that's always hovering haltingly, in the deep, dark recesses of my mind. I look up and see Will standing in the doorway. He's wearing the dark brown wool suit that he looks so good in, the one he was wearing after court on the day he came with me to pick up Ben from Farmer Fred's. I remember that he, too, had smiled a little as I told him why I kept my fruit bowl in the microwave. But his expression had remained sombre, his eyes sorrowful. His reaction was one of tenderness, not one of mirth.

As I sit Ben back down on his chair in front of the computer, I recall the way that Will had jumped up from the sofa and walked over to see what he was watching. And now, as I think of it, I remember that he'd kept Ben company the whole while that I'd cooked dinner. He'd really seemed to want to get to know him. Not until Ben was in bed did he turn his attention back to me.

The doorbell rings, shocking me out of my reverie. I go out into the hallway to let Andy in. He follows me into the kitchen and unwraps our fish and chip supper while I fetch plates, cutlery and glasses. I poke around in the kitchen drawer and hand him a door key. 'Here,' I say. 'You'll need this.'

After dinner I give Ben his meds and put him to bed while Andy clears up the dishes and wraps up the fish and chip papers. When I come back into the kitchen, he's sitting back at the table, scrolling through his phone, a bottle of beer open in front of him. I can see that he's poured me a second glass of wine.

'Hmm. I shouldn't really have another one,' I say, hesitantly. 'I've got a trial tomorrow.'

Andy puts his phone down and looks up. 'Go on. It'll help you sleep.'

'No, it won't! But never mind.' I slip back into my seat at the table opposite him and stretch out my legs. I tease, 'I'll be able to relax when I get home, won't I? I'll go and get Ben's glasses fixed, and meanwhile you'll have picked him up from club and fed him and got him into bed. There'll be nothing left for me to do.'

'Absolutely.' Andy nods, pleased. He adds, 'You can go and visit your bloke again if you like.'

I look at him in surprise. 'Really?'

'Sure.' He studies my face as he says this.

I try to keep mine neutral as I reply, 'Thanks. Maybe I will.' Before he can ask me anything else about Will, I say, 'There's someone else I know on the Critical Care Unit. A copper I used to work with. His name's Mark. He's in a really bad way.'

'Really?'

I nod, and take a sip of wine. 'Yeah. He was attacked in the street, then run over. He's got multiple life-threatening injuries, severe brain damage. He can't talk, he doesn't recognise his own family. It's really, really sad.'

'Jeez. It sounds it. Poor guy. Will he get better?'

'I don't know.' I shake my head, then hesitate. Andy's a civil engineer, not a lawyer or a policeman. He's not involved in any way; he'll keep this to himself. 'I'm not allowed to visit him.'

Andy frowns. 'What do you mean, you're not allowed? Who says?'

'The police.' I stroke the stem of my glass with my forefinger. 'Mark's boss. He came to see me at court yesterday. He warned me off. Told me to stay away.'

'What?' Andy's eyes widen. 'Why?'

'I'm in the way, or so he says. They think this was a revenge attack from an organised crime syndicate that they'd been investigating. Mark was working undercover; they think his cover was blown.'

'Bloody hell.'

'Only I don't buy it,' I tell him.

Andy frowns. 'What? What do you mean, you don't buy it?'

I sigh. 'I just don't think it's as simple as that. There's something the police aren't telling me, something they're covering up. First: they arrest my client, a kid who lives on the estate where the hit-and-run happened. Tried to suggest they had forensics that linked him, that could put him in the car that was seen leaving the scene. But now, they've changed their minds. They're now saying they don't have the car after all, that it was never recovered, that they made a mistake. That if I "cooperate with them" – by which they mean "keep my nose out of it" – they'll release my client from bail. They'll let him go. Which is suspicious in itself, of course. But why arrest him for it in the first place, if they suspected all along that it was the syndicate that was behind the attack?'

Andy takes a sip of his beer and says, 'Go on.'

'Second,' I continue, 'they tell me that Mark's life is now in danger. They have a police presence up at the hospital and no one but his family's allowed in. And yet, for three months, there were no cops there at all. I wandered right in and found him; anyone could have done the same, at any time. If they really believed all along that a deliberate attempt had been made on his life by someone – anyone – they'd have had a police presence there at the outset, wouldn't they?'

'So, you asked him that, right? This copper. What did he say?'

'Just that no one at the hospital knew who Mark was until...'

'Until what?'

'Until I came along and identified him,' I admit. 'But I

don't buy that either. Someone's life is in danger, you protect them, don't you? I'm pretty certain that what he told me is some kind of cover story, that he just wanted to keep me away.'

'Why? Why are they interested in you?'

'Because I'm interested in *him*. Mark. And what happened to him. Because I've been talking to Karen, Mark's wife. They've told me to stay away from her, too. They want to stop me putting ideas into her head. They want to stop us talking in case, between us, we figure it out.'

'Figure what out?'

'Whatever it is they're covering up.'

Andy looks doubtful. 'Why would they be covering anything up?'

I sigh. 'I don't know, do I? But something's not right with the story I've been given. And I've definitely been warned away.'

Andy sits back in his chair and folds his arms. 'Well, maybe you *are* just getting in their way. I think you should do what they've asked you to, and butt right out. Besides, if it *is* something dangerous, I don't want you involved.'

I lift my eyebrows and peer at him over the top of my wine glass.

'As the mother of my child,' he insists. 'That's what I meant.'

I take a sip of wine and give him a knowing smile, meaning that it's a little late in the day for him to be expressing concerns about my well-being, when he's been on the other side of the world for the last two years.

'Anyway, I know you.' Andy smirks. He lifts the bottle and takes a swig. 'You just don't like being told to back off.'

'No,' I agree. 'I don't.'

Andy's eyes gleam and his face lights up as he warms to his subject. 'You never did like anyone telling you what to do. I remember when my mum came to visit that Christmas soon after Ben was born. She suggested to you that he might have too many clothes on. You just gave her this look.' Andy pulls a face. 'And then you leaned over and put a bobble hat on his head.' He leans back in his chair and snorts with laughter.

'It was winter,' I protest. 'He was cold! I felt his hands.'

'Yeah. I know,' Andy teases. 'But, shame, hey. Shame that detective... that...'

'DCS.'

'Yeah. That DCS. Shame he didn't know you any better. If he did, he'd have told you that he could do with your help. He'd have asked you to dig deeper and find out whatever you could.' He leans back in his chair and starts to chuckle again. 'That would be the only way to stop you.'

I wait for him to stop laughing, then tell him sternly, 'Yes, well it's no laughing matter for Mark's family. He's got two children who're in bits. Three months, they went, without knowing what the hell had happened to their dad. And on the one hand I've got this DCS telling me that Mark couldn't let go of the investigation, that he kept going out on assignments and putting his life and the lives of everyone around him at risk. And then on the other hand, he's telling me that Mark's given him strict instructions to protect his children, to keep them away if anything happens to him, to make sure they don't come to any harm. It just doesn't make sense. The risk-taking, cocky, arrogant... adrenalin junkie just doesn't fit with the responsible father who wants to protect his kids. He was either one thing or he was the other.'

Andy puts down his beer bottle and holds his arms out like he's a pair of human weighing scales. 'Shit dad,' he says, looking at one hand. 'Perfect dad,' he says, turning his head and looking at the other. He shakes his head. 'You're so black and white, Sarah. Maybe he was just an OK dad – something in between.'

I consider this for a moment. 'Maybe,' I agree. 'But it still doesn't stack up. When he was a custody sergeant at Farringdon, I saw him most days. I saw the way he was with people. He was reliable, caring. He looked out for people. He looked out for *me*.' I look up. 'He saved me, once, from a violent client. I could have got hurt, but he was watching out for me the whole time, through the window to the conference room.'

Andy shrugs. 'That was his job, wasn't it?'

'I know, but...'

Andy gives me a sympathetic half-smile. 'Are you sure you're not just idolising him? Making him into "perfect dad" because your own dad was so shit?'

He leans back in his chair and folds his arms, pleased with his analogy, with his psychoanalysis of me.

I put my glass down heavily on the table, wishing now that I hadn't told Andy any of this. I wish, suddenly, that I was talking to Will, instead of Andy. Will didn't always agree with my theories, but he would get that there was something amiss here. He'd be asking all the right questions, picking it apart. Andy knows nothing about the police and the way they operate; Will does. He'd offer some theories of his own – theories about SO21 and about Mark Felding.

He'd be keen to talk to me about the case, to scrutinise everybody's motives, without twisting the spotlight back onto me.

'OK. What is this?' I ask.

'What d'you mean?'

'All this stuff about me and my dad?' I place my arms on the table and lean forwards. 'Why are you dragging it up?'

Andy presses his lips together and picks up his beer bottle. 'I'm just questioning your motives, that's all.'

'Why?'

He heaves a sigh. 'Because you're getting involved in something that's nothing to do with you.'

'It *is* to do with me. They arrested my client.'

'It's just a job, Sarah,' he says. 'You don't have to get so hyped up all the time.'

'Hyped up?' I glare at him. 'What's that supposed to mean?'

'It means that you're angry. Face it, Sarah. You're still angry with your dad. You're angry with him for leaving your mum when she had cancer and running off with another woman, and it leaks into everything you do.'

I shake my head, my anger rising at the irony; I wasn't feeling angry until he started all this. 'Maybe I'm angry with *you* for leaving,' I say. 'Maybe this isn't about me at all. Maybe it's about you and what *you* did.'

Andy nods, slowly, then lifts his beer bottle and takes a sip. He says, quietly, 'It's the same thing, though, isn't it?'

I shake my head, infuriated. 'What are you talking about?'

Andy leans forwards. 'Come on, Sarah. Your dad was shit and you've been judging every man you ever met by his shitty standards ever since.'

'That's not what I'm doing,' I object. 'And my dad wasn't shit. He was just... well, he was what he was. I'm over that.' I gesticulate dismissively. Andy raises his eyebrows. 'I *am*,' I insist. 'And don't tell me about my father, anyway. You haven't been here for two years. You don't know how things are between us any more.'

Andy puts his hands up. 'OK,' he agrees, a faint smile now playing on his lips.

'This isn't about me and my father,' I argue. 'This is about him: Mark Felding. A man who's lying in a hospital bed, who's been wronged, badly wronged – but he can't do anything about it, because he can't talk.' I can hear my voice getting louder, more animated, more upset. 'His wife's been fed a load of baloney, and she's buying it, and they're trashing his reputation and... and he has no one to speak out for him!' Tears spring to my eyes suddenly, without warning. 'He has no voice!'

Andy's smile fades. He leans across the table and takes my hand. 'Like Ben,' he says, softly.

I nod, as the realisation hits me. 'Yes,' I agree. 'Like Ben. Someone has to fight his corner.'

Andy says, 'But you have Ben.'

I tug my hand away from his. 'I have lots of people, Andy. I have a job, a career. I defend people. That's what I do.'

Andy lowers his eyes. He reaches out and picks at the foil that's round the top of his beer bottle. 'I know, but... *he's* not your job, is he? He's a cop. You don't defend cops.'

'I defend whoever I want to.' I glare at him until he looks up and his eyes meet mine. 'Look, I'm glad you're here,' I tell him. 'I really am. But please don't think you can come swanning into my life again, telling me what I can and can't do. Not five minutes ago, you said you were here to help me.'

'And I meant it!'

'So, help me, then! Help with your son. But don't even *try* to impose conditions on me, Andy, because I'm telling you now, there are not going to be any. None. OK?'

Andy looks at me in silence for a moment. 'Are you in love with him?' he asks.

I place my elbows on the table and press my fingertips to my forehead. 'No. For God's sake! I'm not in love with him,' I sigh wearily.

'OK.' Andy puts his hands up again, in his habitual gesture of defeat. 'I'm just asking.'

'Well, don't!' I pull down my sleeve and wipe my eyes on it.

Andy stands up, pulls a kitchen towel from off the roll, then hands it to me. I take it and blow my nose. I can feel his eyes on me, watching me in silence until I eventually look up at him. He's standing in front of me, shuffling slowly from one foot to the other and biting his bottom lip.

'Sorry,' he says, softly, eventually. 'You're right. It's none of my business what you do. I just care about you, that's all. I don't want anything to happen to you.'

I scowl at him. 'I can take care of myself. I've done it for long enough.'

A hard silence settles between us. Andy pushes his hands into his jeans pockets.

'Why don't you sit down? Finish your beer,' I suggest, finally, my anger subsiding.

Andy looks relieved. He pulls out his chair and sits down in front of me again.

'So, what time do you want me tomorrow?' He looks into my eyes with the utmost sincerity. 'You just tell me what you want from me and I'll be there.'

push open the door to the opticians. Cathy, one of the optometrists, looks up from behind the reception desk.

'Hello, Ms Kellerman,' she smiles.

'Sarah. Please,' I insist, as I place three pairs of glasses down on the counter in front of her.

'Sarah,' she agrees, as she examines them. 'So, how are you?'

'I'm good, thanks. You?'

'Oh, you know. Mustn't grumble.' She picks up all three battered frames and scoops up an errant lens. 'Got any shopping to do?'

We have this same conversation every time I see her. Going to the opticians is a bit like *Groundhog Day*.

'Take your time,' I tell her, breaking with tradition; it's not often I get to say that to anyone. There's always shopping to do – shopping I can't do when I have Ben with me. But an hour of freedom to just *walk* – a bit of time to myself, space to think about things – is exactly what I need right now.

I exit the store and head down the busy street, my mind soon turning to Will, who still hasn't phoned me since I gatecrashed his parents' visit on Saturday. If I don't go to see him, Andy will inevitably start asking what's wrong between us, a question which I don't yet have an answer to. And if I do go, will I be sidelined by Will's parents and Veronica for a second time? Or worse: Veronica on her own? I imagine her sitting next to Will, her slim legs crossed sideways, her elbows on the bed as she leans over him, her honey-blonde ringlets brushing his cheek.

Who is she? I wonder. Is she his girlfriend? *Am* I now just his 'friend Sarah'? And was he cheating on me... or on us both? Maybe I should just let it go, assume that our short relationship is already over, I consider. Leave him to his family and 'butt out' of it, to use Andy's expression; do what everyone seems to be telling me to do and stay away. But on the other hand, it would be churlish – heartless, even – to do that when Will's so poorly. I think of his dark, swollen eyes, looking beseechingly into mine. *I'm sorry*, they'd seemed to be saying. *This isn't my doing. I didn't ask for any of this.*

I veer off towards Chapel Market and then head south towards Lexington Gardens. As I enter the park, my phone vibrates in my pocket and I reach in to pull it out. It's Andy, telling me that he and Ben are back home, and that Ben's having his dinner. As I pause on the path to text back, a second message pings through with a photo. I open it up and smile to myself as Ben gapes back at me, his fingers curled around a sausage, a streak of ketchup visible on his chin. The meal on the table looks suspiciously similar to the one we had last night, and there's not a vegetable in sight. But in the big scheme of things it hardly matters, does it? Takeaway chips, two nights in a row – who cares? The important thing is that Ben looks happy and that Andy's coping. I text back with a smiley face emoji then send a second text, saying, 'Don't forget his meds.'

The clocks haven't gone forward yet, but it's still pleasantly light; it's on the chilly side, still, but the promise of spring is in the air at last. As I exit the gardens out onto the street again, I realise just how nice it is to be able to walk aimlessly, with no purpose at all. I don't have to do anything, *decide* anything, right now, I tell myself, so long as I'm back for Ben's specs by eight thirty. But for now, I'll just enjoy myself, follow my nose and wander around for a while.

I change direction and head south-east, with the vague notion that I might head down to the Barbican. I'll cut through the back streets, I decide, to avoid the fumes of the evening rush-hour traffic. After fifteen minutes of walking, I stop briefly to get my bearings. I'm in one of the city's elegant eighteenth-century garden squares, but I don't know which one; they all look so similar. I can see a main road up ahead, which is tailed back with traffic, so I turn and head west again, pulling my phone out of my pocket and opening up Google Maps to double check that I'm heading in roughly the right direction. As I zoom in towards the little red pear drop that pinpoints my location, I realise that I'm in Finsbury – and that the adjacent street is Packington Street. Next to it in big grey capital letters are the words 'PEAR TREE ESTATE'.

The instant I see it, the Barbican is forgotten, my legs carrying me swiftly out of the square in the direction of the estate. I could do a bit of a recce, I realise; retrace the steps Mark Felding took on New Year's Eve, check for CCTV cameras, set the scene. Nothing wrong in that. It's what I'd do if this was a trial of mine. I know it isn't, and that I've agreed to butt out and stay out of the way. But I don't see what harm it can do to take a look around. I just want to see where it happened, to satisfy myself that the police haven't missed anything, that they're investigating properly, doing everything they can.

On the corner of the street there's a pub, a shabby, double-fronted white brick building with frosted glass windows and a gaudy band of red and gold signage above the door. The Hope and Glory, I read. Not much hope here, I imagine, and certainly no glory; the paintwork is dirty, the render broken. It's not hard to tell that this is no gastro-pub. I scan the eaves for security cameras, then continue around the corner into Packington Street, checking round doorways beyond the pillars and arches as I go. There are several houses with what look like security cameras, but I know the odds of finding anyone who has kept footage from three months ago are not great.

All the same, I wonder if I should knock, make my own door-to-door enquiries? I pause on the pavement halfway down the street, taken aback by the vastness of the estate which sprawls off to my right. It's a concrete jungle of four- or five-storey council flats; row upon row, block upon block of dull brown brick and white PVC stretching off into the distance as far as the eye can see, the only burst of colour provided by an ugly chain of pale blue metal panels which forms a balcony to one of the blocks nearby.

A car door slams and, behind me, I hear footsteps. I turn to see a middle-aged couple approaching. I watch as they head up the steps into the house next door to where I'm standing, and then move quickly to catch them up.

'Excuse me?' I call out.

The woman stops, first steadying herself on the railing

with one hand as she turns. The man pauses at the top of the steps, his key already in the latch. 'Can we help?' he asks.

'I hope so. I'm... I'm investigating the accident... the hit-and-run that took place here on New Year's Eve,' I tell them.

The couple look at each other and the woman frowns. 'That was a while ago now. Haven't the police finished their enquiries yet?'

'I don't know. But I'm not police. I'm... a friend of the family,' I tell them. 'Of the man who was hit. His family would like to know more about what happened. Peace of mind, you know.'

'Oh, I see.' The woman takes a step back down towards me.

'We were away. Can't help you, I'm afraid,' says the man. He turns the key in the lock and opens the door.

The woman lifts one gloved finger and points. 'You might want to talk to the man at number seventeen.'

'You know him?' I ask her, hopefully.

'We don't know him, as such—' says the man.

'But he was there,' the woman interrupts him. 'He was first on the scene, by all accounts. Such an awful thing to have happened,' she continues. 'Your friend. Did he... did he live?'

'I'm sorry,' I shake my head. 'I really can't say.'

'You're not press, are you?' says the man, abruptly. 'We were asked not to talk to the press. Not that we know anything, anyway.'

'No, I'm not press,' I reassure him. 'And thanks for your help. I'll do as you suggest.'

I walk back down the street a little, counting the

door numbers as I go. As I step onto the path to number seventeen, the curtain to the bay window moves and a male face appears. I smile and give a friendly wave. The curtain drops and a few moments later the door opens and a man is standing there. He's slight, dark, Asian in appearance. He's wrapped in an oversized beige wool cardigan which he's hugging tightly around him. His legs are as thin as stickpins inside grey flannel trousers. 'Can I help you?' he asks.

'I hope so. I'm here about the hit-and-run on New Year's Eve. I understand you were first on the scene?'

The man frowns, then nods. 'Yes, Miss…'

'Sarah. My name's Sarah.' I walk up the steps towards him. 'I'm investigating what happened.'

'Oh.' He scratches his head. 'Well, I already made a statement to police, miss,' he tells me in slightly broken English.

'Of course. I'm not a police officer. I'm… I'm a friend of the man who was hit.'

His face softens. 'Oh. I'm sorry to hear that, miss. I told the police I would speak to his family. Sometimes it helps, you know. But nobody came.'

I nod. 'Yes. I think it *would* help. That's why I'm here now. The family… they *would* like to know a bit more about what happened. If you don't mind, that is?'

The man's eyes narrow. He says, again, 'I'm very sorry, miss.' He looks thoughtful for a moment and I think that maybe he's not going to tell me anything more. But then he says, 'It wasn't too long after midnight. I was asleep. I was woken up by the fireworks and so I got out of bed and looked out of the window. I saw this man. Your friend.' He looks up at me, sorrowfully. 'I'm sorry to tell you this.'

'It's OK,' I say. 'Please. Carry on. I need to know what happened.'

He nods. 'Well, I saw him get up from the pavement and he was stumbling around.'

'You saw him? Before the car hit him?'

He nods. 'Yes. He was lying on the pavement. Just there.' He points across the road to the pavement opposite his house. 'I thought to myself that he was drunk. I mean...' He looks at me, apologetically. 'That's how he seemed. He got up and he was staggering a little. Then he started to cross the road. He bent down to pick something up... and then he fell again. I put on my dressing gown. I thought to myself that I would go outside to be sure he was OK.'

I nod. 'That's... that's good of you.'

He lifts his hands and presses his fingers to his temples, his forehead creasing. 'But as I opened my front door, I saw this car. It was coming slowly at first, but then it speeds up, is going very fast. *Too* fast. And I realised that this man is still in the road, but it's too late because car is there. It is there right in front of me, going much too fast.' His eyes dart towards the road and back to meet mine. His brows draw together. 'People are not supposed to drive so fast down this road, you know? It's a twenty-mile zone. But sometimes teenagers from across the estate, they steal cars and they drive too fast. They bring a lot of trouble to this street.' He nods across the road at a sleek white car that's parked facing us on the corner of the street opposite. 'You see that BMW just there? They pulled wing mirror off it, same night. Owner found it in a skip next day. He was very mad.'

My eyes follow his as he pauses and glances dolefully

across the road in the direction of the estate, which is separated from the street we're standing in by a border of railings and a small desolate park.

He heaves a sigh and turns his gaze back towards the road in front of us. 'Anyway. Then car is gone,' he continues. 'And this man is lying there in the road, just there.' He points, further up the road. 'The car dragged him along. There was blood. A lot of blood. I could see instantly that – boom – car had gone right over him. It was terrible. Terrible.' He shakes his head, sadly.

'So, what did you do?' I ask.

'Well, I called ambulance. And then I stayed with him. I talked to him, tried to tell him help is coming. But I don't think he could hear me. He was not conscious. Then ambulance and police arrive.'

I nod. 'So, tell me about the car.'

'Police car?'

'No, the car that ran him over.'

'Oh. Of course. It was black, Range Rover. Shiny, new-looking.'

'But you didn't get the registration number?'

He shakes his head. 'No. It was an unusual number plate. Private one, I would say. All I saw was the letters "JCV". It was easy to remember, because it is my initials.' He glances up at me. 'I am Jaydeep Chirag Vyas, you see? And the car windows, they were dark. Black—'

'Wait,' I interrupt him. 'You *did* get the registration number?'

He shakes his head. 'Only the first three letters.'

'But that's great,' I say.

The man looks pleased. 'It is?'

'Yes,' I insist. 'It is. Did you tell the police this?'

'Yes. When I gave them statement. I have been waiting to be called as witness but I am thinking they haven't found driver yet?'

I think about this for a moment. 'No. It seems not.'

'And your friend?' Jaydeep's face softens. 'How... how is he? Did he... did he survive?'

I nod. I probably shouldn't be telling him this, but he doesn't look like a member of an Organised Crime Group. He appears so genuine, so kind. 'Yes,' I say. 'He's alive.'

Jaydeep looks at me hopefully and his eyes shimmer. 'Oh, that is such very, very good news!'

'I hope so,' I say. 'Time will tell. I'm afraid I can't say any more than that.'

Jaydeep nods and clasps his hands together. 'I have been thinking about him and his family. They are in my prayers. It's so very good to know that he's still alive. He was very badly hurt. I'm glad you came to tell me this. Thank you, miss.' He holds out his hand towards me.

I take it and squeeze it tight. 'Thank you, too,' I say.

As I head out of the gate and onto the street, I pause. I turn around and go back up the steps. 'Jaydeep,' I call out to him.

He looks over his shoulder as he opens his front door.

'Can I ask you a small favour?' I ask. 'Do you mind?'

Jaydeep looks pleased. 'No, miss. I'd be glad to help you.' He flashes me a broad smile.

'Would you...' I scratch my head and glance round. 'Would you let me know if the police come back to talk to you?'

Jaydeep nods and bows slightly. 'I'd be happy to do that,

miss. Please go ahead and give me your number.' He pulls a mobile phone out of the pocket of his grey flannel trousers. I walk up the steps and watch as he taps my number in.

The sun has started its descent and the light is fading as I walk back up the street, the conversation with Jaydeep playing out in my mind. The police have a make and model and a partial VRN of the vehicle. Surely this would have given them a significant lead? This is a police officer – their colleague – all but killed in the line of duty. Why are they sitting on this? What is it that they're trying to hide? Was Sinclair telling me the truth about the syndicate... and does someone within it have some kind of hold over the police? Is it possible that Sinclair and the powers that be at SO21 know exactly who it was that drove the four-by-four over Mark Felding's body, but are unable or unwilling to prosecute them?

As I round the corner to the Hope and Glory, I pause on the pavement and study the building in front of me. There are now lights on inside and I can see the shadows of figures moving around behind the frosted window panes, the bar area beyond them bathed in an amber glow. To the side of the pub there's a battered gate screening a narrow alley, beyond which I can just see the edge of a weathered decking area. As I stand still on the pavement, the faint, but distinct, scent of cannabis floats out.

This pub is the nearest venue to the crime scene and the police ought to have made enquiries here. But have they? I wonder. It's more than possible that there's someone inside who walked out of the pub and into Packington Street soon after midnight on New Year's Eve; someone from the estate, maybe, on their way home. Someone who might have witnessed what happened; someone the police haven't yet spoken to.

The thought has barely entered my head before I'm pushing open the door to the pub and walking inside. There's a pool table in one corner and a lone man with a flat cap in the other. He has a dog lying at his feet, a piece of string attached to his collar in place of a lead. A middle-aged woman with thick hard eyeliner and dyed black hair piled high on her head is washing glasses behind the bar and she looks up as I walk in. I order myself a lime and soda and take a seat on a stool at the bar, then scan the room, taking in the seemingly inebriated couple by the jukebox, the rowdy group in the bay by the window, the two young men in low-slung sweatpants playing pool and the man with the flat cap in the corner who, I now notice, seems to be missing several teeth. This is estate territory, without a doubt; both the pub and its clientele are far too downmarket for the fine folk of Packington Street. Although the bar is reasonably busy, gut instinct tells me that if I start wandering around, asking questions, I'll draw the wrong kind of attention to myself.

I remain seated on the bar stool while I consider my options. After a while, someone who appears to be the landlord enters the bar from a door at the back of the pub, beyond which I can see a staircase. He's stocky with a bald head and glasses. He lifts up the flap in the bar top and walks behind. I've just decided that he's the person to talk to, when the woman from the jukebox comes over and stands next to me. She says, 'All right, Larry,' to the landlord, who nods back at her and then looks silently from her to me and back again.

'I'm good,' I say, indicating my full glass. 'I'm waiting for someone.'

The woman says, 'The usual, please.'

The landlord pours her a shot of something from an optic behind him and opens a bottle of Coke, which he plonks on the bar. The woman opens her handbag and takes out a handful of coins. She lowers her voice and says to him, 'So. Is Dex here?'

I glance up at her, my heart skipping a beat. Dex; I know that name.

The landlord holds out his hand for the coins. He nods over his shoulder and replies, 'Out back.'

The woman dips her head in acknowledgment, then zips up her handbag and picks up her glass and bottle of Coke.

'I'm looking for someone,' I say, quickly.

The landlord and the woman both turn to fix their eyes on me.

'I don't know his name. He never told me it.' I think quickly. 'But when I see him, he helps me out...'

The woman and the landlord continue to look silently at me. My gut tightens as I feel their gaze intensify.

'With bits,' I improvise, remembering the transcript from the last drugs case I dealt with. 'And bobs,' I add, although I'm not sure I've got that last bit right. 'He has short fair hair and very bright blue eyes,' I continue, hastily. 'And he's got this scar under one eye, just here.' I indicate my right eye. 'You can't miss it.'

The woman stares into my face, scrutinising me carefully.

She has pencil-thin eyebrows which look like tattoos. 'Who are you?' she says, finally, her eyes boring into mine.

'Anna.' My forehead feels clammy, my mouth dry. I pick up my drink and take a sip.

The woman makes an irritated gesture, which says, *So what?*

'Anna...' My brain freezes. *Montana? No!* 'Finch,' I say, before I can stop myself. I hope Anna will forgive me if this ever gets out.

The woman shakes her head, the name meaning nothing to her, of course.

The landlord continues to glare at me in silence.

'I don't know what's happened to him, and I kind of need to find him.' I lick my lips and run my tongue around my dry mouth. 'I met him in here on New Year's Eve. But I haven't seen him since.'

The woman shoots a look at the landlord, whose eyes connect with hers.

'I was wondering if you know him. If you might know where he is.'

The woman says, 'Have you been online?'

Online? *Online?* I think quickly. Ah. On 'line'. I shake my head. 'No. I... I changed my phone, lost the number. I was hoping I'd get a text to say he was back on, that he was... erm, shotting. But... there's been nothing. Not for a while. I was hoping I might bump into him here.'

I pick up my drink and take another sip, conscious that my hand is trembling as my fingers grip the glass.

The woman continues to scrutinise me for a moment and then her face softens. 'You're clucking,' she observes, kindly.

I look back at her for a moment as it registers: she's

mistaken my nerves for withdrawal symptoms. I moisten my lips again. 'Yeah,' I agree. 'Yeah. I am.'

The landlord looks away across the bar.

The woman nods her head towards the back of the pub. 'Come on then,' she says to me.

She moves round the bar and I follow her, glancing over my shoulder as I go. The landlord is now out from behind the bar, collecting empty glasses. His interest appears to be elsewhere, but behind him, from across the pub, the man with the dog is watching me.

I follow the woman out through a door to the beer garden where a group of men is sitting around a picnic table on the wooden decking. It's dusk now, and there are no outside lights; there's just a small flame glowing on and off over the table as one of the group repeatedly flicks a Zippo lighter. The smell of petrol in the yard is strong, intermingled with the smell of weed.

One of the men shifts in his seat and turns to look me up and down. He's white, probably in his early thirties. He has ear-length hair under a beanie hat and dark-coloured joggers with two lime-green stripes up the side.

The woman says, 'Ozzy. This is Anna. She knows ST.'

The man lifts an eyebrow. 'Yeah?'

All eyes are now on me. The male with the lighter has stopped flicking it.

'Yeah, only I've not seen him for a while.' My voice sounds hollow in the half-light. 'Do you know where he might be?'

Ozzy shrugs, and starts to roll a cigarette. 'He had a' accident, innit?'

I can feel my knees weakening. 'What accident?'

Ozzy lifts his eyes from his roll-up and gives me a smirk. 'Car accident. That's what they're saying.'

'Do you know what happened?'

Ozzy ignores my question. His mouth tightens. 'So, you want something, or what?'

The men round the table are all still watching me.

'Oh. Yeah.' I take a deep breath. I'd better do this, I suppose. I'd better go through with it and do what I supposedly came for.

I'm about to ask for 'weed', but then I remember that I'm meant to be clucking.

Ozzy looks me in the eye. 'I got best of both. Can do you three tens for twenty. Special.'

I think, quickly. 'Three tens for twenty'. Three ten-pound deals – that's what he's saying – for twenty quid. And, 'best of both'… that means he's got both heroin and crack cocaine. I open my bag, pull out my purse and take out a twenty-pound note. Thank God I went to the cashpoint on my way to the opticians. Little did I know then that I'd be needing it for drugs.

'OK.' I inhale deeply, my chest fluttering. 'Can I have… erm… one dark,' I say. 'And two light.'

Ozzy reaches into his jogger waistband and pulls out a sock, from which he extracts a handful of wraps. He selects three and hands them to me in exchange for the note in my hand.

The other men round the table are looking at me with interest. 'You speedballing, love?' grins a black male with short, tied-back dreads, wearing a camouflage jacket. He moves along the bench to make room for me. 'You'd better come and sit down.'

'Yeah, come and sit down,' echoes the male with the Zippo.

I realise with alarm that they're expecting me to take the drugs now, here – with them. I thought I could just extract a bit more information from Ozzy about Mark's accident, get a phone number for the drugs line, put the wraps into my pocket and drop them down a drain at the edge of the road on my way back to the opticians. But I'm supposed to be clucking, aren't I? Withdrawing. I need the drugs now. Obviously.

My heart starts hammering in my chest. I open my sweaty palm and peer uncertainly at the cling-film wrapped 'bits' in my hand – one brown-coloured, two an off-white. One deal of heroin and two of crack cocaine; he's given me what I asked for. So, what do I do now? What are they expecting me to do – smoke them or inject them? And if I do neither, how's it going to look?

'You gonna chase it?' one of the men asks me.

Foil. He means heating it up on foil. 'Sure,' I agree. 'But it's cold out here... I think I'll just go in and use the toilet.'

The woman swings an arm out, abruptly, and blocks my path. 'No way. You ain't using inside,' she snaps. 'Larry'll fucking do one!'

'Oh. Right,' I agree. 'OK.'

I stand there for a moment, my knees trembling as I try to think up my next excuse.

Suddenly, Ozzy's face falls and anger clouds his features. He leaps to his feet and, in what seems like slow motion, a metal tobacco tin crashes to the ground. In an instant, the rest of the men seated at the picnic table all leap to their feet as well. A knife appears, then two. The black man with the dreads and the camouflage jacket steps forward, menacingly. The woman – whose name I still don't know – turns and flees into the pub.

A hand grabs my arm tightly, roughly. Before I know what's happening, I'm spinning around and someone is yelling into my face, 'What the fuck do you think you're doing? Huh? What are you doing, you fucking whore?'

The voice is so close that I can't see who it belongs to. All I can see is a snarling, angry male face, pushed up into mine. 'You fucking bitch!' the voice spits at me. 'Think you can mess with me, do ya? You think I'm a fucking dickhead?'

And then I'm being dragged off the decking area, one arm twisted up awkwardly behind my back. I stumble and trip. Two arms catch me, encircle my entire body, squeezing the breath right out of me, and lift me off the ground. I'm completely overpowered by the brute force of the man that has hold of me and so shocked and frightened – it's all happening so quickly – that I can't work out what's going on. But I'm vaguely aware of Ozzy and the other men, still standing on the decking area next to the picnic table, watching in silence, all eyes on me. They continue to watch as I'm half-dragged, half-bundled into the alley, out of the gate and into a waiting car.

8

The rear passenger door slams and the driver's door opens. There's a thud against my back as my bag lands on top of me and the locks clunk shut. I experience a fleeting moment of relief as my phone tumbles onto the floor near my head, which is jammed hard against the armrest of the door. But as I reach for it, the engine starts and the car screeches away down the street so fast that I tumble forward into the footwell. I steady myself with one hand as we take a corner and then another, the car veering from right to left and back again.

My head begins to spin in confusion and a wave of nausea washes over me. I try to lever myself up, but the car continues to lurch across the road and I keep falling back again. I can just about see out of the side window and so I settle instead for staying where I am and trying to monitor the direction the car is heading, but it's too dark to pinpoint any landmarks and the motion of the car, combined with my position, wedged onto the floor behind the seat, is soon too much for me.

'Please. Stop. I'm going to be sick!' I splutter.

The car swings round yet another corner and then comes sharply to a halt. The driver turns off the engine and gets out. A moment later, the back door opens and I take a grateful gulp of air, before pulling myself up onto the seat and lowering my head over the edge. As my stomach heaves and I throw up into the gutter, I'm conscious of the man's feet standing on the kerb above me. He's wearing dark grey Converse trainers with white stars and a yellow stripe. The feet disappear for a moment and I feel his weight in the front of the car. Then he's back, crouching down and holding out a tissue and a bottle of water.

'Sit up. Drink this,' he says, gruffly. 'And then pull yourself together.'

He has a strong Northern Irish accent. I make a mental note; dark grey Converse trainers, Northern Irish accent. Jeans. What else?

I take the tissue from him and wipe my mouth and the strands of hair that I've just been sick over, before pushing myself up into a sitting position. The man is crouching down beside the open car door and I take a good look at him. He's wearing a battered brown leather jacket over a white T-shirt. He's clean-shaven and has cropped, light grey hair, which is receding at the temples. There are bags under his hazel eyes and his forehead is lined. I'd put him in his late fifties.

He pushes the bottle of water into my hand. I glare at him, weakly.

'Go on,' he says. 'Have a drink. Then get yourself into the front seat and I'll take you home.'

'Who are you?' I continue to glare at him.

'My name's Burdie. Pete Burdess. I'm a police officer, and I've just saved your fucking neck. No need to thank me,' he continues, as he glances up and down the street. 'Just get yourself in the front of the car and let's get out of here.

I think you've drawn enough attention to yourself for one day, don't you?'

He stands up, walks around the car and into the road. He opens the driver's door and gets in, leaving me sitting on the back seat.

I peer out through the back door, which he's left open. We're in a residential street and there are houses within a stone's throw. I could easily make a run for it if I wanted to; he's not stopping me. It's early evening and there are lights on in several windows. He's right; anyone could be watching us. If he chased me, there'd be witnesses in double figures. I could dart out and knock on a door – two, even; the houses are terraced and close together – before he could catch me. It seems highly probable, therefore, that he's telling me the truth.

I inhale deeply in and out, the crisp air gradually relieving the fear and sickness that has flooded my entire body. I reach down into the footwell to retrieve my phone from under the seat and drop it into my bag, before taking several more deep breaths and sliding out of the car and onto the pavement.

Burdie looks up as I open the passenger door.

'So, where's your warrant card?' I challenge him.

He shoots me a scathing look. 'I'm undercover. I don't carry a warrant card.'

'So, how do I know you're a cop?'

He sighs heavily and rolls his eyes. 'Fine. Walk home, if that's what you want.' He turns to face me and raises a finger, which he jabs at me accusingly. 'But stay away from that fucking pub.'

I crouch down so that I'm eye level with him. My knees

are still trembling with the aftershock. 'Why? What's going on there?'

'I'm serious,' he warns me. 'You don't know what you're messing with. I don't know what the fuck you think you were doing, but you were told to keep out of it. So, do as you're fucking told.' He starts the engine.

I open the door wider. 'Wait. Wait a minute.'

I slide into the front seat next to him and put my seatbelt on. He glances across at me and sighs. 'So where am I taking you?'

'What time is it?' I rummage in my bag for my phone.

'Just before eight.'

God. Is that all? It seems like a million years since I walked out of the opticians. I find my phone and glance at the clock, but he's right. It's twelve minutes to eight.

'Angel,' I tell him.

'Angel,' he repeats. He glances at me. 'You don't want to say "please"?'

I unscrew the cap of the water bottle I'm holding and turn to face him. 'If you're a police officer,' I say accusingly, 'then presumably you know that false imprisonment is a serious criminal offence?'

A flicker of anger clouds his features. 'Don't be so fucking stupid.'

I argue, 'You had no right to do what you did. You—'

'Don't be so fucking stupid,' he says again, but louder. He glares at me for a moment, before swinging the car out into the road. 'That lot in there that you were just shooting the breeze with might just look like a bunch of dickheads to you. But they're making a lot of money for some *other* fucking dickheads, the kind who carry guns, not knives, and who really aren't gonna like the sound of you.' He glances across at me, sarcasm contorting his features. 'You're not their kind of woman, d'ya see where I'm coming from? You stand out a fucking mile.'

I shrug. 'I don't think I do. I work with people like them. I know how to fit in.'

'You stupid bloody woman!' Burdie bangs both hands against the steering wheel. The car jerks and veers off to the left and a slop of water lands on my knee. I grab hold of the door handle as he continues to yell at me, 'You're reckless! Completely fucking reckless!'

'That's rich,' I say, 'coming from the man who drives like Ayrton Senna.'

His eyes flicker towards me. 'He was a great fucking driver.'

I glare back at him. 'He killed himself.'

'He had a broken steering column.'

'He was driving at a hundred and ninety miles per hour!'

'I was making sure that we weren't being fucking followed!' Burdie explodes, his face flushed with anger. He bangs one hand on the steering wheel again. 'You could have got yourself killed!'

A hard silence settles between us. I screw the cap back onto the bottle and clutch hold of the door handle again. Burdie turns onto Pentonville Road and takes another left turn. I notice Lexington Gardens off to the right.

'Why? What's going on?' I persist.

He continues to stare at the road ahead of him.

'You've been watching the pub,' I press him. 'So, does that mean you know about Mark Felding? About what happened to him?'

Silence.

'I'll take that as a "yes".'

He grits his teeth. 'You need to stay out of it,' he says, sharply.

'That was the location, wasn't it? The Hope and Glory is where Mark was meeting the informant on New Year's Eve?'

More silence.

'They told me he had a car accident,' I tell him. 'The dealers. They *know* what happened to him.' I glance across at him and his eyes flicker to meet mine. 'Did you know that? They talked about him. "ST", they called him. Is that his undercover name?'

Burdie sighs and looks away.

'So, was it them?' I persist. 'Was it them that ran him over?'

'No comment,' he says, smugly.

I shoot him a withering look. 'You know who did it, don't you? Why haven't you arrested anyone?'

'Again – no comment.' Burdie swings the car round the corner into Chapel Market. 'Where do you live?' he asks, sharply.

'This will do,' I sigh. 'You can pull over here. I need to go to the opticians.'

Burdie swings the car over and turns off the engine. He turns to face me, his face screwed up, incredulous. 'You're going to the fucking opticians?'

I nod. 'I need to pick up my son's glasses. They'll be shutting soon.'

'Well, it's a good job I arrived when I did, then, isn't it?' His voice is loaded with sarcasm. 'You might not have made it back to the fucking opticians before they fucking shut.'

I glance over at him.

'Are you for fucking real?' he splutters. 'Were you worrying about your kid's eyesight when you walked into that back fucking yard?'

'Do you think you could stop swearing please?' I wrinkle my nose in distaste. 'I know you're angry and once or twice is acceptable. It's actually good for you, apparently; it relieves stress. But when you use it in every other sentence it's really bloody offensive.'

Burdie exhales and looks at the roof of the car. 'Un-fucking-believable,' he says.

I turn to face him. 'OK. I admit it,' I confess. 'I was scared. I got myself into hot water. And yes, I was worried for my son, if anything happened to me. So, thank you. Thank you for rescuing me. But there's a man lying in a hospital bed with severe brain damage and he's got kids too. So where were you *then*? Who's looking out for *him*? Why the bloody hell has no one been arrested? What the hell is it that you lot are trying to hide?'

Burdie continues to looks up at the ceiling of the car.

We sit there in silence for a moment.

'ST is short for Scar Tissue,' he says, eventually. 'That's what they call him. And yes, that's where he was on New Year's Eve. That's all I'm giving you.'

I think about this for a moment. 'The guy with the flat cap and the dog?' I ask. 'Is he the informant?'

Burdie swings round to face me. 'You need to stay out of it,' he hisses angrily. 'I'm serious. You have no fucking idea what you're getting into!'

He folds his arms and his mouth snaps shut. His shoulders rise, then loosen and sag as he lets out a sigh. I watch him in silence for a moment. He's a 'red anger' person, I can tell; blows up hard but soon calms down again. If I wait a minute longer, will he change his mind and talk to me?

'Go on,' he says, finally. 'You'd better get to the opticians.'

'I've got a minute,' I say. 'Just tell me—'

He swings round to face me. 'Bloody hell, woman! Just do what I fucking say, won't you? Stay out of it. Now go!'

I open the car door and pick up my bag, then step out onto the pavement. I watch as he drives away. His car is an old silver Saab. It has a dent in the nearside wing.

My phone rings. It's in my hand and it makes me jump out of my skin.

It's a private number. I answer it.

'Sarah?' says Will. 'It's me.'

He's sitting up in bed when I arrive. Becky's with him, moving around busily, folding and unfolding his blood pressure cuff, lifting his hand and moving his oxygen saturation probe from one finger to another, picking up a chart on a clipboard at the end of the bed. Will looks up and smiles when he sees me but I stand back and watch in silence until Becky's finished.

'Nearly done.' She catches my eye as she leans forward and adjusts the position of Will's leg slightly on the pillow, then examines his dressing. The crepe bandage has gone and he now has what looks like a black sponge under clingfilm, with a tube coming out of it. There's some writing scrawled onto the plastic in black marker pen.

Becky removes her rubber gloves. 'Right then. I'll leave you to it.'

'How's he doing?' I ask her.

'He's doing well.' Her voice is neutral, giving nothing away.

'So, the infection… is it under control?'

'Well, it seems to be. It's early days.' She glances across at the bed. 'Shall we let Will explain?'

Will's eyes dart up to meet mine. They're still swollen, but less so and he's been shaved, his hair washed and brushed. There's some colour back in his cheeks and he looks much more like the Will I know, which is encouraging. But it's clear from the way both he and Becky are acting that he's not out of the woods just yet.

Becky walks out of the bay. I hang my bag over the back of the chair next to the bed and slip off my coat.

'So, Ms Kellerman.' Will greets me in the same way he always does when we're at court together.

'You're looking good, Mr Gaskin,' I smile.

'As are you, Ms Kellerman,' he grins. 'As indeed are you.'

I sit down next to him, keeping a slight distance from the bed. I'm not going to encourage Will to slide back into the ease of our former fun, flirty work relationship, the one where he manages to keep me at bay. I want to talk to the same Will I spoke to on the phone an hour earlier, the one who was gentle and penitent, who said he was sorry for the way his parents had treated me – and that he had no visitors this evening and could I please come?

Now that we're alone, now that he's looking better than I've seen him in some time, I want answers. I'm not going to let him fob me off this time.

Will continues to smile, his eyes flickering across my face as he notices my body language, tries to gauge my mood.

'So, how do you feel?' I ask him.

'Better,' he nods. 'Better than I was.'

'That's great. And what's going on there?' I indicate his leg. 'What's that tube for?'

Will clears his throat. 'It's called a VAC dressing. It helps bring the edges of the wound together and draws the infection out.'

'So… does that mean it's healing?' I ask, hopefully.

He smiles. 'They think so.'

'They *think* so?' I repeat.

Will clears his throat again. 'It's… it's not guaranteed that they've been able to remove the infection completely, this time round. I'm likely to need more procedures.'

'More surgery?'

Will's eyes meet mine. 'Yes,' he says, hesitantly.

I uncross my arms and lean forward. 'I googled it, Will. I've read all about it: necrotising fasciitis. See? I even know how to pronounce it. I know how serious it is. And I know that you know too. You'd have asked, and they'd have told you. Please, don't try and shield me. Tell me what's going on.'

Will heaves a sigh. He looks away towards the window for a moment, then turns back and looks me in the eye and nods. 'OK. This is what's going on: the infection is still there. It's eating away at my flesh and my muscles and the tissue in my leg. At the moment it's contained to a small area, but there's still a significant risk that it could spread. Worst-case scenario, it could get into my organs and cause… failure, and… and, well, I could die.'

He pauses and gives me a grim smile. My body freezes and my heart skips a beat.

'But,' he continues quickly, 'the good news is that they caught it early and the antibiotics seem to be working at the moment, and it hasn't spread beyond my leg at this stage. They just have to keep removing the infected tissue, and they have to do that in surgery under a general anaesthetic. The procedure is called debridement. If it's successful, I'll need skin grafts. But there's still a chance that I'll develop a resistance to the antibiotics. I could get sepsis or, if the debridements don't work they... they may have to amputate.'

He pauses and presses his lips together.

'Amputate?' I echo.

'Yes. I could lose my leg.' He clears his throat and winks at me. 'But let's hope not, hey?'

I nod and swallow, unable to speak for a moment.

'So, is that all the bad news out of the way?' Will looks up at me. 'Can we talk about something a little more jolly now?'

'Soon,' I agree. 'And... and I know this is hard for you. But there's still stuff you haven't told me. Things I need to know...'

Will closes his eyes. He sighs deeply, then opens them again.

'I need to know what you want from me,' I continue, hoping that my face doesn't reveal quite how churned up I'm feeling. 'Am I *just* your friend, like you told your parents? Because if that's all it is for you, then that's fine. I can be your friend.'

Will turns his head towards me and his eyes seek out

mine. 'You're more than a friend to me, Sarah, you know that.' He sighs again. 'But it's just... not that simple right now.'

I nod and swallow. 'Veronica.'

He says, 'It's not what you think.'

'What do I think?' I ask him.

'You think I have feelings for her.'

I take a deep breath. 'And do you?'

'No.' Will shakes his head, firmly. He swallows hard and his lips tighten. 'No, I don't. At least, not those kinds of feelings.'

I wait for him to elaborate, but he doesn't.

'I wouldn't blame you if you did,' I say. 'She's stunning.'

Will glances up at me and I notice the dark shadows under his eyes. 'She's an attractive girl,' he agrees, finally. 'But...'

'But, what?'

Will's eyes flicker to meet mine. 'But, nothing,' he says.

I look back at him in confusion. 'So, what's the problem?' I shrug.

'The problem?'

'With us, being together. You said it wasn't that simple. So, what is it? Who is she to you?'

Will lowers his eyes and moistens his lips. 'She's a childhood friend,' he explains, looking away down the bed towards his leg. 'A friend of my family. Her parents and mine are old friends. Close friends. So, naturally, they wanted us to be a couple. They'd been pushing us together for years. It wasn't... necessarily what I wanted. But over time, it became a little hard to resist.'

'So... what? Are you in a relationship with her?'

Will shakes his head. 'No. No, I'm not. Not any more.' He looks up at me again. 'But I was.'

'When did it end?'

He shakes his head, dismissively. 'Oh, years ago. It... it didn't last long. A year, maybe.'

'That's long enough,' I observe.

Will's forehead creases. 'Long enough for what?'

'I don't know.' I shrug. 'For her to fall for you, I suppose.'

A cloud crosses Will's eyes. He inhales deeply, then lets out a sigh. 'Yeah. My fault, entirely. I should never have...' He tails off.

'You think you led her on?'

Will nods, decisively. 'Yeah. I did. I didn't mean to, of course. I didn't intend to hurt her. I should never have let it go on as long as it did.' He turns to me. 'We had nothing in common, not really, apart from our shared history, that is. There was never any real spark between us.' He smiles and looks up at me, his eyes shining, suddenly. 'Not like there is between me and you.'

I lean forward, my heart thumping. 'So, what's the problem? She's a grown-up. And so are you. If this all happened years ago, surely she's over it by now?'

He nods. 'I thought so. She met someone else. She married him.'

'Oh?'

'Yes. Yes,' he says again, almost wistfully. 'He was good for her.'

I look at him, confused. 'So... why was she here?'

He sighs. 'Her marriage ended, it seems, and so...' He looks up at me, apologetically. 'And so, my parents gave her my number, put us in touch. They were trying to matchmake again. They shouldn't have done. It seems they may have got her hopes up, so I met with her… tried to let her down gently. I told her that I was with someone else.'

'Someone else?'

'You,' he smiles. 'Obviously. But I didn't tell her who. I just said that I'd met someone.' He turns to face me. 'And then…' His smile fades. 'And then, a few days later, I end up here, and my parents tell her, and obviously she's worried. But they should never have brought her to the hospital. It wasn't what I wanted.'

I think about this for a moment. 'So, how did she take it?' I ask him. 'When you told her you'd met someone?'

Will hesitates. 'Fine, I think.' He considers this for a moment. 'Yeah,' he repeats. 'She was fine.'

'So, why not introduce me?' I look him in the eye. 'Properly, I mean.'

Will scowls as he ponders this for a moment, then sighs. 'It was all… such bad timing,' he says. 'I didn't want to…' He lifts a hand to his forehead. 'Well, it's one thing telling her I'd met someone, but I didn't want to crush her like that, rub her nose in it, I suppose. And, besides, things had barely had a chance to get off the ground between us – you and me, I mean – when… when…'

He holds my gaze as he realises what I'm going to ask him next.

'When *what*? What happened to you, Will?'

He sighs and looks away.

'Is it drugs?' I ask him, finally. 'Are you using drugs? Have you been injecting into your leg?'

Will swings his head round to face me, his expression

incredulous. '*Drugs?*' He grins, widely. 'Bloody hell! No, Sarah. Is that what you've been thinking?'

I shrug. 'Well, yes. Frankly, it is.'

'Sarah!' Will shakes his head and he starts to laugh, then he realises that I'm serious. 'Sarah.' His eyes seek out mine. 'I haven't been using drugs, I promise you.'

Mild relief washes over me. 'Then... then what is it? What happened?'

'Sarah, please.' His forehead creases. 'I just cut myself. OK?'

'*How?*'

'I don't *know* how. I don't remember,' Will pleads with me. 'But I'm not a junkie, or an alcoholic, or... or anything bad. There's nothing terrible you need to know about me. Let that be enough. Please.'

He sighs and holds out his hand towards me.

I look at him for a moment, then nod. I tentatively pull my chair forward and take his hand in mine. He pulls me in close to him. 'Look, I know I've hurt you, and confused you... and... I'm sorry,' he says. 'But this has all been really, *really* hard for me.' He looks into my eyes. His are wide, imploring. 'This is *not* how I wanted my relationship with you to get off the ground. It wasn't meant to happen like this.'

I nod. 'I know.'

'And I certainly didn't want to tell you how I felt about you for the first time in front of my parents and... and bloody Veronica!'

I smile.

His eyes move around the bay. 'Or those two over there.'

I glance over my shoulder at the man in the bed opposite.

'I know, I know,' he jokes. 'I know what you're going to say. That one's unconscious.' He peers at the bed in the opposite corner. 'And… yep. So is he.' He forces a smile and looks up at me. 'But all the same,' he tells me, seriously, 'it's not what I had in mind.'

'Me neither,' I agree.

We sit in silence for a moment. I pour Will a glass of water and help him take a sip.

'Whilst we're on the subject of exes,' I confess, 'mine is also back on the scene. He's at my house now, with Ben.'

Will's face falls. 'Really?'

I nod. 'There's nothing between us,' I reassure him. 'He's here for Ben, not for me.' I know that this isn't one hundred per cent true as far as Andy's concerned and it crosses my mind that maybe I shouldn't have told Will this right now, when he needs to focus on getting well. But I don't want to be a hypocrite, when I've just finished quizzing him about Veronica. At some point he'll ask me who's looking after Ben, and I don't want to lie. I say, 'He's the reason I can come and visit you on a weekday evening.'

'He knows about me?'

I nod. 'Yes. He does.'

'So…' Will raises his eyebrows and moves his head. 'What did you tell him about me?'

'I told him the truth,' I say. 'I told him that I had a boyfriend, and that he was in hospital.'

Will's eyes sparkle. 'Did you tell him how good-looking I am?'

'Of course I did.'

'And that I'm quite handy with my fists?'

I smile. 'Yes. I told him all of that. He's a little scared of you, naturally.'

Will presses his lips together and says, 'I don't suppose there's any chance that he only has one leg?'

I look up at him. A smile is still playing across his lips, but his eyes are glistening. I get up off my chair and squeeze onto the bed next to him, then lean forward and slide my arms around his neck. He puts a hand against my back and pulls me into him. I say into his ear, 'You're not going to lose a leg, Will. Everything's going to be OK.'

He takes my arms and holds me away from him a little. 'I might do, Sarah,' he tells me. 'There's every chance that I might.'

I shake my head. 'It's not going to happen,' I tell him, firmly. 'But it wouldn't change a thing for me if it did.'

He says gently, 'I think it probably would.'

'No.' I shake my head. 'It really wouldn't.'

He shakes his head back at me and his smile fades. 'You have Ben,' he says. 'You need someone who can help you, not someone who...' He lets go of my arms.

I frown. 'Someone who... what?'

He swallows and looks me directly in the eye. 'Someone who you have to push around in a wheelchair.'

'Will,' I object. 'Don't be silly. There are prosthetics. Even if...' I hesitate and peer into his eyes. Will moistens his lips. 'Even if,' I continue, 'and this is the worst-case scenario... even if that was the outcome, it wouldn't have to be as bad as you think.'

'That's not the worst-case scenario,' he points out.

'Yes,' I insist. 'It *is*. You're not going to die, Will. And you're not going to lose a leg. You can do this.' I reach out and take his hand in mine. 'You can fight this. Things are going to work out just fine for you. And for us.'

And then I lean forward and I kiss him, there on the bed with my arms wrapped tightly around him. He grips me just as tightly and kisses me back.

9

As I turn out of the bay I collide with Karen. She drops a plastic cup of water onto my foot, which soaks through my trainer and into my sock.

'Oh no! I'm so sorry,' she cries out in alarm, as she bends down to retrieve the cup. She looks up at me, her face flushed. 'Are you wet?'

'A little, but don't worry,' I reassure her.

She stands up and heaves a sigh as she glances around from left to right.

I duck back into Will's bay and grab some paper towels out of a dispenser near the doorway. 'Here.' I hand some to Karen and we both bend down to wipe up the water that's on the floor.

As I spread out the paper towels, I notice that Karen is crying. I reach over, still on my haunches, and touch her arm. 'Hey. What's wrong?'

She gives a quick shake of the head.

I hesitate and glance round, but there's no one else in the corridor. 'Do you want to talk?' I ask.

She gives me a faint smile. 'I'm fine. It's late. You were just leaving.'

She straightens up and I stand up, too. 'I don't have to hurry home... for once', I tell her. 'My ex is looking after my son. He owes me about...' I wrinkle up my face in an exaggerated manner as I calculate. 'About eight thousand babysitting hours.'

Karen smiles through her tears.

I smile too. 'I have time, if you do.'

She nods. 'Do you fancy a drink?'

'Sure, but... the pubs will be closing soon, won't they?'

She sniffs, her eyes still glistening. 'I know a place.'

I glance over her shoulder as I see a figure walking down the corridor towards us. It's DCI Hollis. His shoulders are pushed back, and he's straining his neck as he observes us together.

'OK.' I lower my voice. 'But let's keep this to ourselves. I'll meet you there. Just tell me where to go.'

Karen's eyes dart up to meet mine. She glances over her shoulder and then back at me. 'The Abbey Lounge in Queen Street,' she whispers. 'It's not far from Westminster Abbey. I'll see you there in twenty minutes.'

'Great,' I whisper back. 'Don't let him follow you.' Out loud, I say, 'Anyway, nice to bump into you again. I'd better fly.'

I give her a wave and stride off down the corridor.

Downstairs on the ground floor I visit the hospital toilets and slip out of my wet trainers, then retrieve my work shoes from my rucksack and put them on. I head out of the hospital doors into the cool night air, past the ambulances and into St John's Gardens, taking a right turn off Horseferry Road in the direction of the abbey. I cross the road and pause briefly in the awning of a shop doorway as I pull out my phone, locate Queen Street on Google Maps, then find Andy's number.

The phone rings just a couple of times before he answers. His voice sounds sleepy. 'Sarah. How's it going?'

'Yes, it's fine. How about you? Can I assume no news is good news?'

'Yup. I told you we'd be right. What time is it?' He yawns as he speaks. I can hear the TV in the background.

'It's around ten thirty. I'm just leaving the hospital.'

A pause. 'So, how is he?'

'He's getting there,' I tell him. 'Fingers crossed, he'll be OK.'

'Oh, well, that's good.' He pauses. 'That's good,' he says, again.

'It's not drugs,' I tell him. 'That's not how he got the scratch.'

Another pause. 'So, what was it then? How'd he get it?'

'He doesn't remember.'

Andy doesn't reply.

'But it's not drugs,' I insist. 'He cut himself, somehow.'

'So, why doesn't he remember?'

'Because he had a life-threatening infection, Andy. He was delirious!'

'All right. Calm down. I'm only asking.'

'Well now you know. And I don't want to talk about it any more.'

'Fine with me.'

I carry on up the road past a row of coffee houses and fast food joints. The smell of fried chicken wafts pleasantly towards me and I realise that I'm hungry. 'So, how was Ben?' I lighten my tone. 'Did the two of you get along OK?'

'Yeah.' Andy yawns again. 'He played on the computer for a bit, we had dinner and then he watched the *Teletubbies*.

And then he went to bed, good as gold.'

'You gave him his meds?'

'I gave him his meds,' he echoes, firmly.

'Great.' I pause at the top of the road and wait at the pelican crossing for the lights to change. 'And thanks,' I tell him. 'Thanks for tonight.'

'No worries. So, are you on your way home?'

'Erm. Kind of. I need to ask you a favour though.'

'Oh. What's that?'

'I don't suppose you could stay a bit longer?'

He hesitates. 'Why?'

'I'm meeting someone. A friend, for a drink. I don't suppose I'll be *very* late, but... but she's upset. I don't want to be watching the clock.'

'Hmmm. I've got work in the morning,' he points out.

I hesitate. 'You could stay the night.'

Andy is silent for a moment. I can almost hear him thinking it through. 'I'd have to go home early,' he says. 'Get some clean clothes.'

'Do you mind?' I ask him.

'Nah, not really. I was already falling asleep. Your sofa is pretty darn comfy, as it goes.'

'Great. Well, make yourself at home. There's a spare duvet in the cupboard in the bedroom. And a toothbrush in the bathroom cabinet. You can just grab a pillow off my bed.'

'OK. Well, have a good one.'

'Thanks. I will.'

I continue up the road and take a right onto Queen Street. I can see the neon-yellow sign for the Abbey Lounge up ahead. Inside, I order myself a glass of Sauvignon and a bag of peanuts along with a platter of bread, cheese and olives to soak it up. I haven't eaten since lunchtime, I realise, and I must have thrown up whatever was left of that.

I take a seat on a stool at a high table near the bar and take a look around me while I eat. The lounge is almost empty. It's decorated in warm yellows, browns and russets and has a sleek, contemporary feel. The wall behind the bar is backlit underneath a long colourful row of shot bottles. Low-hung shades dangle from the ceiling, casting a moody yellow glow over the bar top and over the table in front of me.

It's not long before Karen arrives. She pauses in the entrance while she loosens the belt of her coat, then shakes it off and hangs it on a metal stand that's tucked in the corner behind the door. She gives me a quick wave, then heads over to the bar. The bartender meets her and she, too, orders a glass of Sauvignon.

'So, what's with all the subterfuge?' She takes a seat beside me. She's smiling faintly, but her eyes are red-rimmed.

I pick up my drink. 'Let's just say that I don't think Mark's bodyguards are too taken with me.'

Karen nods. 'You mean... DCI Hollis?'

'Yep. Him and the other one. Sinclair.'

She raises an eyebrow and takes a sip of her drink. 'Oh. You've met John Sinclair.'

'I was paid a visit,' I smile. 'Told to keep my nose out.'

Karen crosses her legs, straightening the pleat in her skirt. 'Well, I wish I could say that I was surprised, but...'

'But...?' I raise my eyebrows.

She hesitates then shrugs and pulls a face, by way of an answer.

I'm interested in what she's got to say about Sinclair

– about SO21 – but I decide not to press her. 'So, how's Mark?' I ask, instead. 'Has something… happened?'

She nods. 'He's gone downhill. It's his chest. He needs more oxygen, more ventilation. They've had to move him to an ICU bed so that they could sedate him.'

'I'm so sorry.' I hesitate, then ask, 'Will he get better?'

She shakes her head, her brow furrowed. 'They don't know. They just can't say. The consultant said that patients can improve and emerge from an unresponsive state up to a year after a brain injury. So, it's not entirely hopeless from that point of view. But because of his chest… his breathing difficulties… he's at risk of other complications.'

'What kind of complications?'

'Well, if it goes on too long, the ventilation can damage his lungs. He could get an infection.' Her eyes glisten. 'And with his chest this bad it's harder… they said it's so much harder to get through any period of critical illness. So…' She pauses and her eyelashes flutter as her eyes meet mine. 'The long and short of it is that he's up against it.'

My heart sinks. 'I'm so sorry,' I say again.

She gives me a wry smile and takes another long sip of wine. 'God, I needed this.' She closes her eyes, then yawns. 'It's been a long day.'

I nod. We sit in silence for a moment, both sipping our drinks.

'You got food,' Karen observes.

I push the platter towards her. 'Help yourself.'

Karen takes a cocktail stick and selects an olive, but then just holds the stick between her fingers, twirling it around on the plate. 'Can I ask you something?' she says, still looking at the olive.

I shrug. 'Sure.'

'I hope you don't mind,' she says. 'But I need to know.'

'Ask away. Ask anything,' I say.

She looks up at me and her forehead creases. She hesitates for a moment, then says, 'Were you and Mark... together?'

'What?' I shake my head, incredulous.

She reaches out and touches my knee, then fastens her eyes on mine. 'You can tell me,' she insists, her face full of warmth. 'Really. I can handle it. It used to eat me up inside, thinking about where he was and who he was with, but now that he's... like this, I just want to know the truth. It sounds strange but I'd almost feel... like the burden had lifted a little. I'd feel that I could grieve.' She throws out her hands in a gesture of defeat. 'At least I'd know what I was grieving for.'

'Karen—'

'And if I knew that it was you,' she continues, her eyes pleading with me, 'it would be... it would actually be a comfort to me. I'd rather he'd left me for someone like you, than some... nineteen-year-old bimbo. Sorry.' She looks at me awkwardly. 'I don't mean that you're not...'

I shake my head. 'Karen! Stop!'

Her eyes swim with tears and she looks away.

'I have never, *ever* been in a relationship with Mark,' I insist. 'Even if I'd wanted to, he was... he was a family man, through and through. He talked about you all. He talked about his kids as though they were everything to him. I promise you, he was just a friend to me, nothing more.'

She continues to look at me, doubtfully. 'So why are you so...?'

I shrug, baffled. 'So... what?'

'So *interested* in him?' She says 'interested' as if it's a dirty word.

I think about this for a moment. I don't quite get it. She'd seemed perfectly pleased with my *interest* the last time I saw her. Why the suspicion now? 'Well,' I begin, 'like I told you, I... I came across him, by accident. I realised I knew him. I think of him as a friend. I don't think it's particularly strange that I want to know what happened to him. Do you?'

I peer at her, waiting for an answer, but Karen looks into her lap.

'There's something going on,' I explain. 'With SO21. I'm sure of it. Something's not right about their explanation of what happened to him. And it bothers me.' I pause as the realisation hits me. 'Wait a minute.' I put my glass down clumsily onto the table top. The stem clinks loudly against the plate. 'What have they said?'

Karen lifts her eyes. 'Who?'

'Hollis. Sinclair.'

She lowers her eyes. I can see instantly that I'm on the right track.

'What've they been feeding you, Karen? Because whatever they've told you about me, it isn't true.'

Karen looks back at me, doubtfully.

'Can't you see what's happening?' I persist. 'They're trying to drive a wedge between us, to stop us from putting our heads together and joining the dots. First they tell me to stay away from you...'

Karen looks surprised. 'From *me*? They said that?'

I nod. 'Sinclair did. And now they're trying to poison you

against me. Telling you stuff… stuff that's absolutely not true!'

I watch her face for a moment as she tries to figure out what to believe. Eventually her shoulders relax and she flashes me a hesitant half-smile.

'Mark was a work colleague,' I explain. 'That's all. And, yes, I liked him. I liked him a lot. But the reason I liked him was because he was so… right-minded. So caring. I liked him because he was the last man I'd ever have suspected of cheating on his wife. That's the point! If anything, I was… a little jealous of you all. Of the way he talked about Sophia, as if she was his little princess. I was never anyone's little princess,' I explain, feeling self-indulgent as I say it. 'I never had a dad like that.'

Karen laces her fingers together on her lap. 'I'm sorry,' she says.

'So, was it them?' I press her. 'Hollis? Sinclair? Did they put this idea into your head?'

'What idea?'

'That Mark was having an affair.'

She shakes her head. 'They didn't need to. You may think you knew him, Sarah, but… he changed. Everything you've described… well, he was like that once. But that was before he went undercover. And I know what the deal is there; I know what goes with that. I'm not stupid. You read about it all the time. Undercover officers getting into relationships, leading double lives.'

'Not him, though, surely?' I protest.

'Sarah, he was never home!' Her voice is thick with emotion. 'Once he joined SO21, within weeks of being put on the op, that was it. He was lost to us. We never knew when we were going to see him, not from one day to the next. He would come home in the middle of the night and leave again before the children had even had their breakfast.' She grabs her glass and takes a swig of her drink. 'Sometimes he was gone for weeks at a time.'

'But that was the nature of the job, surely? He'd infiltrated a crime group. He was pretending to be a drug dealer. He had to play the part.'

'I know that. And I could have lived with that. But, believe me, it went much deeper. He didn't just get into character, he... he *became* that character, that *person*.' She spits out the word 'person'. 'He shut me out. He was always preoccupied, always checking his phone, his laptop, or standing outside in the garden, staring out into the dark. Anything, so long as he didn't have to spend any time with me – with us. He became more and more distant. It was obvious that there was something on his mind, but he wouldn't talk to me.' She looks up at me, wistfully. 'We used to talk about everything, at one time. There were no secrets between us. But in the last few months, it was like living with a stranger. And then the moodiness,' she continues, before I can answer. 'You have no idea. Yelling at me. Yelling at the kids. It got so that we were walking on eggshells around him. It got to the point that I was glad when he didn't come home.' She stops and her expression changes. I can see that she's thinking about what she just said – that maybe, now, he never *will* come home. But she shakes it off. 'I couldn't live like that,' she says, decisively. 'And it was really affecting the children – Jack, in particular. They'd been so close. Jack looked up to him. In the end I'd had enough. And when I asked him to move out' – her eyes meet mine and she looks hard at me, making her point – 'he didn't even argue. He just packed his bags and went. One minute he was there – and then the next he was gone.' She sighs and says, bitterly, 'He couldn't wait to get away.'

I think about this for a moment. Something about it just doesn't seem right. I think back to what Sinclair had told me: that when Mark first agreed to the assignment his instructions were that his family were to be protected at all costs, that they had to be kept as far away from him as possible if anything went wrong. This is the one thing Sinclair told me that actually rang true.

'But if he was in danger,' I suggest, 'he might just have been scared?'

Karen shakes her head. 'That doesn't explain...' She breaks off and looks up at me, her eyes wide. 'He could have *talked* to me.'

'But what if he couldn't?' I say. 'What if he'd got in so deep that he couldn't get out without putting your lives at risk? What if he was deliberately pushing you away? What if he deliberately engineered the breakdown in your relationship so that he could put as much distance as possible between you and the crime group? Because it was the only way he could protect you and the kids?'

I watch as the colour drains out of her face, as her skin pales from porcelain white to an ashen grey, her red lips parting in evident acknowledgement and surprise.

'Don't,' she says, abruptly, and shakes her head rapidly from side to side. 'Don't say that.'

I reach out and put my hand over hers. 'Karen, I really think that—'

'No!' she utters, loudly. The barman looks up from behind the bar. Karen snatches her hand away from me and looks, unseeing, across the room at him for a moment before fixing her eyes on her wine glass. After a moment, she pushes it away across the table top and places her elbows on the table, her head in her hands. 'I don't need to hear this. I just need to forgive him and move on,' she says, through her fingers, her voice muffled.

'You need to grieve,' I remind her. 'That's what you said. You said you needed to know the truth. And I think the truth is that he loved you, all of you. He loved you so much that he had to let you go.'

'But why would he do that?' She lifts her head and looks up at me, her eyes stricken, wide. 'Why not just leave? The police, I mean. The op. Why not just tell them he wanted out?'

'Maybe he couldn't,' I suggest. 'Maybe he was in too deep.'

Karen shakes her head. 'No. No, that's not right. He loved his job. He loved being undercover. He was unstoppable. *They* had to stop him. They suspended him. They took him off the op, well before Christmas…'

I shrug. 'So they say.'

'So, he could have easily—' Karen stops in mid-sentence and frowns. 'What? What do you mean, "so they say"?'

I shake my head. 'I don't know what I mean. But what I do know is that they lie. They lie about everything. I know they lied to me. They're bound to have lied to you too.'

Karen thinks about this for a moment and then her back straightens. 'Well,' she says, stiffly. 'We'll probably never know for sure.'

I frown. 'What?'

She looks at me sympathetically, almost condescendingly. 'I know how they work, Sarah. The squads. SO21. They'll never tell me the truth about what Mark was involved in.'

I narrow my eyes. 'And that's good enough for you?'

She shoots me a tight, tolerant smile. 'You said it yourself: they lie.'

'Well,' I say, angrily, 'if it was me, I'd make it my business to find out.'

She looks at me despairingly. 'How?'

'You said you wanted the truth,' I point out.

She clenches her jaw. 'About his other women. Not about his work. I don't need to know about his work!'

I hold out my hands. 'They *took* him from you, Karen. Hollis, Sinclair... SO21. They *stole* your life together, they stole your husband and then when they'd finished with him they put him in a hospital bed—'

'You don't know that!'

'—and then they didn't tell you where he was for three months. How can you not be angry?'

Karen shakes her head and her eyes light up in despair. 'Don't you see? I don't *want* to be angry! I can't *let* myself be angry, because I can't do anything about it! I don't want to be burning up inside – I just want peace! I just want to say goodbye to Mark and move on.'

'But that's my point. You might never have had that peace, that... closure. Thanks to them, he might have died without you ever knowing where he'd gone!'

Karen's eyes meet mine and then flicker down towards her lap. Her face flushes, distinctly.

I continue to watch her for a moment, and then I realise. 'You *knew*,' I accuse her. 'You knew where he was all along.'

She holds up a finger. 'No, I didn't! Not... not all along, I didn't.'

I sit up straight in my seat. 'When? When did they tell you?'

Karen bites her lip and squeezes her eyes shut tight. 'I challenged Hollis about it. I made him tell me.'

'When?' I persist.

She drops her hands into her lap. Her shoulders sag. 'In January,' she confesses. 'A couple of weeks after New Year.'

I look at her in disbelief. 'You *knew*. You knew all this time what had happened to him... and you didn't tell your kids?'

Karen doesn't answer.

'Were you ever going to tell them?' I press her. 'Or were you just going to let him disappear into thin air?'

Karen presses her fingers against her temples for a moment. 'I was told... No. I wasn't told. I was *ordered* not to tell them!' She looks up to face me, her eyes swelling with tears. 'I was told that Mark's life was in danger, that if the kids found out – if they told anyone at school – that it would put Mark in serious jeopardy, that they'd come back to finish off the job.'

I lean forward. '*Who?* Who would?'

'I honestly don't know!'

I think about this for a moment. 'You told me that it was an accident,' I accuse her again. 'You said that what happened to Mark was a random accident; a random mugging and a hit-and-run.'

'I had to,' she says. 'They told me to say that.'

I look up. 'They told you to lie to me? They sent you to my office?'

She swallows and nods.

'To throw me off the trail?'

Karen looks back at me, guiltily. 'They asked me to come and talk to you. To explain.'

'So, what happened? What *really* happened?'

'I don't know, Sarah! I don't know any more than you do. You need to stop interrogating me.'

I think for a moment. 'You told me that he'd left custody and gone to CID.'

'Because he'd gone undercover.' Karen raises her shoulders, then drops them again. 'I wasn't allowed to tell you, obviously. But now you know. You know everything *I* do. And you know what? That's *all* I want to know.' She swings her seat away from me and stares down at the table in front of her. 'You don't know who you're messing with,' she warns me. 'You need to be careful.'

I ask, 'Of who?'

Karen doesn't answer. She drains her glass and picks up her handbag, then slides off the stool. 'Whatever you think of me,' she says, shakily, her eyes still glistening, 'I'm just trying to protect my children. That's all.' She unzips her handbag, takes out her purse and places a twenty-pound note on the table. She looks me directly in the eye. 'Thanks for the chat,' she says, her voice loaded with irony. 'I feel so much better now.'

She turns and heads for the door.

'Karen, wait.' I jump up. 'I'll… I'll get this.' I snatch the note up from the table and root in my bag for my purse. I have no cash. I've spent it all in the Hope and Glory. I pull out my credit card and snap it down onto the bar, then stride after Karen who is at the door, putting on her coat.

'I'm sorry,' I tell her, pushing her money back into her hand. 'I'm really sorry. I understand that you were just doing what you were asked. I had no business telling you how to deal with any of this.'

She fakes a smile. 'That's one thing we agree on.'

I reach out and touch her shoulder. 'Please, Karen. I'm on your side. Don't let them come between us. Don't let them win.'

'Don't let them win?' Karen repeats, her eyes flashing. 'For Christ's sake, Sarah, listen to yourself. This isn't a bloody game. Look at Mark. He's already lost. You think you're cleverer than him?'

She shakes her head and gives me a pitying glare before yanking the door open and walking out onto the street.

The door closes on me. I remain standing where I am for a moment, then turn around and walk back over to the bar.

'That everything?' asks the barman, picking up my credit card.

'Yes. Thanks.'

I settle the bill, then step over to the table. My phone is ringing. I snatch my bag up from the floor and root around in the side pocket before remembering that I've left it in my coat pocket. I pick up my coat and pull it out. I have a missed call, but it's not from Andy, it's from Matt. I sink back down onto my stool and stare at the phone for a moment, waiting for my voicemail to send me a text. Matt must be on call tonight. But why's he calling me? It must be one of my clients. Maybe he needs some advice.

I pull on my coat and head for the door. Outside, I dial Matt's number. He picks up as soon as it rings. 'Sarah. You're needed,' he says, in his usual abrupt manner. 'Client's asking for you. I think you're going to want to get a babysitter this time.'

'What? What are you talking about?'

'It's Jerome Thomas,' he says. 'He's been arrested. Attempted murder. Of a cop.'

10

The officers are from Major Crime. They show me into a room and sit down at the table, notebooks and pens in front of them, fingers folded, faces inscrutable. I sit down opposite and ask for their names.

'DS Jim Trafford,' says the tall, thin one, with the cropped grey hair, who's wearing a suit. He gesticulates toward his younger colleague. 'This is DC Justin Flint.' He pushes a piece of paper across the desk towards me.

I skim the page in front of me. 'What *is* this?'

'It's written disclosure.'

I look up at DS Trafford. 'So, where's the disclosure?'

His green eyes narrow as he surveys me in silence.

'All it actually says,' I continue, 'is that my client's been arrested on suspicion of causing serious injury to a plain-clothed police officer, based on a... on a mind-blowingly generic description. And, once again, an undisclosed forensic link. On *New Year's Eve*. We've been through all this before. You've already arrested him for this. You had nothing to connect him. It was NFA'd.'

Trafford's voice is measured and controlled as he says, 'Your client was arrested for this offence for the first time at twenty forty-five hours this evening.'

'Different offence, same circumstances. So, what are you

suggesting now? That he ran over the victim in the four-by-four? And if so, why didn't you mention that last time? Why wait until now to arrest him for this?'

I look at each one of them in turn. The officers remain silent.

'So what's the link?' I persist. 'What's the forensic? And where was it found?'

DS Trafford leans back in his seat and rubs his clean-shaven chin, his long, slightly crooked nose raised defiantly in my direction. 'Your client will be offered the opportunity to account for his movements on the night in question. We want to test his veracity. We're not prepared to disclose any more at this stage of the investigation.'

I write this down. 'Witnesses?' I ask.

'Possibly.'

'Who? How many?'

Trafford purses his lips. He says, sombrely, 'We've given you sufficient disclosure to enable you to advise your client.'

I look him in the eye. 'With respect,' I tell him, 'it's my job to decide that. And paragraph 11.1A of PACE Code C would beg to disagree with you.'

Trafford merely stares back at me in silence. He picks up a ballpoint pen from the table and rolls it back and forth between his thumb and fingers.

'So, will there be any ID procedures?' I ask.

'Depends what he says in interview.'

'Any CCTV?' I continue, knowing the answer already.

'We're not prepared to disclose anything further at this stage of the investigation.'

'Cell site evidence? Phone data?'

'We're not prepared to disclose anything further at this stage of the investigation.'

'Searches?' I ask. 'Anything?'

I look up as DC Flint shoots a glance at his colleague.

Trafford says, 'A number of items were seized on the section 18 this evening. We'll be asking him about them in interview.'

I think about this for a moment, while I survey my hand-scribbled Q and A. What could they have found at Jerome's home address that connects him with the four-by-four?

'Anyone else arrested?'

'We're not prepared to disclose anything further at this stage of the investigation.'

'Any significant comment on arrest?' I ask, finally.

'"It's a fair cop, guv",' says Flint, and Trafford's mouth curves into a smile.

I give them both a hard stare.

'No,' says Trafford. 'No comment on arrest.'

'Right.' I gather up the disclosure notice and pick up my iPad. 'I'm guessing we're done here. I'd like to speak to the custody sergeant now.'

I follow the officers out of the conference room and up to the custody desk. 'Do you want your client out?' asks the custody sergeant. 'His mum's out at the front desk.'

I nod. 'Yes please.'

The custody sergeant hands the cells keys to an assistant and the officers head off out to the SDO.

'I want to make representations,' I say, when they've gone.

The custody sergeant pulls the computer monitor towards him, clicks his mouse and starts typing. 'OK,' he agrees. 'Go ahead.'

'If this is another fishing expedition,' I say, angrily, 'then it needs to stop now. This is a child at the end of the day—'

'He's nearly sixteen,' observes the custody sergeant.

'He's a child,' I insist. 'A child who's trying to stay on the right tracks, to get on with his life. This is effectively the second arrest for the same offence and disclosure has been wholly inadequate, both times.' I pause to allow the custody officer to catch up with me, then tap on my iPad and read aloud, 'Code C, paragraph 11.1A states that, before a person is interviewed, they – and if they are represented, their solicitor – must be given sufficient information to enable them to understand the nature of the offence and why they are suspected of committing it.'

'However,' the custody sergeant lifts up a finger and reads from his computer screen, 'this does not require the disclosure of details at a time which might prejudice the criminal investigation.'

He surveys me from behind his monitor for a moment, as he waits for my response.

'What is sufficient,' I counter, looking back down at my iPad, 'will depend on the circumstances of the case, but should normally include *a description of the facts* relating to the suspected offence – note 11ZA.' I look up again. 'I've had no description of the facts. I've had no description of anything that links my client to an offence.'

'"Normally",' the custody sergeant reminds me. 'The key word here is "normally". And,' he continues to read, 'the decision about what needs to be disclosed rests with the investigating officer.'

I say, 'A discretion which is not to be blatantly abused.'

The custody sergeant shoots me a bemused smile. 'So, where does it say that?'

'It doesn't,' I shoot back. 'It's implied.'

He closes down his web page and leans forwards, his arms on the desk. 'I'm sorry, Sarah. This is a highly sensitive investigation. The officers need to be allowed to do their job. You'll have to save your arguments for court.'

There is a rattle of handcuffs behind me and I turn to see Jerome. He's shivering in a white paper jumpsuit and custody standard canvas slip-ons; the police have seized his clothes.

'Hey,' I say to him.

'Hey,' he mumbles back, looking at the floor.

The custody assistant removes his handcuffs.

'Room one,' says the custody sergeant.

I follow Jerome inside and we both sit down.

'You're cold,' I observe. 'I'll ask them for a blanket and a hot drink. Your mum will be here in a minute. But I need to talk to you first.'

He nods.

'Are you OK?' I ask him.

He nods again and rubs his eyes.

'Do you know why you're here?'

He hesitates for a moment, then shakes his head.

I stand up. 'I'll get that drink.'

I step outside, where I catch the custody assistant's eye. In the opposite direction I can see that DC Flint has re-entered the custody area. Georgina is behind him, wearing a white puffa jacket and pink tracksuit bottoms. Her eyes meet mine. 'He's fine,' I reassure her as they approach me along the corridor. 'I'm with him now. But I need to talk to him on his own for a bit. I'll come and get you. OK?'

She clutches her handbag against her chest and nods.

I step back into the conference room and slide back into my seat in front of Jerome. I place my iPad and disclosure notes on the table in front of me and then look him in the eye. 'OK, Jerome. This is what I've been told: the police are saying that you were involved in a serious assault on a plain-clothed police officer. It happened in a street near the estate where you live in the early hours of New Year's Day. Not long after midnight,' I clarify, watching his face carefully for a reaction. 'And they're saying that it was deliberate. A deliberate attempt to kill the police officer, not just to injure him. That's what attempted murder means.'

Jerome looks back at me in silence, his dark eyes fixed on mine.

'The police officer *was* badly injured,' I tell him. 'There's no doubt about that. He's in hospital, fighting for his life. The investigating officers haven't told me much, but... but I know some things. I found out some things. And what I know is that something happened to him in the street. It seems he was assaulted; possibly robbed. And then he fell into the road. He was run over by a car. The car was going too fast. It sped up when it reached him. Deliberately, it seems. With the intention of... of doing more than hurting him. Then it ran over him and it didn't stop.'

Jerome folds his arms and shivers. I can see the outline of his narrow shoulders and his bony chest through the thin paper of his suit.

'The car crushed his chest and collapsed his lungs,' I continue. 'It broke his pelvis and his ribs and his shoulder, and he had two separate head injuries. This happened in Packington Street,' I explain. 'Do you know where Packington Street is?'

His eyes flash with recognition.

'It's the road that runs along the edge of the estate, where the small park is,' I clarify.

'It weren't me,' he says, abruptly. 'I weren't driving no car. I didn't run no one over.'

I nod. 'Well, the police have told me very little, except that you've been linked forensically. They won't say how, and I don't know if they're bluffing, like last time. But if they have something, it's going to be a fingerprint, or your DNA, or... or something from your body or your clothes that connects you with what happened. Any idea what that might be?'

Jerome grips the sleeves of his paper suit and shakes his head.

'They've searched your home this evening and seized some items,' I continue. 'Which they're going to ask you about. What have they found?'

He shrugs. 'A bit of weed, maybe.'

'Anything else?'

'No. Nothing else.'

'So... nothing to connect you with any of this?'

Jerome looks me in the eye. 'No. Cos I didn't do it.'

'OK.' I agree. I look down at the disclosure notice on the desk in front of me. 'They also have a description of a suspect,' I continue. 'A black teenager with short dark curly hair, wearing a dark-coloured hoody and dark jogging bottoms, which could be you or... or half the kids on the estate.' I pause and look down at my notes. 'So, what were you wearing when you were arrested this evening?'

'A hoody,' he says. 'Black. And grey joggers.'

'What make?'

'Nike.'

'Trainers?'

'Black. With orange stripes – and an orange sole.'

'Orange?'

He nods.

I think about this. The clothing could be anyone. The trainers... not so much. 'OK. Well, they may want them for description, or fibres or footwear marks... I just don't know yet. What I *do* know... and they haven't told me this. It's something I found out for myself. But the car that ran him over was a four-by-four. Dark in colour, with blacked out windows.'

Jerome's eyes flicker up to meet mine.

'Yes,' I say. 'The same one they interviewed you about already.'

Jerome's eyes widen as he makes the connection. 'It weren't me,' he protests. 'I told you. I didn't steal no four-by-four. I didn't run over no fed.'

'No.' I hesitate. 'But you know where you were on New Year's Eve, right? And what you were doing?'

Jerome doesn't answer. I can see him thinking, working it out.

There's a knock on the door. The custody assistant appears with a blanket and a plastic cup of watery hot chocolate. He hands Jerome the blanket and places the cup on the table in front of him.

The door shuts. Jerome unfolds the blanket and pulls it around his shoulders. He picks up his drink.

'So, New Year's Eve,' I press him. 'Where were you?'

'At home.' He lifts the cup to his mouth and blows into it. 'In my bedroom. On the Xbox.'

I look him in the eye. 'All evening?'

He nods.

'Are you sure?'

He nods again.

'Can anyone confirm this?'

Jerome hesitates, taking a slurp of his drink. 'Yeah,' he says, finally. 'My friends. I was playing Xbox with the boys, innit?'

I hesitate. 'What about your mum?'

He nods. 'Yeah.'

'So, can I ask her?'

'Yeah,' he says. 'You can ask her. She'll tell you: I was at home.'

I stand up and open the door. Georgina is in a room opposite. I wave her into the conference room, where she takes a seat next to Jerome.

She places her handbag on the floor and looks from Jerome to me and back again. 'Attempted murder?' she hisses, when the door shuts. 'Of a policeman?' She stares at me in disbelief. Her face is devoid of make-up, her eyes ringed with tiredness. 'This has got to be a joke, right?'

'It *is* a joke,' Jerome mutters. 'Cos it weren't me. I ain't done nothing wrong.'

'Where?' she persists. 'And when did this happen?'

'Packington Street. Opposite the estate,' I tell her. 'New Year's Eve. Well, not long after midnight, so early hours of New Year's Day.' She shakes her head, her eyes still wild and disbelieving. 'Jerome says that you can give him an alibi. You can say that he was at home on New Year's Eve?'

Georgina thinks for a moment. She turns to face her son and says, accusingly, 'Not all evening you weren't.'

'Mum!' Jerome spins round to face her. 'You don't remember? I looked after Kaleisha and Jordan while you went with Lanecia to Aunty's house.'

'For a couple of hours, earlier in the evening. But then, later, you went out.' Georgina's voice starts to rise, her head bobbing animatedly. 'I heard the door shut. I'm not going to lie for you, Jerome!' Her face crumples and her eyes fill with tears. 'I swear, I can't take much more of this. If you was involved in this you need to tell Sarah the truth!'

'OK. Thanks, Georgina.' I hold my hands up. 'There's no need to say any more.'

'I didn't do anything!' Jerome pleads with his mother. 'I didn't do nothing to no police officer! I didn't drive no four-by-four.'

Georgina flings her own hands up in the air. 'Then why are they saying it was you?'

'I don't know, do I?'

'And, to be fair… neither do I,' I jump in, quickly. 'They haven't told us anything much at all. So please, let's all calm down. Let's take this one step at a time. If they've got no evidence then Jerome won't need an alibi. So, let's go and find out what they've got.'

It's warm and airless in the interview room, which is effectively a cell with a table and five bolted-down chairs. This room, with its dated fluorescent strip lights, its hard wooden seats, its enforced intimacy – five of us, sitting so close in such a warm, small space that we can smell each other's skin – will be my workplace for the next few hours, potentially all day tomorrow, too. DC Flint asks Georgina if she's happy with the childcare arrangements that she's put in place for her younger three, but he doesn't ask me. My heart flutters a little as I think of Ben. I silently pray that Andy will hear him if he cries, that he will instinctively wake the way I do if Ben wakes, if anything happens, or – the thought that's always there, tugging away at the back of my mind – if Ben falls ill.

DC Flint takes out a set of discs from its cellophane wrapper and inserts them into the machine. He taps our names into a computer monitor attached to the wall and then the familiar buzzer sounds. There is the usual preamble while he states the date and time and the room number, while we all give our names and Jerome is cautioned and given his rights. Then the interview begins.

Trafford leads with the opening I'm expecting. 'Jerome, I want you to account for your movements on the thirty-first of December into the early hours of the morning on New Year's Day. Let's go back to the beginning of the day, to what happened after you got up. Tell me everything you did.'

I clear my throat. 'As your colleague has just reminded Jerome, he has the right to silence. He's going to exercise that right. He's not going to answer your questions; not until you tell him what you suspect him to have done and why you think he's done it.'

Trafford gives me a long, penetrating stare. He turns to Jerome. 'May I remind you that your solicitor's advice is just that: advice. It's your decision. It's you, not your solicitor, who would have to explain to the court why you didn't answer them here, when you had the chance—'

'And may I remind *you*,' I interject, looking back at Trafford, 'that you are not here to advise my client. You're here to try and get him to incriminate himself. Please don't pretend to be looking out for his best interests, when what you are actually here to do is to try and get him to confess to a crime.'

Trafford's jaw tightens. 'We're here to investigate,' he says. 'To look at all angles. To find out what happened.'

'If that were true,' I counter, 'you'd have told him what you suspect him of before you asked for an explanation. Until you do, he'll be making no comment and the court will be satisfied as to why. Check out the judge's comments in the case of Roble. Nineteen ninety-seven. Court of Appeal.'

Trafford ignores me and turns to Jerome. 'Of course, you have the right to silence. But I'm still going to need to ask you some questions. So, Jerome, going back to the morning of the thirty-first of December... where were you? What were you doing that day? Who were you with?'

Jerome's eyes flicker to meet mine. I give him a nod. 'No comment,' he replies.

'What time did you get up?'

'No comment.'

'What did you do?'

'No comment.'

'Who did you call?'

'No comment.'

'Where did you go?'

'No comment.'

'Who do you hang out with, Jerome?'

'No comment.'

'Do you know Desharn John?'

'No comment.'

'How about Nathan Scott?'

'No comment.'

'Luke Clayton?'

'No comment.'

'Romy Lane?'

'No comment.'

'They're friends of yours from the estate, aren't they, Jerome?'

'No comment.'

'Where did you all meet?'

'No comment.'

'Do you know the shops on the corner of Holford Street?'

'No comment.'

'What are they called?'

'No comment.'

'Penning Parade, is that right? Did you meet them there?'

'No comment.'

'What were you wearing, Jerome?'

'No comment.'

Trafford opens a plastic wallet and pushes a CCTV still across the desk towards us. 'Is this you?'

I stop writing and look across the table at the still. It's taken from outside a newsagent's at a small row of shops. There are four boys present, two of whom are on bicycles. Trafford points to one of them. I don't need to look twice; it's clearly Jerome. The time on the still is 12:43:03 on the thirty-first of December.

Jerome looks up at me. I shake my head. 'No comment,' he replies.

'What are you wearing, Jerome? Can you describe your clothing for me?'

'No comment.'

'Well, I'll describe it, then, shall I? You're wearing a black hoody with a white Nike swoosh logo, grey joggers with a white stripe up the side... and black trainers with... with what looks like three thick orange stripes on the outer side.'

'No comment.'

'Jerome, can you confirm what you were wearing when you were arrested this evening?'

'No comment.'

DC Flint reaches down to the floor and pulls up a large clear evidence bag. 'Was it these clothes here? The ones we seized from you when you came into custody?'

'No comment.'

The clothes in the bag are clearly identical to the ones in the still, but DC Flint takes us through them one by one anyway, moving the items around through the plastic so that everyone can see. 'This is exhibit JMF/12. A black hoody with a white Nike swoosh logo... a pair of grey joggers with a white stripe, tapered round the ankles... and a pair of black trainers with three orange fluorescent bands on the side and which...' He turns the bag over and shakes one of the shoes a little. 'Which have orange soles. The label on the tongue says... Adidas Palace. Would you agree with that description, Jerome?'

'No comment.'

'Can we agree that these are your clothes, Jerome? Is this what you were wearing when the police arrested you tonight?'

'No comment.'

Flint lifts the evidence bag up off the table and onto the floor.

'So, this is Luke, here.' He points to the still. 'Is that right?'

'No comment.'

'Romy's the other one on the bike. And that's Nathan, standing next to you.'

'No comment.'

'Where's Desharn?'

'No comment.'

'So, how long did you stay at the Parade?'

'No comment.'

'Where did you go after that?'

'No comment.'

'Nathan went home, didn't he?'

Jerome says nothing. I make a mental note: they've already talked to Nathan – or someone. They already know where everyone went.

'Where did you go...' persists Trafford. 'You, Romy and Luke?'

Jerome looks into his lap. 'No comment.'

'Did you go to the Drag?'

'No comment.'

'You know what the Drag is, don't you, Jerome?'

'No comment.'

'It's the stretch of wasteland from Freight Lane up to Macey's at the back of the estate. It's where stolen cars get dumped. You were up there for the afternoon with Romy and Luke.'

'No comment.'

'So, who else was up there? Who did you meet?'

'No comment.'

'Did you meet Desharn?'

'No comment.'

'Did you meet Jaden Spence?'

'No comment.'

'What about his brother, Jemal?'

'No comment.'

'How long were you there?'

'No comment.'

'What were you doing?'

'No comment.'

'Were you drinking? Taking drugs?'

'No comment.'

'What time did you leave the Drag, Jerome?'

'No comment.'

'Where did you go after that?'

'No comment.'

'Did you go home?'

'No comment.'

'Who left with you?'

'No comment.'

'What about Romy and Luke?'

'No comment.'

'What did they do?'

'No comment.'

'So whose idea was it to go out again, later?'

'No comment.'

'Was it Romy's or Luke's? Or Desharn's? Who called for who?'

'No comment.'

'If you were at home, why don't you just tell me, Jerome?'

His eyes flicker towards Georgina, then back to Jerome again.

'No comment.'

'If you have an alibi, someone who can say where you were, then just tell me?'

'No comment.'

'It's because you *weren't* at home, were you? It's because you were out, on the estate. You were out late at night, on foot, this time. No bike. You didn't need a bike, did you? Jerome?'

'No comment.'

'You didn't need a bike, because you were going to steal a car.'

I lean forward. 'Where's the evidence? You can't assert that without evidence.'

Trafford looks at me for the first time since the interview started. He then glances at DC Flint and nods.

DC Flint reaches down to the ground and lifts up a laptop, which he opens and places on the desk. 'I'm going to show you some camera footage now.'

'For the benefit of the tape,' I say, 'this was neither shown nor disclosed to me or my client prior to the interview.'

'Agreed,' says Trafford, stiffly. 'But we're showing it to you now.'

'What kind of footage is it? Where's it from?' I ask.

Both officers ignore me. DC Flint clicks on a file and opens it and a video screen appears. The screen capture is dark, the sky black, the streetlights glowing ink-spots of yellow light. At the forefront of the shot there's an expanse of black tarmacked road with a faint broken white line behind it, beyond which I can see buildings: a row of houses fronted by white pillars and arches, which I immediately recognise as Packington Street. Off to the left, I can see what appears to be Jaydeep's front door. I lean forward to get a closer look, glancing down to the bottom left of the screen for data about the recording. I can see that the date is the first of January. The footage is paused at 00:08:18.

'This is exhibit JMF/1. Footage,' says DC Flint, 'of Packington Street, recorded soon after midnight on New Year's Day. I think you know Packington Street, don't you, Jerome? Does this street look familiar?'

Jerome doesn't reply.

DC Flint leans forward and presses a button and the footage begins to play. 'Look familiar now, Jerome?' He looks across the table at Jerome and their eyes meet, momentarily. 'So...' DC Flint points to the screen. 'Here's the park area that borders the estate, off screen to the right, here. Here's the railings and the bushes beyond, down here. Then across here,' he points to the left side of the screen, 'is the north-east side of the street that leads up to Hope Square. You know where that is, Jerome? It's where the pub is, on the corner, the Hope and Glory.' He glances at Jerome again. 'I think you know where I mean.'

DC Flint falls silent. For a moment, nothing happens, and we're all sitting watching an empty road. Then a male in dark clothing crosses in front of the screen, just a few feet away from the camera. I can see that he is white – his hands and part of his face are visible – but he's facing away from us, his back to the screen.

DC Flint pauses the footage. 'Who's this?' he asks.

Jerome's eyes are fixed on the screen in front of him, his shoulders tensed, his head immobile. 'No comment,' he says.

'Is it Luke?' asks DC Flint.

No comment.'

'What's he doing?'

'No comment.'

'Is he trying car door handles? Trying to find a car to steal?'

'No comment.'

'OK.' DC Flint starts the footage again. The white male is joined by a second, taller, black male, wearing a white bodywarmer with a long-sleeved top underneath. He too has his back to the camera. When he turns to speak to the first male, his face is obscured by a hood.

'Who's this in the bodywarmer?' asks Flint.

Jerome says nothing.

'Is it Desharn?'

No reply.

'And how about this?'

A third male enters the screen. I can see that he's black, but he too has his hood up.

'Who's this, Jerome?'

'No comment.'

'Is this Romy?'

The third male points towards something off camera a few feet away and all three turn to look in the direction that he's pointing before moving off to the left of the screen. The male in the bodywarmer can be seen to bend down briefly before following the other two out of sight.

DC Flint pauses the footage.

'Where are they going?' he asks Jerome. 'What have they seen?'

I glance at Jerome out of the corner of my eye. He glances back at me. 'No comment,' he says.

DC Flint presses play. For a moment nothing happens.

We all sit and stare at the empty road. At the top of the screen, behind the houses, shimmering trails of light are now zigzagging up into the sky as fireworks appear and then disappear.

We all sit and watch for a moment. A fourth male moves from behind the camera into view. He's black and is wearing a dark-coloured hoody and grey jogging bottoms. His face is partially obscured as he stops and glances briefly to his left in the direction the other males have just gone then looks purposefully around to the right. He has something in his hand, I notice, some kind of baton or stick. He crosses the road away from the other males and, as he does so, his footwear comes into view: dark trainers. Light-coloured soles. Orange soles. Next to me, Georgina shifts in her seat. My heart begins to sink.

'And here...' says DC Flint, slowly, 'is you.'

He pauses the video. 'That *is you*, right, Jerome? I mean... tell me if I've got this wrong?'

I take a deep breath in. 'Jerome, we need to stop the interview for a further consultation.'

DC Flint says, 'Up to you, Jerome. We can take a break. But you might want to watch this next bit first.'

Jerome looks at me and I nod. DC Flint presses play again.

The first three males remain out of camera shot, off to the left of the screen. The male with the orange soles walks over to the opposite pavement, in front of the houses, then steps back into the road again and walks back towards the camera. He appears distracted, glancing to his right across the screen in the direction his friends have gone and then to his left, to where the dark metal railings to the park can just be made out. As he comes closer towards the camera, he lifts the object in his hand and swings it around, first slowly, then faster, in swift movements, as if he's a martial artist with a samurai sword.

We all watch as the male in the footage comes closer. He continues to swing the object, moving it from left to right, up and down. As he nears the camera, he turns directly to face it. DC Flint pauses the footage and there's silence in the room as we all look at the screen. It's unmistakable. It's Jerome.

'That's you, Jerome,' says Trafford. 'It's clearly you. The question is, what's that in your hand?'

I look across at Jerome. 'Don't answer any more questions,' I say, quickly. 'This wasn't disclosed to us. We need to take a break.'

'Was it this?' asks DC Flint, lifting a clear plastic evidence bag up from the floor and placing it on the table. Inside is a thick black metal bar, approximately a metre long.

'Stop the interview,' I say, firmly.

Trafford leans over and presses a button and the recording stops.

I gather up my papers and my iPad and jump to my feet. Georgina and Jerome follow my lead and stand up too.

As we head out of the interview room, Trafford hands me a sheet of paper. 'Further disclosure,' he says.

Jerome sits across the table from me and sinks his head into his hands.

'Do you need a break?' I ask him. 'You're entitled to a rest period. I can make representations to the custody sergeant that we start this again in the morning.'

'No.' He looks up, through his fingers. 'I want to get it over with. I don't want to sleep here. I want to go home.'

I take a deep breath in and clasp my hands together on the table in front of me. 'Jerome,' I say, gently, 'I don't think you're...' I hesitate as his eyes dart up to meet mine. 'I'm sorry, but I don't think you're going to be going home.'

Jerome's forehead furrows. 'What?' He stares at me, uncomprehending. 'They're not gonna let me out of here?'

I bite my lip. 'No. I don't think so. Not tonight.' I hesitate. 'And maybe not for a while.'

His eyes widen in terror. 'What do you mean? They're going to lock me up for this?'

I lean forward. 'Jerome, the exhibit they just showed you, the metal rod. It's the weapon, the weapon that was used to assault the police officer. It has his blood and particles of his hair on it and... and it has your fingerprints.'

He surveys me uncomprehendingly for a moment.

I lift up the disclosure notice that I've just been handed and read from it. 'The police say that the metal rod is one of the railings from the park. It was found in a skip near the scene. SOCO – Scenes of Crime Officers – examined it. A palm print and three horizontal fingerprints were recovered in a tape lift and sent to the Fingerprint Bureau for comparison. A computer search has resulted in the palm and fingerprints being identified to you.'

'But... I found it.' Tears begin to form in the corner of his eyes. He blinks them back. 'I found the pole and picked it up. And then I threw it in the skip. That's all.'

'Where did you find it?'

'In the park, on the grass, near the railings.'

'When?'

'Just before... just before... what you saw on the video, me swinging it around and that. I just picked it up. I was playing with it, that's all. I didn't hit anyone with it, I swear down. I didn't. I wouldn't.'

I look hard at him. 'What about your friends?'

Jerome looks back at me, his eyes wide.

'What were they doing, Jerome? While you were swinging the piece of railing around?'

Jerome's expression closes up. 'They can't pin this on me. I found it. Anyone could have picked it up before me and... anyone could have done it. They ain't got nothing!'

I nod. 'You're right. It's a moveable object. Without anything else we could argue that. But someone hit the police officer over the head. He was knocked to the pavement not long after midnight and you're there, you're there in the street where it happened, round about the time that it happened, holding the weapon in your hand, and...'

Jerome's forehead creases. 'And what?'

I say, 'The police searched your bedroom, Jerome. They found a wallet.'

Jerome's eyes widen.

'With bank cards inside,' I tell him. 'It's the wallet belonging to the police officer. It was hidden at the back of the radiator behind your bed.'

Jerome stares at me, open mouthed.

'Did you put it there?' I ask him.

He shakes his head.

'Did you know it was there?' I ask.

He shakes his head again.

'Did you rob the police officer?' I press him.

Another shake of the head.

'Did your friends?'

Silence. And then, 'No.'

I sigh. 'Jerome, you need to tell me what happened. I can't help you otherwise.' I pause and watch as he visibly turns in on himself, his eyes clouding over and his shoulders hunching forwards inside his blanket. 'I know you,' I persist. 'All you've ever done is steal cars. This is too big a leap. This isn't you. Who are you covering for?'

Jerome looks down at the desk in front of him, then mutters, 'No one.'

'Is that what they were doing?' I ask. 'Were they robbing him? The police officer? Is that why you walked away across the road? Because you didn't want to get involved?'

Silence.

I hesitate. 'Or were you keeping lookout for them?'

Jerome's head swings up to face mine. '*No*,' he says, scornfully.

'Did one of them have the piece of metal railing first?' I ask. 'Did they hit him with it? Did you take it off one of your friends? Is that what happened?'

Jerome's eyes burn with indignation. 'You're not listening to what I'm telling you,' he cries. 'I found it – I found it in the park. My friends didn't do nothing to that fed! And neither did I.'

I sit back in my seat and rub my temples, then look despairingly across the table. 'Are you seriously going to do this?' I ask him, staring purposefully into his eyes. 'You're only fifteen. You have your whole life ahead of you. Are you really ready to take the blame for this?'

Jerome doesn't reply. I continue to look hard across the table at him as he sits there, immobile, his narrow shoulders dwarfed by his big blue blanket, his dark eyes fixed back solemnly on mine. I wonder if he has any idea what is in store for him, what it's really like inside a secure training centre or a young offender's institution. I wait for a few moments longer, then stand up and open the door. It's time to let his mother in, to see if she can get through to him, if there's anything she can do to help. But I already know that this is as much as he's going to say to either of us. I already know how this is going to go.

I'm let out of a side door at the back of the police station, where I'm shown through a yard full of police cars and out of an electronic gateway to the rear. A security light blinks on and off again as the gate closes behind me, and then it's dark, the sky above me empty and black. I'm in a narrow back street. Up ahead, there's a single police street lamp casting a circle of light over the royal-blue railings of the station duty office below. I can see that it's closed, the shutters down. No one's there. They don't keep these front offices open at night-time any more.

I walk towards the streetlight, then pause on the pavement by the railings underneath, taking in a breath of crisp, cool air while I switch my phone back on, quickly checking that there have been no missed calls. Nothing, thank God. Ben's tucked up, fast asleep. Of course he is. It's one thirty a.m. I consider my options: night bus or Uber. If it wasn't so late, I'd enjoy the walk.

As my eyes adjust to the light, a figure steps out of the shadows behind me. I stiffen, and my heart races. I push my bag back onto my shoulder and tighten my grip on my phone.

'I suppose you'll be wanting a lift?' says a familiar voice.

I let out a sigh of relief. 'The way you drive?'

'Suit yourself,' says Burdie.

I shake my head. 'You frightened the bloody life out of me. What are you doing here?'

'Keeping an eye on things.'

'Keeping an eye on *me*?'

He shrugs. 'If you like.'

'So presumably you know what's going on?'

He takes a pack of cigarettes out of his pocket, taps one out and lights it. He leans back against the railing, his foot raised up against it, and puffs on his cigarette, contorting his mouth to blow the smoke out to one side.

'Don't you have something of a conflict of interest?' he asks me.

'Not necessarily.'

'You know the victim. You seem to be pretty pally with his wife. And now you're representing the suspect accused of trying to murder him. How's that not a conflict?'

I push my phone into my coat pocket and pull up the zip. 'It's only a conflict if he's guilty.'

Burdie peers back at me, his expression one of disbelief. 'He's got the wallet of a seriously injured police officer in his bedroom and he's on camera with the weapon in his hands! He's going to be charged. You know it.'

'I know he'll be charged with something.' I look straight back at him. 'But the question is, with what?'

He snorts. 'Are you serious?'

'Two things,' I say. 'Firstly, you've arrested and questioned him for attempted murder. But from where I'm looking, I see no more than a random mugging. So, where's the intent to kill? Secondly,' I continue, 'what's happened to the four-by-four? To the hit-and-run? It wasn't even mentioned this time, but Mark got run over minutes later and you lot obviously believe it's connected. You've already arrested Jerome for stealing the car. Major Crime interviewed him about it. So, what...? Are you going to try to suggest that he hit Mark Felding over the head, emptied his pockets, ran off down the road, stole a vehicle and drove back and ran over him to finish him off? It's a bit bloody much.'

Burdie takes a last puff of his cigarette, drops it onto the pavement and smothers it out with his foot.

'Why would he want to kill a police officer?' I persist. 'And why would anyone think that he did?' I pause and think for a moment. 'Unless...'

Burdie watches me, and waits.

'Unless...' I continue. 'Unless it's gang-related. Or... or drug related.' I seek out his eyes. 'You think he's connected to the crime group. To the drugs line,' I press him. 'To Dex. Is that it?'

He shakes his head, but it's an expression of exasperation rather than denial.

'You said that the crime group was responsible for the hit-and-run,' I remind him.

'I never said that. I said we didn't know.'

'You were watching them! You rescued me from them! You told me not to mess with them,' I point out. 'You told me they were dangerous.'

'Obv-ious-ly,' Burdie stretches the word out.

'I know Jerome,' I insist. 'Whatever he's done or not done, he's done it out of loyalty to someone else. If he or any of his friends are connected to the crime group, if they're being used as runners, if they're being exploited, compelled to commit a crime... then they will have a section 45 defence, under the Modern Slavery Act. And you lot,' I point at Burdie, accusingly, 'you have a duty to follow the protocol. You have a duty to go through the National Referral Mechanism to establish whether he's a trafficking victim before a charging decision is made. If this is what's happened... then it's your job to protect him. And you need to act now.'

'Whoa. Slow down.' Burdie lifts up his hands. 'There's no evidence that anyone's been coerced by anyone else.'

I shrug, impatiently. 'So, why else would he do it? What other reason could he have to deliberately attack a copper?'

'Maybe he didn't. Maybe they'll charge him with robbery. No intent needed. What's the difference? The sentence is the same; life imprisonment. That's all they'll need to put him away.'

I put my head to one side. 'They?'

Burdie says nothing.

'Not you?'

He merely looks back at me.

I peer at him in the darkness. 'You're part of this investigation, aren't you?'

He raises one eyebrow. 'Am I?'

'You told me you were on the surveillance team.'

'So I did.'

I glare at him, frustrated. 'Are you going to look into this? Flag up the protocol?'

He says nothing for a moment. Then, 'I'll mention it.'

I shake my head and turn on my heel.

'Sarah—'

'I'm wasting my time,' I shoot back at him. 'You don't want the truth. You just want to put him away.'

I pull my bag over my shoulder and stride off down the street.

'Sarah, wait!' he calls after me.

I stop and turn round. He strides after me and catches me up. 'It's late,' he says. 'Let me give you a lift home.'

I shake my head. 'I'm fine, thank you. I'll call a cab.'

He says, 'I have some information for you.'

I look back at him, suspiciously. 'What information?'

He nods towards his Saab, which is parked just across the street. 'Get in the car,' he says. 'Let me run you home. I'll tell you on the way.'

11

To be fair to Burdie, his driving is better this time, although, given the late hour, there's very little traffic on the road and very few people. And we're not escaping from a bunch of drug dealers with knives this time, of course. Fewer hazards all round. There's less swearing, too. I'm almost relaxed.

'So?' I ask, as we drive up Rosebery Avenue, past Sadler's Wells and onto St John Street. 'What is it that you were going to tell me?'

He clears his throat and shoots me a quick glance. 'First, I need you to agree to something.'

'What's that?'

'If you're going to represent this kid, you need to keep Mark Felding's identity to yourself. And where he is. Which hospital. It won't be in any of the paperwork and it won't come out in court. He'll be referred to by his undercover name.'

'Of course,' I agree. 'I want to protect him as much as you do. You know that.'

He nods. 'Good. So that's settled, then.'

'Is that it?' I ask.

He nods again. He pulls up at the traffic lights at the Angel as they turn to red.

'So?' I turn to face him.

'So,' he replies, glancing back at me. His mouth twitches into something resembling a smile. 'I've had a geographical search run through the ANPR system on the partial number plate for the four-by-four. We got a local match not too far away from Packington Street at eleven thirty-five on New Year's Eve.'

I stare back at him in surprise.

'There was just the one hit,' he continues. 'The image is grainy, but it's clear enough. Black Range Rover Sport, tinted windows, of course, as per the witness description, and there's some glare anyway, so you can't see who's driving, but the VRN is there. I can't say for certain that it's our vehicle. There are not enough cameras to cover all the roads in and out of the area. But the vehicle was there at the right time, travelling in the right direction, so it's a pretty good start.'

I watch his face, riveted. 'Are you serious? You think you've found the car?'

'We'll see. I've run it through PNC. It's a private plate. Its registered to an address in Gravesend.'

'*Gravesend?*' I frown.

'Gravesend,' he echoes.

'And was it reported stolen?'

He shakes his head. 'No. Not according to PNC.'

'Which means…' I pause as I take in what he's said.

'Which means,' he continues, 'that your client didn't steal it. And all in all, if this is our car, the evidence points away from him being inside it.'

The lights change to green. Burdie checks his rear-view mirror then revs the engine and crosses the junction.

I eye him suspiciously. 'Why are you telling me this?'

Burdie exhales loudly. 'I suppose I'm trying to help you.'

'But, why?'

'Because you're obviously not going to back off.' He glances across at me. 'And because – believe it or not – I want the truth, too.'

I consider this for a moment as I watch the lights of Upper Street sweep past us. 'So, you have the name of the registered keeper. Have you talked to them?'

He shakes his head. 'Not yet. But I will.'

'OK. But whoever it is, they're not just going to put their hands up and admit that they were driving, are they? What if the car's not there? What if the owner says he's sold it and the buyer's not sent off the paperwork?' I think out loud. 'But… there would have been damage. So now that you have the full VRN, what's next? Contacting garages, body repair shops? Putting a marker out for the car?'

'Good God, woman. You're exhausting,' Burdie says. 'Like I said, leave it with me.'

I turn to him, exasperated. 'How can I trust you, though? How do I know you'll do what you say? How do I know you're even telling me the truth? You're with SO21, at the end of the day – and all I've been fed is lies.'

Burdie doesn't answer. He turns left at Highbury Corner, onto the Holloway Road. He grinds the gears and swears a little. I look away, out of the window as we pass my office, a reminder that it's only a few hours until I have to get up for work again. I'm going to be shattered tomorrow and I'm likely to have a full day of police interviews. I wonder if Andy would pick up Ben again and give him his tea. Something other than sausage and chips, this time, hopefully.

'I'm not,' says Burdie, out of nowhere.

I turn to face him. 'You're not what?'

'I'm not with SO21.'

I shrug. 'The outside surveillance team then. Whatever. You're part of the drugs operation.'

He hesitates. 'No, I'm not.'

I look at him, confused. 'So, who are you with, then? Which department?'

He nods pointedly at the road ahead of him. 'Are you going to tell me where I'm going here?'

'Sorry. Take the next right.' I direct him up Jackson Road and into my street. He pulls over opposite my house. Andy has left the hall light on for me, which feels comforting, somehow.

Burdie switches off the engine and turns off the lights.

I scan his face in the darkness. 'Who are you?'

He shifts in his seat and pulls his cigarettes out of his top left-hand pocket. As he lifts his arm, I breathe in the scent of old leather from his jacket, the smell of cigarettes on his fingers as he taps the pack and empties one out.

'Burdie?' I press him.

He shifts in his seat again and pulls a lighter out of his jeans pocket.

'Don't tell me,' I say, half-joking. 'You're anti-corruption?'

He smiles. 'Yeah. Maybe I am.'

I peer back at him. 'Are you a PI?'

He laughs. 'Yeah. Maybe I'm that too.'

I fall silent for a moment, then look up at him again. 'But you're on my side? Is that what you're saying? You're willing to help me?'

I can see his eyes twinkling in the dark. 'Don't push your luck.'

I pull my bag up onto my shoulder. 'Can I have your phone number, then?'

A grim smile. 'I thought you'd never ask.'

'Don't go getting any ideas,' I tell him. 'I only want you for one thing.'

'Story of my life.' He puts the cigarette and lighter onto the dash and holds out one hand. 'Give me your phone, then.'

I pull it out of my pocket and unlock it. I create a new contact and hand him the phone. He taps in his number and hands it back to me. I press dial and I hear a bleep from his pocket.

'There,' I say. 'We're connected.' I look at him with curiosity.

'Go on. Get yourself indoors,' he says, stiffly. 'I need a smoke. Then I'll be on my way.'

'Wait.' I take hold of his arm. 'You can trust me. I promise. Please, tell me who you really are.'

He leans his head back on his headrest for a moment, his eyes trained upwards onto the roof of the car. 'You never give up, do you?'

'No. Not really.'

He lowers his eyes to meet mine. His face is sombre and drawn. The intensity of the moment makes me feel suddenly awkward and I let go of his arm.

'I'm Mark's handler,' he says. 'Or, at least, I was. I've been suspended from the police. Pending dismissal.'

'What?' I ask, astounded. 'Dismissal for what?'

He gives me a sardonic smile. 'For trying to get him out.'

I look back at him in stunned silence as he picks up his cigarette and his lighter and opens the driver's door. I feel a blast of cool air and then it slams shut behind him. I watch as he cups one hand over the flame and lights his cigarette, then leans up against the car, his back pressed up against the window.

I sit in the darkness and look at the clock on my phone. It's gone two in the morning; I should go in and check on Ben, then get myself off to bed, get some sleep. But I can't bring myself to leave. I need to talk to Burdie, I need to hear this; I need him to tell me what else he knows.

I wait, patiently, while he finishes his cigarette, watching the leaves on my neighbour's overgrown hedge moving around in the breeze and listening to the occasional swish and hum of traffic coming from the Holloway Road. After a few moments, Burdie turns around, opens the car door and gets back in again. He gives me a look which says, 'Are you still here?'

'Mark?' I ask him. 'You were trying to get Mark out? Out of the op? The undercover job?'

He nods. 'Yep.'

I hold his gaze. 'Why?'

'Because he was in danger. He knew he was in danger. He was begging me to find him an exit. But they wouldn't let him go.'

'SO21?'

'Yep.'

I think about this for a moment. 'So, all that stuff Sinclair told me about him loving the thrill of it, taking too many risks, getting cocky, having to be taken off the job...?'

'... was all royal bullshit.'

'And the desk job at Farringdon CID?'

'Never happened.'

I nod, slowly. 'Which is why no one missed him when he disappeared. No one missed him because he was still working undercover for SO21 when he went to the Hope and Glory on New Year's Eve?'

'Uh-huh,' says Burdie. 'Unfortunately for him.'

We both fall silent. Everything is now starting to make sense. 'So, they made that up, all that stuff about him being suspended?' I ask him. 'Before Christmas?'

'Yep. That wasn't Mark. That was me.'

I shake my head. 'I don't understand.'

Burdie looks out of the window into the darkness. I wait for him to continue. 'As Mark's handler, I was his only confidant for almost two years,' he says, finally. 'He reported back to me every step of the way. He had to. It was part of the job. When he was first recruited onto the op, he was deployed to the south coast. He did a fantastic job there, infiltrated the network, got us the intel we needed on almost all of the runners and a few of the main men too, without giving anything away. That should have been it. Job done. He should have gone home to his family. But then things shifted up a gear. The op got bigger and more complex. The bigger it got, the more frightened he became – the more he wanted out.'

'So, why didn't he just quit?'

Burdie sighs. 'It's not as simple as that. You can't just quit. You can't just disappear, not when you're working at that level. There has to be a properly planned exit strategy to avoid raising suspicion.'

'But surely, if he felt he was in danger…?'

'He was a good UCO, Sarah. Very good. He'd won the respect of several major players within the syndicate. It all started to move to London – way too close to home. Mark was asked to drive to meets with the ringleaders in pubs in various parts of the city. Sinclair told him he needed to agree, to go along every time he was asked, otherwise it would look odd.' He looks up at me. 'He was actually ecstatic, of course.'

'Mark?'

'Sinclair. Mark was bringing him closer and closer to the top of the supply chain. He was perfectly placed, right there in the centre of it all, observing everything, gaining valuable evidence which he was filtering back through me. In return, Sinclair promised Mark his get-out, plus full anonymity for any court proceedings, a new job and home for him and his family well away from London. Witness protection. A new ID. If he just stayed with it a bit longer, that's what he said. Just until he'd got them that golden nugget of intel that they needed to secure a conviction against their primary targets, against the men at the top.'

'And so Mark agreed?'

He shrugs. 'He had no choice. He couldn't get out of it alone. He needed their help. They kept promising him his exit, but it never came. Mark was terrified. He became paranoid. He was constantly looking over his shoulder, expecting to be recognised at any moment.'

'And was he?'

'I honestly don't know.' Burdie shakes his head. 'And neither did he. But let's face it, he'd sat behind a desk in Farringdon custody for the previous eighteen months with every Tom, Dick and Harry who'd ever been arrested in central London passing through his door. The risk was enormous. He'd changed his appearance, of course. Grown his hair, was wearing all the right gear, driving the flashy cars, doing a pretty damned good job to blend in, but it was only a matter of time before he was spotted and he knew it. He had good reason to be paranoid.'

He exhales, deeply.

'I can't believe it.' I shake my head. 'How could they do it? How could they let him put himself in danger like that?'

Burdie's mouth tightens. 'Because Sinclair is an arrogant, selfish...' He glances at me, then breaks off. 'Fucker!' he explodes, simultaneously hitting the steering wheel with the flat of his hand. '*He's* the one who got cocky. He just kept saying that we'd deal with it if it happened, we'd come up with a cover story that Mark was a bent-copper-turned-drug-dealer or something equally unconvincing. Sinclair thought he could outwit anyone. But the truth is, he lost sight of what mattered once he'd got his eye on the prize.'

'The prize being someone at the Hope and Glory, I'm guessing.'

Burdie looks at me, but he doesn't speak.

'It's OK,' I say. 'I don't need to know the details. But what happens to the op without Mark? Without his testimony?'

'Well, they've blown it,' he tells me. 'They're back to square one. Sinclair has fucked up and he knows it. If Mark doesn't recover, he's got no witness. It's his own fault. He pushed him too far and this is the result.'

'Jeez,' I say, taking it in. I turn to face him. 'So, what happened? To you, I mean?'

'I stuck my head up above the parapet, I got shot down.' He shrugs, then catches my expression and clarifies. 'I tried to tell them that Mark was in danger. I'd been trying for months. Mark's a good friend and a fine detective. I told them they needed to do what they'd promised and find him his way out.'

'Don't tell me. They didn't like it?'

'They thought I was influencing Mark, putting ideas into his head. They gave me a few pep talks to start with, told me that I needed to be positive, to encourage and support him to "be the best that he could possibly be". Apparently, there was no place for my "negativity". But I couldn't just stand by and watch them throw him to the sharks. One day, just a few weeks before Christmas, I cornered Sinclair. Threatened to go above him, to blow the whistle on the whole thing if they didn't get him out.'

'What did he say?'

'Nothing.' He shoots me a smile that's tinged with bitterness. 'But he beat me to it. I turned up for work the following day and was hauled up in front of the ACC.'

'What for?'

'What do you think?'

I think about this for a minute. 'Don't tell me. They found drugs in your locker?'

He nods. 'A hundred and twenty-nine individual wraps of diamorphine and twenty-five wraps of crack cocaine. Street value of fifteen hundred pounds. Oh, and seventeen-fifty in cash.'

I shake my head. 'I'm so sorry.'

'Me too.'

We sit in silence for a moment.

'So, if you'd already been suspended, taken off the job... if you weren't on surveillance... why were you there, watching the pub?'

'Same as you. Trying to find out what happened. That's all I'm trying to do.'

I turn to face him. 'We can help each other. Right? If we find out the truth about what happened to Mark, expose Sinclair, we can get you your job back.'

Burdie smiles. 'Yeah. And pigs might fly. I think I'd just settle for getting justice for Mark.'

'Yeah,' I agree. 'That'd be a start.'

He gives me a wry smile by way of an answer.

We sit in silence for a moment. I think about everything I've been told, how it's all been twisted on its head. 'His family have a right to know,' I say, finally.

'No,' he warns me. 'You need to stay away from them. You need to keep this to yourself. I have to be careful how I do this. I'm relying on the goodwill of former colleagues to keep me in the loop. Dig around too much and they'll be onto me.' He glances at me. 'Onto us. That can't happen.'

I nod, uncertainly.

He looks at me, his eyes wide and intense. 'It's what he would have wanted, Sarah. He loved his family. He loved his kids. He was scared for them. He never wanted to break up with Karen, but he saw no other way. He had to make her hate him so that she wouldn't try to stop him leaving. He rented a bedsit in King's Cross, where he could blend in with the transient population; only saw the kids when he was one hundred per cent certain that he wasn't being followed. It was the only way he could sleep at night. He never wanted any of this to happen. But now that it has, they need to be protected, at least until there's enough evidence to lock away whoever ran him over. You need to keep a low profile and let me sort it out.'

'I have to defend my client,' I point out.

He nods. 'I know you do. But please, Sarah, for the love of God, will you now just do what I'm asking? Stay away from the Hope and Glory, stay away from Karen Felding – and leave the four-by-four to me.'

12

A ndy wakes me with a cup of coffee. Now that the mornings are getting lighter, the sun normally rouses me, but I'm so soundly asleep when Andy walks in that when I first open my eyes I don't remember what he's doing here. I blink at him in confusion for a moment, then pull the duvet up around me and drag myself up into a sitting position. He hands me the cup and I take a sip. He's remembered how I like it: strong, milky, no sugar.

'Do you need to leave?' I ask him, noticing that he's fully dressed and is holding his jacket. He looks really nice in his work shirt and smart trousers, albeit that they're yesterday's clothes. I pull the duvet higher, feeling conscious of my flimsy nightdress and bare shoulders. 'What time is it?'

'It's just after seven. And yeah, in a minute.'

'Is Ben awake? Is he OK?'

'Yeah. He's fine. He's got a drink. He's on the computer.' He frowns. 'You look shattered. What time did you get home?'

'Late. I got called to the police station.' I look up at him, apologetically.

Andy frowns. 'You went to the police station? I thought you were just going for a drink.'

'So did I. But it was my client. The kid I told you about.'

'The one they arrested for nicking a car?'

'Yes. Only it was far more serious this time. I wanted to deal with it myself.' I hesitate, then decide to fill him in. I'm going to have my work cut out for me today. I'm going to need Andy's help. 'He was arrested for attempted murder,' I explain. 'Of the copper I told you about. The one who's in hospital.'

'The hit-and-run?'

'Yes.'

Andy frowns. 'I thought they said that was a revenge attack from a drugs gang?'

'That's what they said. They let him go but now they've arrested him again.'

'Jeez.' Andy shakes his head. 'How much sleep have you had?'

'Just over three hours,' I calculate. 'I'm going to suffer for it later.'

'Do you have to go to work?'

'Yes,' I sigh. 'You don't get to lie in just because you've been working half the night. Not where I work, anyway. And besides. I'm going to have to go back to the police station. Second interview this morning.'

Andy pulls his jacket on. 'Will you be OK?'

'I'll survive. But if you're free later and want to come back and give me a hand after work, I could do with the help. The police have over fourteen hours left on the custody clock. I could be stuck there all day. Getting home in time for Ben might be tricky.'

Andy nods, without hesitation. 'Sure. I'll pick him up again and bring him home. I'll call you later.' He looks at his watch. 'I'd better go.' He looks at me fondly for a moment and then leans down and plants a tentative kiss on my cheek. He turns around and stops in the doorway. 'Sorry I can't stay.'

I nod. 'I'll manage. Don't worry. You go.'

I wait for the front door to slam and then get out of bed and go into the living room. As soon as Ben sees me, he looks around for something for me to do. He spots his sippy cup on the table next to him, picks it up and holds it out to me, even though it's already full. 'You've got juice already,' I tell him, and wag a finger. I pick up his Picture Exchange Communication System book from the table and hold it out to him. 'Look. What do you want to eat?'

He leans forwards and tugs a Velcro-backed card out of the book.

'Raisins? You want raisins?' I say emphatically. 'Ben wants raisins. Good choosing, Ben.'

I head down the hall and into the kitchen, the PECS card in my hand. It's not actually very good choosing, because he chooses raisins every time. I put the card on top of the microwave, open the door and take out the fruit bowl, then put my mug of coffee inside to heat up while I make him something more substantial: hard-boiled eggs, toast and slices of banana. I put a handful of raisins onto a separate plate.

Once Ben's sat in his chair at the table eating, I call the police. Custody is busy but after three tries I manage to get through. There's been a change of shift and it's a different team from the one last night. I give an assistant the custody number and wait while he gets me an update. After a moment, the custody sergeant comes on the line.

'The CPS have authorised charges,' she says. 'It's going to be a remand because of his previous, so if you have any representations—'

'Are you serious?' I ask, surprised. 'No second interview?'

'Sufficient evidence to charge. We want to get him into court this morning.'

I think about this for a moment. 'What are the charges?'

'GBH. Section 18. And robbery.'

'Has anyone else been charged?'

'No one else at this stage.'

I make my representations about the decision to remand Jerome, knowing that it won't change a thing. I then ask to be put through to him and reassure him that I will see him at court in a little while, that I will do everything in my power to get him bail. I phone Georgina and, finally, Gareth, my boss. I then clear up the mess of Ben's breakfast from the floor, wash and dress us both and strap Ben into his buggy, ready for my frantic version of the morning buggy run.

When I get into the office Matt and Lucy are in reception, heads together. They stop talking when I walk in.

'Gareth wants to see you,' says Lucy, to me.

'I already spoke to him an hour ago,' I say, surprised. 'Jerome Thomas has been charged. Gareth knows that I'm going to court.'

Lucy and Matt exchange glances.

'What's going on?' I ask.

'I'll see you later,' Matt says to Lucy. He opens the door to the street and walks out.

'Yeah, see you later,' Lucy calls after him. She sits back down at her desk and puts her headphones on.

I head up the stairs and along the corridor to Gareth's

room and tap on the door. He gets up and pulls it open. His features are clouded with ill-suppressed anger. He nods at the empty chair by the window then puts one hand out behind him and pulls his own chair forward. He backs down into it, all the while still glaring at me.

'What's this I hear about Jerome Thomas?'

I drop my bag down onto the floor and sit down. 'I told you. He's been charged and remanded. They're getting him over to court this morning. I was just about to—'

'I've been told that you've got yourself involved with the victim in the case. Is this true?'

I sigh. 'Who told you that?'

He leans forward abruptly, shoulders hunched, palms clasped between his knees. His eyes flash, furiously. 'I've been told that when you've not been busy representing the client at the police station, you've been down at the hospital, visiting the *victim*. A *police officer*. Is it true?'

'Yes, but—'

'For crying out loud, Sarah. Do you not think you've got a conflict of interest here?'

'Maybe not,' I say, hesitantly. 'I can explain.'

He leans back in his chair. 'Well, let's hear it, then. But it better be good. Because from where I'm sitting, you've just lost us a case.'

My heart sinks. 'No,' I say, quickly. 'No. We can act for him. It's not a conflict. Or, at least, it doesn't have to be. Jerome didn't do it. He says he didn't do it. He's covering for someone. I'll tell him I know the victim. He won't mind. Why would he? If it wasn't him that hurt the victim, then it doesn't matter that I know him, surely?'

'Of course it matters,' Gareth retorts, angrily. 'How can

you not see that? And why would you go and get yourself involved with a police officer anyway? How do you know him?'

'Only from the police station,' I admit. 'He used to be a custody sergeant at Farringdon. But then I bumped into him in hospital. I was there visiting someone I know and I came across him and…'

'And what?'

'Well, he was in a bad way. He'd suffered a severe brain trauma. And I recognised him and I wanted to help. And then…'

'And then his wife came to see you. Here, at the office. You talked to his wife, about the case? Is that right?'

'Yes,' I concede.

He shakes his head. 'You have a conflict, Sarah. You have a clear conflict. You should have called it. We're going to have to get rid of the case.' He swings his chair round to face his desk. He says, over his shoulder, 'You'd better find out who's duty at Highbury this morning.'

'No!' I protest. 'Jerome's expecting me. His mum's expecting me. He's going to struggle to get bail but he might just get it if I can explain to the judge – to the court – that…' I tail off as Gareth swings back round to face me, his eyes blazing. 'I know Jerome,' I plead. 'There are things I can say to help him. We can't give it away to duty. He's not guilty. I know it. There won't be a conflict if he pleads not guilty.'

Gareth's face widens in disbelief. 'Yes, there will. Of course there will. Your *friend* has life-threatening injuries. If he dies, they're going to lay a murder charge. How can you possibly represent someone in a murder case – in *any* case

– if you're friends with the victim and his family? How do you think it would look? What if he was found guilty after trial and wanted to appeal? What would an appeal court say? You're an experienced solicitor, Sarah. I can't believe you're even sitting here arguing with me about this.'

'But I know things about this case,' I protest. 'It goes deeper than the police are admitting. It's not Jerome they're after, I'm sure of it. I have good reason to believe it's drugs-related. Even if he *was* involved, he may have a Modern Slavery defence. But he'll go down for it if he doesn't get the right help. And that can't happen. He's vulnerable. He won't cope inside.'

Gareth turns back to his desk. 'Well, unfortunately, that's not our problem any more, is it? The duty solicitor will have to take care of him. So, go across the road and hand it over – and keep your phone on. There are two in at Farringdon that need covering.'

'What?' I shake my head in despair. 'Are they ready?'

'Speak to Lucy. And, Sarah,' he adds, as I stoop to pick up my bag. 'Next time, you need to think a little more carefully about where your priorities lie.'

The duty solicitor is a man named Neil Grainger. I check with the usher and am told he already has a list of six defendants to see. It takes me a good twenty minutes to track him down. Meanwhile, Georgina is waiting for me. She's sitting on the concourse, looking exhausted and bewildered. I follow her into a conference room where I explain my predicament. As I anticipated, she doesn't care that I know the victim and insists that she wants me to stay on Jerome's case. I explain that I can't and how sorry I am to be abandoning them both, but that I will be sure to brief the duty solicitor about everything he needs to know. I promise to go and see Jerome in the cells before I leave and explain this to him, too. Her forehead furrows and her eyes glisten, but she eventually nods, brushes her eyes with the back of her hand and rises to her feet.

The duty solicitor walks past as she's leaving, a laptop under one arm. I jump up and call his name. He turns and walks back towards me and I introduce him to Georgina. He smiles amiably and shakes her hand, asks her to take a seat, then follows me into the conference room.

'Do you have the papers yet?' I ask him.

He nods and slides into a seat, placing his laptop on the table and opening it up. 'They've just arrived. I've had a glance through.'

'OK.' I pull out the chair opposite him and sit down. 'Well, I promised his mum that I'd give you the lowdown. He knows his chances of getting bail are—'

'Around about... zero,' says Neil, squinting pensively at the screen in front of him and tapping with one finger on the arrow key.

'They're not good,' I agree. 'But they're not zero.'

He looks up and pushes his black-rimmed spectacles up onto his head. He has a thin, waxy, pallid face and thick, bushy salt-and-pepper eyebrows which knit together as he frowns at me in disbelief. 'He's hit an undercover police officer over the head with a metal bar and nicked his wallet,' he says, shaking his head. 'It's not good. Not good at all. And it's late at night, drug fuelled—'

'What?' I interject. 'Who says it was drug fuelled?'

'They found cannabis in his bedroom. Ergo, he takes drugs.' His grey eyes flicker up and down over me, as if he's seeing me properly for the first time. 'The police officer's in hospital with life-threatening injuries. He's not in a good way at all, by all accounts. It's a grave crime, a category one. He's looking at up to sixteen years for this.'

'For an adult,' I say. 'But he's only fifteen. The guidelines say...'

'... that he's going away for a very long time.' He draws in his breath. 'High culpability, serious harm, overwhelming evidence. Lock-'em-up Long is presiding in the remand court. So, all in all, he's in trouble. I hope you haven't told him he's getting out today.'

'He'll be pleading not guilty,' I say, firmly. 'He didn't do it. He's covering for someone.'

Neil Grainger blinks and looks back at his screen. 'He's caught on camera with the weapon in his hands and his fingerprints all over it. And the copper's wallet's in his bedroom. He's handed it to them on a plate,' he insists. 'What defence is he going to run?'

'The weapon is a moveable object...'

'But he's there! He's there and there's an injured cop on the ground.'

'How do you know?' I ask. 'Have you seen the footage?'

'No, but—'

'So, you need to watch the footage. There are other people there. His friends. He's covering for one of them.'

He shrugs. 'I'm not going to get to see the footage unless he pleads not guilty.'

'So, he needs to plead not guilty.'

He shakes his head. 'We'll see what he says, but he'll

need to think about the credit he'll lose on sentence if he's convicted after trial.'

I lean forward. 'He didn't do it.'

'Well, what was he doing there, then?' he frowns. 'And why has he got the weapon in his hands? How did the wallet get into his bedroom?'

'He was just playing with the weapon, swinging it around. He didn't know it was a weapon. As for the wallet, I don't know yet. He won't say. He just froze up when I tried to ask him. But he's covering for someone. One of his friends, possibly. They haven't enough evidence to charge anyone else. But there were other people there. There was a whole group of them.'

He frowns again. 'Well, that's not helpful is it? A group attack? That's an aggravating feature.'

'But it's also a defence,' I insist. 'Someone else did it and Jerome just happened to come along and pick up the weapon after the event.'

'If he's there with his mates, the prosecution will argue that he was party to the attack, that it was joint enterprise.'

'Then it's down to us to...'

Neil raises his eyebrows.

'It's down to the defence, I mean,' I correct myself, hastily, 'to rebut that. In the footage you can see that he walks away from them. It's credible enough that he didn't like what was happening, that he wanted no part in it – and that one of his friends stole the wallet and hid it in his room.'

'But what jury's going to believe that, when he's holding the weapon?' Neil objects, impatience creeping into his voice.

'Well, I'd believe him,' I say.

'I wouldn't.' He catches the expression on my face and

sighs. 'Look, I'm not saying I'm not going to do my best to help him, but – objectively speaking – he hasn't got a hope in hell.'

'It's not cut and dried,' I insist. 'There's also the issue of causation. Whoever carried out the attack didn't cause all of the injuries. There's a witness to the fact that the victim got up after he was attacked, that he was walking, that he fell into the road and was then crushed by the wheels of a car, a car that deliberately sped up and ran him over. Is that mentioned anywhere in the case summary?'

He sighs. 'There's something about an ongoing investigation into what happened to him after he was attacked. But the head injury is significant. It's still a category one. It's enough to sustain a manslaughter charge if the victim dies. At the very least. So for the purposes of bail—'

'They should be calling a witness,' I continue. 'An Indian gentleman named Jaydeep Vyas. He lives in the street. He saw the victim get up and try to cross the road. He saw the car that ran over him. Is he named in the case summary? Is there any mention of the four-by-four that came along afterwards? You'll need medical expert reports regarding which injuries were caused afterwards by the car and—'

He snaps his laptop shut. 'With respect, Sarah, you've told both the prosecutor and the usher that you have a conflict of interest. This is my case now and I'm not prepared to discuss it with you any further. I'll go and see the client and we can take it from there.'

'Wait. Please,' I say. 'I'm just trying to give you a heads-up that there's more to this case than meets the eye. Even if Jerome *did* do it, I have good reason to believe it may be connected with a County Lines crime gang. He may have been exploited. He may have a Modern Slavery defence. That needs to be explored too.'

He pushes his chair back and stands up. 'Thank you for the briefing. Like I said. I'll take it from here.' He picks up his laptop.

I jump up, too, and seek out his eyes. 'There are things I need to tell you,' I persist. 'About Jerome. Things he won't tell you himself. He's vulnerable. He won't cope well inside. There are things you can tell the judge.'

'Like what?'

'He has social anxiety.'

'Diagnosed?'

'No, but he has all the hallmarks. The same hallmarks that make him an easy target for a crime gang: social isolation, absent father, single parent mother, several younger siblings, all living in overcrowded social housing on an estate that's rife with crime. He feels angry and rejected by his father and he can't identify with his mother, because she's female, and she's got her hands full with the younger ones anyway. There's an emotional gap to be filled. There have been studies done on it. It's always the same kinds of children who are targeted, those who are looking for some kind of connection, a "family" to belong to, or otherwise escaping problems at home. The people he was with may be gang members too. He may have been following orders. He's just a kid at the end of the day. Please... please look after him.'

He nods and his face softens. 'OK. I'll look into it. I'll see what I can do.'

'Thank you,' I say. 'I'll come down with you and say goodbye.'

My phone rings. It's sitting on the table in between us. We both look down. It's the office.

I pick it up. 'Ready to go at Farringdon,' says Lucy.

'No! Really? Can they wait? I'd just like to—'

'It's ready,' says Lucy, firmly. 'Gareth told me to make sure you were on your way.'

'Fine.'

I end the call and glance up at the duty solicitor, who is still hovering in the doorway.

'There's really no need for you to come down,' he says. 'Like I said, I'll take it from here. I'll say your goodbyes for you, tell him you came.'

When I leave Farringdon police station it's five o'clock. I switch my phone back on and check for messages. There's one from Andy, to say that he's just finished work and is on his way to pick up Ben. I immediately feel the tension easing out of me. Even though I'd expected this, there's always the potential for something to go wrong while I'm inside the police station with my phone switched off. But not this time. No need for my usual power-walk to the nearest Tube station, the stress of the journey home or the sprint up the escalator to pick Ben up on time.

I stand on the steps of the police station and take a deep breath in and out. It's a beautiful evening. I'll walk up to Angel and take the bus home from there. As I wander through the back streets towards St John Street, my phone vibrates in my pocket to tell me I have another missed call. I pull it out and check my call log. It's Georgina. I tap on the slider and call her straight back.

She answers on the first ring. As usual, there's a child crying in the background. Georgina is crying too.

'They've taken my boy, Sarah,' she sobs as if her heart is breaking. 'They've taken him. My boy's been sent to jail.'

13

Jaydeep places a tray on the coffee table in front of me and walks across the room. He draws back the curtain that frames the bay window and peers out.

'He should be home soon,' he says. 'He normally gets home around about this time.'

'Thank you.' I pick up my mug of tea from the tray and take a sip. 'And I'm really sorry, again, for just turning up on your doorstep like this. But I was in the neighbourhood and I realised that I hadn't heard from you, even though someone has been arrested and charged and the case is now in court. And then that got me thinking about the footage.'

He waves his hand. 'It's not a problem at all, miss. I am glad to be of help. But the police, they have not contacted me at all. I would have called you like I promised you I would. Surely they will call me soon.'

'Yes,' I say. 'I hope so. We'll see.'

'Can I get you anything else?' he asks. 'A sandwich, perhaps?'

I look down at the plates and dishes that are sitting on the tray in front of me. I reach out and select a round cracker and a handful of nut and seed mix. 'No, really. These will be just fine. They look delicious.'

Jaydeep beams at me. 'That one is *khakhra*. And this dish

here, *chavanu*. And that one there, *sing bhujia*. My mother has sent me these via parcel from India.'

'Lovely,' I nod as I take a bite.

There's a wooden thwack and a burst of applause from the wide-screen television across the room, where a cricket match is playing. 'Whooooey!' Jaydeep turns his head to watch for a moment and then turns back to me again. 'You see that? You like cricket?' he asks me, his smile wide, his teeth white and even. 'This is Indian Premier League.'

'Erm… sorry,' I admit. 'I can't really say that I'm a cricket fan.'

Jaydeep immediately leans over, picks up the TV remote and turns it down.

'No. Please,' I say. 'Don't let me interrupt your match.'

He shakes his head. 'It's not a problem. I just have it on in background while I am working. My favourite team is not playing again until tomorrow: they are CSK – the Chennai Super Kings.' He gives me a wide grin. 'I have prayed to Ganpatiji earlier this morning and I am sure CSK is going to win.'

'Well, I hope so too,' I smile. 'I'll keep my fingers crossed.'

I glance around the room. On the wall next to the television is a picture of Ganesh, the Hindu god with an elephant head, seated on a gold and jewel-encrusted throne. Underneath it, next to the window, there's a laptop open on a desk.

'So, you work from home, then?' I ask him.

He sits down in a chair opposite me. 'Yes. I am IT professional. I run a software development company in Gujarat. I have team of developers in Ahmedabad.' He glances over towards the window and gives me another of his wide smiles. 'But today I am private investigator. I am very happy. I have always wanted to be a private investigator.'

I laugh. 'Well, actually, an IT professional turned private investigator is exactly what I need.' I take a last sip of my drink and put my cup back down on the tray. 'So, how much do you know about dash cam?'

Jaydeep smiles. 'I know some things. Main thing is that it is usually well hidden, tucked up as tight as possible to top of window, just under rear-view mirror. You can angle it if you want more sky or more bonnet. You also need external power source to run motion and impact detection in parking mode.'

'Would most people have this?'

He shrugs. 'If they want to run in parking mode, yes they would. You will need permanently powered twelve-volt socket. You can wire up to battery pack. This can last many weeks, as long as memory card does not get overwritten.'

'And how much will it record, once it detects motion?'

'It depends on the model. But most motion-sensing based models have pre-buffer which record few seconds before and can continue to record up to five minutes of inactivity after motion is no longer detected. Can be longer if you deactivate parking mode and run in normal.'

I nod. 'So, although they only showed us a few minutes of footage, potentially there is more?'

He nods. 'Oh yes, very possible. Ah.' He glances towards the window and his eyes light up. 'I can see his car. He is home.'

We both get up and Jaydeep follows me out of the front door and across the road. The BMW is now parked in its regular space, facing us, on the corner of the street opposite. It's still light outside, but now that I'm looking for it, I can see a blue light blinking on the rear-view mirror. I walk over and stand in front of the car, then turn to face the row of houses behind me.

I immediately realise that I'm right about this. The view that I'm looking at is identical to the screen capture area on the video footage. Straight ahead of me there's the gap between the houses where the fireworks had been visible, with Jaydeep's house to the left. To my immediate left is the corner of the street where the road leading to the estate turns into Packington Street, and to my right are the railings of the park.

'Can I help you?' calls out the owner of the BMW, who is standing at his front door, his hand poised, key in the lock. He's smart-looking, wearing a beige trench coat over a navy suit and tie.

'I hope so,' I call back to him. 'Could we have a word, please?'

The man pulls his key out of the lock and pulls his front door shut. He walks over to meet us.

I step forward and hold out my hand. 'I'm Sarah Kellerman. I'm a...' I glance round at Jaydeep, who is standing behind me. He flashes me a smile. 'I'm a private investigator,' I say. 'I understand that your car was damaged on New Year's Eve and I wondered if I could ask you a few questions.'

The man nods a 'hello' to Jaydeep. He steps forward and gives me a gentle but firm handshake then says, in a well-spoken voice with a hint of a London accent, 'I'm guessing you're more interested in what the police pulled out of the skip than what those kids did to my wing mirror.'

I hesitate, then nod. 'Sorry. Although, of course, if we find out what really happened that night...'

'Forget it.' He shakes his head. 'It's the car they wanted. They only pulled the wing mirror off because they weren't able to steal the car. It's got an immobiliser. They'd have needed the keys. Anyway, I found my wing mirror and they've left it alone since then. They've got more than that to worry about, from what I've heard.'

'So, what have you heard?' I ask.

He shrugs. 'Just that someone got hit over the head with that pole the police found in the skip.'

'You didn't see what happened?'

He shakes his head. 'I was at a party in a hotel in Pimlico on New Year's Eve. I only heard about it afterwards.'

'After... what?'

'Well. You know, after I handed the footage over to the police.'

'And the footage was dash cam? From your car?' I ask, trying not to let the excitement creep into my voice.

He nods. 'That's right.'

'So, when did you call the police?'

'The next day – after I found my wing mirror.'

'So, if you weren't here, the dash cam was running in parking mode?'

'Yeah. I always leave it in parking mode. You're on camera now,' he smiles.

'That's fine,' I smile back. 'I have no plans to damage your car.'

'Yeah, you'd better not,' he says, then laughs.

'So, did you watch the footage?' I ask him. 'Before you gave it to the police?'

He shrugs. 'Of course.'

'And what did you see?'

'Well, just what I told the police. A group of kids, circling the car and... one of them must have touched it, tried the door handle no doubt, which triggered the motion sensor... and then—'

'Hang on,' I say. 'The camera starts recording *before* the motion detector is set off?'

'Yes. That is what pre-buffer is,' Jaydeep explains. 'It records all the time but does not write to memory unless something happens.'

The man nods. 'And then it releases what it has buffered which will be up to about five seconds before.'

I nod. 'OK. Carry on. What happened next?'

'Well, they walked off camera for a bit, one of them came back, had a metal pole, was swinging it around a bit. I stopped the footage at that point and checked the car again for damage. Wasn't sure if he'd hit the car with it, but no. Thankfully not... and then the car starts shaking, moving. That's when they're pulling the wing mirror off. And then they all ran off.'

'You saw them run off?' I ask.

'Yeah,' he nods.

'Which way?'

'In the direction of the estate.' He turns and points. 'It's gone now, but there was a skip just there, outside the garages, with a load of old wood and furniture dumped in it. After I watched the footage and saw them running off up there, I retraced their steps and had a poke around inside it. Saw my wing mirror straight away and called the police. Rest is history.'

'Well, not quite,' I say. 'Did you watch the footage right to the end?'

The man peers at me, confused. 'The end of what? I told you, they ran off.'

'And did you see anything else? After that?'

He shrugs. 'No. But to be fair, I wasn't really looking. I'd already seen what I needed to see. The forensic people took a lift from the driver's door-handle. Then I downloaded the footage onto a USB stick and gave it to the copper who came to the door.'

'Did you keep a copy?'

He shakes his head. 'No. Sorry. The police asked me that.'

'Did you upload to the cloud?' asks Jaydeep.

'No. I didn't enable it. Didn't see the need.'

My heart sinks. 'So, what did they tell you?'

'About my wing mirror?' He shrugs. 'That they'd look into it.'

'And about the assault?'

'They just told me they were investigating something more serious and that they would be in touch if they had any leads.'

Jaydeep steps forward. 'You still have same memory card?'

The man nods towards the BMW. 'It's in there now.'

'Same one?'

'Well, yes,' he says. 'But—'

'What kind?'

'It's a micro SD card. But,' the man looks confused, 'I leave it in parking mode most of the time. For protection, you know. I've got it hardwired to an external power source, but even so, it'll have been overwritten by now.'

Jaydeep says, 'Do you have a spare one?'

The man nods. 'Well… yes.'

'Can we please borrow this one?' Jaydeep asks, nodding towards the car.

I turn to Jaydeep. 'You can recover it?'

He shrugs. 'I can try. The deleted file may still be there. It all depend on how much data is on there and how much has been overwritten. I will need to see if I can find the correct recovery software.'

The man looks doubtful but pulls his car keys out of his pocket anyway and points the fob at his car. I see the lights flash and hear the doors clunk open and then he reaches inside and fiddles with the dash cam and removes the memory card. He hands it to Jaydeep.

'So, what's this you're investigating, then?' he asks, glancing from me to Jaydeep and back again.

Jaydeep looks at me.

I hesitate. 'A missing child,' I say.

The man's eyes widen. 'From round here?'

'Yes,' I nod. 'From round here.'

'Oh, gosh.' The man frowns back at me for a moment. 'How old? Do you have a description?'

'Fifteen,' I say. 'And he's black.'

The man looks momentarily confused and then his face relaxes. He glances knowingly in the direction of the estate. 'Oh. Well. Good luck with that.'

'Thanks,' I reply.

He turns and glances from me to Jaydeep and back again, then locks his car and walks off in the direction of his house.

★

When I get home, Andy and Ben have eaten dinner and there's some waiting on the stove – and on the floor – for me.

'Spaghetti bolognaise,' says Andy, proudly.

'I can see that.' I reach down and grab a cloth from out of the cupboard under the sink, then get down onto my hands and knees. 'You need to clear it up as soon as he's eaten, Andy. Otherwise he'll tread it all around the house and into the carpets. And you need to wash his hands, otherwise there will be bolognaise sauce all over everything.'

'I cooked for you,' Andy throws back. 'I thought you'd be pleased.'

I sigh and stand up, tipping the discarded strands of spaghetti and sauce into the food waste bin. 'Yes, of course I'm pleased. But you really can't let him eat spaghetti bolognaise with his fingers.'

'Why not?'

'Because it's sauce, Andy! It's messy. And because Ben has sensory issues with spaghetti. Same with grated cheese. He doesn't like the texture. He picks it out and flings it.'

'Ah. OK. So, that's why he was doing that.'

I walk into the front room. Ben is still wearing his school uniform, which is covered in bolognaise sauce. 'Andy, it's all over him!' I wail. 'You could have changed him first! This was his last clean school sweatshirt. Now I'm going to have to put some washing on!'

Andy appears in the doorway behind me. 'No, you're not. Just send him in in his civvies. What are they going to do – give him detention?'

I swing round to face him. 'That's hardly the point.'

'Yes, it is,' says Andy. 'It's exactly the point. Look, I'm

sorry I let him make a mess. I'll clear it up. I'll clean *him* up. But you,' he grabs my arm, 'are coming with me. You're tired and you're ratty. You need to sit down, put your feet up and let me dish up your dinner and pour you a glass of wine.'

He's right. I'm exhausted. I allow him to lead me down the hallway back to the kitchen, where he pulls out a chair for me, gets a wine glass from the cupboard and opens the fridge. I sit down and watch as he takes out an expensive-looking bottle of Chablis and pours me a glass. I realise, suddenly, that he's gone to a lot of trouble to make things nice for me. He hasn't even asked me why I've been so long getting home.

I take a sip of wine and force myself to put Ben's bolognaise-stained clothing to the back of my mind while Andy busies himself at the stove. A minute later, he places a plate of food in front of me. 'Enjoy,' he smiles. 'I'm off to change Ben. And I'll find him something to wear tomorrow for his free-dress day.'

'Ben's school calls them mufti days,' I correct him.

'Well, Ben's having a mufti day tomorrow,' he says, 'and you're putting your feet up. So, are we good?'

'We're good,' I smile. 'And I'm sorry for snapping.'

The bolognaise is good too. I've nearly finished when Andy comes back into the kitchen a few minutes later with a pyjama-clad Ben in his arms.

'Look what I've got, Mummy,' he says, playfully, in his squeaky fake-Ben voice.

I look up. Ben's holding his iPad, which is sitting inside a thick rubber case.

'You got a shockproof case for it,' I smile.

'Yep. He can throw it around as much as he likes now.'

'That was very thoughtful,' I say.

Ben wriggles out of Andy's arms and takes his iPad into the living room. Andy takes a beer out of the fridge and sits down at the table opposite me. He twists the top off his bottle. 'So how d'you go today?'

I put down my fork and pick up my wine glass. 'They charged him with GBH and robbery. They've remanded him. He's just about to start his first ever night in prison.'

Andy's face softens. 'You're really upset.'

I nod. 'I guess I am. He's never been inside before.'

'I'm sure you did your best,' Andy reaches out a hand, tentatively, across the table, but it stops just short of mine.

'I didn't, though,' I tell him. 'I wasn't there.'

'Huh?' Andy frowns. 'What do you mean? Why not?'

I look him in the eye. 'I had a conflict of interest, because I know the victim. My boss made me give the case away.'

Andy sucks his teeth with his tongue and takes a swig of beer. 'Well then, it's not your fault he got remanded, is it? It's somebody else's.' He looks hard at me. 'To be fair, most likely *his*.'

I shrug.

'Well, they must think he did it, Sarah. Otherwise they wouldn't have locked him up for it.'

'It doesn't exactly work like that,' I say. 'He's not on trial yet. He's not guilty until a court says that he is.'

'So why did they lock him up, then?'

'Because it's serious. And because of his previous convictions.'

Andy raises his eyebrows again. 'He has form?'

I shake my head. 'Not for anything like this.'

We sit in silence for a moment. I twirl the remaining forkful of pasta around on my plate. Once again, I wish that this was Will I was talking to, not Andy. I wouldn't have to explain the way I'm feeling; he'd intuitively know. I desperately wish that I could finish my dinner, thank Andy, then get up and go off to the hospital and sit beside Will's bed to talk to him, to mull it all over, the way we used to do. He'd listen without prejudice, and then he'd offer some words of wisdom. *If he wasn't trying to fight off a serious infection, of course*, I reprimand myself for my selfishness. *If he wasn't trying his hardest not to lose a leg.*

I can feel Andy's eyes on me as he sits across the table, one hand on his beer bottle.

'The food was really good,' I say.

He beams. 'Want some more?'

He starts to get up, but I stop him. I put down my fork and fiddle with the stem of my wine glass.

'Talk to me,' says Andy. 'Tell me what you're thinking about.'

I'm thinking about Will. I sigh. 'I'm thinking about his mum, how she must be feeling right now. She rang me a little while ago. She was in bits.'

'Bound to be,' says Andy, sympathetically.

I look up at him. 'It's one of the hardest parts of my job, when a kid gets locked up for the very first time. You know there's a really good chance that it's going to happen. But at the same time, there's never any warning. The judge just comes back in and sits there,' I continue. 'He never says anything until the cells staff are there. Someone, somewhere, has made a phone call to them, but you don't see that happen. It's not until everything goes quiet, and you hear the rattling of handcuffs, of keys on a chain and the cell doors opening and you spin round to see the look on the kid's face as the jailers walk into the dock and handcuff him. It's not until then that you really believe it and have that horrible feeling that he's been failed, somehow.'

'Unless he's guilty,' Andy points out.

'But what if he's not? What's this going to do to him – to his view of the world – if he's been locked up for something that he hasn't done? He's still a kid. He's too young to process this, to regulate his emotions. He's not old enough or tough enough to deal with what's coming, and deep down – although he'd never admit it – he still *really* needs his mum. He's about to experience the most severe form of homesickness he's ever known.'

Andy doesn't reply.

'Not to mention the other stuff.'

'Well,' Andy shrugs. 'You know, some people might say that's his own fault for hanging around with the wrong crowd.'

'He's a kid! Imagine if it was Ben?' I say. 'Imagine how you'd feel?'

Andy lowers his eyes. 'Ben's never going to prison, is he?'

'No,' I say. 'But imagine how you'd feel if he did. He's somebody's son,' I say. 'That's what I mean.'

Andy peers at me for a moment over the top of his beer bottle. 'He'll cope,' he says. 'He'll survive. He'll have to.'

'Maybe. But what will it do to him in the meantime? What sort of person will he be when he comes out?'

Andy shrugs. 'A tougher one, I guess.'

'Yeah, but not necessarily in a good way. His perception of himself and of the world has already been fucked up by his father walking out on him, rejecting him, wanting nothing to do with him. And now this. I'm worried about what it will do to him if he's allowed to carry this, if he's allowed to take the blame for something that's not his fault. You do that to kids and there are consequences. Potentially serious ones.'

Andy puts down his beer bottle and rests his tanned forearms on the table.

'There've been studies on this kind of negative reinforcement,' I continue. 'There's a risk that he will develop a view that he's fundamentally not OK, and that the rest of the world is not OK, either. This ultimately leads to self-harm – emotional or physical – or the inflicting of harm on others. Hence, your knife crime. These kids have a deep-rooted sense of shame and worthlessness and are really, really angry with the world. Their dads are violent or in jail or otherwise emotionally absent and they've got a struggling mother who doesn't have the time or the energy to help them through the turmoil of the teenage years. They've nothing else left to care about.'

'So, if you don't want to lock them up, what are you going to do?'

I shrug. 'Lift them out of poverty, provide them with a good male role model. And teach them to believe in themselves.'

Andy tightens his lips.

'What?' I look up.

He grins. 'I dunno. Just sounds a bit woolly liberal to me.'

'OK,' I say. 'Well, then they should stick with the knife ASBOs. See how that goes.' I push back my chair. 'I'd better go and see what Ben's doing. It's time he was in bed.'

'No. I'll go. Stay where you are.' Andy leaps up. I leave him to get Ben into bed and go into my own room to change out of my work clothes. I then watch from the bathroom doorway as Andy sits Ben on the toilet seat, gives him his medication and tries to brush his teeth. As usual, Ben fights and pushes and tries to grab the toothbrush and throw it onto the floor. When Andy turns back to face me, there's toothpaste spatter all over him and all over Ben.

'Is there a knack to this tooth-brushing lark?' he asks me. 'Got any tips?'

'Not really,' I say. 'Just... wear old clothes.'

'Great.' He grins and picks Ben up, sets him on the floor, then walks him to the bedroom. I kiss Ben goodnight and go back to the kitchen where I sit back down at the table and take another long sip of wine.

A few moments later, Andy sits down in front of me again.

'You know your problem,' he says. 'You over-identify.'

I look up. 'What?'

'Because of what happened to you,' he explains. 'When you were a kid.'

I heave a sigh. 'Andy, you've cooked me dinner, you've looked after Ben, you've got him to bed. You've done a great job here. But starting a sentence by telling me what my problem is – that's really not the best way of cheering me up right now.'

He shrugs. 'Sorry. I didn't mean it like that.'

'Well, you always say it like that. You always bring everything back to me, as if I'm walking around with some enormous chip on my shoulder.'

'OK. I didn't mean to. But this kid has lost his father,

and now he's lost his mother. Just like you did. That's what you're thinking, isn't it?'

'Maybe,' I agree. 'But it's more than that. Maybe it's because I'm a mother myself. Maybe I just know how strong that bond is between a mother and her child.' I look up. 'It's a love like no other. It's… it's beyond anything you could ever have imagined.' I wipe a tear from my eye. 'You know from the moment that they are born that you will never be able to sleep again without knowing that they're safe from harm.'

Andy shrugs. 'It's the same for men. Men feel that too.'

'Then why did you leave!' I explode. I catch my breath as unexpected tears stream down my cheeks. 'If you feel what I feel in here,' I tap my chest with my fist, 'how could you have possibly gone?'

Andy's face falls. A patch of crimson creeps up his neck and he looks down at the table. 'You know why,' he says. When I don't speak, he continues. 'It was hard. It was too hard. Ben was so difficult. He cried all the time. We had no life together, you and I… any of us. I just couldn't…' He doesn't finish. He stares down at the table, shaking his head and biting his lip.

'You couldn't deal with it. I know,' I say. 'But *I* had to. *I* had to deal with it. I stayed. I got on with it. I've had to be both his father and his mother for the past two years.'

Andy nods. 'I know you have. And I'm sorry. I'm so sorry that you had to do that all alone. But I'm here now. I'm trying to make it up to you.' He pushes his beer bottle to one side and leans forward, so that his face is looking up into mine. 'You think that all men leave, Sarah. That's the bottom line for you. But I'll prove you wrong. I'll prove to you that you can trust me. I'll be there for you this time. I had a blip. I had a crisis. It was so... unexpected, finding out all of a sudden that my son was... was different to other children, that he was not going to be all the things that I had thought he was going to be. I couldn't cope. I needed time to deal with it. But I'm here now. I want us to be a family again, if you'll just – please... *please* – give me another chance.'

A heavy silence falls between us. I'm exhausted, too exhausted to know what to say. Andy leans forward, his eyes looking up into mine. There was a time when those blue eyes, that yearning in them, could make my stomach flip.

And then my phone rings. I realise that I don't know where it is. I jump up to find it quickly, in case it wakes Ben.

I find it in my coat pocket and pull it out. I glance at the screen, then over at Andy, who's sitting at the table, watching me expectantly.

'It's Will,' I say. I push the slider across before it cuts out, and walk down the hall into the living room. Behind me, I can hear Andy's chair scraping back and then the clatter of dishes in the sink.

'Hello, you,' I say, softly, conscious that Andy can still hear me. This flat's not big enough to have a private phone conversation.

'Sarah.' Will's voice sounds gravelly again. 'How are you?'

'I'm OK,' I say. 'More to the point, how are *you*?'

The line goes quiet for a moment and then, 'Still here,' he says.

Something's wrong. My legs feel shaky suddenly. I sink down onto the sofa. 'What is it, Will?' I ask. 'What's happened?'

Silence. I can hear Andy opening and shutting the fridge.

I say, 'Tell me, Will. Please.'

And then Andy's in the room, holding my wine glass. 'You forgot this,' he says, loudly. He places it on the coffee table in front of me and disappears again.

Will's voice is slightly muffled as he says, 'Is there someone there?'

I curse under my breath. I can't lie to him. But I don't want him to get the wrong idea. I could kill Andy.

'Andy's here,' I say.

A pause. 'Again?'

'He picked up Ben for me again, that's all. I had an attempted murder in at the police station. I didn't know how long I was going to be.'

'That's good. That's good that he's helping you.' Will gives a fake laugh. 'It's not as if I'm any bloody use to you at the moment, is it?'

'I'm coming to see you,' I say, decisively. 'Tonight. I'll get him to stay longer.'

'You don't need to do that,' he says. 'It's late.'

'No, I want to.'

'Really,' he says. 'I'm tired. I just wanted to hear your voice.'

'I'm glad,' I say. 'I'm so pleased that you called.' I lower my voice. 'I miss you so much.'

Will hesitates, then says, 'Do you?'

'Of course I do,' I insist. 'Look, if not tonight, I'll come first thing tomorrow. I'll get the day off work. I don't care what my boss says. I'll make some excuse.'

'No,' says Will. 'Please don't do that.'

'You don't want me to come?'

Will clears his throat again. 'I'm having surgery,' he says.

Fear clutches at my chest. 'When?'

'Tonight.'

'*Tonight?*'

Will doesn't reply.

'What for?' I press him.

Will says, softly, 'The infection has spread.'

I take a deep breath in. I feel tears springing to my eyes again. I try to keep my voice steady as I say, 'How far? How far has it spread?'

'Into my thigh,' says Will. 'Possibly into my hip. They won't know for sure until they operate.'

'OK,' I say, wiping my eyes and taking control. 'But we knew that could happen, right? They've just got to remove the infection. It's another debridement. You got through the last one and you'll get through this one too. You're going to be absolutely fine.'

Will says, 'We'll see.'

'I'm so sorry, Will,' I tell him. 'I'm so sorry that you're going through this. But I want you to know that—'

'Phone battery's going,' he interrupts me. 'I'm going to have to go.'

'OK. I'll come tomorrow. Just try to stay positive,' I say, talking quickly, thinking quickly. 'This is just one more step on the road to recovery. And then, when you're better, we'll do something *really* nice. I'll get a babysitter. We'll go away for a weekend together. Shall we? Where shall we go?' I pause. 'Will?' I press him.

Nothing.

'Will?' I say his name again.

14

It's warm again on the ICU when I arrive the following afternoon. I shrug off my coat and enter the waiting area. Both Sophia and Jack are there. Sophia's watching a video on her phone, while Jack is staring languidly up at the TV on the wall in the corner, where a nature programme is playing with the volume down low. I can't help being drawn to his face as I notice how much he looks like his father. He has the same earnest expression, the same square jawline. He's taller and thinner than his dad, I note, as he sits slouched in his seat, leaning back against the chair with his head against the wall, his long legs stretched out in front of him. He's wearing his school uniform: a smart black blazer with a blue-and-white crest on the upper pocket over a white collared shirt and burgundy tie. Next to him, Sophia's dressed in an emerald green sweatshirt and a grey pleated skirt. Her hair is tied up in a long ponytail.

She looks up as I enter.

'Hi.' I smile.

'Hi.' She smiles back.

Jack turns his eyes in my direction and gives me a vague nod of recognition, before looking back up at the telly again.

I hang my coat on the back of a chair. 'So, have you two just come from school?'

'Yes,' says Sophia. 'We've just broken up for the holidays.'

'Nice.' I'm about to ask her what she's got planned, but then think better of it. 'So, which school do you go to?' I ask instead.

'St John's.' She turns back to her video. 'But in September I'll be going to Goswell High with Jack.'

Jack shoots her a contemptuous glare. 'You won't be going *with* me.'

Sophia swings round to face him. 'Who will I go with then?'

Jack shrugs his shoulders in a gesture of irritation. '*I* don't know, do I?' He makes a 'pffft' sound. 'But you're not walking with me and my mates.'

Sophia frowns at him for a moment before her face brightens and she turns to me with an audacious grin. 'Have you got any Maltesers?'

I shake my head. 'Sorry. Not this time. I was in a hurry to get here.' I raise my eyebrows and stifle a smile. 'I've just skived off work for the rest of the afternoon.'

Jack shoots me a look of mild interest. Sophia looks concerned.

'Will you get into trouble?' she asks.

'Yes,' I say. 'Probably.'

'Is your boss mean?'

'A bit,' I confide. 'He doesn't like me much.'

'Why not?'

I think about this for a moment. 'Because I break the rules,' I tell her. 'I think *he* thinks that *I* think that I'm special.'

Jack turns and looks me up and down.

Sophia's eyes meet mine.

'But I don't,' I tell her.

Sophia says, 'You don't *seem* special.'

'Thanks a lot!'

'It means weird,' she explains.

'Oh,' I say. 'It never used to mean that. Well, hopefully I'm not too weird.'

'No,' she says, kindly. 'I don't think you are.'

'Thank you,' I smile.

'Welcome,' she says.

'I just don't always like the rules,' I explain.

Sophia thinks about this for a moment, then says, 'Neither do I.'

Jack rolls his eyes. 'What are you on about? You're a bloody *sheep*.'

'No, I'm *not*,' Sophia retorts. '*You're* a sheep. No, you're a cat. You're a big scaredy-cat.'

Jack glances at me and flushes, visibly. A patch of red creeps above his collar and across his cheek. He turns to his sister and sneers, 'You don't know what you're on about. You chat such a load of—' He stops mid-sentence, his eyes flickering towards me. He sighs heavily and pushes himself to his feet. 'I've had enough of this.'

Sophia's eyes widen. 'Where are you going? Mum said you have to wait here with me.'

'I don't care what she said,' Jack snaps back at her, angrily. 'I'm going in to see Dad.'

He walks abruptly past me and out of the door. Sophia watches him go for a moment, then looks back down at her phone.

'So, where's your mum?' I ask her.

She doesn't reply.

'Sophia?' I press her. 'Is she in there with your dad?'

'She's talking to the doctors.' Her lip quivers as she speaks. I peer into her face and notice that her eyes are welling with tears.

I reach out and stroke her arm.

'He hates me,' she says.

'Jack?'

She nods.

'Brothers can be mean,' I tell her. 'Especially at that age. Mine was just the same.'

She raises her glistening eyes to meet mine. 'Was he? Was he really?'

'Oh, yes,' I sigh. 'He was horrible to me.'

'Why?'

'I guess he was angry.'

'With you?'

'With everyone.'

'What was he angry about?'

I sigh. 'How long have you got?'

'Ages,' she says.

I laugh. 'I'll tell you another time. Now, come on. Dry those eyes. I'll go and find your mum for you. And then I *must* go and see my boyfriend. But,' I add, winking at her, 'if I see any chocolates lying around near his bed, I'll pinch a few and bring them back for you. Deal?'

Her face brightens. 'Will he mind?'

I shake my head. 'I don't think so.'

'OK.' She wipes her eyes. 'Deal.'

I get up and walk over to the door.

'Don't forget to check his pockets,' she calls out after me. 'There might be some sweets in there.'

Karen walks out of the ICU as I walk in. She's wearing the obligatory white plastic apron. She gives me a half-smile. Her eyes are red-rimmed and swollen and she has a scrunched-up tissue in her hand.

'Hi,' I say. 'I told Sophia I'd find you. Jack's gone—'

'I know.' She nods back towards the ward. 'I've seen him. He's in there now. I'll go and sit with her.'

I nod and hesitate, unsure whether I should ask about Mark, heeding Burdie's warning to me and also remembering how angry Karen had been with me when I saw her last.

'How's your boyfriend doing?' she asks me, breaking the ice.

'I'm about to find out.' I breathe in deeply. 'He had more surgery last night.'

'Really?'

I nod, blinking hard as I feel tears springing to my eyes. 'It's not good news. The infection's spread.'

Her face softens in sympathy. 'I'm so sorry, Sarah,' she says. 'It's so hard, isn't it?'

I nod, unable to speak for a moment, but feeling comforted by her kindness. She, of all people, knows how I'm feeling right now.

She hesitates, then says, 'I'm afraid it's not looking good for Mark, either. He has pneumonia.' She catches my expression. 'It's common when you've been on the ventilator a while.'

'Can they treat it?' I ask.

'He's on antibiotics. But his oxygen requirements have gone up, so they can't reduce the ventilation. Even if he gets through this, they don't think he will ever…' She pauses and swallows.

I shake my head. 'Ever… what?'

'Be able to breathe independently.'

I nod, slowly, taking it in.

Her red-rimmed eyes meet mine. 'He'd have no quality of life. He'd have to go into a nursing home. Paired with a significant brain injury, it's just not… it's not an outcome that they think is…' She hesitates. 'It's not a good outcome,' she says. 'Sorry, Sarah. I'm glad I saw you. I wanted you to know because… well, because you've been a good friend to him and I know you care.'

I nod. For a moment, neither of us can speak. Tears shimmer in her eyes and she squeezes them shut and tilts her head away. She raises one hand to cover her face.

'It's OK,' I say. 'You don't have to—'

She turns back to face me. 'The doctors have started talking about withdrawing life support.'

I feel a weight drop in my stomach, even though I'd known what she was going to say. 'And you've agreed?'

She nods. 'He wouldn't want to live like that. It's no life for him. For anyone.'

I reach out and put my arms round her. She clutches me tightly. 'I'm so sorry,' I say, into her shoulder.

'Me too.'

After a moment she releases me and wipes her eyes with the tissue that's in her hand. 'I'm sorry if I…' she starts to say.

'Don't be silly.' I shake my head, dismissively.

She says. 'I suppose I'd better—'

'When will it happen?' I ask, simultaneously.

She takes a deep breath. 'Whenever we're ready, they said. But probably within the next forty-eight hours. That's if he survives until then.' She looks up at me, her eyes pained. 'I've signed a form to say that they shouldn't apply CPR.'

I touch her arm. 'That's so hard. But you did the right thing, I'm sure.'

'Yeah,' she agrees.

I say, 'Do the children know?'

'Not yet. I'm going to tell them tonight.' She shoots me a despairing smile and her chest rises and falls as she contemplates this. 'Sophia still doesn't want to come in,' she confides. 'I'm worried that she's going to regret it.'

'Maybe when you tell her what's… going to happen?' I suggest.

'Maybe. Although that might just make it harder. She doesn't really talk about him at all. She seems to be… focusing on other things. She was like that after he left. Didn't really ask about him, seemed not to care. Didn't want to see him. A defence mechanism, I suppose. Whereas Jack was very vocal, got angry, demanded to know why his dad hadn't called. But Sophia just blocked it all out, as if she didn't need him any more.'

I nod in recognition. What she's saying rings uncomfortably true.

She smiles. 'I'd better go and see if she's OK. And I'd better let you get to your boyfriend.'

'Sure.'

'I'll keep my fingers crossed for you,' she says, her eyes still glistening.

'Thanks,' I say. 'And I hope that—' I stop mid-sentence, both of us knowing that there are no words of comfort for her.

When I reach Will's bay, I wash my hands again at the sink in the corner. I pause and look round for Becky, but she's nowhere to be seen. I peer across to Will's bed. He's still in the same spot by the window and I'm pleased to see that he's alone. I walk over to his side. He's fast asleep and doesn't stir at the sound of my footsteps. I catch my breath as I take in his appearance. He looks so poorly again. His face is pale and clammy, his eyes swollen. He has all the same tubes reattached to his neck, his nose and his arms, which are trailing off into machines beside the bed. His left leg is propped up on its usual position on the pillow, but the black sponge and clingfilm have gone and in their place is a huge expanse of crepe bandage which stretches all the way along his leg, from calf to thigh. The machine's back at his feet, inflating and deflating in a steady rhythm which seems to coincide with the rising and falling of his chest.

I put down my bag and pull up a chair.

Will's eyelids spring open and his eyes dart up to meet mine. His expression is one of shock.

'Hi,' I say, softly.

His eyes flicker from me towards the door and back again. 'What are you doing here?' he whispers, hoarsely.

I lean forward. 'I came to see you,' I smile.

He shakes his head. 'But I told you not to come.'

I nod. 'I know, but—'

He fixes his swollen, dark eyes on mine. 'I don't want you here,' he says, abruptly. 'I want you to go.'

I look back at him in confusion. 'Will? What's going on?' I say. 'Are you expecting someone else? Your parents?'

He doesn't answer.

'Will?' I reach out and try to take hold of his fingers but he moves his hand away. 'Please,' I say. 'Talk to me. What is it that's upset you?'

'What the hell do you think?'

I recoil at the tone of his voice. He turns his head away.

'Is it because of Andy?'

Silence.

'Then, what is it?' I ask him. 'What have I done?'

Will's face contorts in pain as he hisses, 'You know what you've done!'

I sit back in confusion for a moment, trying to figure it out. 'No,' I say, finally. 'I don't.'

Will moves his head. A tear slips out of the corner of one eye. 'Christ. You're really enjoying this. There's something wrong with you. You've just come here to gloat.'

'Will, please... I haven't! I don't know what you think I've done, but...' I rack my brain as I try my hardest to figure out what on earth he's talking about. Will shifts on the bed and tries to lift his head up. His forehead is glistening with sweat.

'No,' I say, reaching out a hand towards him. 'Don't try and move.'

He flinches. 'Don't touch me!' he screams out.

I snatch my hand back. 'OK. OK. Look,' I say. 'I'll go.

If that's what you want.' I push my chair back and pick up my bag. Will watches me, but I notice his eyes moving towards the bed remote, which is hanging on the side rail of the bed.

'Are you in pain? Do you want me to call the nurse?' I say, leaning forward again.

'Nurse!' Will cries out, hoarsely, before I can press the button.

I activate the alarm and there's a monotone beeping sound.

'Nurse!' Will's voice gets louder.

'Will, calm down,' I say. 'I've already called for the nurse.'

He shoots me an angry, frightened glare and calls louder, 'Nurse!'

I hear movement and voices in the corridor and turn around, dazed with confusion, as Becky strides into the bay and over to the bed.

Will is really agitated now. He's trying to lift his head off the pillow again. 'Nurse!' he keeps saying loudly, even though Becky's right there in front of him.

Becky leans over and turns off the buzzer. 'All right, Will. What is it? What's wrong?'

Will eye-points at me.

Becky glances at me, then moves around the bed, checking that all his tubes are still attached, fiddling with cables and tightening his blood pressure cuff. She presses a button on a machine behind the bed. 'All right,' she says soothingly. 'It's fine, Will. Everything's OK.'

'No, it's not. You need to get her out of here,' Will says, excitedly, looking up at Becky, then intermittently glancing at me. 'I don't want her here!'

'OK. All right.' Becky turns to face me. 'I'm sorry. It's best if you leave.'

I pick up my bag and move away towards the end of the bed.

'I don't understand,' I say, under my breath. 'I don't know why he's being like this.'

Becky moves after me and says, in a hushed voice, 'Please don't worry. It's really common for people to get distressed following surgery. It's likely to be the medication he's on. But we'll do some further tests, just to be sure that there's no secondary infection.'

I gaze back at Becky as the realisation hits me: she's right; Will's delirious. He doesn't know what he's saying. I suddenly recall his words to me when he told me about his arrival in hospital. *I thought I was on a film set. I congratulated one of the nurses on her acting.* I smile at the memory, reassured by the fact that this is what happened post-surgery last time and that he'd come through it. When he's better, we'll laugh about this. Hopefully.

'It's OK, Will. I'm going,' I reassure him. I lower my voice. 'Can I have a word?' I say to Becky, under my breath.

She nods and indicates that she'll follow me out in a moment. I cross the bay and step out into the corridor. After a few moments, she appears in the doorway, squirts alcohol gel onto her hands and walks out to where I'm waiting.

'Bottom line. How is he doing? How worried do I need to be?' I ask.

Her face is warm but inscrutable as she tells me, 'It's very early to be able to tell you very much, but the surgery went well. We've removed the infected tissue. He's on a course of strong antibiotics.'

'They didn't stop it spreading last time,' I observe.

She nods. 'Unfortunately, it's difficult for us to get ahead of the infection, but we're doing everything we can.'

'And the things he just said? Is that really normal?'

'Very. He may well be confused for several days.'

'But it could be due to another infection?'

She hesitates. 'It can happen for many reasons. We'll keep an eye on his temperature. But more commonly it's a reaction to the drugs we've given him. Morphine and general anaesthesia are notorious for this.'

'And he got confused last time, didn't he?' I ask, hopefully. 'But then he got better?'

'Yes,' she says. 'That's right.' She says, earnestly, 'We hope to see an improvement. I wish I could give you odds or guarantees but you know that's not possible. Only time will tell, I'm afraid.'

Back in the waiting area, Karen and Sophia are sitting side by side.

Karen looks up, her eyes questioning. 'You weren't long?'

'He wasn't really up to seeing visitors,' I explain. 'He's very poorly. But he was awake – and talking.'

'Well, that's a good sign. Isn't it?' Karen forces a smile.

'I hope so.' I nod. 'They said it's too early to say, really, but...'

'I'm sure...'

'Yes,' I finish for her.

Karen inclines her head, the weight of what she's bearing hanging silently between us.

'He was delirious,' I tell her. 'He didn't know who I was.'

Sophia looks up from her phone. 'What does delirious mean?'

'Well...' I begin.

'Is it, like... stupid?'

I smile. 'Not quite. More like... confused.'

'Oh.' Her eyes flicker up to meet mine. She raises her eyebrows and grins at me. 'So, did you get any, then?'

Karen glances from her to me, questioningly.

I shake my head. 'I'm sorry.'

'What are you up to, young lady?' Karen smiles at her.

'I was supposed to see if Will had any chocolates,' I confess.

'Sophia!' Karen reprimands her. She turns to me. 'Sorry.'

'Don't be daft,' I say. 'It was my idea.'

I reach over and pull my coat from the back of the chair.

'So, what now?' she asks me. 'Heading home?'

'I guess so,' I say. 'What about you?'

She gives me a meaningful look. 'Waiting for Jack, I guess, and then...' She glances at Sophia, who's now bent over her phone again.

I think about the conversation that Karen is soon to have with her children. 'Do you want me to wait with her?' I offer. 'So that you can go back in, spend a bit of time with him? And with Jack?'

She lifts her eyes, hopefully. 'Do you have time?'

I nod and shrug my coat off again. 'Yes. As it happens, I do.'

'She skived off work,' says Sophia, without looking up.

I grin, penitently. 'It's true.'

'That would be great,' she says. 'If you're really sure you don't mind. I won't be long.'

'Go.' I gesture towards the door. 'Take as long as you need.'

Karen stands up and turns to her daughter. 'Soph. I'm just going to get Jack.'

Sophia nods.

Karen hesitates, looking at the top of Sophia's head as she hunches over her phone. 'Do you want to stay here with Sarah?' she asks. 'Or do you want to come with me, to see your dad?'

'Stay here.' Sophia doesn't look up.

Karen heaves a sigh, then looks at me and shakes her head. She takes a deep breath and then says, 'Right.'

When she's gone, I sit down next to Sophia and place my coat down on the chair. 'So, what are you watching?' I ask her.

'Cats,' she says. 'Doing funny things. Do you want to see?'

'Sure.' I lean over her shoulder. She plays a YouTube clip of a cat swiping playfully at itself in the mirror, then at another one purring blissfully as its head is massaged by a machine. We both laugh. 'Have you got any photos of your rabbit?' I ask her.

She glances at me and grins. 'Yes.' She closes down her browser and flicks open her photo gallery. 'Here,' she says, swiping through her photos and clicking on a video. 'Here's me giving her a banana.'

'A banana?' I ask in surprise.

'Yes,' she giggles. 'She loves bananas. What did Tallulah Louisiana like?'

'Carrots and hay, mostly,' I say. 'I don't think I ever tried to give her a banana. My brother gave her a doughnut once.'

'A doughnut?' she frowns. 'That's stupid.'

I nod. 'I know. He was a bit stupid, sometimes. It was my doughnut. He put it in her cage to hide it from me.'

'Because he was angry?' she asks, remembering our earlier conversation.

'Yes,' I agree. 'Probably.'

She closes down her photo gallery. 'Why was he angry?'

I let out a long breath. 'I guess because my dad left my mum when we were kids and he didn't want him to go.'

Sophia looks up, uncertainly, her mouth falling open. Her eyes flicker over me.

'Deep down, he missed him,' I explain, 'and he was actually very, very sad. But he didn't want to be sad, so he was mean instead.'

'Why?' she asks, her curiosity trumping her disquiet regarding the direction of the conversation. 'Why didn't he want to be sad?'

I shrug. 'Because being sad was too hard for him, I suppose.'

Sophia's mouth sets in a tight line. 'He still shouldn't have been mean to you,' she says, defiantly. 'He was *your* dad too. He wasn't the only one who was sad.'

'No,' I agree, glancing across at her, and nodding. 'That's absolutely right.'

Her eyes meet mine for a second, then she lowers her head. A tear squeezes out of the corner of one eye and runs down her cheek. She lifts her hand to wipe it away, on the pretext of rubbing her nose.

I hesitate. 'I was pretty much the same age as you,' I tell her. 'I was nine when my dad left us.'

'I'm ten,' she objects, her voice muffled. 'I'm nearly eleven.'

She looks hard into her lap and for a moment we don't speak. Her voice is barely audible as she says, 'Did you cry?'

'No,' I say. 'But I wish I had.'

A pause. And then, 'Why?'

'Because I think it would have helped.'

Sophia continues to hang her head, but I can see that tears have started to trickle down her cheeks.

I root around in my bag and, miraculously, find a clean tissue. I hand it to her. She takes it without looking up. 'It didn't work,' I say. 'Bottling it up inside. It took up a lot of my energy. And it didn't make it hurt any less. So I wish, now, that I'd just let myself cry.'

Sophia gasps as a sob escapes from her throat.

I say, 'Your dad loved you, Sophia. He loved you very, very much.'

She looks up, her freckled cheeks wet with tears. 'How do you know that?'

'Your dad and I used to work together. We're friends,' I say.

'Did he tell you?'

'He didn't have to.'

She dabs at her eyes with the tissue. 'So how do you know, then?'

'Because of the way he talked about you. Because of the way his eyes lit up when he mentioned your name.'

She shakes her head, disbelievingly. 'I don't think he loved me. If he did, he wouldn't have gone.'

'It's not as simple as that.'

She shrugs.

I look her in the eye. 'OK. Close your eyes. Close your

eyes and think of him. Think back to a really happy memory of him, of a really happy time.'

She obediently squeezes her eyes shut, lifting her wet cheeks towards the ceiling, gripping the seat underneath her, her knuckles red.

'Have you got one?' I ask.

She frowns in concentration, her head tilted upwards, her mouth quivering and her front tooth digging into her lip. Then she nods.

'OK. What is it?' I ask her.

She smiles, her eyes still closed. 'When he gave me my rabbit,' she says. 'On my birthday.'

'OK. Tell me about it.'

'So.' She shifts in her seat. 'He came home from work in the morning and he was whistling and pretending everything was normal. I was in the living room. I was wearing my pyjamas. I heard the door slam. And then he was standing there in his coat, with his hands in his pockets and he didn't have a present for me. And I said, "Dad. Have you forgotten?"' Tears begin to trickle out of the corners of her eyes again. 'And he said, "Forgotten what?" And I said, "Dad, it's my birthday!" And he said, "Oh yes. So it is. Happy birthday, Squiggle."' She looks up at me, her eyes glistening. 'That's what he calls me: Squiggle.'

I nod. 'OK. Close your eyes again.'

She does as I ask.

'Carry on.'

'And then,' she continues, 'he pulled some sweets out of his coat pocket and gave them to me. But that wasn't very special, because he always did that. And then he smiled and he said, "What? You don't like sweets any more?"' She starts to giggle through her tears. 'And then I said, "Yes, I do, but it's my birthday, Daddy!" And he started smiling. And then he went out into the hallway and brought my rabbit in, in her cage, and he got her out of the cage and he put her in my arms and she was so soft and warm and furry. And then he gave me a little bottle of water so that I could feed her and… it was just so, so amazing.'

Her eyes are shining as she opens them. She looks at me and quickly shuts them again.

'What did you say?' I ask her.

'I said, "Thank you, Daddy. I've always wanted a rabbit!" And he said… he said, "I know you have. Happy birthday, Squiggle."'

She pauses for breath.

'And then?' I ask.

'And then he hugged me.'

I nod. 'Can you feel his arms, wrapped around you?'

She nods, her nose in the air.

'How do they feel?'

She thinks about this for a moment. 'Nice.'

'Does it feel as though he loves you?'

She nods, vigorously, then sniffs, then says, chokingly, 'Yes.' She unscrews the tissue that's in her hand and blows her nose.

'So, there's your evidence,' I tell her. 'That he loves you. It's all about evidence. If you want to know the truth, you just have to find it.'

She looks up at me, her lip quivering. 'Then why did he go?'

I hesitate, Burdie's voice in my ear again. 'He had his reasons,' I reassure her. 'He had some very, very good reasons. But they were absolutely nothing to do with not loving you to the end of the world and back again.'

Mark is in a single room in the corner of the ward. I'm relieved to see that there's no sign of DCI Hollis or any other police presence in the room. Karen and Jack both look up in surprise as I walk in, Karen's face softening into a gentle smile as she sees Sophia standing next to me, holding my hand. I can feel Sophia trembling and I grip her hand tightly to reassure her.

'Come here, baby,' Karen calls out to her, standing up and stretching out her arms. She moves round the bed towards us. 'Come and say hi to your dad.'

I wait until Sophia loosens her grip on mine, then I let go of her hand and watch as she walks tentatively over to meet her mother, glancing across at Mark's bed as she goes. He's lying very still, his head tipped up on his pillow, his eyes closed and his mouth slightly ajar. The tracheostomy tube is partially concealed inside a wide collar around his neck and lies across one side of his chest. The ventilator and all the other machinery is bleeping and whirring quite loudly, and Sophia glances at it momentarily before lowering her eyes down to her father's face.

'Am I allowed to touch him?' she asks her mother.

Karen nods. 'Yes. You can kiss him if you like.'

She shakes her head. 'I don't want to wake him up.'

'You won't,' Karen reassures her. 'They've given him something to make him super sleepy. Just try not to move the tube in his nose, or the one around his neck.'

I notice Jack standing up and moving to one side so that

his sister can get closer to Mark. I catch his expression. He appears to be pleased that Sophia has come.

I watch for a moment as Sophia first hesitates then finally leans over and kisses her father's cheek. As she does so, from the doorway, I say my own silent goodbye. I take a mental snapshot as I move my eyes across his face, noticing the scar under one eye, the gentle expression. I imagine him dressed in his white collared shirt with black epaulettes and silver stripes and buttons on the shoulder. I imagine him, fit, strong and healthy, moving around behind the custody desk at Farringdon, booking in prisoners, releasing others on bail, and all the while, caring about everybody and what happened to them.

'Bye,' I say, to Karen, Jack and Sophia.

Karen glances up and nods.

'Goodbye,' I whisper, again, to Mark.

As soon as I exit the doors to the Critical Care Unit, I pull my phone out of my pocket and find Burdie's number. I press the green 'call' button and put the phone to my ear then pace up and down on the landing outside the lift. My stomach is churning with rage.

'Yeah,' he says, simply, when he answers.

'It's Sarah,' I say. 'Sarah Kellerman.'

'Oh.'

'So,' I say, curtly. 'What have you found out?'

'About what?'

I huff. 'About the four-by-four!'

Silence. And then, 'Not much, to be fair.'

'What?' I try to keep my voice steady. 'What do you

mean, "not much"? Have you talked to the registered owner?'

A pause. 'No. Not yet.'

'For fuck's sake, Burdie! Why the hell not?'

'Because I haven't. OK? What do you want me to say?'

'Oh, I don't know,' I retort, scathingly. 'How about, "My good friend and colleague is about to have his life support machine switched off, so maybe I'd better crack on with speaking to the person that ran him over"?'

Burdie doesn't reply.

I hesitate. 'You knew, right? That Mark…'

He sighs. 'Yeah, I knew.'

'Then why haven't you done anything?' I say, exasperated. 'Why haven't you been down to Gravesend and talked to the RO?'

There's a long pause on the other end of the line before he says, 'We don't actually know that the RO is the driver.'

'What?' I say, sharply. 'I don't believe this!'

He hesitates again. 'Look. As you pointed out yourself, whoever it is is just going to say that they didn't have possession of the vehicle that night.'

'Then you ask him who did!'

'And then what? What is he going to say? Oh, OK. It was me. No. Wait. It was my friend Bob. No, wait. I think I'd sold the car by then. So, anyway, yeah. It wasn't me.'

'OK. What the fuck's going on?' I sink down onto a wooden bench that's set back on the landing, opposite the lift.

He coughs. 'I'm trying to come up with a strategy. That's what's going on.'

'A strategy? How much of a bloody strategy do you need to talk to the registered owner of a vehicle that's run over and killed your colleague in the execution of his duty?'

'It's not quite as simple as that.'

'Why the hell not?'

'Because it's not. It's just not.'

I shake my head. 'This whole thing stinks! It doesn't make any sense. Why has Jerome been arrested and charged, but not the driver of the four-by-four? Are you part of it? Is that what this is? Was that all just a load of bullshit that you fed me about getting suspended and wanting to help me? Are you still with them? With SO21?'

'No. I'm not with them, Sarah. What I told you is the truth. I'm trying to find out the truth.'

'Then just fucking tell me. Tell me what's going on. Either help me – or fuck off out of it and I'll do it by myself.'

'And how are you going to do that, exactly? You're not a copper.'

'Neither are you.'

A pause. 'Thanks for that.'

'You're welcome,' I retort.

Another pause and a long deep breath. 'You need to calm down.'

'Are you not getting this?' I leap up out of my seat again. 'He's going to die! Mark's going to die! They don't know it yet, but I just watched those two kids say goodbye to their dad. Karen's lost the love of her life. And Jerome is going to end up charged with some kind of role in a conspiracy to murder. He'll go to prison for life. There are lives being ruined here. And it's on you. It's all on you! If you don't help me, goddammit, I'm going to get in the car tomorrow with my little boy in the back and drive down to Gravesend myself.'

A sigh. 'You'll be wasting your time.'

'Oh yeah. Because I'm not a copper. Because I don't have access to your systems.' I parody his accent. I march forward and whack the lift button hard with the flat of my hand. 'Just watch me try. Maybe I'll just go back to the Hope and Glory and see what I can find out there!'

'Jesus fucking Christ!' Burdie groans into the phone so loudly that my ear rings.

I stop still. 'What's going on?'

'Look,' says Burdie. 'You just have to trust me on this. I know what I'm doing. OK?'

'No.' I give the lift button another whack. It finally starts its ascension, rattling slightly as it draws closer to our floor. 'It's not OK,' I hiss back at him. 'I don't trust you. That's the problem: I don't believe a bloody word you say.'

'Sarah—'

'I'm going to find out the truth,' I insist. 'With your help or without it.'

'No,' he says, sharply. 'Just wait!'

'What for?' I eject, bitterly. 'For you to stare at the ceiling, have a few more *smokes* and come up with your *strategy*? No thanks. I think this conversation is over.'

Burdie's voice cracks slightly as he says, 'It's a job car.'

The lift doors slide open. DCI Hollis and DCS Sinclair are standing there, suited and booted, their faces sombre. Both pairs of eyes lock onto mine. For a moment we stand face to face, nose to nose, almost.

I take a step backwards to let them pass.

'What?' I whisper to Burdie. 'What do you mean?'

Sinclair and Hollis step out of the lift, their eyes still locked firmly on mine.

'I mean,' says Burdie, his voice solemn and low. 'That the four-by-four belongs to SO21.'

15

drive through the gates that lead into Alexandra Palace and follow the winding road up and around the perimeter. It's dark and the grounds are deserted, but the palace is lit up by glowing orange lights. I spot Burdie's Saab, a lone vehicle sitting at the top of the hill. As I pull in and park nose to nose with him, he sees me through the windscreen and lifts his head. I glance over at Ben, who's fallen asleep in his car seat, then tug my coat from the back seat, open the driver's door and step out.

Burdie opens his door and steps out to meet me. He tilts his head towards his car. 'Do you wanna get in?'

I shake my head. 'My kid's in the back.'

He nods. 'Is he OK?'

'It's fine. He's asleep. Let's talk out here.'

'Fine.'

I zip up my coat and push my hands into my pockets. I lean up against my car and Burdie joins me, opening his jacket and pulling out his pack of cigarettes.

'Great view, huh?'

'Yeah,' I agree, following his eyes across the rooftops and chimneys towards the distant city skyline. I hesitate. 'So, have you heard anything?'

He taps a cigarette from the packet and lights it, then exhales a long, slow, steady stream of smoke. 'He's gone, Sarah.'

I catch my breath and feel my stomach sink. Even though I'd known this moment was coming, his words still cut me to the core. 'When?' I ask.

'An hour ago.'

'Poor Karen,' I murmur. 'Poor kids.'

Burdie's eyes shift towards me, but he doesn't answer.

We both stand in silence for a moment, looking out at the twinkling sea of lights that sprawls beneath us, at the skyscrapers of Canary Wharf which stand illuminated on the horizon. I love this city, I tell myself, as I fight back the urge to cry. I'll never stop loving this city. Through darkness or through twinkling light, it will always be my home.

A gust of wind blows through the trees in front of me, catching and cooling the trickle of a tear on my cheek. 'I don't understand,' I say, finally. 'Why would someone from SO21 want Mark killed? He'd cracked the drugs case for them. He was their chief prosecution witness. They needed him. Why would they want him dead?'

'Good question.' Burdie lifts his eyes towards mine.

I meet his gaze. 'You think one of them was bent?'

'Possibly.'

'But you must have known,' I accuse him. 'You worked there. You must have known it was an SO21 car.'

'No.' He shakes his head, grimly. 'I had no idea. It's not one I recognised from the fleet. Vehicles get called in and shifted out again all the time. Especially when you're working on Special Ops.'

'Do you know where it is now?'

He turns his head away and blows out a cloud of smoke. 'No.'

'Back to the owner, maybe?' I suggest. 'You told me it was registered to an address in Gravesend.'

He drops his cigarette and grinds it into the gravel with his heel. 'Forget about the RO, Sarah. Forget about Gravesend. It means nothing. That's what happens with vehicles that are being used for undercover work. They just get registered to an unoccupied address somewhere so that they can't be traced.'

I glare at him in the dark. 'And you knew that all along, right? You were just trying to throw me off the scent?'

Burdie stiffens next to me. 'I gave you information about the vehicle that I didn't have to give you.'

'You strung me along,' I say.

He shoves his hands in his pockets and raises his eyes. Above us, the sky is black, any stars obscured by cloud.

'I suspected,' he says, finally. 'I didn't know for sure. There's a difference. I needed time to follow it up, to see if my suspicions were correct.'

'And? Now that you know? What are you going to do about it?'

He sighs. 'Obviously, I'm trying to find the car.'

I fold my arms. 'Well, take your time.'

'Look.' He spins round to face me. 'I've been calling in a lot of favours here. I've friends who've stuck their necks out big time. I have to be careful.'

'Of what?'

'Of being cut off! Blanked completely.'

'So, you lose a few friends. So what?'

He looks back at me and shakes his head, his expression

one of disbelief. 'I'm investigating my own colleagues. Without any support or authorisation from up above. Just put yourself in my shoes for five minutes, can't you? I'm risking everything here.'

'You've already been suspended on a drugs allegation,' I point out. 'What exactly are you risking?'

'Everything!'

'Your pension. Is that it?' I ask. 'Has Sinclair offered you some kind of a deal? Keep quiet about the four-by-four and he'll make the drugs go away?'

Burdie claps his hands to his head. 'For crying out loud, Sarah. If that were true, do you think I'd be standing here with you now?'

I hesitate, feeling ashamed suddenly. I've gone too far. 'So, why *are* you here, then?'

'You said you wanted answers.'

'I do.' I glance at him. 'But what's in it for you?'

He hesitates, then takes a deep breath in and out, his shoulders heaving visibly under his jacket. Eventually he sighs and shakes his head at me, resignedly. 'I suppose you never know when you're going to need an irritatingly persistent lawyer.'

I look back at him, uncertainly. 'Are they going to charge you? With a crime?'

He rubs his temples. 'No. They won't do that. That would put their internal investigation under the kind of scrutiny that they really don't want or need. But I'm under no illusion. I crossed them. I'm finished. They'll make sure of that.'

'So, why don't you just report this?'

Frustration creeps into his voice again. 'To who? I've no

idea who's involved in this, or how big it is. Who am I going to tell?'

'The CPS,' I suggest. 'You could go directly to them.'

'I don't have enough evidence. I'd be discredited. I can't prove a thing. Not yet.'

I look up at him. 'So, are you going to let me help you?'

He sighs. 'Well, you're clearly not going to back off.'

'You won't be sorry,' I say.

'Fucking hope not.' He looks away, out into the darkness, but then glances back at me, a gentle smile playing on his lips.

We fall silent.

I think about the four-by-four. 'There must be a vehicle log.'

'There was a log. But it's gone.'

'Gone?'

'Disappeared.'

I shake my head. 'What a coincidence.'

'Yeah, isn't it just?'

'So, what now? What happens next?'

He lifts his jacket and takes out his cigarettes again. 'I've a colleague – an intelligence officer – doing a specialist search on PNC for the vehicle. I've also made enquiries around police repair shops. But I've found no trace of it so far.'

'Could it have been disposed of somehow? Or given false plates?'

He sticks a cigarette in his mouth and flicks his lighter. 'Easier to clean it up and repair it than to explain a missing car.' He exhales a cloud of smoke. 'But it's Special Ops, at the end of the day, so theoretically, yes. Access on PNC would be legitimately restricted. You could probably make it go missing for a while without too many eyebrows being raised.' He sounds more resigned than bitter as he says, 'We have to be realistic, though. We're a few months down the line. Even if I find it, anything of forensic interest is likely to be long gone by now.'

I sigh heavily and lean back against the car. 'So, we're still no closer to knowing who was driving it that night?'

'No.' He hesitates then says, 'At least, not directly.'

I look up at him, expectantly. 'What do you mean?'

Burdie takes another long draw on his cigarette, turning his head to exhale. He turns back to face me. 'DCI Hollis is in a relationship with Karen Felding.'

I straighten up. 'What? Are you serious?'

He nods, slowly.

'How do you know?'

'Word of mouth.'

'So, it might not be true?'

He shoots me a contemptuous glare.

'You've been following him.'

'It's called surveillance.'

It takes me a moment. 'And that's why you wanted me to stay away from her?'

He raises his eyes. 'Finally.'

'Well, why didn't you just tell me this sooner?' I shoot back at him.

He gives me a weary look. 'I didn't think I needed to.'

I turn my mind back to every conversation I've ever had with Karen, a knot of unease tightening in my gut. 'There was something going on between them at the hospital,' I say. 'The first time I saw them together, I... I saw the way that they looked at each other. It suggested intimacy, that they knew each other as more than the wife of an injured copper and his boss.'

Burdie looks back at me silently, flicking ash on the ground.

'But she seemed so cut up about Mark that I didn't clock it. I thought... I thought that she was still in love with him. With Mark, I mean.'

Burdie stubs his cigarette out, listening in silence as I speak.

I shake my head. '*That's* why she didn't want to know. When I confronted her with my suspicions about SO21, when I told her that I thought they were involved somehow, that they were covering something up... she just kept batting me away.' I hesitate, and turn to Burdie, confused. 'But then again, she seemed so genuine. She seemed... genuinely cut up about Mark. And frightened.' I cast my mind back to the conversation in the Abbey Lounge. 'She said she didn't know anything, that she didn't *want* to know anything. And when she said that, she looked so scared...' I look up at Burdie, searching his face for a clue. 'Do *you* think she was involved?'

He looks back at me for a moment, chewing his lip. Then, 'I don't know.'

I clap one hand to my mouth. 'She signed the forms! She signed the DNR forms at the hospital. So that they wouldn't resuscitate him if his heart were to stop.'

Burdie shakes his head. 'He wasn't well, Sarah. He wasn't going to make it. The doctors wouldn't have let anything improper happen to him.'

'You're right. What am I thinking?' I look up at him, still turning it over in my mind. Karen wouldn't have wanted to hurt Mark. She loved him. You could see it in her eyes. But Mark had left her. She thought he didn't care. Why shouldn't she get into a relationship with someone else? 'Just because she's seeing Hollis, doesn't mean that she wanted Mark dead,' I say, finally. 'And let's be honest, anyone at SO21 could have been driving the four-by-four that night.'

'Agreed. Except…'

I turn to face him. 'Except what?'

'Except that the ANPR hit we got at eleven thirty-five was two streets away from Karen Felding's house.'

I look at him, shocked. 'There's a camera there?'

He shakes his head. 'No. But there was a triple nine call to a burglary in an adjacent street at eleven thirty. The uniform who responded had in-car ANPR. It coincidentally captured the four-by-four as it was passing. The direction of travel would have taken it away from her house in the direction of King's Cross.'

I look at him, stunned. 'But why King's Cross? That would have taken it away from Packington Street, wouldn't it?'

He nods. 'Yeah, it's not yet clear where it was going.'

'King's Cross. That's where Mark lived. To his flat, maybe?'

'Maybe.'

'But there would still have been time to drive there and back to Packington Street before midnight, right?'

'Uh-huh,' he agrees.

I think about this for a minute. 'Any hits after midnight?'

'Nothing. Nothing at all. Whoever was driving knew where the cameras were and which route to take to avoid them.' He looks at me. 'There are also certain avoidance tactics that can be used to throw the cameras off.'

'Which would be known to an experienced police officer?'

He nods.

'Or,' I concede, thinking aloud, 'to a career criminal.'

He nods. 'True.'

I look up at him. 'Maybe the number plate was modified in some way to avoid detection?'

He shakes his head. 'No. You'd be putting up a red flag. If the vehicle was stopped it would be obvious on inspection. Better to avoid the cameras.'

'Unless you're unlucky enough to pass a police vehicle,' I comment.

He nods and smiles. 'Whoever was driving would not have anticipated that.'

I turn to check on Ben, but he's still fast asleep.

'But, if Hollis was driving the four-by-four,' I ask, 'why would he go to King's Cross? As Mark's boss, he'd have known exactly where Mark was that evening. He'd have known that he was in the Hope and Glory.'

'Not necessarily. Maybe they'd lost touch with Mark, weren't sure where he'd gone and went looking for him. Or maybe Hollis needed to pick someone else up along the way.'

I shiver at the thought of the planning that might have gone into Mark's murder. 'He could have delivered the car to someone else. Someone else could have been driving after Hollis left Karen's house.'

Burdie shrugs. 'It's possible.'

'So, we still can't prove a thing.'

'No,' he concedes. 'Not yet.'

We fall into silence.

'So, what's next?' I ask.

He rubs his forehead. 'To be honest with you, Sarah, I'm

pretty lost for leads at the moment. The forensics would have been key.'

I gaze back at him. 'There must be something…?'

'Continued surveillance,' he says.

I turn to him, eagerly. 'Karen trusts me. I can talk to her, try and find out if—'

He shakes his head, quickly. 'No. Too risky. She already thinks you're onto something. If Hollis is bent, he'll show his hand before long. Leave this one to me.'

I look at him. 'Don't cut me out.'

'I'm not cutting you out.'

'So how can I trust you?'

'I've told you everything I know, for Christ's sake.' He takes hold of my arm and swings me gently round to face him. 'How about you show me that *I* can trust *you*?'

We look hard at each other for a moment.

He lets go of my arm. 'When I need you, I'll call you. OK?'

I nod. 'OK.'

He fixes his eyes on mine, his brow furrowed.

'OK,' I say again, more firmly.

He hesitates, then turns to look at Ben through the car window. 'I'd better let you get your little lad back home to bed.'

I follow his gaze. 'I'm amazed he's still asleep.'

'They all drop off in the car, don't they?'

'Yeah, but he normally wakes as soon as the engine stops.'

He crouches down and peers through the glass. 'He's got a *lot* of hair, hasn't he?'

I smile. 'He's got my hair. Thick and unruly.'

Burdie stands up straight and casts his eyes over my hair, then over my face.

'How about you?' I ask. 'Do you have any kids?'

He straightens up. 'Two. A boy and a girl. Both grown up now.'

I smile. 'Your work is done.'

'You could say that.'

'Lucky you.' I heave a knowing sigh.

'Yeah,' he says. 'Lucky me.'

I look at him, questioningly.

'They hate me,' he explains. 'I haven't seen them for twenty-two years.'

'I'm sorry.'

'Me too.'

After a moment, he adds, 'I was a terrible husband and father.'

I pull a face. 'I find that hard to believe.'

He frowns. 'Are you messing with me?'

'No,' I protest. 'I'm serious. It's just… well, you're kind, aren't you? Caring. You saved me from those drug dealers.'

Muscles move beneath his jaw. 'Now I *know* you're messing with me.'

'OK,' I agree. 'How were you a terrible father?'

He lets out a sigh. 'You'd have to ask my wife.' He's silent for a moment, then he says, 'Just so that we're completely clear on this, you're not to ask my wife.'

'As if,' I smile.

He doesn't smile back.

'Right.' I open my car door. 'I'll be on my way, then.'

'Right,' he agrees.

I unzip my coat and slide into my seat. Burdie catches the edge of my door and crouches down beside me. He says, 'I need to be careful. Play my hand too soon and I'll cut off any legitimate lines of enquiry that I have. I'll be completely discredited. And then we'll never get justice for Mark.'

'OK,' I agree.

He turns to me, 'You need to be careful, too. They've a lot to lose.'

I hesitate. 'Who?'

He looks back at me intently. 'All of them,' he says. 'Hollis. Sinclair. Whoever else is involved in this whole sorry mess. Please believe me when I tell you,' he insists, his eyes widening earnestly, 'that a senior ranking officer in a regional crime squad can turn your life upside down.'

I nod. 'Understood.'

'We both want the same thing,' he reassures me. 'We both want to nail those bastards. But if we do it, we have to be sure to nail them well and good.'

I nod my agreement. 'I'm sorry if I was a bit… earlier. What I said about your pension. I was out of order. I was upset about Mark.'

He nods back. 'I know.'

'You're a good friend,' I say, after a moment. 'To Mark, I mean.'

He shrugs. 'Mark was a decent bloke. He wanted what was right.'

I peer at him in the half-light. 'All the same, not everyone would put their career on the line for someone else. You're a good person.' I hesitate, then add, 'Someone should tell your kids that.'

Burdie looks back at me for a moment, his expression inscrutable, then stands up and closes the door.

16

Andy selects an album on his iPod and starts the engine. 'Ed Sheeran?' I frown as 'Shape of You' starts up.

'What's wrong with Ed Sheeran?'

'Nothing. It's just that Ben normally has nursery rhymes in the car.'

Andy moves the Laguna out and heads along my road. 'He'll be fine. We can't listen to nursery rhymes for ever.'

I glance across at him and then back over my shoulder, but Ben's sitting happily in the back, grasping his portable DVD player in his hands.

We turn onto the Holloway Road. 'So, does he know you're coming?'

'No.' I shake my head.

'He hasn't called you since...?'

I look up at him. 'It's only been a few days. He's still recovering.'

He doesn't reply.

'He was delirious, Andy. He didn't know what he was saying.'

'Even so, what if he doesn't want to see you?'

'Then I'll just come straight back out again.'

He brightens. 'OK. So, I'll just go for a little drive with

Ben, shall I? We'll head south across the river. I'll take him on the London Eye, maybe.'

I glance at him, anxiously. 'You're kidding, right?'

'Why not?'

'He'd hate it. He'd freak out. That's why not!' I gasp. 'Please tell me you're not going to attempt it?'

Andy smiles. 'All right. It was just a little joke.'

I shoot him a warning glare. 'Not funny.'

'Hey. Listen to him.' Andy nods over his shoulder.

We listen silently for a moment as Ben makes a tuneless 'Oooh-wah' sound from behind us, over the music. Andy glances across at me and grins. We listen again and – again, on the chorus – Ben starts up with the same sound.

'That's incredible,' I smile at Andy. 'He's singing along! And he knows the words!'

'He has a *terrible* singing voice,' Andy observes. 'He doesn't get that from me.'

I smile. 'Me neither.'

'Maybe he's not ours?'

I nudge him, playfully, but inside I'm glowing. Ben likes Ed Sheeran! For just a few moments he's come out of his closed-off world and into our world with us.

There's a build-up of traffic near Highbury Corner. 'Turn here,' I suggest.

Andy indicates right and crosses the lane, then turns into Liverpool Road. He heads on past the Angel and down through Clerkenwell. As we drive along Rosebery Avenue, I find myself instinctively looking up for cameras, wondering which route the four-by-four took from the road near Karen's house and where it was heading next.

When we reach the hospital Andy pulls up outside, then

turns to me, a look of concern on his face. 'Don't take *too* long, will you? Ben's just getting used to me again and I'm out on my own with him and...'

'Do you want to take him back to mine?' I offer. 'I can get the Tube home.'

He wrinkles his nose and shakes his head. 'You don't want to do that.'

'I don't mind. If it's easier.'

'No. It's fine. We'll wait for you.'

'OK. If you're sure.'

'I'm sure. Just...'

'What?'

'Well. You know. If he starts going off again, you don't need to put up with it.' He reaches up and strokes a strand of hair from my face, an act of unexpected intimacy which takes me by surprise. 'You've got me and Ben, remember?'

I hesitate, feeling briefly confused at his touch. 'Andy, let's not have that conversation again.'

'Think about it,' he presses me. 'We get on so well.'

I give him a sideways glance. 'Not always.'

He smiles. 'Most of the time we do. We have fun. And there's Ben to consider too.'

'Don't bring Ben into this,' I shoot back at him. 'That didn't stop you leaving me!'

'I didn't leave *you*. I didn't leave *Ben*. I left the situation. You know that – and you know that I'm sorry. But now that he's got both of us back in his life again, it makes sense for us to be a family again.'

I look up at him. He fixes his beautiful blue eyes on mine and smiles, disarmingly. 'I have a boyfriend,' I say. 'He's in hospital, fighting for his life. Your timing sucks.'

'Are you saying that if he wasn't in hospital then you'd consider it?'

'I'm not saying anything, Andy.' I pick up my bag and grab my jacket from the back seat of the car. 'Except that I need you to back off. I'm not having this conversation with you. I'm going in to see Will.'

He looks down into his lap and nods dejectedly. I glance across at him. Feeling the weight of his disappointment, I reach out and squeeze his arm.

'Please,' I say. 'I can't do this. Don't put pressure on me.'

He nods, silently.

'I'm sorry.'

'That's OK.'

'I'll see you in a bit.'

He lifts his head. 'Give me a call when you're done.'

The waiting area is empty. I glance through the glass window as I'm buzzed into the unit and it makes me wonder what Karen and the children are doing right now. Making plans for the funeral, no doubt. I think of Jack and Sophia as I put on my apron and then I think of Karen as I wash my hands. I can't believe she'd want Mark hurt. I can't believe that she feels anything but pain. How is it possible that she could have been involved in anything so sinister? Mark was the father of her children. She loves her children. Not telling them he was in hospital is one thing, but surely she wouldn't have knowingly taken him away from them?

Will looks up as I cross the bay towards him. My heart sinks as I see his parents sitting there, one either side of him. His bed is raised to a forty-five degree angle, so that he's sitting up a little. He looks slightly better than he did, although his hair is dishevelled and he has a few days' worth of stubble on his chin.

Will's expression when he sees me is one of discomfort.

His father follows his gaze and smiles at me.

I stop just short of the bed. 'Should I go?' I ask, hesitantly.

Will turns his head and says something under his breath to his father who nods and stands up. 'No. *We'll* go,' Nick says, cheerfully. 'We'll let you two young people have some space to talk.'

Will's mother looks up at him, about to protest, but her husband gives her a nod of the head and says, 'Come. We'll go and get some tea.'

I watch as they leave, then move closer to the bed.

'Can I sit down?' I ask.

Will nods. 'Of course.'

I sit down on the chair that his mother had been sitting in and draw it closer to the bed. Will watches me, expectantly, his expression solemn. His eyes are still swollen, but he looks less pale and clammy than he did.

'How are you—'

'I'm sorry,' he says at the same time.

We both fall silent.

'About the things I said,' he continues. 'When you came before. I wasn't myself.'

'I know,' I smile. 'Don't worry. I realised that. How are you feeling now?'

'A little better.'

I smile and reach out for his hand. He moves it gently but discernibly away.

I hesitate, watching his face. 'What's going on?' I ask him.

He gives a gentle shake of the head. 'Nothing.'

I look into his eyes. 'You don't seem the same.'

He swallows, then clears his throat and says, 'I'm not the same, am I? Look at me.'

I hesitate. 'You're feeling low. You're bound to be feeling low. After the anaesthetic and all the drugs and everything that's happened. It's inevitable that you'd be feeling—'

'I don't think we should see each other any more,' he says, abruptly.

'What?' I breathe, looking into his eyes. 'Are you serious?'

He swallows again, then nods. 'I'm sorry. But it's just not going to work.'

My heart flutters in my chest. 'Is it Veronica?' I ask. 'Are you back together? Is that it?'

He shakes his head, quickly. 'No. No, it's nothing like that.'

'Then what is it?'

'It's… nothing. It's just… how I feel.'

Tears spring to my eyes. I blink them back. 'If it's her you want to be with, then you can just say that. It's fine. I'd rather know the truth.'

Will looks up at me. He looks pained. 'There's no one else,' he says. 'I just don't think we're right for each other, that's all.'

I hold his gaze for a moment then look beyond him towards the window, where the afternoon sun is glinting through the trees that border the square.

'I don't believe you,' I tell him. 'I don't believe that this is what you want.'

'I'm sorry,' he says again. 'But it is.'

'Is it your parents?' I ask him. 'They don't like me. Is that it? They want you to be with *her*?'

Will sighs, but he doesn't answer.

'It's your parents?' I quiz him. '*Seriously?*'

'Don't be ridiculous,' he says. 'It's not my parents.'

'Then it's her,' I say. 'Veronica.'

Will makes a gesture of impatience towards me, but his eyes betray him and it falls flat.

Anger grips me. 'What hold does she have over you, Will?'

He looks anxious. 'What are you talking about?'

'Are you frightened of her?'

'Don't be silly,' he huffs, unconvincingly.

I watch his face for a second, then cast my mind back. 'The things you said the last time I came. The way you were with me. You said I was happy that you were in hospital, that I'd come to gloat. What did you mean?'

'Sarah, I'd just had surgery. I didn't know what I was saying. I barely remember you being here.'

'You thought I was someone else,' I accuse him. 'You thought I was her!'

Will squeezes his eyes shut and tilts his head towards the ceiling.

I lean in closer. 'Oh my God. Did you think I was Veronica?' My heart leaps and my eyes move down the bed towards the expanse of crepe bandage. 'Oh my God!' I gasp again. 'Did *she* do this to you? Did she do this to your leg?'

Will's eyes spring open, darting first at me and then around the bay.

I look at him, incredulous. 'I'm right.'

He doesn't answer.

I ask, 'Do your parents know?'

'No!' Will raises one hand and runs it across his forehead. He looks distraught. 'You can't talk about this,' he says. 'Please. I mean it, Sarah.'

I lean forward again, my teeth clenched, anger rising in my chest. '*She's* done this to you? Goddammit, Will! Why are you defending her?'

Will's voice is cracked and nervous as he says, 'She wasn't well. She wasn't… herself.'

I look back at him in stunned silence for a moment, my eyes searching his.

'How?' I stutter. 'How did it happen?'

Will brings his hands up to his face and presses his fingertips against his eyelids. For a moment he remains so still that I wonder if he's crying. 'It was an accident,' he says, finally. 'She just lashed out.'

'Tell me,' I say. 'Tell me from the start.'

He swallows, heavily. His expression is gaunt and haunted. 'That night,' he says, softly. 'That night I was supposed to be meeting you.'

I cast my mind back. 'When you phoned and cancelled?'

He nods and swallows. 'Yes. She called me to say that she was coming over. That she wanted to talk.'

'About what?'

'About us.'

I hesitate. 'Us? As in… you and her?'

He nods, slowly, fixing his dark eyes on mine.

I think about this for a moment. 'You told me that your parents had been trying to matchmake. That they'd got her hopes up. That you met with her to let her down.'

Will nods.

'It was that night?'

He nods again. He says, 'She seemed to think that we had something going. She and I, I mean.'

I look him in the eye. 'And did you?'

He shakes his head. 'I told you. I don't feel that way about her. I cared about her, but... but that's all.'

'So, did she come over?'

He shakes his head. 'No. I didn't want that. I wanted to meet somewhere... neutral. We went to a restaurant. Brown's. We talked. She was very excited.'

'About what?'

He sighs. 'About us. About our future together, as she saw it. I realised that it was going to be a difficult conversation to have.'

I look at him carefully. 'Were you sleeping with her?'

He shakes his head. 'No, Sarah. I'd already started seeing you by then.'

'Before that, I mean.'

He hesitates. 'Once. It happened once, when she first came back to town. Her marriage had ended. She was going through a rocky patch. I felt sorry for her, and before I knew what was happening...' He looks up at me, earnestly. 'But that was before you and I... I swear, I wasn't with you then.'

I nod.

'I didn't hear from her for a while,' he continues. 'I assumed she was back together with her husband and I was pleased for her, genuinely pleased. But then she started calling me and... and my parents started talking as though we were a couple again and I realised...'

'That she thought you *were* a couple? And that you needed to break it off?'

He nods, sorrowfully. 'Yes.'

'So, what happened at the restaurant?'

'We ordered our food. I tried to broach the subject.' He sighs, heavily, his eyes darkening. 'But she started talking over me instead, about how we were destined to be together. She'd had signs, she said, dreams about our future children, stuff like that.' He pauses and catches his breath. 'While we were eating I... I just came out and told her that I was seeing someone else.' He adds, 'You, of course. But I didn't tell her who.'

He closes his eyes for a moment. I wait for him to open them again.

'And what did she say?'

'She was upset.' His eyes move up to meet mine, his brow creasing and his eyes flickering at the memory. 'She was really upset. I tried to calm her down, but she got really... animated. And then – I can't remember exactly; it all happened so quickly – but she somehow knocked her wine glass off the table and onto the floor.' He takes a deep breath. 'Anyway, I turned around to catch the waiter's attention, but she got down onto her knees and started to clear it up. I tried to stop her and ran around the table to help her.'

He pauses for breath again. I wait for him to continue.

'I could see that she'd cut herself; her hand was bleeding. She was looking at it and crying. People were glancing over by now, but still no waiter. I crouched down next to her and asked her to let me see her hand, but...' He hesitates, seeming lost for words. 'She was really crying. She was... hysterical. She told me to fuck off and get away from her. And then, when I tried, again, to take hold of her hand...'

His eyes move up to meet mine. He looks bewildered. 'Well, that's when she picked it up.'

My stomach flips. 'Picked what up?'

'The glass.' He takes a deep breath. 'The broken stem of the wine glass. And then I felt it. This *incredible* pain in my lower thigh.'

'Jesus fucking Christ, Will! She stabbed you in the leg with it? She *glassed* you?'

My eyes seek out his and he nods.

'Jesus fucking Christ,' I say again.

Will blinks back at me, his eyes widening and his mouth falling open in response to my reaction. I realise that this is the first time he's told anyone – the first time he's seen the enormity of what's been done to him reflected back at him in another person's eyes.

We look at each other in silence for a moment while we both process what he's just told me.

'You told me it was just a scratch,' I say, bewildered.

'I know.'

'So, how bad was it really?'

He closes his eyes. 'Bad enough.'

'So, what did you do?' I ask, finally. 'Did you call for help?'

He shakes his head. 'No.'

'Did you call the police?'

'No.'

'Jeez, Will. Why not?'

'Because she was...' He opens his eyes and looks at me, apologetically. 'Because she was sorry. She was so bloody sorry. She was beside herself, as soon as she realised what she'd done. She just kept saying how sorry she was, over and over again.' He raises a hand and smooths his hair back from his forehead. 'And because it was so... unexpected. I think my body must have gone into shock.'

'So... what did you do?'

He frowns at the memory. 'I sat down.' He hesitates, his eyes moving back and forth. He blinks. 'That's what happened. I sat down to try and stem the blood flow with a napkin and then she got up and tried to help me and I told her to sit down too, so she... she did.' He licks his lips and looks up at me, his eyes expressing a blend of shock and bemusement. 'And then I... I think I paid the bill.'

I stare back at him in disbelief. 'You paid the bill?'

Will nods, then starts coughing and I pour a glass of water and help him to take a sip.

'And then what did you do?' I press him.

'We left the restaurant,' he croaks. 'I went home.'

'You didn't call an ambulance?'

'I couldn't call anyone. I couldn't tell anyone. She'd be arrested.'

'But there must have been witnesses,' I say. 'People must have seen what happened?'

He shakes his head. 'No. We were behind the table, in a secluded corner of the restaurant. I mean, people could see that we were having an argument. But no one saw her...'

'Stab you in the leg!'

Will recoils at my words. 'She didn't *stab* me, Sarah. It was just a jab.'

'A jab that put you in hospital with a life-threatening infection! Jesus Christ, Will. Are you trying to tell me that you let her get away with it?'

He sighs. 'You didn't see her. She was in bits. She was crying and apologising, over and over again. She told me that she'd been really depressed, that she would see the doctor. She promised me that she'd get herself sorted out.' He lifts his eyes to meet mine. 'Thing is, Sarah... she's a pupil at Dean Street Chambers.'

I look back at him in surprise. 'She's a lawyer?'

He nods. 'She's just starting out. You and I both know that once you call the police with something like this, there's no going back. With really strong mitigation, she might avoid prison, but it would be the end of her career. I had to make a snap decision. I had to think of the repercussions. I didn't want to do that to her. Surely you understand?'

'For fuck's sake, Will. She put you in intensive care! There are major arteries in your leg. She could have killed you!'

'I know,' he pleads. 'But she didn't mean to. It was a moment of madness. It was a mistake that she regretted instantly.'

I take a deep breath. 'So, what did you do?'

'Well, we managed to conceal the blood. Got outside. She found a late-night chemist for dressings and antiseptic, then she called me a taxi. When I got home, I washed it and dressed it and then I went to bed.'

'And then?'

'In the morning I had a fever and the pain in my leg was excruciating.' He looks at me, sheepishly.

'And you still didn't go to hospital?'

He shakes his head.

'Bloody hell, Will. You must have known it was infected. You should have called me... someone. Anyone. Why didn't you call your parents?'

'I promised her I wouldn't tell anyone.'

I look back at him, uncomprehendingly.

'By that point, I wasn't thinking straight,' he explains. 'The infection came on quickly. My thoughts were muddled. I don't remember much, just thinking that I had the flu, that I needed to take painkillers and sleep it off. I may have taken too many painkillers. I don't know. Anyway, after that I only remember going out for milk and then waking up in here.'

I shake my head in disbelief. 'And she had the nerve to come and visit you, to sit there holding your hand, as if she cared.'

Will lowers his eyes. 'I think she does care, Sarah. Too much. That's the problem. She's beside herself with guilt.'

'And jealousy,' I remind him. 'Which is presumably why you're trying to break it off with me.'

He looks at me, thoughtfully. 'I just think it's for the best. You've got Ben to think of. I don't want you caught up in any of this.'

'So, you acknowledge that it's not over? That she hasn't learned her lesson, given up on you and walked away?'

Will hesitates. 'I don't know,' he confesses, eventually. 'I really don't know. But, please, Sarah – do as I ask. It's for your own good. And,' he glances up at me, 'probably for mine, too.'

He closes his eyes and I watch him in silence for a moment. I have questions, more questions, but I can see that our conversation has exhausted him. I wait until I can see that he's asleep, his breath slipping through his open lips in soft gentle gasps. Then I lean over and press my mouth to his forehead and stroke his tousled hair.

As I leave the ward, I pull my phone out of my bag. I have one missed call and a message; Andy, I assume. But when I go into my call log, I see that it's not Andy, but Jaydeep who's called.

I read his text. *Good afternoon, Sarah. I have recovered data from memory card. There is something very interesting for you to see.*

17

When he opens the door, Jaydeep looks beyond me to the Laguna. He spots Ben's head in the back and smiles. Andy gives him a wave.

'It's my son and his father. School holidays,' I explain.

Jaydeep flashes his teeth and waves back at Andy. 'Come. Bring your son,' he then says to me. 'You must all come inside. I will make us some tea.'

I smile, gratefully. 'It's OK, Jaydeep. Thanks, but don't worry. They're going to go on home. I'll get the Tube back later.'

Jaydeep's dark brows knit together. 'No, no, no. I must insist. Your husband and your son are most welcome in my house.'

I hesitate. 'He's not my husband,' I say, to avoid any potential for confusion. 'We're not together. He's just helping me look after our son.'

'Well, he must come in,' says Jaydeep, gesticulating again to Andy. 'All of you. You must all come inside.' His smile widens. 'I think your son will like some *khakra* or some Gujarati *sing bhujia*. Don't you?'

I shoot him a look of apology. 'Erm, actually, Jaydeep, my son can't swallow too well. I can't give him nuts.'

Jaydeep looks disappointed. 'A sandwich, maybe?'

I smile. 'He'll be fine. Honestly. Thank you. He's not very good in other people's houses, especially if he's never been there before. He gets anxious.'

'Oh.' Jaydeep scratches his head and waves at Andy again. I wave too and we watch for a moment as Andy drives away with Ben.

I follow Jaydeep up the steps. Inside, he makes tea, while I sit on his sofa. I glance round the room. The cricket is on again on the widescreen TV and the laptop is set up on the desk with two monitors attached. As I look up at Jaydeep's god Ganesh, who is looking solemnly back at me from the wall above his desk, I wonder, somewhat cynically, what sign Veronica saw that told her that she and Will were destined to be together. Presumably a similar one to the one which told her to glass him in the leg.

Was it just a moment of madness, I wonder, brought on by alcohol, depression and disappointment? Or was it a symptom of something more? I don't know whether Veronica's to be pitied or hated, but if Will doesn't want the police involved, then who am I to interfere? It's his decision to make, not mine, and he won't thank me for getting myself involved. Besides which, he's the only witness to what happened. If he doesn't support a prosecution there'd be nothing the police can do.

Jaydeep walks in with a tray containing two mugs of tea and some bowls of Gujarati snacks. He places the tray on the coffee table.

I nod at the TV. 'How's the cricket going?'

'It's going really great,' he grins. 'CSK was the first out of eight teams to clear the play-offs.'

'Brilliant!' I smile. 'No more prayers needed?'

'Oh, yes.' He smiles. 'I never stop praying. I am praying every day. So,' he raises his eyebrows, 'you want to see what I have found?'

'Yes please.' I pick up my mug and follow him over to his desk.

He fetches another chair and I take a seat next to him, watching as he clicks his mouse onto an icon on his desktop and opens up a software program that I don't recognise. He drags and drops a file onto the main viewer screen and then duplicates the viewer onto the second monitor. A moment later, we are looking, in duplicate, at the exact same view of Packington Street that I saw in the police station a week ago. As previously, to the forefront of the screen, there's the road outside Jaydeep's window. To the right I can see the edge of the railings to the park and the bushes beyond. To the left is the corner of the street that leads up to the Hope and Glory. I peer up out of the window across the road and take in the mirror image of the view, piecing together what lies to the side and beyond the screen in front of me.

The footage begins to play automatically and Jaydeep pauses it. I can see that the time on the clock is 00:07:03 on the first of January. I glance across at Jaydeep and smile. 'I can't believe you've done this.'

He grins back at me, clearly delighted. 'Yes, it wasn't easy. But I eventually found correct software. We were very lucky to find this. You will see.' He presses play. 'OK. So, this is the beginning. Pre-buffer recording. Here,' he waves the mouse pointer over the black band that lies on the lower part of the screen, 'here is the bonnet of BMW and here...' he zooms in a little as the footage continues to play, 'you can see that the vehicle is moving. Rocking.'

'Yes,' I agree.

'So those kids, they are there. Someone is touching the car.'

'They're trying the door handle.'

'Hmm. Yes. As my neighbour said, that is most likely what has triggered the motion sensor.'

Jaydeep zooms back out again. We wait a moment, watching the empty road.

'It's good quality,' I comment.

'My neighbour, he has WDR technology. Better for night-time.'

'Better for us,' I agree. 'And here they are,' I observe, as the first male crosses the front of the screen, just in front of the BMW.

'OK. Nothing happening yet. Keep watching,' murmurs Jaydeep.

The second, taller male in the bodywarmer comes into view, speaks to the first male and then they are joined by the third. As previously, the third male points towards something off camera a few feet away and all three turn to look in the direction that he's pointing before moving off to the left of the screen. The male in the bodywarmer can be seen to bend down briefly before following the other two out of sight.

'Where are they going?' I ask.

Jaydeep pauses the footage, glances at me, then points to the left of the screen in the direction the other two males have gone.

'Off camera here,' he moves his hand and glances up at me again, 'this is where your friend is.'

'Really?' I breathe. 'He's on the footage? You've seen him? You know for sure that he's there?'

Jaydeep nods. 'Yes. I'm sorry.'

I nod. 'It's fine. Carry on.'

Jaydeep presses play. We watch as the male in the bodywarmer straightens back up again. Jaydeep says, 'It's possible that your friend has dropped something out of his pocket and that this kid is picking it up.'

'OK.'

'And now he's dropped it into the road again,' says Jaydeep. 'There. You see. He doesn't want it.'

I squint at the screen. 'Yes, I see.'

We watch the empty road. At the top of the screen, behind the houses, the fireworks have now started to zigzag up into the sky.

'And here comes Jerome,' I say, as, from the left of the screen – from the direction the three males have just gone – the fourth male moves into view.

I peer with renewed interest at the object in his hand, which I know now is a piece of metal railing. As he walks across the screen and crosses the road, I'm unable to rid my mind of the image of what is in all likelihood happening off-screen. If Mark's there, as Jaydeep suggests, he's presumably lying on the pavement by now, surrounded by Jerome's three friends, who are going through his pockets and taking his things.

I turn my attention back to Jerome. Seeing the footage for the second time, with the firm knowledge that Mark's there on the pavement, is causing me to see everything with fresh eyes. If Mark's there, being patted down by Jerome's friends, and if Jerome is just a few feet away with the weapon, I have to concede that the case against him now appears much stronger. And I can't, of course, rule out the possibility that Jerome – who is now swinging and twirling the metal pole around – was the one who put Mark there.

I watch Jerome's body language carefully for clues as he walks over to the opposite pavement, in front of the houses, then steps back into the road again and walks back towards the camera. As previously, he appears distracted, glancing first to his right across the screen in the direction his friends have gone and then to his left, to where the dark metal railings to the park can just be made out. As he comes closer towards the camera, I'm able to track the movements of his eyes. He appears to be more than aware of what his friends are doing. He appears to be acting as lookout for them.

I glance at Jaydeep out of the corner of my eye, to gauge his reaction. This is not looking good for Jerome so far. He'd told me that he was just playing with the pole, but now, on a second viewing, it doesn't really seem that way to me.

'You think he's keeping lookout?' I ask Jaydeep.

'Hmm. Yes. Keep watching,' murmurs Jaydeep, his eyes focused intently on the screen. 'Interesting bit is coming soon.'

'Sure,' I agree, realising that what Jaydeep thinks is interesting might not necessarily be something that helps Jerome.

We continue to watch as Jerome pauses directly in front of the BMW and continues to look in the direction of the park. For two or three seconds he appears to freeze, like an animal caught in headlights. You can see his expression change and his eyes move so that they are gazing intently as he focuses his attention to the right of the screen. I follow his gaze, but I can't see what he's looking at. Is it something off-screen? Is there someone else there?

A few seconds later, he swings his head round in the direction that the first three males have gone as they appear briefly in the left-hand corner of the footage and disappear again, just as quickly, out of view. Jerome then darts forwards to the right of the BMW and after glancing twice over his shoulder, disappears too.

'OK, now they are running,' says Jaydeep. 'All of them.'

I nod.

The sky lights up momentarily as an explosion of fireworks breaks out overhead. The footage then begins to move slowly from left to right in a rocking motion.

'And now, they are pulling wing mirror off of the car,' Jaydeep observes.

'Seems that way,' I agree.

The car continues to rock side to side for several moments. I continue to watch. Nothing happens. And then, just as suddenly, the rocking stops.

'They've gone,' comments Jaydeep. 'You don't see them again. They must have gone in that direction.' He lifts his eyes from the screen and points out of the window directly ahead of us. 'In the direction of the estate.'

'Makes sense,' I agree. 'That's where they live.'

The car is now still, the road empty. I feel strangely apprehensive as I realise what we are now watching for; what must be coming next. Sure enough, a figure soon appears to the left of the screen. My heart leaps a little as I see that it's Mark, now standing and walking as if he's come back to life again.

'Your friend,' says Jaydeep, gently.

I nod, unable to speak. It's a strange, eerie sensation to see him moving around on the screen in front of us, knowing at the same time that he's soon going to be fatally run over by a car.

'This is what I saw from my window,' says Jaydeep. 'This is the exact place he was, what he was doing when I first saw him. He got up from pavement and he was moving around on street corner here, directly opposite my house.'

I nod.

Jaydeep pauses the footage. 'You OK?' he asks.

I swallow, and nod again, more firmly.

Jaydeep presses play. We both watch as Mark walks towards the road at the edge of the pavement in the corner of the screen, then stops and lifts a hand to his face. He appears to lose his footing and stagger and sway a little, before regaining his balance again. I can see why Jaydeep had assumed he was drunk. We watch as Mark steps unsteadily out into the road and then hesitates as he appears to spot something on the ground. He bends down to reach for the object, the same object, it seems, as the kid in the bodywarmer had dropped, but then he stumbles and falls into the road.

For a painful moment, we watch him tumbling forwards, then landing on the ground. My heart jolts. I will him to get up. I know that what's about to happen next is inevitable, irreversible, and yet I find myself willing him to get up again.

And then my heart races as I see it. The four-by-four. It's there and gone in a flash, taking Mark with it. A moment later the road is empty again.

I sit in stunned silence for a moment until the footage cuts out.

I glance across at Jaydeep, a lump in my throat. 'I haven't seen that part before.'

Jaydeep nods. 'The Range Rover has dragged him up to here.' He points off-screen to the right, beyond the park. 'I found him there.'

'Can you go back? Can you freeze frame?' I ask.

'Yes. But it did not capture the registration,' says Jaydeep, sadly. 'I already checked but it's completely wrong angle. I will give you micro SD card so you can look for yourself. But nothing visible from number plate, even enlarged and enhanced.'

'Damn,' I say. I glance at him. 'Thanks for trying, anyway.'

'But there is more,' says Jaydeep, raising his eyebrows.

I frown. 'Really?'

He smiles and takes hold of his mouse and pulls the slider slowly back across the screen. He stops midway through the footage then moves it carefully from left to right a little to find the correct point, then starts it up again.

We watch as the fireworks zigzag up into the sky once again and as Jerome emerges for a second time from the left of the screen and walks over to the opposite side of the road. We watch, again, as he then turns and walks back again, spinning the metal pole back and forth, up and down, for a second time.

This time, watching his movements, I'm less sure about what Jerome is doing. Maybe he's just looking left and right for traffic as he crosses the road. And it occurs to me that there's still no explanation for the fact that the police retrieved this footage from the BMW owner over three months ago, but have only just arrested Jerome. It wouldn't have taken three months for the forensics to come back from the weapon in a case like this. They would have been expedited, pushed to the front of the queue. I wonder which version of the footage was sent by the police to the CPS; the edited highlights that I saw at the police station – or this one, showing the four-by-four at the end?

'Here,' says Jaydeep, pausing the footage as Jerome turns his head towards the park railings. 'What is he looking at? What can you see?'

I lean forward and peer more closely at the screen. 'Nothing,' I confess.

'Watch now. Look just here.' Jaydeep moves the cursor across the screen to some bushes just beyond the park railings. 'Don't watch the kid. Watch the bushes here.' He shakes the pointer over the bushes and then moves back and presses play again. 'OK. How about now? What do you see?'

I open my mouth to say, 'Still nothing', but then I see it. The bushes are moving, just slightly. There's a shade of something pale just about visible behind the leaves.

'Now,' says Jaydeep. 'I am going to zoom in. Like so.'

He zooms in on the railings and the bushes so that Jerome and the rest of the street disappears.

'Now what do you see?'

I shrug. 'I'm not sure, to be honest.'

'OK,' says Jaydeep. 'I have taken screenshot and exported it to PNG. So now I will use other program.' He minimises the dash-cam viewer and clicks on another icon. A picture editing dashboard appears on the screen. Inside it, he opens the screenshot he has taken and zooms in.

'The resolution is not great,' he explains. 'It is heavily pixelated. But you can see I have selected the region of interest and I am resizing it. Then you can play with resolution... like so.'

He creates a new frame within the leafy area that he has selected, zooms in further and moves several sliders on a panel to the right to improve the clarity of what we are looking at on the screen. All we can see now are the bushes, magnified into a dark green mass of leaves and stems. But behind them is the outline of what is clearly skin, and eyes, and the distinctive curve of a face.

I turn, slowly, to face Jaydeep. He looks back at me and smiles and nods.

'There's someone there in the bushes,' I gasp. 'Watching.'

'Yes.'

'Can you zoom in any further?'

He shakes his head. 'This is clearest image we can see. Enlarge any more than this and it becomes over-pixelated.' He zooms in to demonstrate. 'You see. Image is distorted.' He zooms back out again. 'Like this, we can see much more clearly. This is as good as we can get.'

I think about this for a moment. 'Can we see the dash cam again?'

Jaydeep minimises the picture editing dashboard and maximises the dash-cam viewer again. He starts to zoom in on the bushes.

'Wait.' I put a hand on his arm. 'Stay there. Go back out again so that I can see the kid with the pole again.'

Jaydeep zooms back out so that we have both Jerome and the face in the bushes visible in the capture window.

'Take it back a little.'

Jaydeep moves the slider.

The video starts up again. Jerome starts walking towards us, swinging the pole up and down, back and forth. He glances across at his friends then back towards the park railings as he moves closer towards the camera, pausing in front of the BMW and then freezing, as previously, as if he realises that he's being watched. When I'd viewed this the first time, I'd thought there was someone there, off screen, behind the park. But now I can see that it's the bushes he's watching. He's looking directly towards the bushes. He's seen that there's someone there.

'Stop. Can you freeze frame?' I say quickly to Jaydeep.

Jaydeep pauses the dash cam then starts it up again, frame by frame. I'm holding my breath as I watch Jerome's eyes move so that they are gazing intently into the bushes at the image we just saw. And then his expression changes. He's smiling. His arm – with the metal pole – drops to one side. He relaxes, visibly.

A few more frames and I let myself breathe again. I turn to Jaydeep. 'They know each other,' I say.

As I round the corner of Packington Street on my way to the Tube station, the door to the Hope and Glory opens and a dog runs out. It trots towards me, pausing to sniff excitedly at the pavement around my feet.

There's a loud whistle from the doorway of the pub and then a voice, commanding sharply, 'Jasper, come here!' It's the man with the flat cap, the one who was watching me closely when I was last in the pub, when I went out to the yard with the woman with the tattooed eyebrows to buy drugs.

The dog ignores its owner and looks up at me instead.

'Hello, Jasper.' I hold out the back of my hand to let him sniff it, then reach down and grab the end of the piece of string that's trailing behind him in place of a lead.

'Here.' I hold it out to the man in the flat cap. He steps out of the pub, letting the door swing shut behind him. He walks over and takes the end of the string from me.

'Cheers,' he whistles slightly through missing teeth. Like his dog, he's thin, with an unhealthy, undernourished complexion. His hair is long and lanky under his cap, I notice, and there's a growth of stubble over his chin. He cocks his head to one side. 'Do I know you?'

I glance with trepidation towards the battered gate that's screening the alley that leads to the yard beyond. Burdie will have my head on a plate for this but it's too good an opportunity to miss.

'I've been in the pub before,' I say, then add, 'I'm a friend of ST.'

His expression changes, his eyes becoming a little less friendly now. He looks back at me, silently for a moment, then nods and turns to leave.

'Wait. Can I talk to you?'

The man ignores me.

'Please. It's important.'

He licks his lips and tugs the string. 'Jasper. Come on, boy,' he says to the dog, who's still sniffing the pavement around my feet.

'I have money,' I say, under my breath.

I can see him hesitate for a split second, before holding his arm out to guide the dog away from me. He walks on past me, the dog trotting along behind.

I turn to watch him go, expecting him to turn the corner into Packington Street, and head in the direction of the estate, but, instead, he crosses the road away from me and walks along the pavement which circuits the square. I continue to watch him for a few moments, while I try to decide what to do next. As he turns the corner into a narrow street beyond the square, almost out of sight, he turns to look back at me.

I peer back at him. Is he giving me a cue to follow him? I hold eye contact with him for a moment as he lets the dog sniff around on the pavement, then – conscious of the eyes that may be watching me from the pub behind – I turn and walk in the opposite direction, circuiting the square the other way.

Once I've rounded the next corner, out of view of the pub, I cross the road and cut diagonally across the park that centres the square. I exit through the railings at the other side, then hesitate, looking up and down the main street in both directions, to be sure that he hasn't decided to take an alternative route. But I can't see any sign of him, so I cross the road into the same narrow, cobbled street where I'd seen him standing a minute ago. I follow the road to a dead end at the bottom. Facing me is a row of imposing Georgian houses, to my left a tennis court. On my right is a church fronted by iron railings. I hesitate for a moment, then walk through the gate, following a path that weaves round the side of the church, beyond clusters of headstones, to the rear. There, sitting on a bench in the corner of the churchyard, is the man with the flat cap, Jasper lying on the ground at his feet.

I walk across the springy turf towards him, the smell of cut grass blending synonymously in my mind with the lighter evenings. It will be at least an hour before it's dark, thankfully, and, anyway, the atmosphere is a very different one from the backyard of the Hope and Glory. The churchyard feels peaceful and this guy doesn't come across as the type to pull a knife on me.

I sit down on the bench beside him. He doesn't acknowledge me, continuing to focus ahead of him instead, as if I'm a ghost who's risen up from one of the nearby graves. I glance around the churchyard. There's no one else here. The only sound I can hear is the enthusiastic tweeting and caw-cawing of the birds from the trees above our heads. I take my purse out of my bag and open it. I slide a twenty-pound note across the bench towards him. He picks up the note and looks at it, but doesn't respond.

I open my purse again and slide him another twenty. 'That's all I've got,' I say.

He picks up the second note, then folds them both and tucks them into a pocket in the leg of his cargo trousers.

'So, what do you want to talk about?' he says, finally.

'New Year's Eve.'

He looks me up and down for a moment, simultaneously reaching out to stroke his dog. His pale bony wrists protrude from his ill-fitting denim jacket. He has a musty smell.

'So, are you filth?' he asks me. 'Like him?'

I hesitate, then shake my head uncomprehendingly. 'Filth? What do you mean?'

He lifts his head to look at me, his mouth widening into a toothless smile. 'You don't have to play the innocent with me, love,' he says. 'I know he's a copper. I know everything there is to know about Mark Felding.'

'Well, then you know he's dead.'

He nods. 'Yeah. I know he's dead.'

I look him in the eye. 'So, do you know who killed him?'

He raises his eyebrows. I can hear the lisp in his voice again as he says, 'Seriously?'

'Yes.' I shrug. 'Seriously.'

He shakes his head and pulls a face. 'You think if I knew the answer to that I'd be giving it to *you* for forty quid?'

'Who would you give it to?' I ask.

'No one,' he says, firmly. 'Because I don't know.'

'But you were there, right?' I insist. 'On New Year's Eve. You saw Mark Felding in the pub?'

He shrugs. 'Maybe.'

'So, who else was there? Who did you see?'

He makes a point of thinking about this for a moment, then tuts and says, 'Nah. Too long ago. Sorry.'

'OK, forget the regulars.' I look at him pointedly. 'Forget the dealers. I'm not asking about them. OK? Someone else was there in the pub that night, someone who didn't normally go there. Someone who knew Mark as a police officer and recognised him that night for the very first time.'

He glances up at me, questioningly.

'It's what the police told me,' I explain. 'And don't get me wrong. They told me some bullshit, too. But this makes sense to me. I think he was followed from the pub. Someone recognised him and they followed him and then... I don't know. But they hid. They hid in the bushes near where it happened.'

He frowns. 'How do you know that?'

'It doesn't matter how I know,' I say. 'I just want to know who it was. If I can find that person, they may have witnessed what happened to Mark.'

He shrugs. 'Or done it,' he suggests. 'Robbed him. Run him over.'

I think about this for a moment. 'Maybe.'

He sniffs and takes a small pouch out of his pocket, opens it and takes out some Rizla papers and a pinch of tobacco. 'So, who do you think it was, then?'

'Well, I was hoping *you* might be able to tell *me*. Cast your mind back. Who was there? Who did you see?'

He looks at me with disdain. 'Like I said, it was a long time ago. I don't have a photographic memory for faces. And I'm not a bloody spook.' He glances over at the gravestones to the side of us. 'No offence,' he says to them.

'Please,' I say. 'Just tell me what you remember from that night.'

'Not much,' he says. 'It was New Year's Eve. It was a party, wasn't it? The pub was packed. And I'd had a few as well.'

'Did anyone speak to him? To Mark? Anyone you hadn't seen before?'

He finishes rolling his cigarette and lights it. 'Not that I can think of. No.'

'Are you sure? Think carefully. Did anyone come up to him and say hello?'

He rubs his forehead with his bony wrist. 'Well, he weren't there for long, was he? Less than an hour, from what I recall.'

'So, who did he speak to in that hour?'

'No one, really,' he says. 'Just the usual.'

I sigh.

He scratches his chin. 'There was that kid,' he says.

I hesitate. 'What kid?'

'I don't know.' He shrugs. 'Just some kid from off the estate. Some poor fucked-up junkie. Came in, off his head, looking to score. Made a right bloody show of himself, he did.'

I turn to face him. 'How? What did he do?'

'Well, he wanted gear, obviously. Weren't very subtle about it, though. Comes straight in and makes a beeline for Mark. Mark told him he had nothing for him, but the kid wasn't getting it. Even though the pub was packed, he was drawing way too much attention to himself. I could see Larry weren't happy. So, Mark bawled him out, basically. Told him to get out, go home.'

'How old was this kid?'

He shrugs. 'Dunno.'

'What colour?'

'White.'

'And what was he like? Can you describe him?'

He frowns. 'Not being funny, love, but they all look the same, don't they? The amount of kids that come into that pub looking to score. They all wear the same gear: same hoodies, same joggers, same kind of trainers. They're all off their heads. They're just junkies at the end of the day. No one takes any notice of them, unless they're causing a scene.'

I sit back. 'So, what did this kid do? After Mark told him to go?'

He shrugs. 'Well, he went on his way, like he was told, didn't he?'

I think about this for a moment. 'Is it possible that he was angry enough to wait for Mark outside – and to follow him, and attack him?'

He scrunches his face up, dubiously. 'Didn't look like he had it in him, from what I remember. Possible, I suppose. Mark gave him a pretty good bollocking.'

I nod, thinking it through. This doesn't sound like Mark. He was more caring than this. But he was undercover. Undercover-drug-dealer-Mark had to be a lot tougher than his real-life counterpart – especially with Larry standing there behind the bar and other scrutinising eyes on him.

'No one wants users being that obvious about it,' he says.

'No,' I say. 'No. I don't suppose they do.' I glance up at him. 'So, is that it?' I ask him. 'No one else you can think of that spoke to Mark?'

'Nope. Just the regulars. The ones he came to see.'

We pause our conversation for a moment as the church bell tolls seven, then he finishes his roll-up and stubs it out.

'Time's up,' he says, after the clock has chimed its last stroke. He stands up and Jasper stands up too. He taps the side of his nose. 'Pleasure doing business with you. Now, if you don't mind, it's time I was heading back for my tea.'

18

It's a level B rub-down search at HMYOI Barley Hill. I walk through the detector and hold my arms in the air while the female officer moves her hands down my body from my chin to my waist, over my bottom and down my thighs. I then stand in my socks on a mat in front of her while she checks inside my shoes. When she's finished, I pick up my laptop and secure all my remaining belongings into a locker. I put the key in my pocket then walk over to the reception office and hand my driving licence over to the officer behind the desk.

The officer looks up to greet me, her eyes immediately moving down to the laptop in my arms.

I show her the printout of the email from the prison bookings department. 'I have laptop permission. It's all there.'

She cross-references my details with the legal visits list in front of her. 'Jerome Thomas?' She frowns. 'We already have a lawyer on the list for him.'

'Today?' I ask, my heart skipping a beat.

'No.' She clicks her mouse and peers at the screen. 'But we have a list of approved lawyers and you're not on it.'

'Jerome's normally my client,' I tell her. 'I've been through this already with your bookings department. He's been in touch with me. He wants to see me about his case.'

She clicks her mouse and peers dubiously at her computer screen. 'Like I say, you're not on the list.'

'He wants to transfer to me,' I lie. 'I'm here for him to sign the forms.'

She studies my face for a second then gets up and walks over to a colleague on the opposite side of the office. They confer for a few moments before she comes back and pushes a form to me under the glass. 'Sign this please.'

I pull the sheet of paper towards me. It's just the standard form that I've read numerous times, asking me to agree to abide by their rules. I breathe a sigh of relief as I sign it, then add my licence to my locker before walking through the gate into a small sectioned-off area, to wait for more lawyers to arrive. Once a few of us are crammed in together, a prison officer joins us and presses a button, which causes the big glass partition door to slide shut. The officer takes her keys from the bunch attached to her belt and unlocks a gate to her left. We all stream out along a path which crosses an outdoor section of well-tended grass and flowerbeds to the legal visits area, which is housed in a building on the opposite side. We wait, silently, while the officer unlocks a second gate and then a third, locking each one behind her before we move onto the next. Finally, we walk up the stairs and along a corridor to a desk where we are shown into our individual rooms.

Inside mine, I sit down at the table and open my laptop. A few minutes later the door opens and Jerome is shown in. He's wearing a yellow prison sweatshirt under a burgundy visits bib. I notice straight away that his left cheek is badly bruised and swollen and one of his eyes is half-shut.

'My God, Jerome. Are you OK?' I gasp.

He sits down in front of me and looks back at me in silence.

'What happened to you?'

'Got into a fight.' When he speaks, I can see that one of his front teeth is broken.

'You mean, someone started on you?' When he doesn't answer, I say, 'You're not a fighter, Jerome.'

He shrugs.

'Does your mum know about this?'

He shakes his head. 'I don't want her to know. I don't want her to be worrying about me.'

'Well, she *is* worrying about you,' I tell him. 'I spoke to her yesterday and again this morning. She says you're pleading guilty. She's not happy.'

He shrugs, indifferently. 'It's my decision, innit?'

'Is it?' I ask, looking him squarely in the eye. 'Is it really your decision, Jerome?'

He hangs his head towards the table to avoid my gaze. I look hard at him until he looks up again and fixes his eyes on mine. His expression is one of defiance, telling me that he's a big guy who makes his own decisions. But his gummy, weepy closed-up eye tells a whole different story.

'Is this what you want, Jerome?' I indicate his eye. 'Another ten... maybe fifteen years of this?'

He shrugs again. 'It is what it is, innit?

'But you're not guilty,' I say.

'You don't know that.'

'Yes,' I say, softly. 'I do.'

He frowns, then winces, the movement of his facial

muscles clearly causing him pain. 'You don't know nothing,' he challenges me.

I swipe the touchpad of my laptop and click on a folder on my desktop before turning the laptop round to face him. 'Take a look at this.'

Jerome glances at the laptop, on which the dash-cam footage is paused at the beginning. The expanse of road in front of the BMW stands deserted, an empty stage set ready for a drama to unfold.

'I saw this at the police station,' he mutters, derisively. 'I don't need to see it again.'

'Who told you that? Your solicitor?'

He shrugs. 'I know what's on it.'

'So, do you know where the footage was taken from?'

He hesitates, then purses his lips and shakes his head.

'It's taken from the BMW,' I inform him. 'The one that you and your friends were trying to steal.'

He looks back at me, disbelievingly. 'Does it show that? That we tried to steal it?'

I nod. 'Pretty much. But that doesn't matter. You're not here for trying to steal a car.'

He shifts in his seat. 'So, what then? What else does it show?'

'You said you knew what was on it,' I remind him.

He looks back at me and swallows. 'I do.'

I nod. 'Well, so do I, Jerome. I've watched it multiple times. I spent all of yesterday evening watching it. And it's as clear to me as the bruise on your face that the police officer was already on the ground when you and your friends came along.'

Jerome thinks about this for a moment, his cheek

twitching. He runs his tongue over his broken tooth and around his upper gum.

'OK. Show me,' he says, finally.

I press 'play' and move the pointer across the screen. 'So,' I say. 'Here's the park area that borders the estate, off to the right. Here are the railings and the bushes…'

'Yeah, yeah,' he cuts in. 'I know where it is. Just show me.'

We watch in silence for a moment until the first three males have appeared on the footage. I press the pause button and point to the male in the bodywarmer. 'This is Desharn, right?'

Jerome's eyes flicker, but he doesn't reply.

'Watch what he does,' I say.

We watch.

'What's he picking up?' I ask.

Jerome shrugs. 'Nothing.'

'OK, well whatever it is, he doesn't want it. He throws it back on the ground again. See?'

Jerome shrugs.

'Then Romy…' I hesitate and point to the second black male on the screen. 'That's Romy, right?'

Nothing.

'Romy points to something further up the street, on the pavement there,' I point. 'And then… here's you.'

We watch as Jerome enters the footage.

'You've come up along the nearside of the BMW. From the direction of the estate, like your friends. Right?'

I glance up at Jerome but he doesn't respond. His eyes are firmly fixed on the screen.

'So, here you are.' I track his on-screen movements with my finger. 'You've found the metal pole, you've picked it up. You walk up to the corner of the street, you look round, you see what your friends are doing. And you immediately cross the road. You walk away. You're trying to distance yourself. You look awkward, Jerome, as if you don't know quite what to do next. If you turn around and go back home, they're not going to like it. But you can see by your body language that you don't want to get involved. So, you cross the road, instead.'

I glance up at him. He's watching the screen intently. He hasn't yet contradicted me.

'Then,' I continue, 'you turn around and you see something move in the bushes, here.' I point. 'So, you cross back over the road again to take a closer look. You're walking towards the park, looking directly towards the bushes. You're anxious. You're not sure who's there, but there's someone. You start spinning the pole around. Posturing, showing that you're armed. Scaring them off.' I hesitate to wait for the footage to catch up with me. 'And then you stop. You pause and you take a good look at them.' I glance up at him, locking eyes with him, watching for his reaction. He doesn't blink. I pull the slider forward. 'And then, here are your friends again. And... here you all go. Running off back past the BMW in the direction of the estate.

'Then here...' I pause and wait for Mark to appear on the footage. 'Here's the man that Romy spotted on the pavement. The man who happens to be a police officer.'

I look up at Jerome, watching his face carefully. I can see that he's as shocked as I had been to see Mark getting up and staggering around on the screen for the very first time.

'He didn't get run over?' Jerome utters, his face incredulous, confused.

'Yes,' I say, gently. 'He did. That comes next. But, first, watch and see what he's doing now.'

We watch as Mark stumbles around on the pavement for a moment, then steps out into the road.

'See that he's bending down?' I say. 'He's reaching down to pick up the item that Desharn picked up, then dropped again, a moment ago.'

Jerome's eyes move from the screen to my face and back again for a moment, as he tries to work out where I'm going with this.

I pause the footage and sit back in my seat. 'You and your friends all come from behind the BMW,' I explain. 'From the direction of the estate.' I lean forward and point to the right of the screen. 'Your friends all come up along the offside of the vehicle here. They're walking in the road that borders the park. Several moments later you come up along the nearside, here.' I move my hand. 'You're on the pavement. But you're all coming from the direction of the estate. Right?'

Jerome hesitates, then nods.

'One of your friends tries the driver's door of the BMW...' Jerome raises his eyes to object, but appears to think better of it, 'and triggers the dash cam,' I say. 'Meanwhile, you're over here, picking up the piece of metal railing from wherever you found it. On the pavement right there next to the BMW, quite possibly – not too far away from where the police officer fell.'

Jerome falls silent.

'Luke, or Romy, or Desharn – or all three – look inside the vehicle,' I continue. 'It has an immobiliser. They can't steal it. They'd need the keys. They all, one by one, walk round in front of the car. And then Romy spots the police officer lying on the pavement.' I pause. 'Plain clothes, of course. Romy wouldn't have known he was a police officer. And he wouldn't have noticed him before that point, because the man was around the corner, out of sight.' I look Jerome in the eye. 'None of you could have seen him from the direction you were coming. You'd have had to have been walking along Packington Street.'

Jerome looks at me, tight-lipped, neither denying nor confirming that I am right.

'So,' I continue, 'Romy spots the man on the pavement and he and Luke go over to investigate, while Desharn spots something on the ground and bends down to pick it up. I don't know what it is, but it's something that belongs to the man on the pavement, something that has fallen out of his pocket.' I pause. 'We know that, because he's going to get up in a minute and try to retrieve it. It's something important, not to Desharn – he throws it away – but to him, to the police officer. Whatever it was, it must have flown out of his pocket when he was attacked. Or been taken and dropped by whoever attacked him, maybe. But whatever it was, it was already on the ground when you and your friends came along – and, therefore, so was the police officer. He can't have dropped it himself; he was coming from the direction of the Hope and Glory and he hadn't yet walked that far up the road. I have a witness who can testify to that. So, either it flew out of his pocket when he was attacked, back here' – I point off screen – 'or someone had taken it from his pocket and dropped it into the road as they ran.'

I pause, waiting for Jerome to speak, but he just looks at me in silence.

'Either the person who attacked the man stole from him and gave one of you the wallet – or, alternatively, you disturbed whoever it was as you all came along, causing his attacker to run and hide in the bushes before he'd had time to take anything. That would be my guess. And then Romy and Luke see the man lying on the pavement and go over and empty his pockets. Then you all run off back past the car again, stopping to pull the driver's wing mirror off on the way.'

Jerome studies my face, silently.

I fold my arms. 'You clearly came from the estate, Jerome. And you clearly then went straight back to the estate again afterwards. Whereas the police officer came from the direction of Hope Square – as did the car that then runs him over.'

I lean over and press 'play'. We wait for just a moment. My words are soon borne out. The four-by-four comes whizzing across the screen, taking Mark with it as it goes.

Jerome's jaw drops. His good eye widens and horrified tears immediately appear. 'I didn't... I didn't... that wasn't me, driving that car,' he stutters.

I nod. 'I know. It couldn't have been you. Like I said, the car came along Packington Street from the direction of Hope Square. Whereas you and your friends are down here,' I point, 'heading back to the estate. It's a dead end down here,' I tell him. 'I've been on Google Maps. There are just the garages and the flats which all lead on to alleys. There's only one road, which goes the opposite way out of the estate. Even if you'd had time, it's not possible to get back round to Hope Square from the estate without going around the park and coming back along Packington

Street in the opposite direction.' I pause for breath. 'Which you didn't. Which means that you can't have been in that car. You didn't attack him – and you didn't run him over. This footage proves it. I can help you. I can take it to your solicitor, get him to point all of this out to the CPS.'

When he shakes his head, his entire body shivers. 'No,' he says, his face now animated. 'You can't show this to anyone.'

'What?' I peer back at him, dismayed.

'You're forgetting about the wallet,' he says, anxiously. 'The wallet was in my room.'

I nod. 'I know. But you didn't steal it. You didn't go anywhere near the police officer. You came straight up to the street corner and immediately crossed the road. The footage proves that.'

Jerome looks into my eyes and says, firmly, 'I was there. It's joint enterprise. That's what my solicitor said.'

I sigh. 'Joint enterprise to what, Jerome? To theft? OK. Maybe – if you knew that your friends were going over there to steal his wallet and you helped or encouraged them in some way, and I'm not convinced that you did. But if none of you attacked him or threatened violence towards him then it's not robbery, it's not GBH. It's not murder and it's not manslaughter. It's just theft. Just an opportunistic theft. Don't get me wrong, it's not pleasant, stealing from an injured man and leaving him there on the pavement, but it's a far cry from what you're accused of. You need to tell your solicitor that.'

'And snitch on my mates? No way. I ain't no snitch.'

I look back at him, questioningly.

He says, 'If I didn't go anywhere near that man on the

pavement, how can I explain how the wallet got into my bedroom without snitching on them?'

I watch his face. 'So, they did take the wallet, then?'

'I never said that, did I? I never told you that.' He flushes, as he realises that he, in fact, did tell me that, albeit indirectly. He leans forward, anxiously. 'You can't tell anyone,' he says. 'You can't tell anyone what I say to you without my permission, right? That's what you're always telling me. That's what your rules say. You're not allowed.'

I nod. 'That's right. I can't.'

He heaves out a sigh of relief, then lowers his eyes and stares at the table as he says, 'OK. So, they took the wallet.' He hesitates. 'And his phone and that, too.' He looks up, plaintively. 'But they didn't know he was injured, I swear down. And we didn't know he was no police officer. We just thought he was some wasteman who'd drunk too much and fallen over on his way back from the pub. We didn't know he was hurt. We thought he was just sleeping it off. Desharn saw the keys in the road and he thought they might be for the BMW. It was a nice whip. A nice car,' he clarifies. 'We only wanted to take it for a spin.'

He stops, abruptly.

'You thought the BMW was his?'

He nods.

'But the keys in the road were only his house keys,' I continue, for him. 'So, Romy and Luke went over to check his pockets – and found the wallet instead?'

Jerome flushes, then nods. 'But you can't tell anyone,' he insists. 'I was there too. It's joint enterprise, innit. I'm pleading guilty to whatever my... my other solicitor says. And I ain't taking no one with me.'

'But you didn't do anything wrong.'

He shrugs. 'I was watching their backs, wasn't I?'

I shake my head. 'No. You weren't. I don't believe that. You didn't like what they were doing. You just had no power to stop them. And then you see someone in the bushes, and you start to figure it all out.'

He hesitates. 'What? What are you talking about?'

'You know what I'm talking about, Jerome.'

I reach out for my laptop and swipe the touchpad. I open up the file that Jaydeep has sent me enclosing the resized screenshot of the bushes.

'Here.' I point to the outline of the person that's hiding behind the leaves. 'Who's this?'

Jerome looks at the image and shakes his head.

'You know him,' I say, watching his expression.

He hesitates, fixing his eyes on the image and avoiding my gaze.

'You know him,' I repeat. 'And you're not scared of him. If it was a stranger hiding there, you'd have told your mates to leave the wing mirror alone and you'd have all scarpered. But you knew him – and you didn't care. For two or three seconds you stand there watching him. You take a really good look at him. And when you see who it is, you're unconcerned. You smile. You smile because you know that he's not going to grass any of you up.'

Jerome shrugs.

'Why? Why is that? Who is he? Is he someone from the estate?'

He shakes his head.

'Is he a drug user?' I ask.

Jerome looks at me as if I'm mad.

I say, 'Jerome, I think this might be the person who attacked the police officer.'

He shakes his head, dismissively. 'He wouldn't attack no fed.'

'So, you *do* know him?' I jump on this.

He shrugs.

'Why are you protecting him?'

'I'm not.'

'So, why don't you tell me who he is, then?'

Jerome looks hard at me. 'He ain't no one. He ain't nothing to me. But, like I said, I ain't no snitch.'

For a moment, we sit there looking at each other silently across the table.

'Man ain't no snitch,' he says, finally, his words coming out like some kind of creed. He looks me hard in the eye. 'No matter what anyone does. Even if they stab you, you don't say nothing to the feds. It don't matter whether you're in this place or on the outside, you ain't never gonna be safe if word gets out that you're a snitch.'

I look back at him, silently. I don't have an answer for this.

He nods towards my laptop. 'So, is that it? Is there anything more to see?'

I shake my head.

He slides his chair back. 'Then we're done here, innit?'

I watch as he walks over to the door and opens it, beckoning to the prison officer who's standing nearby.

'Jerome, just think about what I've told you,' I say, uncertainly. 'We'll sort it. We'll get protection for you. I can help.'

He turns in the doorway. 'No offence,' he says. 'But you can't. And you ain't my solicitor any more.'

*

When I take my phone out of my locker there are three missed calls. One is from the office. The other two are from Gareth's mobile, made over an hour ago. My heart sinks as I gather my things together and walk out into the car park. I've been rumbled; it's obvious. Gareth's onto me.

I wait until I'm inside my car before I return the call.

'Where are you?' he asks abruptly.

'Barley Hill,' I say.

A pause. 'What are you doing at Barley Hill?'

'Visiting a client.'

'Which one?'

I hesitate.

'This is not good enough, Sarah,' he says, angrily, before I can speak. 'There's no prison visit in the diary. And now we've got two ready to go at Colindale and no one to cover them.'

'Where's Matt?'

'Matt's got a private client coming in.'

'OK,' I say. 'I'm on my way.'

'Not if you're at Barley Hill you're not.' I can hear him huffing on the other end of the line. 'You're going to be at least an hour and a half, if not more.'

'I'm sorry.'

'So, who've you been to see?' he asks, again. 'And why wasn't it in the diary?'

I hesitate. I can't lie to him. 'Jerome Thomas,' I say.

The line goes silent. 'Jerome Thomas?' he repeats, suspiciously. 'Something new, is it?'

'No,' I confess.

His voice rises angrily. 'Not the same case? Not the section 18?'

'Yes, only the victim has died and it's actually a murder and—'

'But we can't represent him!' Gareth cuts in, impatiently. 'I told you to get rid of him. You told me he'd gone elsewhere.'

'I know I did. And he has. But I needed to see him. I have some new evidence that proves he's not guilty, and—'

'How did you get in?' he demands.

'I booked a visit.'

'A *legal* visit?'

'Yes,' I admit. 'I needed my laptop.'

'And you said you were his lawyer?'

I sigh. 'Not exactly. I said he wanted to transfer to us. Which he might have done,' I say, quickly, 'if I could have persuaded him to plead not guilty. But he's frightened. He's being influenced. He's been beaten up.'

'You're giving advice?' says Gareth, his speech rapid and excitable. 'You can't give advice, Sarah! Not if we don't act for him. And we can't act for him. We have a conflict, remember? I expressly told you that. What do you think the judge would have to say about this?'

'I don't know,' I concede.

'You've just spent the morning visiting a client for whom we're not allowed to act. You've used your position to do so and, on top of that, I'm going to have to instruct an agent for the two cases at Colindale while I'm paying you to drive around the countryside.'

'I'm sorry,' I say. 'I'll make up the time. I promise.'

'That's just not good enough!' Gareth bellows down the phone. 'What the hell's going on with you, Sarah? You're never in the office. No one has any idea where you are half the time. And now this.'

'I'm sorry,' I say. 'But I can explain.'

'Get back to the office,' he says, sharply. 'We need to talk. No diversions, no trips to the hospital. No fictitious clients. I want you straight back here – right now.'

19

When I get home, Andy has already picked Ben up and fed him. He pours me a glass of wine then heats up my dinner while I take Ben into the front room. I push a DVD into the Panasonic, then sit him on the sofa with his iPad. I take a long sip of my drink before placing the glass on the window sill behind the blind, where it's hidden from his view. Ben watches me solemnly for a moment, then his face breaks into a grin.

'I know,' I say. 'Mummy's crying. You think crying's funny.'

He lets out a giggle. I put my arms around him, burying my face in his wild, wonderful hair.

He pushes me away. 'Get off me, Mummy,' I say for him, letting him go. 'No hugs. No hugs for you today.'

I get up and pull a tissue out of my bag and blow my nose and wipe my eyes. I reach up behind me and pull my wine glass out from behind the curtain and take a long, deep swallow.

'So, what happened?' Andy asks, as I go into the kitchen.

He places a plate of food on the table. It's some kind of pasta dish again. It smells nice, but I'm feeling too churned up to eat.

'I got suspended.' I pull out a chair and sit down.

'You've got to be kidding me?' Andy grabs a beer from the fridge and sits down opposite me.

I shake my head. 'I wish I was.'

'How? On what grounds?'

'I made an unsolicited visit to a former client.'

'What does that mean?'

'Being a solicitor is a bit like being a prostitute,' I explain. 'You're allowed to do it, but you're not allowed to tout for business. It's against the rules.'

Andy shoots me a sympathetic smile. 'You might want to use "taxi driver" as your example when you explain that to anyone else.' He puts his elbows on the table. 'So, did you? Tout for business?'

I peer at him. 'No. But I broke the rules.'

Andy frowns. 'I don't understand.'

I pick up my fork and give my pasta a stir. 'This is the kid I told you about, the case I had to give away. He's fifteen and he's making decisions that aren't the best for him, ones that will ruin his life. His new solicitor doesn't get it. His mum wanted me to go and see him but I should have booked a social visit, not a legal one.'

'So why didn't you?'

'I wouldn't have been able to get my laptop in.'

'Why did you need your laptop?'

'I had something to show him and… and anyway, the point is that my intentions were to help the client. That's all. But I shouldn't have done, because I also know the victim. So, it's a conflict. And blah-dee-blah. Which would make it ethically immoral, of course, if I were advising the client to plead guilty to something he hadn't done, but I was doing the opposite. And as for touting for business, he was my client before Gareth made me give the case away. I never tout for business. Matt – my colleague – does it all the time, with Gareth's blessing. He's the biggest prossie going – pinches other firms' clients all the time. Brings in loads of new business this way, which is why Gareth loves him.'

'So why the double standards?'

I look up. 'Because Gareth hates me. That's why.'

Andy looks dubious. 'Why does he hate you?'

'Because I don't toe the line. Because I work the cases according to what's best for the client, not what's best for business. I break the rules – but not the ones he wants me to break. And, because I have Ben, basically. I can't stay late in the office or go to the police station at night like Matt does. Therefore, I don't bring in as much money as Matt does, and that's all he cares about. Why have one me and one Matt when he could replace me and have two Matts and more money?'

Andy shakes his head. 'But he can't get rid of you because of your parental responsibilities. That's discrimination.'

'It's not if you dress it up as something else. Trust me, if I fight this, he'll find plenty of ammo against me. Strictly speaking, I broke the rules. I used my position to get into a young offender's institution. Telling the truth about why he wants rid of me is not going to help anything.'

'So, what happens next?'

I shrug. 'Wait and see, I suppose. He'll have to go through the formal procedure. There'll be a hearing in a couple of weeks' time.'

'It'll be OK,' Andy says, reassuringly. 'Come on. Eat up. Your food's getting cold. I'll go and give Ben his meds and get him into bed and then I'll pour you another glass of wine.'

I've just eaten my last mouthful of food when my phone rings. It's sitting on the table in front of me and I pull it towards me. It's a withheld number. I push the slider with my thumb before putting the phone to my ear.

'Is that Sarah?' asks a familiar voice.

'Speaking.'

'It's Becky here, from the Critical Care Unit at St James's Hospital.'

My heart skips a beat. 'Is it bad news?' I ask her, breathlessly.

'On the contrary,' she says, cheerfully. 'Will's made a really good recovery. We're about to move him off the ICU and onto a ward.'

I drop my fork and clap my hand to my mouth, my spirits lifting. 'Oh, my goodness, that's amazing news!' I hesitate, my heart sinking again, just a little. 'But he didn't want to tell me this himself?'

She hesitates. I can hear the trepidation in her voice as she sidesteps my question. 'He wanted you to know that he's out of any immediate danger. It's early days, obviously, but I think we can safely say that we've beaten the infection and that he's on the mend.'

'Thank you, Becky. Thanks so much for letting me know. Please tell him that I'm so happy for him… and that I send my love. And that I'd love to hear from him. Please… ask him to call.'

When I hang up, Andy's standing in the doorway behind me. He asks, 'Who was that on the phone?'

'It was the hospital.' I turn around to face him, unable to hide my pleasure. 'Will's better. He's out of the woods.'

Andy's face falls as he sees mine light up. 'Why are they

phoning you?' he frowns. 'I thought he didn't want to see you?'

'It seems he wanted me to know that he was on the mend. He would know that I'd be worried about him. But it's really good news. They're moving him out of the Critical Care Unit and onto a ward.'

Andy takes another beer out of the fridge and sits down at the table opposite me. 'That's great,' he agrees, his tone flat. 'Let's hope someone gives him a haircut,' he adds, sarcastically.

I look across the table at him. 'What did you say?'

Andy flushes and licks his lips. 'I just meant... nothing. It was just a joke.'

I watch him as he picks at the label on his beer bottle, avoiding my gaze. A patch of crimson spreads up his neck and a hard lump appears in his throat.

'What did you just say?' I repeat my question.

A faint smile crosses his face. 'Calm down,' he mutters. 'It was just a joke.'

'You've been to the hospital? You've been in to see him?'

He exhales heavily and closes his eyes.

'Andy?' I persist. 'What the hell's going on?'

'It was just a throwaway comment.'

'OK.' I lean my arms on the table. 'I'm going to ask you one more time. And don't even think about lying to me. I want to know when you went to the hospital and I want to know what you said to Will.'

He hesitates for a moment, then looks up. 'I was passing, OK? I thought it was time that he and I met. We had a chat, that's all.'

'And you didn't think to tell me about this?'

'It was no big deal.'

'What did you talk about?'

He shrugs. 'Nothing much.'

I lean forward. 'Andy, I swear, if you don't tell me the truth, I'll go down to the hospital right now and I'll ask him myself.'

Andy looks at me blankly for a moment, then lets out a sigh. 'We talked about you, and me, and Ben,' he says. 'He agreed with me that Ben needs his father, and that... and that you and I should have some space, a chance to try and work things out.'

I shake my head in disbelief. 'Are you serious? You went in there flexing your muscles and warned him off?'

Andy groans. 'I didn't have to flex any muscles, Sarah. He's a reasonable bloke. We just talked and I told him that I still loved you and that I wanted a chance to put things right with you for Ben's sake, and he agreed with me.'

I leap up out of my seat and lean over him. 'Of course he bloody agreed! What choice did he have? He could hardly fight you, could he?'

'It wasn't like that. It was a proper chat, man to man—'

'Where you both decided what was best for me!'

'For Ben—'

'Don't give me that! This wasn't about Ben. This was about you getting what you wanted – and, meanwhile, getting to lord it over a sick man in a hospital bed!'

He shakes his head at me, his face expressing hopelessness in the face of my fury.

'When did this happen?' I ask.

'I dunno.' He blinks. 'A couple of weeks ago, maybe?'

'Before I went to visit him last time? The time you took me?'

He nods.

'Jesus fucking Christ, Andy!' I hiss at him. 'How could you do that to him? He was in intensive care, fighting for his life!'

'And I was fighting for my family,' says Andy, stubbornly.

I spin round and open the fridge door. I grab the wine bottle, then pour myself another glass. 'I am so angry with you,' I say. 'You had no right to interfere in my life.'

He says, 'I'm sorry. OK? But, be honest with yourself, Sarah. Things have been pretty good between us, haven't they? We've been getting on really well.'

'As friends, Andy! You're the father of my child.'

He shakes his head. 'There's something there between us, still. I can feel it and I know you feel it too.'

'It's Will that I want to be with! Not you!'

My words come out too abruptly and the colour drains from his face. His lips tighten.

'You need to wake up, Sarah,' he retorts. 'He's got someone else. Why do you think he agreed to give you up so easily? Why do you think he didn't fight for you?'

I feel my pulse quicken. 'What are you talking about?'

'I saw her at the hospital,' he says. 'She was there when I arrived.'

'Who? Who was?'

'A woman. A young, elegant, attractive woman.'

I shake my head. 'That's not his girlfriend.'

Andy leans across the table towards me. 'She wasn't his aunt, Sarah. She was all over him like a rash!'

'She's his ex-girlfriend,' I say, defensively. 'He told me all about her. He doesn't want her there. But she won't leave him alone.'

Andy smiles and lifts his eyebrows. 'Bloody hell, Sarah. And you really fell for that?'

'Don't patronise me,' I shoot back. 'You have no idea what you're talking about. Their relationship is complicated.'

Andy looks me up and down. 'He's really sucked you in, hasn't he?'

I turn away, putting the wine bottle back in the fridge. I take several long deep breaths in and out and count to ten. 'Was he OK?' I ask, when my trembling subsides. 'When she was there? How did he seem?'

'What do you mean, "How did he seem"? He seemed like a bloke who'd got a beautiful young woman draped over him. He was in his element.'

I take another deep breath. 'Right. OK. I don't have to discuss this with you. I'm going to check on Ben.'

When I come back into the kitchen, Andy hasn't moved. He's picked the label off his beer bottle and shredded it into a pile on the table in front of him.

'I know what this is about,' he says to me as I enter the room.

'What are you talking about?' I say, sharply. 'You've interfered in my relationship and I'm pissed off with you. That's what it's about.'

He shakes his head. 'Except that it's not. It's about more than that. You've got a chance to be happy, but you're not going to take it. You're picking a fight with me to push me away and you're chasing after someone who doesn't want you, instead.'

I pick up my empty plate from the table and place it in the sink. 'Don't be ridiculous. You don't know anything about Will and me.'

'And what do *you* know about him, Sarah? Not a lot, by the sound of things.'

I turn the tap on. 'Like I said, it's complicated.'

He nods. 'And complicated is good, isn't it? It's like a red rag to a bull where you're concerned. There's another woman on the scene and you're not going to let her steal him away from you, like your stepmum did to your dad.'

'Oh, please.' I spin round to face him. 'Not this again. Can't we just talk about what's happening in the present without coming back to my supposed Daddy Issues every time?'

'Are you denying you have Daddy Issues?'

I rinse off the plate in the sink. 'I have ex-boyfriend issues,' I spit.

'You have issues with men, Sarah. You have issues with me, you have issues with your work colleague, you have issues with your boss…'

I spin round to face him. 'I can't believe you, Andy. I just confided in you. How dare you turn it around and use it to score points off me!'

He shakes his head and his face softens. 'I'm not trying to score points, Sarah. Can't you see? I'm trying to stop you sabotaging our relationship. I'm trying to make you see that it's your dad that you're really angry with, not me.'

'And doesn't that just suit you, that little theory?' I put my hands on my hips. 'A woman stands up to you and she has "Daddy Issues". While you… you're just the innocent victim of my craziness, my unpredictable moods. How well does that work out for you, Andy? You get to project your shit onto me and then absolve yourself of any responsibility for what you did. It's every man's perfect solution when a woman stands up to him: call her crazy, tell her it's her hormones. That way, you always get to be right and I always get to be wrong.'

Andy smiles and looks down at the table.

'What's so funny?'

'It's just the generalisation: the way you talk about "every man" wanting to push women down.'

I shake my head. 'That's not what I said…'

'Yes, you did.'

'Well, then, I meant you!'

Andy nods, slowly. 'But not Will.'

I shake my head. 'No. Not Will. Will has never called me irrational. And he doesn't bring up my father every time we disagree.'

'Ah, yes.' Andy swings back on his chair. 'Perfect Will. Bad Andy. Well, give it time. We all fall from our pedestal eventually.'

I look at him in silence for a moment, then lick my lips. 'OK. You've convinced me.'

He looks thrown, briefly. 'Of what?'

I say, 'I'll admit it. I wasn't sure about Will. I wasn't sure about you. There have been moments when I've wondered whether I wanted the same thing that you wanted. I've asked myself that question: should we make another go of it? But, you know what, Andy? You've now made me surer than I've ever been that it's truly over between us.'

He looks at me for a moment, then looks down at his beer bottle, shaking his head.

'And, you know what else?' I continue. 'Men have issues with their fathers too. They just express it differently.' I add, 'Usually with violence.'

And then it comes to me in a flash.

Andy is speaking, but I don't hear what he's saying. A rush of adrenalin surges through me as I realise what's been right in front of my nose all along. I stand next to the sink, looking at Andy, watching his lips move, watching him swinging back on his chair and playing with the pieces of his shredded beer label as he makes his next point, authoritatively.

For a moment I stand stock-still, looking at the bits of paper and hearing, but not listening, to the monotone of his voice. And then I stride down the hallway into the living room, where I pull my laptop out of its bag and open it up on the coffee table. I click on the file containing the PNG image of the face in the bushes that Jaydeep had created from the dash-cam footage. I look hard at the features, the shape of the nose and eyes and the outline of the jaw. And then I open up Google Maps.

Andy appears in the doorway. 'What are you doing?'

I look up at him. 'I have to go out. You need to look after Ben.'

I jump up and grab my bag then walk past him into the kitchen to get my phone. He follows me. 'What do you mean?' he asks. 'What's going on?'

'It's work,' I explain.

'How can it be work? You've been suspended.'

'I know, but… something's come up,' I say. 'I need to go.'

Andy shakes his head. 'You can't just dump on me, Sarah.

You can't just go out whenever you feel like it. You have a child.'

I grab my phone from the table. 'And so,' I retort, 'do you.'

I type out a text to Georgina and then a second one to Burdie.

Andy hovers by the table, watching me. 'No,' he says, after a moment. 'I'm not having this. You've made your choice. You're not going to use me as a babysitter whenever it suits you.'

I look up at him, aghast. 'You're not my babysitter! You're Ben's *father*.'

Andy is defiant. He stands in front of me, his shoulders raised. 'You're not using me, Sarah. I don't see why I should do you any favours. You said it was over between us.'

'Between you and me!' I scream at him. 'Not between you and Ben!'

'But—'

I face him head on. 'I'm not asking you for a favour here, Andy. I'm asking you to be a father. It's unconditional. There are no rewards, no prizes, no strings attached. We're parents because we chose to be parents. That's it; end of story. And, most of the time, it's mucky and it's dirty and it's fucking hard work! If Ben's lucky, you'll see what I see and you'll realise that the occasional smiles and fun and rewards that you get from him in between make it worth it, because – as they say – love really does conquer all. But you can get rid of whatever rosy image you have in your head of the three of us sailing off into the sunset together and living happily ever after, because there isn't one big sunset, Andy, and there isn't any happy ever after. There's only this, what we're living, right here, right now.' I wave my arm expansively around my kitchen. 'I'm sorry to disappoint and disillusion you. Whatever hopes you had of there being something between us – well, I'm sorry to shatter those for you, too. But I am *not* going to thank you for looking after your own son. If you truly believe that fathers are important enough to fuck up our lives, then stick around this time and be one!'

My phone bleeps. It's Georgina. I open up her message, my heart pounding; it's as I thought.

Andy opens his mouth to speak, but I don't wait for his answer. Instead, I push past him out of the kitchen and down the hallway and out of the front door.

20

It's just a ten-minute drive to Karen Felding's house at this time of the evening, a straight route south down to St John Street and then off towards Goswell Road. I talk to Burdie en route, making my case to him through the Bluetooth, persuading him – finally – that my plan is best and – finally – he agrees.

When Karen opens the door and sees me standing there, her face first expresses surprise, then pleasure. 'How did you know where I live?' she asks.

'A little birdie told me,' I say. 'I need to talk to you. It's important.'

Her face is drawn and tired, her brow furrowed in confusion, but she steps back and opens the door wide. 'Come on in.'

I follow her down the narrow hallway to an open-plan kitchen-diner at the rear of the house. The floor is dark oak, the table French farmhouse. Orange cotton drapes hang from the window and there are pretty matching cushions on a sofa set back from the patio doors.

'You have a lovely house,' I say.

'Thank you.' She gathers up a pile of papers and magazines from the grey and white linen tablecloth and invites me to sit down. 'Can I get you anything?' She nods towards a bottle of red wine that's open on the counter. 'That's what I'm drinking if you fancy a glass?'

'I'm driving. Just tap water please.'

She goes over to the sink and picks up a tumbler from the drainer.

'Where are the children?' I ask.

'Soph's at a friend's, having a sleepover. Jack's upstairs.'

'How are they?'

She fills the tumbler with water, then hands it to me before pulling out a chair and joining me at the table. 'Oh, you know. Doing OK, I think. It's early days. We're taking it one step at a time.'

I take a sip of my water.

'How's your boyfriend?' she asks me.

'Much better. They're moving him onto a ward.'

'That's great news,' she smiles. 'Such great news. You must be over the moon.'

'Yes,' I agree. 'I really am.'

Her eyes track mine. 'So, what is it?' she asks. 'Has something happened?'

I look down at my hands. 'You've probably heard that a fifteen-year-old kid has been charged and locked up for attacking Mark. He's going to go to prison for a very long time.'

She nods. 'I've been told that there's not going to be a trial.'

I look at her intently. 'And how do you feel about that?'

She picks up her wine glass. 'How do I feel? Relieved, of course, as anyone would be. No one wants to have to drag it all up and live through it a second time, do they?'

'No,' I agree. 'No, they don't.'

342

'So,' she says, taking a sip of her drink. 'After all the speculation, all the talk of targeting by...' she shrugs, 'whoever Mark was involved with. In the end, it seems it was just a random attack, after all. A robbery. Nothing more.'

'Was it?'

She glances at me, questioningly. 'Well, yeah. It seems that way.'

'And what about what happened after that? The hit-and-run?'

'Unfortunately, that remains unsolved. It's unlikely that they'll ever find the culprit.'

'Is that what you've been told?'

She nods. 'There's no car. No CCTV. No witnesses. So, no leads.'

'There's a witness,' I point out.

She takes a sip of her wine. 'He didn't get the vehicle registration though.'

'He got a partial registration.'

'It's not enough.' She shrugs. 'Even if they spoke to every registered owner of a four-by-four beginning with that partial registration that hit a local camera around that time...'

'I know. It's not enough to be sure they've got the right one. There aren't enough cameras to cover every exit and every entrance to that street.'

'Right.' She looks at me, sideways. 'They'd need the vehicle. The forensics.'

'Who told you all this? DCI Hollis?'

'Yes.'

'And what did he tell you about the vehicle?'

'Just that it's never been found. And that there's not much prospect of finding it. That at least they've caught Mark's original attacker. And that I should accept that and try to move on.'

I nod. 'Good answer.'

She looks up at me, mistrustfully. 'Sarah, why are you here?'

'I'm here,' I say, 'because the kid who's been charged isn't the person who attacked Mark.'

'What do you mean?' Her expression is more weary than surprised. 'What are you talking about?'

'He didn't do it.'

She frowns. 'But he's pleading guilty. Why would he plead guilty to something he didn't do?'

'Because he's protecting other people and because he's frightened,' I tell her. 'Because he's been badly beaten up in prison. Because being a snitch is as good as being dead in the culture that he lives in. It's the very worst thing that you can do. It's worse than killing someone.'

She looks at me, dubiously. 'So, how do you know all this?'

'I just do.'

She sighs heavily and rubs her forehead. 'Well, I'm sorry, but... I don't know what you want me to do with that.'

I say, 'I want you to tell me what happened here on New Year's Eve.'

She looks at me, alarmed. 'What? What are you talking about?'

I meet her gaze. 'I'm talking about DCI Steven Hollis,' I say. 'About your relationship with him.'

She flushes then, her neck turning crimson. She lifts

one hand to her throat, taking hold of the pendant that's hanging there and rolls it back and forth. 'What's that got to do with anything?'

'Everything. It's got everything to do with it.'

'I don't understand—'

'Just tell me,' I insist. 'About you and him.'

Her eyes flash. 'It's not a relationship,' she says. 'It's not like that. Steve's a friend, that's all.'

'That's not really true, though, is it?'

She looks back at me, her chest rising and falling. After a moment, she lets go of the pendant and pushes her chair back. 'I think you need to go now,' she says.

'There's evidence,' I say, quickly, 'that suggests that Steve Hollis may have been driving the four-by-four that night, the one that hit Mark.'

She looks up at me, her shoulders rigid, her mouth gaping. 'What are you talking about?' Her words come out in a single breathless gasp.

'There's also evidence that he was here that night, shortly before it happened. He was here. He came to your house.'

Her eyes widen and a flicker of fear crosses her face. 'What evidence? Who has this evidence?'

'I'll tell you,' I say. 'But first, you need to tell me what happened that night when Steve came over.'

Karen reaches down and drags her chair back in. She closes her eyes, resting her elbow on the table and leaning her forehead into the palm of her hand. 'He was comforting me,' she says, softly, after a moment. 'That's all.'

'On New Year's Eve?'

'After Mark left.' She looks up at me, her eyes expressing

a blend of guilt, disbelief and fear. 'He just started coming over to see if I was OK, if the kids were OK.'

'And then?' I prompt her.

She hesitates, her eyes moving back and forth, her voice wavering uncertainly. 'And then last Christmas... it became obvious that he wanted something more.'

'And you didn't?'

She looks into her lap. 'I was confused.'

'So, something *did* happen.'

'He told me that he wanted to be with me. I told him that I still loved Mark. But... but that night, we'd had a few drinks and...' She looks up at me, her expression one of bewilderment, then says, 'I was upset. I was upset that Mark hadn't come over to see his children. The kids were upset. Jack was upset,' she corrects herself. 'Sophia... well, you know how it's been with her. And I felt bad for them. So, I asked Steve what was going on with Mark. I wanted to know, once and for all. Steve told me that Mark was seeing someone else, that he was having an affair. I was really hurt. And... and I guess I was lonely.'

I nod. 'So, you and Steve...?'

'It was nothing, not really.' Her lashes flutter and she inclines her head. 'We kissed. It was just one kiss, here in the kitchen. That's all it was. And as soon as it happened, I wished it hadn't. I knew it was a mistake and I told him that. I told him that I wasn't ready for anything, that I still loved Mark and then... and then I went to check on the kids, to tell them it was nearly midnight, to ask them to come downstairs to watch the fireworks, and I realised that Jack wasn't in his room. He wasn't in the house. And that's when I realised that he must have walked in and seen us, that he must have been upset and that's why he'd gone.' She looks up at me. 'Jack didn't like Steve being here. They didn't get on.'

'Why not?'

'He thought he was here too often. He thought he was trying to take his dad's place.'

I nod. 'So, where did he go?'

'To look for his dad.'

'What time was this?'

'Some time after eleven. I don't know for sure what time he left the house. Like I said, I thought he was in his room.'

'And then Steve went after him?'

She looks up at me. 'Yes. As soon as we realised Jack was missing, he said he'd go and find him. He went to Mark's flat in King's Cross and then he drove around the streets looking for him.'

'And did he find him?'

She nods. 'Yes. Eventually.'

'What time did they get back?'

'Some time after one, I think. It's hard to remember now.' She lifts her glass to her lips and takes a sip, but I notice that she's trembling.

I say, 'You must have known what car he was driving that night.'

'No.' She shakes her head, quickly, but her eyes look frightened. She puts down her glass and twists her hands together on the table top. For a moment she doesn't speak. 'No,' she says again, eventually. 'He just turned up here. I let him in. I didn't see his car.'

'Really?' I look at her, doubtfully.

'Really.' She turns to me, speaking rapidly. 'Steve went to find Jack. He brought Jack home. And then he left. I was inside the house when they came back. I didn't see his car. I didn't look outside. I wasn't concerned about anything else at the time, except that he'd found my son and brought him home safely. I was grateful to him. He said that it was best if he left, and I agreed. Jack was upset. But Jack was home. That's all I cared about. I didn't see Steve again that night.'

'You must have questioned it?' I suggest. 'Later. When you found out what had happened to Mark? Come on, Karen. Steve leaves the house and, half an hour later, Mark gets run over…'

'No.' Karen shakes her head. 'No. Why would I? He's a police officer. He's Mark's boss, for God's sake. He told me that Mark was in all kinds of trouble with drugs and the wrong kinds of people… why shouldn't I believe what he said?'

'If you know anything you're not telling me, Karen, now is the time to say. They're onto him,' I warn her.

Her eyes flicker. 'Who are?'

'Someone within the police,' I say. 'It'll go to Professional Standards. It's all going to come out. It's only a matter of time. If you helped in any way, now's the time to say so. Assisting an offender is a serious criminal offence. Steve Hollis will go to prison for this and, if you helped him, so will you.'

'No!' cries a voice from the doorway, emphatically. 'She didn't help! She didn't know! She's not involved in any of it. Leave her alone!'

My eyes move across to the doorway in the direction of the voice.

Karen reaches out her hand, her face crumpling. 'Jack, darling. It's all right. You don't have to—'

Jack steps into the room. 'They can't send her to prison,' he says to me, his eyes shining, animatedly. 'She hasn't done anything wrong.'

'Jack, it's OK. Sarah didn't mean it,' begs Karen, her eyes glossing over. 'I'm not going to prison. You don't need to worry about anything.'

Jack continues to look at me truculently. I turn to Karen. 'And did you ask Jack what car Steve was driving that night?'

She shakes her head, looking genuinely baffled. 'I don't know. I honestly can't remember. Did I, Jack?'

Jack nods. 'Yes. You did.'

She looks from Jack to me and back again.

'And what did you tell me?'

Jack says, 'I told you that he was driving a Merc.'

She nods at me. 'Well, there you go, then.'

'But he wasn't,' says Jack, tears shimmering in his eyes.

Karen turns, wide eyed, to look at her son. We both do.

'What car was he driving, Jack?' I ask him gently.

'A four-by-four,' he replies, silent teardrops rolling down his cheeks, streaking his skin. 'A Range Rover Sport with blacked-out windows. I saw it happen. It was him. It was Steve. He's the bastard who ran over my dad.'

Karen lets out an agonised groan and slumps forwards, her arms splayed across the table. Her elbow knocks into her wine glass, which topples over and a streak of red seeps into the tablecloth.

'Mum!' Jack cries out, rushing over to her side and flinging his arms around her. 'It's OK, Mum. Please don't cry.'

Karen reaches up and encases her son in her arms and then

pulls him down into the seat next to her. 'What happened, Jack?' she sobs. 'Tell me what happened.'

I reach over and pick up the wine glass, then get up and fetch a cloth from the sink and press it against the tablecloth.

'Jack?' Karen persists, her face stricken, her hands still gripping his upper arms. 'How could you have kept this from me?'

'He made me!' cries Jack. 'He made me keep quiet. I wanted to tell you, all this time, but I couldn't.'

'Why on earth not?'

'I was scared. He said we were in danger.'

I slide back into my seat. 'Danger?'

Jack glances at me. 'He said that some police operation had gone wrong and that there were people after us, criminals with guns who would kill us, and that we had to get out of there.'

'What people?'

He shakes his head. 'I don't know. But he said if I told anyone what had happened to my dad, they would come and find me and—' He breaks off and frowns, despairingly, at his mother. 'He said they would kill you and Soph!'

'Jack…'

'I wanted to go back and help my dad,' he pleads with us both. 'But he wouldn't let me! I told him it wasn't gangsters that did that to my dad. I told him it was me. It was all my fault!' Jack collapses forward onto the table, his head in his arms, his shoulders heaving as he sobs, violently.

I look across at Karen, who looks back at me. All the colour has drained from her face.

She reaches over and rubs Jack's shoulders. 'Jack, what

are you talking about? Talk to me. Tell me what happened.'

Jack continues to cry, shaking his head, his face in his arms.

'I think I know, Jack,' I venture. 'And I don't think you meant for any of it to happen. You were angry and you were upset. But there's a kid who's locked up for this, a kid who is very frightened. I can help you. I promise I'll help you. But you need to tell us the truth.'

Jack looks up, eventually, and licks the teardrops away from his lips. I reach down into my bag and pull out a bundle of tissues, handing them to him.

He wipes his eyes and looks at his mother. 'I saw you,' he says, unhappily. 'You and that bastard. I saw you, kissing in here. It made me so angry. I wanted to find my dad. I wanted him to know that he needed to come home, that his arsehole of a boss was moving in on you.'

Karen sighs, heavily, and closes her eyes.

'So, I went to his flat. And I saw him. He was just leaving as I turned into his street.'

'You told me you didn't find him!' says his mother, her eyes springing open, aghast.

'I know,' he says. 'But I did.'

'What time was this?' I ask him.

'I dunno. Late.' Jack looks up at his mother, plaintively. 'I wanted to know where he was going. I wanted to know what he had to do that was so important, more important than being with us. So, I followed him.'

I nod. 'To the pub. To the Hope and Glory.'

He nods and sniffs, choking back another sob. 'Yeah. To the pub.' He turns to his mother. 'He went to the pub, Mum. I was so angry. Instead of being with us for New Year, like he promised, he went to the pub.'

Karen glances at me, then back at her son.

'So, you followed him in?' I suggest.

'Not straight away, I didn't. I waited for him outside for a while.'

'For how long?'

He shrugs. 'I dunno. I can't remember. Some old boy came along and gave me a can of lager. I drank that first, and then I went in.'

Karen shakes her head. 'Jack, you'd already been drinking my brandy. I found the empty bottle in your room.'

'Were you drunk?' I ask him.

He nods and starts to cry again. 'All I could think about was, why didn't he care about me?'

'Jack, he did care about you,' Karen protests. 'He loved you!'

'Not enough, though,' cries Jack, his words tumbling out, angrily. 'Not enough for him to be pleased to see me, not enough to stop him from going ape and bawling me out in front of his friends. Telling me to go home, talking to me like I was just some stupid kid that he wouldn't even piss on if I was on fire!'

'I'm sure he didn't—' begins Karen, wiping her eyes.

'He did, Mum! You weren't there! First of all he ignored me, pretended like he didn't even know me! And then he was, like, shouting under his breath at me. "Go. Get out of here."' Jack hisses, to demonstrate. 'Like that. Like he didn't want anyone to hear. Like he was ashamed of me. And then, when I wouldn't go, I saw him looking at his friends, and then he started shouting out loud, calling me names, telling me to fuck off. He said I was just a useless, pathetic piece of shit.' He breaks off and looks at his mother, heaving a sob.

'Everyone was looking at me. He made me feel like... that big.' He indicates with his fingers.

Karen claps her hand to her mouth and says, 'Oh my God, Jack. What did you do?'

Jack frowns and shakes his head, his eyes glistening. 'Well, I went, didn't I? I left the pub, like he told me to.'

'Where? Where did you go?' Karen presses him.

Jack lowers his eyes. 'I went back along the road, the way I came.' He hesitates as he thinks about this for a moment. 'I was gonna go home, and then... and then the fireworks started and I changed my mind. I thought to myself, No. He's not getting away with this. He's not going to talk to me like a piece of shit, showing off in front of all his friends like that, acting like I mean nothing to him, acting like he doesn't even have a son.'

Karen looks at him in silence. Her fingertips remain pressed against her mouth.

'So, I decided to wait for him.' Jack's eyes begin to well up again as he looks up at us.

'Where?' I ask.

'On a bench next to a... kind of park. There were railings. I dunno...' He heaves a sigh. 'I was just trying to figure it all out. You know, should I go back to the pub, or should I go home?' He leans forward in his seat and puts his head in his hands. 'I was so messed up,' he murmurs through his fingers. 'I can't really remember what I was thinking.' He hesitates. 'But then I heard noises and I realised I was near this estate.'

'The Pear Tree Estate?' I suggest.

He nods. 'Yeah. I think so. I've never actually been there. I just know about it because some kids from school live there and it's meant to be rough.'

'So did you see anyone you knew?' I ask.

He nods. 'But, first, I just heard some noise and some shouting and stuff in the distance. I got frightened.' He looks up. 'I mean... I was on my own and I didn't know who it was. Some of the kids in my year have a bit of a rep, and...' He hesitates. We wait for him to continue. 'I looked around and I saw this loose railing that was sticking out from all the rest of them that go round the park and so I pulled it out just to arm myself, like, in case anyone started on me. Something like that. I don't remember much, just that I was frightened and so I decided to get away.'

'Where did you go?'

He thinks about this for a moment. 'I crossed the road. I think I was going to go back to the pub again, but then I heard someone coming and... I hid behind a car.' His face falls and tears spring to his eyes again. He looks up at his mother. 'And then I saw him. It was him. Dad.' He lets out a sob. 'Seeing him just walking along like that, going home, with his hands in his pockets, all casual, as if nothing had happened, like he didn't even care – it just made me so... so fucking angry again.'

We wait as Jack places one arm on the table and sobs into the sleeve of his hoody. It's Adidas, I notice. Light grey, white stripes on the arm. Logo on the chest. Generic. The sort you'd see any fifteen-year-old kid wearing, no matter where he was from – be it a two million pound Georgian townhouse off St John Street, or an overcrowded council flat half a mile up the road on the Pear Tree Estate.

Karen reaches out and strokes his back. 'Just tell us, Jack,' she says.

'I don't know... I don't know...' he mumbles.

Karen looks up at me, and sighs. Her eyes brim with tears.

'Jack.' I lean forward. 'It's going to be OK. I'm going to help you. Whatever it is that you did... you can tell us.'

He lifts his head. His cheeks are red and streaked with tears. 'I don't know what happened to me,' he wails. 'I wasn't thinking. I just totally lost the plot. He walked right past me and it all just got to me. Him not caring about us, him bawling me out like that. I was off my head, and it's no excuse but I didn't know what I was doing. I was just burning up with anger inside. And before I even knew what I'd done, I'd gone up behind him and... I hit him with the bit of railing.'

'Oh my God, Jack.' Karen's hands fly up to cover her mouth. Her eyes peer at Jack, wide and frightened, over her fingertips.

'Where did you hit him?' I ask.

Jack looks up, a bewildered frown etched across his forehead. 'On his back. I meant to hit him on his back. But he stepped off the kerb into the road and I... I got him on the head. But I thought he was all right! I mean... he turned around and he looked at me. In the eye. He saw me,' he says, sobbing hard again. 'I was the last person he saw. And then he fell on the floor. I didn't even think I'd hit him that hard.' He shakes his head. 'I've... I've never hit anyone before. I didn't know that he would fall over. But he fell onto the pavement and he must have banged his head. He was out cold.'

'Oh my God, Jack,' his mother says, again.

'What did you do?' I ask.

He looks up at me, then at his mother, his eyes full of

remorse and self-loathing. 'I ran. I ran away, up the street. I was scared. So, I ran. I'm sorry,' he sobs, looking up at his mother, plaintively. 'I'm so sorry. I didn't mean it. I didn't mean to hurt him. I don't know what the hell happened to me to make me do a thing like that.'

Fresh tears trickle down Karen's cheeks. She puts her head in her hands.

'And then you went back?'

Jack turns to face me. 'How did you know that?'

'I've seen some footage,' I say.

'It's on CCTV?' He sits up in alarm.

I shake my head. 'No. None of that's captured. But I've discovered that there was someone hiding in the bushes next to the park,' I say. 'I'm guessing that was you.'

He nods, swallowing. 'I realised I'd made a mistake. I realised my dad was hurt.' He hesitates. 'I've been over this in my head so many times and I think… I think I was expecting him to get up and chase after me, but when he didn't, I got really scared.'

'So, you came back to help him?'

He nods.

'But then you saw some boys from the estate. Boys from school?'

He nods again. 'There was a few of them. I was on my own. It seemed like they were out looking for trouble.'

'So, you hid in the bushes?'

'Yeah. I was just waiting for them to pass. And then I was going to go back and help my dad.'

'But they saw him first and emptied his pockets?'

He nods and sniffs, his jaw quivering. 'Yeah.'

'And when they'd gone?'

'I went to cross the road again, to go and help my dad, but then I saw him getting up. He was OK.' His face brightens, the hope and fear that he'd simultaneously felt now shining in his eyes. 'He started walking towards me, and I waited and I didn't know what to do. I mean…' He looks down at his hands. He picks up a tissue from his lap and wipes his nose. 'Part of me was so glad that he was OK and part of me was really worried that he was going to be so angry with me. And then I saw him bending down to pick something up – and then he fell forward, into the road. And he didn't get up again.'

Karen removes her hands from her face. She looks as though she's seen a ghost. 'Jack,' she murmurs. 'Oh my God, Jack.'

'What did you do next?' I say.

'I didn't do anything!' he cries out. 'I didn't do anything, did I? I should have gone and helped him but, like a big fat coward, I ran!'

His sobbing starts up again.

I ask, 'Why did you run, Jack?'

'Because I… I saw a car coming and the headlights were on me and I was scared. I was really scared.' He shakes his head. 'The car started speeding up, like it was chasing me. I didn't know who it was, I just got paranoid and I thought someone was after me.'

'But it was Steve Hollis? In the four-by-four? Is that right?'

He nods.

'He was out looking for you?' I ask.

He nods again, unable to speak for a moment. 'But I didn't know that,' he says. 'I didn't know that then. I was really scared. And so I ran.'

'And that's why he sped up. He was driving down the street looking for you and then he spotted you and sped up to catch you up.'

Karen closes her eyes.

'I didn't know it was him!' cries Jack, turning to her.

'I know…'

'I just panicked,' he explains. 'And I… I ran. I looked over my shoulder and my dad was still in the road, and I thought the driver would see him and stop. But he didn't. He was going too fast, trying to catch me up and so I stopped but…' He catches his breath. 'But he didn't! He just went right over him. He just drove straight over my dad.' Jack lets out a strangled cry.

Karen closes her eyes again. Tears squeeze out and stream down her cheeks. After a moment, she reaches over to Jack and takes his hand, curling her fingers round his. 'You should have told me! Why didn't you tell me?'

'He wouldn't let me,' Jack sobs.

'He stopped? Picked you up?' I ask.

Jack nods. 'I got in the car and I screamed at him. I said, "You've just run over my dad!" and he was like, "What the fuck…?" And I told him that we had to go back. But he said that we couldn't.'

Jack covers his face with his hands.

'Did he say why?' I ask.

Jack sobs, gently, into his hands for a moment. Karen looks over at me and then at her son. She reaches out and removes one hand from his face.

'Why, Jack? What exactly did he say?'

Jack shakes his head, and sniffs as he casts his mind back. 'He was panicking, saying it was too late. I told him, "You're an arsehole, Hollis!" and I tried to get out of the car… but he locked the doors and he just kept driving and he told me that we couldn't stop, that we couldn't go back now.'

'Why?'

'Because it was too dangerous. That's what he said. I was, like, "What are you on about? You need to turn this car round, right now!" But he didn't. He wouldn't. He just kept driving. He said that he didn't have time to explain it to me, but that there were people after my dad – drug dealers, dangerous people, and that we couldn't be in that street any longer. He said he'd call someone, get help.'

'And did he?' I ask.

Jack nods. 'He made a call. He made a couple of calls. Some police talk that I didn't really understand. But I remember he said, "I need a car." And then he told me someone had called an ambulance. That it was on its way.'

'So, then what happened? Where did you go?'

'To some industrial estate. It was dark. We waited and then a car pulled up and Steve told me to stay there and he got out and the other driver got out and they spoke for a moment and then we swapped cars with the other driver.'

'Did you get a look at him?' I ask.

He shakes his head. 'He had his hood up. It was dark.'

'And then?'

'And then Steve took me home. I told him that we had to go to the police. I told him that it was my fault that my dad was lying in the road. I told him what I'd done and that we both had to turn ourselves in, but he said that it was more complicated than that and that we both needed to keep quiet. He said that the ambulance was with my dad by now and that we just had to keep this to ourselves.' He takes a deep breath. 'That's when he told me that my dad was a drug dealer and that he had people after him – and if I told anyone what had happened, the drug dealers would come after me, too, and that they'd kill my sister and my mum.'

I shake my head. 'None of that's true, Jack. Your dad wasn't a drug dealer. He was an undercover police officer – a bloody good one too. He was trying to *catch* drug dealers. But he was also trying to protect you. That's why he shouted at you in the pub. He was undercover at the time. He needed you to leave because he was afraid you'd blow his cover. He didn't want the drug dealers to know that you were his son. He loved you so much. He didn't want any harm to come to you.' I glance at Karen. 'That's why he left you and your mum and Soph and went to live in that flat.'

Jack looks up in surprise. 'So, Steve was telling the truth about them coming after my dad?'

I shake my head. 'I don't think so. I think that Steve made a mistake in running him over and was trying to cover his own back.'

Karen shakes her head. 'He was drunk. He'd been drinking that night. That's why he didn't stop. And the spineless shit has been using a fifteen-year-old boy to keep his dirty secrets for him.' She turns to Jack. 'You've been carrying this by yourself, all this time?' she sobs. 'It must have been torture for you. I'll bloody kill him! I'll bloody kill him when I get hold of him.'

As she speaks there's a knock at the door. My phone beeps simultaneously. Karen gets up to answer the door.

I look at my phone. The text from Burdie says, 'He's at the door.'

I call his number. 'We've got it,' I say. 'We've got enough.'

'Right,' he says. 'OK.'

'Jack,' I say, looking into his swollen, tear-streaked face. 'It's all about to kick off. But you don't need to worry about anything, OK? I want you to stay calm. I'm going to make sure you're looked after. You have to listen to me. Please stay calm. You're going to be OK.'

He nods.

At that moment, I hear the sound of a male voice in the hallway and the high-pitched tones of Karen's voice. I jump up and move out into the hallway, where Karen is raining blows over Steve Hollis's body while he tries to catch hold of her arms. As I pull her away from him, he looks from me to Karen and then sees Jack standing in the kitchen doorway behind me, and I can see the hostility in his face.

I open the front door and let Burdie in.

'What are you doing here?' Hollis swings round and sneers at him. 'You're not a police officer any more. You don't have a badge. You should be home, right now, tucked up in your little bed.'

'Ah, no. I don't think so,' says Burdie, pleasantly. 'I wouldn't miss this for the world.'

'I'm ordering you—' begins Hollis, but he doesn't finish, because the hallway is now flooded with uniformed police officers. And then Hollis is being cuffed – rear-stacked, I notice with pleasure – and, as he struggles violently, he is winded with a deft knee to his stomach and is taken to the floor.

DS Trafford leans back in his chair. 'Let me get this right,' he says to Karen. 'He went out to find your son. At your request?'

Karen shakes her head. 'I didn't have to ask him. As soon as he realised that Jack was missing, he was gone. He was out of the door. He was thinking of his police operation, not my son. I didn't ask him to run over my husband and I didn't ask him to leave him in the road and bully my son into harbouring his horrible secret for months. It must have been eating him up inside.'

'But,' says DS Trafford, 'if there was a risk that your son would blow your husband's cover and if DCI Hollis was trying to prevent that from happening – and if he then believed at the point that he ran your husband over that your husband had been attacked by a member of the criminal fraternity and that – for his own safety and for the safety of your son – he had to leave the scene—'

'My husband is dead because of him!' explodes Karen. 'Because of them! Because of all of them at SO21! Mark should never have been in that pub that night. He wanted out. He should have been listened to. He should have been safe. SO21 put their undercover operation ahead of my family, they intruded in my life and they treated me and my children as if we were nothing, as if our lives were unimportant. If they'd listened to Mark, if they'd taken his warnings seriously, if they'd got him out of the dangerous situation they'd put him in, I'd still have my husband – and my son would never have been driven to do what he did. Not only that, but Hollis deceived me and he manipulated me and he wormed his way into my affections by making me think that Mark didn't care about me, when nothing could have actually been further from the truth. I have a witness to all of this.' She flings her arm out, and points at Burdie who's standing near the door.

'Hollis perverted the course of justice,' chips in Burdie. 'He hid the car. He hid the evidence. He prevented Jack from admitting what he'd done and allowed you to arrest and prosecute an innocent person. Not trying to tell you how to do your job here, Jim, but you've got plenty, mate.'

Trafford looks across at Burdie and colours slightly. He then turns to Karen. 'You know that we're going to have to take Jack in for questioning.'

She swallows and nods.

Trafford stands up as a uniformed officer appears in the doorway.

I jump up. 'You don't need to handcuff him.'

Trafford turns to the officer. 'No cuffs.'

We watch as Jack is led down the stairs and out to the police car. My heart aches for Karen as the officer holds his head and guides him into the back seat.

pause for breath. Will props himself up onto his elbows and I tuck another pillow behind his head.

'So, what about Sinclair?' he asks, leaning back again.

'Totally implicated by Hollis in his police interview. Fortunately for us, the code of honour that Jerome lives by doesn't apply at SO21. "Man look out for himself,"' I mutter, in a gangster accent.

Will shoots me a bemused smile.

'A reduced sentence in exchange for his cooperation was clearly way too tantalising for Hollis to resist,' I continue. 'Suffice to say that conspiracy charges will be brought against Sinclair and some lesser charges against a number of others at SO21.'

'Why would Sinclair – or anyone else – get involved, though?' Will asks. 'Why not just look out for themselves and turn Hollis in?'

'They'd bodged the op. Hollis had run over their own undercover officer and the chief prosecution witness in the case against the crime gang. It wasn't just Hollis's head that would roll for this. They'd made a real mess of everything and it would reflect badly on all of them. Sinclair's reputation was on the line. How was he going to explain this to his superiors? Better to make it Mark's fault instead of theirs – make out that he blew his own cover, that the crime gang had got to him. It was the logical answer. Mark was so severely injured that he was unable to tell it otherwise. And they'd already discredited Burdie, turned both him and Mark into bent coppers, drug dealers. The only witness to the truth of what Hollis did was Jack, who was easily silenced by pretending that the OCG were after him.'

'And were they? Is there any evidence that the gang had wind that Mark was a copper?'

'Not according to the informant. When I talked to him, I realised that he totally bought it, Mark's act. He really thought Jack was some junkie from the estate, as Mark had intended. Mark played his part well. If his cover had been blown, if Larry or anyone else in the pub had worked out who Jack really was – who Mark really was – the informant would have gone to ground. He'd have been begging for protection, not offering his services again – which he is, by the way. Burdie says he's still ratting, that the net's closing in again on the OCG.'

'And Jack?'

'He's been granted full immunity from prosecution in exchange for his evidence against Hollis. It's been decided that there's no public interest in prosecuting him, given the role of the police in what happened to his father. The Feldings have been offered witness protection. They're going to be moving away out of London to the countryside.' I muse, 'It looks as though Sophia's going to get her horse, after all.'

'So, did Burdie get his job back?'

I shake my head. 'He's got his disciplinary hearing this

week, but in all the circumstances he shouldn't have too much trouble convincing the panel that he was set up. He was coming up for retirement anyway. I expect he'll take it.'

Will grins. 'And get his pension back.'

I smile too. 'Looks that way.'

'So, what's happened to Jerome?'

'It looks as though the prosecution may accept a plea to attempted theft of the BMW on a joint enterprise basis – no names, of course. They agreed to review the other charges with a view to discontinuance, on the basis that SO21's conduct calls into question the reliability of the evidence in relation to the stolen wallet.'

'As in, someone – including the police – could have planted it behind Jerome's radiator?'

'Precisely. I don't think they want to go there, frankly. Jerome's been released on bail until the next hearing. No pressure, but if you could try and get yourself out of here and back on your feet by the twentieth of July, that would be extremely helpful. I had to instruct a different barrister for the plea hearing, of course.'

Will frowns. 'What are you talking about? You're suspended. And it wasn't your case. How are you involved in any of this?'

I grin. 'Oh. Didn't I mention? When Georgina went to visit Jerome and told him what had happened, Jerome sacked his solicitor and insisted he wanted me to represent him instead.'

'But…'

'Judge Kingsley readily agreed to allow the transfer to my firm, on the basis that a gross miscarriage of justice could have occurred, had I not involved myself. He commented that I knew more about the case than anyone else – including the police – hence was the only person who could do Jerome justice in my negotiations with the CPS. He also agreed that there was no longer any conflict of interest in acting for Jerome. On the back of that, Gareth had no choice but to make a finding in my favour in the employment proceedings and lift the suspension against me.'

Will's eyes are shining as he lifts them to meet mine. 'In that case, Ms Kellerman, I should be delighted to accept the brief. I have a question, though,' he says, scratching his chin, thoughtfully. 'What was Jerome's role in all of this? As far as SO21 were concerned, I mean?'

'OK,' I say, leaning forwards in my seat. 'I've been thinking about this too. Initially, they had no need to arrest anyone. They had a sighting of the vehicle – which could easily be a drug dealer's vehicle – and a sensitive undercover operation, hence a legitimate reason for keeping it from the press. Within hours, SO21 had taken over the investigation from Major Crime and by that time the SO21 four-by-four had been removed from the picture, taken to a repair shop somewhere. Twenty-four hours later the dash-cam evidence is seized from Jaydeep's neighbour and the weapon is recovered. The dash cam is of no use to them. They can sit on that along with the partial VRN. The weapon has Jerome's fingerprints all over it but Hollis knows that Jerome wasn't the one who attacked Mark. They're not going to arrest Jerome for it. It's the crime gang that's done this, not Jerome, right? Mark's blown his own cover and they want him to take the blame. That's the story SO21 are telling on a need-to-know basis and that's the story they're sticking with. There's no public pressure to find the perpetrator, after all. There's only Karen, who is already angry with Mark and continues to be fed all sorts of lies about him by Hollis, all designed to turn her against her husband. Otherwise, no one is demanding a result... in fact, no one outside SO21 even knows where Mark is...'

'Until...'

'Until I walk onto the ward and start poking my nose in. That's when the game changes: Mark's identity is out. People are going to start asking questions, now – nurses, doctors, family members, other police departments. So, now, there's a new cover story: it was a random hit-and-run. There's a sighting of the vehicle, so let's suggest it was stolen, and let's have Jerome for it. He's the perfect suspect – he has form for nicking cars, he lives on the estate, he's there on the dash cam and his fingerprints are on the weapon. Questions are now being asked as to where the car is – so they'd better make an arrest. Of course, that's just a cover story for me and anyone else who's asking. In the upper ranks of the Home Counties Regional Crime Squad, they're still telling the story that Mark blew his own cover and what happened was a revenge attack from the crime gang. Sinclair, meanwhile – realising that I'm asking too many questions and drawing way too much attention to the four-by-four – pays me a visit and lets me in on the "truth", or the story he's been telling his bosses. On realising that Jerome – their patsy – is my client, he offers me a deal, tells Major Crime to take no further action on the car theft. They'll have to make the car go missing another way. He warns me away from Karen, worried that I'll get to the truth about Jack and – in turn – Hollis. He thinks he's got it all wrapped up, covered himself and Hollis. But I don't back off. They're now worried. They need a suspect and they need a conviction, so they dig out the dash-cam footage and fingerprint evidence and call in Major Crime to arrest Jerome again. Legitimately, this time, or so it seems on a first glance at the footage. If they, at least, get Jerome for the assault on Mark, then they might be able to divert interest away from the four-by-four.'

Will nods. 'So, how did you work out that it was Jack hiding in the bushes?'

'Jerome knew him. He admitted that he knew the person in the bushes. He said that person was "nothing to him" but he clearly knew who he was. "He wouldn't attack no fed," he said, which was an odd thing to say. Why not? Why wouldn't he? Then something Andy said got me thinking about how, as well as loving his dad, Jack had to be pretty angry with him that he'd left the family just like that – especially after they'd been so close. He had to be pretty mad that his dad had just abandoned him, had kept breaking his promises to him. He'd failed to turn up for Christmas and then done the same thing again on New Year's Eve. And then it all fell into place: Jack's moodiness, his spitefulness towards his sister, his surliness with his mother, the way he snapped at Hollis when they were all standing next to Mark's hospital bed. Jack's sister had told me he went to Goswell High. Something Sinclair said and a quick Internet search told me that Goswell High is the catchment school for the Pear Tree Estate. A text to Georgina confirmed to me that it was indeed Jerome's school, too. Jack and Jerome might not be friends but they'd be in the same year. They'd know each other by sight. Put that together with Hollis being at Karen's house that night and… I suddenly realised that it was Jack. That it had to be him.'

'And the four-by-four? Has it been found yet?'

I nod. 'It was moved out of force. All cleaned and fixed up, of course, as Burdie suspected. No forensics – clean as a whistle and bumper and undercarriage as good as new. But with Hollis's admissions and Jack's evidence they'll have enough to convict. It was certainly enough for me to get the CPS to drop the most serious charges against Jerome and to agree to review the rest.'

Will nods. 'So, who was the barrister you instructed for his plea hearing?'

I take a deep breath. 'It was a pupil, actually.'

'A pupil?' Will peers up at me.

'From Dean Street Chambers,' I add.

Will looks back at me, his face falling. 'No, Sarah. No way.'

I grin. 'She did a pretty good job, actually.'

'Why?' Will gasps. 'Why would you instruct Veronica?'

'You weren't available.' I shrug.

'Sarah!'

'You know what they say,' I tell him, smiling. 'Keep your friends close, and your enemies closer. Better to pour hot coals on her head or whatever it is that the Bible tells you to do. Awaken her conscience instead.'

Will doesn't look convinced.

'Look, Will.' I lean forward. 'I spend my working life – as do you – persuading judges to give people a second chance. I realised that I'd be a hypocrite if I didn't give her the same benefit. If she's truly sorry, she'll stay away from us.'

Will flinches just a little at the word 'us'. 'Sarah,' he sighs, searching for the right words. 'You know how much I want to believe that. Maybe in time, once she's had a chance to move on, find someone else...'

'And what, we put our lives on hold until then? Will, she put you in hospital! You nearly lost a leg. You could have died, but you didn't. Don't let her take another minute of your life away from you. Every minute is precious. If nothing else, what happened to you has shown me that.'

Will gives me a sideways look. 'So, how was she? With you, I mean.'

'Surprised, I think, that I'd instructed her.' I grin. 'Baffled, even, I'd say. Of course, she got the brief via her clerk and when we met at court we didn't talk about what had happened. We kept it strictly professional... just talked about the case. She doesn't know for sure that I know anything. But, she'll have wondered. She'll still be wondering. And she'll no doubt be wondering if I'll talk to her bosses at chambers, or to your parents, or... or if I'll persuade you to talk to the police.'

Will shakes his head.

'But she also seemed quite pleased,' I continue. 'You remember how it was when you were a pupil, trying to get solicitors to instruct you, to build up your reputation, get your career off the ground?'

'Yes...'

'So, as well as being baffled, she'd have also been dead chuffed, I imagine, that I gave her the brief.'

Will scratches his chin. 'Well, yes. She would,' he concedes.

'And, as I say, she did a good job,' I smile. 'So, my "message" to Veronica is that – so long as she behaves herself – I'll be sure to instruct her again.' I seek out Will's eyes. 'Or I could just send an anonymous note to her at chambers saying "I know what you did." Would that work?'

Will looks startled. 'You'd better be kidding me!'

I laugh. 'Of course I'm kidding. That would be illegal.'

'Bloody hell, Sarah. Are you trying to give me a heart attack?'

'No, I'm not. I'm trying to make you see that we have two choices here: we run and hide or we live our lives.'

He exhales deeply. 'So… what about Andy?'

I shrug. 'He won't stab me.'

'No, I mean…'

'Or you,' I say. 'Especially if you keep wearing your lucky socks.' I point down to the end of the bed at the socks that I've just tugged onto Will's feet. They're the royal blue and red superhero socks that he was wearing when we first went to court together on our last case.

Will smiles, defeatedly, and takes hold of my hand. 'Will he stick around?' he asks.

'I don't know. I honestly don't know,' I sigh. 'I hope so. Because, in spite of everything, in spite of all the hard work, I think he knows that Ben is a gift. If he leaves again, he'll miss out on Ben's wonderful uniqueness, on everything that Ben has to teach him about himself and about the world. Andy will get used to the idea of us,' I reassure him.

He sighs. 'I wish I could say the same about Veronica.'

'Will… what are you going to do? Are you going to spend your life looking over your shoulder? What she did to you was an awful, awful thing. What you've been through is horrific. But if you don't leave this hospital and start living the life that you want to live, then everything you've been through will be for nothing. If I'm not worth the hassle, then that's fine. But if it's not me, it will be someone else. It's like having children. You have to establish boundaries, don't you? And you have to do that straight away.'

He nods and squeezes my hand tighter. 'Come here then,' he says. I snuggle in closer and he kisses me.

'Talking of life being too short,' I say. 'I've handed in my notice.'

'Seriously?'

I smile. 'The minute Gareth withdrew my suspension I told him that I no longer wanted to work for him.'

Will looks slightly alarmed. 'What did he say?'

I laugh. 'Not a lot. He acted surprised and said that he was sorry to hear that. He wasn't,' I point out. 'He was glad. But not half as glad as me.'

Will frowns. 'Where will you go?'

I shrug. 'I don't know yet. But I'll find something. Maybe I'll freelance for a bit. Maybe I'll set up my own law firm. Maybe I'll set up my own cleaning company, or my own corner shop. I've got three months' contractual notice to work it out. It's a little scary financially, but sometimes you have to take a leap of faith… right?'

He smiles. 'If your name's Sarah Kellerman, then, yeah. I'd say you probably do.' He pulls me towards him. 'I'm glad he didn't lock you up,' he says, smiling.

'Who?'

'Lock-'em-up Long. For contempt of court. Who knows how things would have turned out?'

I shake my head and pull a face. 'Doesn't bear thinking about.'

Acknowledgements

Huge thanks to my fabulous editor, Madeleine O'Shea, to everyone else at Head of Zeus and to Sophie Robinson, who was there in the beginning. I owe so much to my dear friend Tracey Ann Wood – yet again – for her meticulous early edits and to Simon Kingston for the detailed feedback, support and advice. Ian Astbury – thank you, once again for fitting this book and my endless questions into your busy life. Karen Draisey, Shannon Draisey, Catherine Scammell and Helena Eastham – thank you too.

I'm so grateful to Paul Organ for his considerable help and advice regarding police procedure. Pete Gotch – thank you for the chat! It was inspirational. Thanks, too, to Victoria Pitt and to the Roads Policing Unit in Abingdon. To Sarah Flint for our fascinating conversation about the use of informants. And to the medical professionals: Mahala Bradford and Becky Froggatt, who gave me extensive advice about intensive care and other aspects of nursing, and to Dr Kunal Shah. Also, to Professor David K. Menon for answering my questions about traumatic brain injury and end of life procedure. Any remaining errors are, of course, mine and not those of the people who helped.

I'd like to thank a number of my friends and colleagues at Tuckers Solicitors in London, Kent and Sussex: Suzanne

O'Connell and Ian Powell, our resident experts on youth crime and gang culture. Robin Murray for his helpful articles on disclosure. Kelly Thomas, Fiona Dunkley, Kirsty Craghill and Cath Diffey for their valuable feedback as readers and as lawyers. And our fabulous tech guys, Chirag Pareek and Laurence Edwards (dash cam, cricket – you name it, they knew it). But, again, if I've got anything wrong legally or technically – it's me, not them. I'm just grateful to work with such a brilliant and dedicated team of people. You're the best.

To my brothers: Mike Lomond for contributing to the Australian aspects of the storyline. And to Simon Lomond for offering – with his usual warmth and humour – some of his own horrific story to my plot.

Finally, thanks a million to my husband Mark and my son Tom, to my mum, and to all the other people in my life who have given me the space, support and encouragement I needed to write. And to you, dear reader, for reading; and to all the bloggers and reviewers for taking the time to tweet, post, blog and review. People always ask me how I manage to find the time to write, to work as a lawyer and to parent two children (one of whom is my very own 'Ben') and the answer is that it's been pretty tough at times. But it's your words of encouragement that have kept me going, so I thank you from the bottom of my heart.

ABOUT THE AUTHOR

Ruth Mancini is a criminal defence lawyer
and author. She has written three other novels,
In the Blood, *The Lies You Tell* and *His Perfect Lies*.
She lives in Oxfordshire with her husband
and two children.